DEATH IN THE DUSK

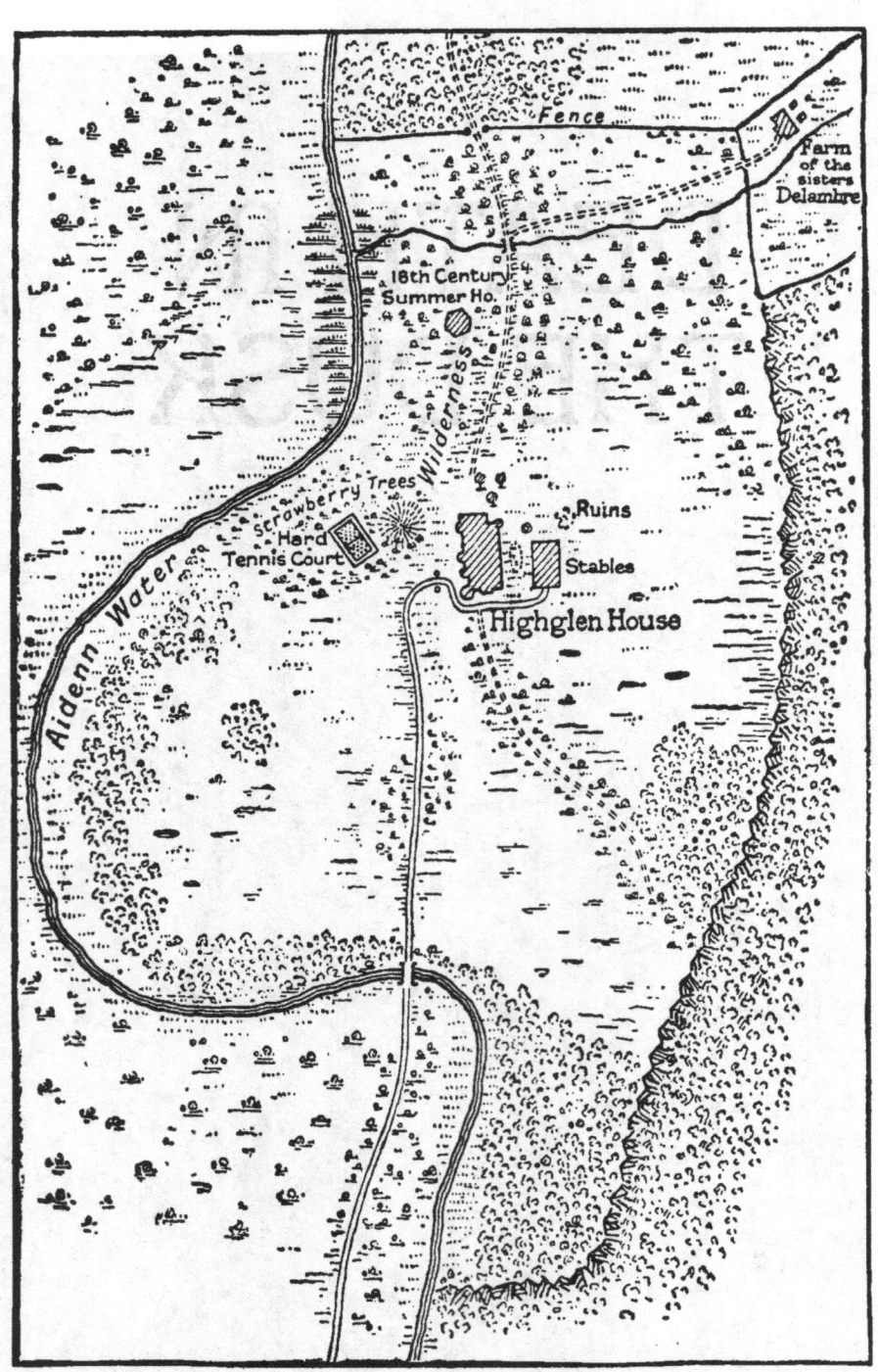

DEATH IN THE DUSK

VIRGIL MARKHAM

INTRODUCTION BY
KARL WURF

WILDSIDE PRESS

To
Paula Andrews
in loving memory of
Paula Lebetwood
and to
Mrs. Robert Cullen
in grateful memory of Lib.

Originally published in 1928.
Published by Wildside Press LLC.
wildsidepress.com

INTRODUCTION

Virgil Markham (1899–1973) was an American author known for his contributions to the mystery genre during the early 20th century. Born in Oakland, California, he was the son of the esteemed poet Edwin Markham, best remembered for his poem "The Man with the Hoe." In 1901, the Markham family relocated to New York, initially settling in Brooklyn before moving to Staten Island. Growing up amidst literary figures such as Ambrose Bierce, Jack London, and Carl Sandburg, Virgil was immersed in a rich cultural environment that undoubtedly influenced his literary pursuits.

Markham's academic journey led him to study literature and education. He later taught at the Markham Intermediate School on Staten Island, an institution named in honor of his father. Between 1926 and 1936, Markham authored nine mystery novels, showcasing his flair for intricate plotting and atmospheric storytelling. Among these works, *Death in the Dusk* (1928) stands out as a testament to his ability to weave suspense with gothic elements.

Death in the Dusk transports readers to a remote Welsh mansion shrouded in mystery and local legends. The narrative follows antiquarian Alfred Bannerlee, who, after losing his way in a dense fog, seeks refuge in the enigmatic estate. There, he becomes entwined with a peculiar household preparing for a wedding. The mansion's eerie ambiance is heightened by tales of Parson Lolly, a spectral figure believed to have died three centuries prior. As the story unfolds, a series of inexplicable events and murders ensue, challenging Bannerlee's perceptions of reality and the supernatural.

While *Death in the Dusk* is a product of its time—it does have a sometimes overly-verbose style—it remains a noteworthy entry in the annals of early 20th-century mystery fiction. Markham's ability to blend elements of gothic horror with the classic whodunit formula offers a unique reading experience that continues to captivate enthusiasts of the genre.

Beyond his literary endeavors, Markham managed his father's literary estate following Edwin Markham's death in 1940. He also imparted his knowledge of English literature at Wagner College on Staten Island. Virgil Markham's legacy, though overshadowed by his father's prominence, endures through his contributions to mystery literature, with his 9 novels showcasing his talent for crafting compelling and atmospheric narratives.

—Karl Wurf

PREFATORY WORDS

The journal of Alfred Bannerlee, of Balzing (Kent), is at last to be published practically in full, and without the alteration of any name. I say "at last," but I suppose there are some who would leap with joy if the closely-written pages of the Oxford antiquarian and athlete were utilized, like Carlyle's first "French Revolution," for building a cheery fire. Lord Ludlow certainly is one.

It seems incredible, but Mr. Bannerlee has requested Ludlow to write an introduction to the book. Perhaps Mr. Bannerlee was pulling the baronial leg. Of all the party of poor half-maddened people who emerged from Aidenn Vale after the powerful doings recorded in this Journal, I can imagine none less likely to perform this service for the diarist who clung faithfully to the task of recording terrors in the midst of terror and didn't hesitate to display the baronial character at its craftiest. Small wonder, I should think, that on the eve of publication of what he himself admits is "an unbelievable and utterly veracious narrative" Lord Ludlow sails for unknown seas, and makes no secret of the fact that England's loss is permanent.

Now, since his Lordship promises never to come back, I don't see any reason why I shouldn't publish his recent letter to me, and thereby, perhaps, satisfy Mr. Bannerlee.

Brillig, Ambleside, Westmorland,
December 27, 1927.

My dear Markham:

One can scarcely conjecture what maggot of audacity was in the brain of Alfred Bannerlee, Esq., when he forwarded me his diary with the request that I write a foreword to accompany it 'to give the stamp of reality.' When you perceive the light in which I am placed in this unbelievable and utterly veracious narrative, you will not need to reflect in order to understand why I decline to have anything to do with the document. In accordance with Mr. Bannerlee's wish, I am sending the diary to you, 'an obscure but ambitious author,' and I do not suppose that you will object to having your name upon the title-page. The whole arrangement impresses me as asinine, but, after all, the manuscript is Mr. Bannerlee's and he should be allowed full scope to play the fool with it.

In fairness to the author, however, I must abate the indictment. I do no more than allude to what seem to me distinct virtues in this account. They will appeal to others likewise, if they are virtues. In the first place, there is nothing of that grisly, putrid stuff going nowadays under the name of modern psychology, although a pedlar of this 'science' could have found no end of matter for his hole and corner methods. Second point: I am not a devotee of the enormous literature dealing with the hounding and capture of wrongdoers. But I will venture a pronouncement in my egregious innocence, to wit, that not in any half-dozen combined of these would-be 'shockers' published in a lifetime will be found as many trials and alarums and as much genuine mystification as make up this compendium of the bedevilment of Parson Lolly, the mad behaviour of the milkman, the invisible omnipresence of Sir Brooke Mortimer, the enigma of the mystic bone, the Legend of Sir Pharamond's imperishable arm, and the machinations of the ultimate contriver, I will not call him 'fiend,' working through and behind all.

And here it is my wish to express my wholehearted esteem for (then) Miss Paula Lebetwood. I dislike the whole species of American girls, but intelligence compels exceptions to every rule. Some of us judged her harshly, no doubt, but she took the road leading to success, and if she seemed cold-hearted, she chose wisely. Had she been a weaker woman, snuffling and inept, the narrative would not now be on the verge of publication. In spite of this, wherever she is, I wish her well.

I myself shall not remain in England to witness the effervescence of the multitude over this narrative. Democratic outbursts rather gall me. On the eve of the publication of the Journal, my yacht, with me on board, sails for waters unknown. I seek as far as I may a shoreless cruise. I am old, and mankind is not my hobby. Perhaps I shall linger in the beauty of the Mediterranean where there are two skies, perhaps drift endlessly in the steady strength of the Trades, perhaps dare the dark Antarctic seas—or find beyond the sunset. One thing stands sure; it is unthinkable that I shall ever set foot in Britain again. So here I take farewell of those who with me shared the dread, wonder and aftermath of *Death in the Dusk*. (By the way, I don't like that title of Bannerlee's.)

Pray accept my congratulations on your recent appointment, and believe me your sincere friend, and

Faithfully yours,
Ludlow.

It is well, I believe, to point out that the minds of all those present at Highglen House among the sorcerous hills of Wales during the early autumn of 1925, the mind which directed the writing of this Journal was, save perhaps one, the best fitted for presenting the closest account possible to the truth. The one other mind which could possibly equal this record in truthfulness would be that which actually contrived the series of demoniacal events in the Vale of Aidenn Water. The strange, tense, potentially tragic, and ultimately fatal situation discovered by Mr. Bannerlee after his serio-comic descent from the Forest through the fog contained so many cross-currents and tangled nets of misunderstanding, prejudice and enmity that no other could have pretended to the shadow of fairness in his (or her) statement of the case. For the sake of truth, then (though God knows what disadvantages offset that!), it was well that Mr. Bannerlee was plunged into the seething midst of the Bidding Feast.

I shall not dilate upon the morbid eagerness with which the public will seize upon this Journal. This is no hackneyed chronicle of raw head and bloody bones. The consternation caused by the events in Aidenn Vale, constituting, upon their emergence after the flood, a problem of what may genuinely be called universal interest, will never be forgotten by those old enough to realize their dreadfulness. The nine days' terror became a nine days' wonder, and without hyperbole it may be said that the fate of one nation hung upon the Radnorshire riddles. The public has never been informed of all there was to be told, nor, as sporadic (and totally erroneous) statements and versions in the press signify, has the public lost its interest. Here, for the first time, is offered for general perusal this unbelievable and utterly veracious document. Need I comment further?

This is not, of course, the original form of Mr. Bannerlee's diary. What he wrote until the turmoil of events forced him to stay his hand on the evening of the 9th of October was necessarily briefer, more compact, and—to a reader not in touch with the circumstances—unintelligible. His recasting of the manuscript, which involved its enlargement to thrice its original length is, it seems to me, one of the most notable of his feats. Hard it must have been for him to alter this account from the sketch-book manner of an ordinary diary, to give the convincing gloss of rumination and reflection, to reveal precise details of fact, the links of cogitation, and the phases of feeling which poured in upon him. I think, too, that he has well preserved the sense of imminence, the uncertainty as to the morrow, which was, I am told, present in the original version. If portions of the work seem lacking in spontaneity, let me remind the reader that it was impossible for Mr. Bannerlee to limit himself to a mere polychronicon of episodes, frilled with running comment on persons, and edged with a neat pattern of emotions. Clearness demanded he should sometimes *elucidate* and the white heat of events must have time to cool before they can be handled analytically.

Only last month I myself visited New Aidenn again. A word of self-introduction to Superintendent Salt made that rather wonderful policeman my good friend at once, and he personally conducted me through the Vale where death and terror had danced. It is all as Bannerlee describes it; even the atmosphere of mystery has not departed, and while Salt and I came down by Aidenn Water through the dusk, I was glad to have him there, glad and nevertheless uneasy. The villagers and the folk of the countryside know well that Parson Lolly is not dead yet, though his age is nearer five hundred than four hundred years, and often they see his black cloak whisk through some twilight copse, or see him far off above the hills, poised against the sunset.

Some day I shall write my own book about Salt: that other mystery of East Wales, the frightful affair of the Straight Road. But enough.

Virgil Markham
St. John's Wood,
London, February 26, 1928.

PERSONS IN THIS CHRONICLE

The Narrator

Alfred Bannerlee of Balzing in Kent, athlete and antiquarian

Host and Hostess of the Bidding Feast

The Honourable Crofts Pendleton
Mrs. (Alberta) Pendleton

The Betrothed

Sean Cosgrove
Paula Lebetwood

Guests

Herbert Pinckney, Baron Ludlow and Ditherington
Ted Belvoir
Mrs. (Marvel) Belvoir
Gilbert Maryvale, Esq.
Mr. Charlton Oxford
Mrs. Eve Bartholomew
Miss Millicent Mertoun
Dr. Stephen Aire
Lib Dale
Bob Cullen

Servants

Blenkinson, patriarch
Soames, footman
Hughes, gamekeeper
Finlay, head gardener
Wheeler, chauffeur and handy man

Morgan, handy man
Tenney, handy man
Toby, boy
Rosa Clay, cook
Ruth Clay, housekeeper
Ardelia Lacy, lady's maid
Jael, parlourmaid
Harmony, housemaid
Em, kitchenmaid

Nebulous or Mysterious Persons

The gorilla man
The menagerie keeper
Sir Brooke Mortimer
The sisters Delambre
The red-bearded runner
The youth in the library
The man in the tower

Officials

Superintendent Salt
Dr. Niblett, Coroner
"Scotland Yard"

Super-Sleuth

Harry Heatheringham

Arch-Lord of Disorder

PARSON LOLLY

CHAPTER 1

THE OBTRUSION OF PARSON LOLLY

Highglen House, Aidenn Vale, Radnorshire,
October 3, 1925. 12.30 A.M.

Heaven smile on us if it can! Heaven watch and ward us. This is a wedding party!

Crofts Pendleton has just brought me the fresh candles and this writing-book. He wished me God-speed in my endeavours and good-night.

"Good-night!" It sounded like a travesty, or a challenge.

Surely I am the sane one here if anyone is. Yet I cannot name the curse that lies on my spirit and keeps in my eyes the vision of the two faces, the golden hair above the black! Never-to-be-forgotten moment! But I shall not let it unnerve me now, as it seemed to then.

The worst of it is that I am confined in a musty chamber (among store-rooms!) on the second floor where the web-scribbled ceiling slants down with the roof and the eaves murmur uncannily just above my window—a room to make flesh thrill and creep. It looks like a chamber where murderers may have lurked in bygone days. The narrow, deep-set window, the old twisty candle-brackets high on the stone wall, the joined chest with never a nail to fasten its boards, the severely plain four-square bedstead—they all remind me that I am in a building centuries old where any or every fiendish deed may have been performed. I wish that this storey, like the rest of the house, were equipped with a good up-to-date electric service. The blinking light of candles is not very comfortable in the gloom.

Nearly a page written, yet nothing pertinent said. This isn't economy in words. But now I'll banish megrims, cease rambling, and come to the situation.

I have been in Highglen House for a scant six hours. Events have been moving with intermittent swiftness ever since I came, and they had not been precisely quiet before my arrival. Tonight, though it takes until dawn, I shall describe as far as I can the happenings of the last day unless I drift off to sleep in the process. But no, even with doors locked, sleep is not likely to trouble anyone much tonight, not after the alarm all of us—I don't except myself in this case—have just had.

Moreover, until the nowhere-to-be-found Sir Brooke puts in an appearance, or some word is heard from him, there will be little rest for me, with Eve Bartholomew knocking at the door every fifteen minutes, with, "I'm so sorry, Mr. Bannerlee; are you still up? It's *so* silly of me, of course—Sir Brooke can take care of himself as well as any of us—better, I'm sure, than most—and yet I'm not so sure—but it's really odd, isn't it? Now I know it's silly of me—but I've just had another idea. Don't you think it's possible that Sir Brooke took the wrong train? Of course I don't know whether you can do that in Shrewsbury in the afternoon—but perhaps he got on the wrong platform, or something—he never was an expert on getting about, poor dear—and then he may have gone to sleep and not noticed where he was going. He has a way of doing that in trains—I know him so well, you see. Perhaps he didn't learn until he got off at some scrubby little place where there's no telegraph. And then, of course, that explains why there's been no message from him."

I have learned a good deal about Sir Brooke's character since Mrs. B. began her raids with a Macbethean knocking and a stage whisper. His chief trait seems to be utter fickleness of memory, his next that something, or lack of something, which makes able-bodied women like Mrs. B. call men "dear" with "poor" prefixed. He is near-sighted, liable to vertigo philanthropic, and a nuisance.

I said Macbethean knocking—I suppose that proves I'm a little highly-strung myself. Certainly she caused a warm, douche-like sensation to pass clear over my scalp to the nape of my neck. We have had an evening which would make the staidest—

I have a severe mind to draw a line through these pages and begin anew. This isn't what I intended at all. My candles are bearded now, and I haven't scratched my subject. I repent and reform this very instant. I am going to try to put down things in order, as they have unfolded themselves in the course of one of the most amazing days I, or any human being, ever lived through.

Yet first (before taking my way back to the hilltop where I wandered this afternoon, never having so much as heard of Highglen House!) while the spirit is urgent and the clutch of sense is keen, I'll transcribe the maddening events of the half-hour just past. Before I forget—but shall I ever forget?

There they were in the Hall of the Moth, civilizees of assorted temperaments, ignoring their alarms, submerging their differences, and levelling their intellects in the fascination of a card game. How "instructive and amusing" had been my introduction by Pendleton to each of them in this very Hall scarcely more than an hour before! Save for Alberta, that luscious wife of his, I had never laid eyes on one of them previous to this evening.

Straight on my entering the Hall, Pendleton had cavalierly handed me around from person to person.

First he revealed me to his wife, who set down her cards and rose with one of the gladdest smiles I have ever seen. She was tall and gracious. Her face, surrounded by its lustre of close-clipped, wavy hair, was a joy to look at, being both pearly-clear and firm, like an exquisite lily-petal of classic marble.

"Alfred! We hear that you have been raiding Aidenn Forest."

"Please!" I laughed. "I wouldn't call it anything so forcible as—"

But already Pendleton had presented me to Mrs. Belvoir. I withdrew my hand from its clasp of Alberta's and took the cold fingers of the colourless man's wife. What thoughts lay behind those brooding lids and that close-lipped mouth? Her face had a wavering indistinctness, like a face seen under flowing water.

"How do you do?" she said in that rich voice, gave me one full look with eyes cold and pale as sapphires, and blinked languidly, as if the discussion were closed.

Pendleton did not let me linger in perplexity. He gave me up to Belvoir, who shook hands with a faint smile, saying, "Mr. Bannerlee and I spelled our names to each other in the hall a little while ago."

Next was Lord Ludlow. "I've seen him," remarked his Lordship, gazing at me with a little asperity, crinkling the skin over the high-pitched bridge of his nose, and sat down, for he was wishful of continuing the game, or of giving the impression that such was his desire.

I was whisked to the second table and made acquainted with the sole woman there. Eve Bartholomew (God give her peace!) grasped my hand for a tug or two, exclaiming hurriedly, "Oh, how do you do?" And she added, with ill-feigned casualness, "They say you've been out on the hills today. You're sure you haven't seen Sir Brooke?"

"Quite sure, Mrs. Bartholomew."

"Or hear of anyone who might be him—he?"

"No."

Next I was set face-to-face with her partner, the red-faced young man, who I was not surprised to learn was Sean Cosgrove. His head was large, his features large, too, without being lubberly. The ruddiness of his complexion was accentuated by his very black and shining hair, short and thick. There was something grim and settled in the line of his jaw, and his blazing black eyes bore out the character of determination. He shook hands unsmiling, gravely.

"My congratulations," I offered.

He gave a short bow, looking at the floor. Then, "I have heard of you," he said, with not a trace of Irish lilt or accent in his speech.

"Is it possible?"

"You are a searcher for the buried lore of antiquity. Is not that so?" he asked with a certain lofty seriousness.

"I have done a little research among the British saints, but I hardly expected my labours—"

"They honour you," asserted Cosgrove, but my smile of deprecation and anything further he was about to say were cut off by Pendleton, who relentlessly kept me on the go, and I faced the next guest.

Two men had been partners at this table; I now found myself staring at a waxed moustache, and a very elegantly tapered and needle-pointed specimen of craftsmanship it was. The rest of his face was nothing remarkable, only a little swarthy-purplish with brandy, and a trifle stary-eyed. I was not prepossessed with this gentleman, judging him to be the sort who shows his cleverness to an assorted public in quips to barmaids and dance-hall musicians. His name, "Mr. Charlton Oxford," struck me as strainedly aristocratic, though no fault of his.

"Chawmed."

"Aesthete," flashed through my brain, but a query-note raised itself after the word. "Just plain fool," I concluded.

"You *are* being bandied about, aren't you?"

I was surprised by the fluence and ease of his voice, and his lightening smile, the big darkish man's who had been dealing the cards so ritualistically a few minutes before. He lifted his weight as if it were that of a bubble, and I saw that indeed he was big, bearing his torso on stanchion-legs. His mass must have been twice mine.

"Gilbert Maryvale, our complete man of business—iron-castings," said Pendleton, with evident gladness that his tale was over.

I saw a quick brightness come and go in Gilbert Maryvale's eyes at that description, as if the eyeball had darted out a little from its station under thatch-brows.

"The winner of the Newman Prize for Lucid Prose, I think, in—let me see—Nineteen-nineteen? May I congratulate you, Mr. Bannerlee, although the time is past? I have read your 'Poets of Enervation' with delight."

"No, Mr. Maryvale, that was not my essay."

"Surely I haven't mistaken the name?"

"You have mistaken only the man. 'Poets of Enervation' was the overflow of my cousin Norval's pen. We were in the University together. I made a bid for the Newman myself, but was buried. Norval and I are often mistaken for each other, even in our literary occupations."

"No doubt you ran him close," observed the big man twinkingly.

"I'm afraid not. And now, as Mr. Cosgrove has said, I am devoted to dustier things, and the prose I give my time to is far from lucid."

"But you wring lucidity out of it."

Maryvale resumed his seat, picked up his hand, as did the rest, for in spite of much invitation I insisted on remaining aloof from the game. Broad capable cheek-bones, sudden forceful chin he had, but I had an awareness there was much more than capability and force in this "complete man of business." That allusion to the Prize Essay for Lucid Prose was a poser. Was there another trafficker in iron-castings in the United Kingdom who had read "Poets of Enervation"?—or one who would speak of it kindly if he had?

Well, all this was past, half-forgotten in ensuing talk. But now, at one minute to midnight, a new presence was in the Hall, threatening the mirth of the Feast! Anger!

For Lord Ludlow and Sean Cosgrove were having a beautiful row.

The Irishman's gaze was hard and heavy, and seemed to bore into his antagonist. His face, I noticed, was still suffusing with blood. No one else ventured to intervene as madly as I had just done, and the silence when the two men ceased parleying was like the yawn of ocean after a gigantic wave.

Cosgrove's bitterness seemed to be growing steadily, like the awful momentum of a railway train, and I had no doubt that the time was not many seconds away when he would arise and beard his foe with menacing hands. Lord Ludlow's acerbity was like the nervous, sputtering viciousness of a dynamo. From his eyes seemed to come green electric sparks, while he shifted his ire from me toward Cosgrove again.

"As for you, sir—"

"I accuse you—"

Hark!

The great Hall of the Moth where we stood was gripped in a new hush, for the clock in the corner was speaking. I had regarded it curiously in the evening, a fine old carcase with hood, waist, and base enveloped in spider's web marqueterie which obliterated the graining of the wood. The brass dial was finely engraved, and Cupid's head appeared four times delicately chiselled in the spandrils.

Now its chime gave the burden it has tolled for two hundred years, and midnight was ringing sternly through the House from the Hall of the Moth. It is a strange clock, devised by some brooding or twisted or philosophic mind long ago: it strikes, they say, only at midnight, proclaiming the death and the birth of a day. The tones, vigorous and vibrant, were mellow with centuries, and their song was poignant.

Like some greybeard councillor's, the old clock's voice appeared to abash the hasty peer and the slowly enraged Irishman. They stared at each other in grimness for an interim of seconds before his Lordship shrugged his shoulders, cackled "Humph!" loudly, and turned to the disrupted card-table.

Cosgrove's clenched hands came down in his lap relaxed, and he, too, turned back to his table, moving his lips without utterance.

But the game did not go on. It could hardly have pursued its placid course again after this very distressing interruption of our peace, even if the crying sound had not begun from somewhere outside the Hall.

A low, tremulous, wheedling cry, strangled sometimes into a moan—it froze every face and turned every eye to stone.

"What's that?" gulped Eve Bartholomew....

"*Where* is it?" asked Belvoir, and one could tell that the "stick of dynamite" had not much breath to spare.

But no one seemed to have the breath or the brain to answer him. My own belief for a moment was that it proceeded from a plane above our heads, instead of from somewhere in the long portrait-lined passage outside the Hall of the Moth. This seemed to be Pendleton's notion, too, for with a tense "upstairs!" our host moved to the nearest door to the corridor. But Alberta Pendleton, dismayed (like all of us, no doubt) by the thought of the hovering menace that had shadowed Highglen House, hurried across to her husband and clung to him, positively clung to him, as I have seen actresses do in plays.

"No, Crofts dear—no, no! Wait—let someone go with you!"

"It's up there," declared Pendleton with steel-trap enunciation. "The damned thing's come again—up there."

"That's why you mustn't go."

"It's up there," he said doggedly, and tugged to loose himself. But she took step for step with him, finally turning in his path with her back against the door.

"We'll all go," said Maryvale.

"All the men," said Cosgrove. "The women lock the doors behind us."

"Ring for the servants," said someone shakenly, I think Charlton Oxford.

"Listen!... It's not there any more.... It's stopped." We listened with Mrs. Bartholomew; beyond our taut breathings and the tick-tack-tock of the carcase in the corner—nothing.

"Ring for the servants, I tell you!"

"Listen! It's out there."

"Out there!"

"On the lawn."

Unmistakably now the low wordless cry came through the half-opened french window leading to the broad lawns beyond the entrance drive. Pendleton was across the room in a trice, heedless of Alberta's protest; so were Maryvale and Cosgrove and I; so were all of us. We followed our host through the window-entrance. Out to the darkness we went from the bright-lit hall in a little throng, and when we were outside, hearing the lonesome, half-whining cry no more, we recoiled and huddled a little, like scared titmice.

Hardly a quarter of a minute—prolonged by our bewilderment and dread—could have gone by, and we stood irresolute upon the fringe of the lawn, when the cry came toward us again, and now it was followed by a woman's voice, different from the cry:

"Oh, come here, come here! I couldn't call you and leave her alone."

At the sound of that voice Cosgrove stamped like a raving beast. "Paula," he bellowed, and plunged across the obscurity of the lawn.

Following among those whose urgence was less than his, my eyes, which deviated from straight ahead, caught sight of a spine-stirring thing. It was motion, but of what? A darker mass on the dark sward. Size, shape, untellable—but moving, moving to the right, now seeming to crawl, now leaping—only an amorphous blob of black—moving, and swiftly, toward the north, moving stilly, with only a small rustling sound at whiles.

"Look there!" I exclaimed to someone who was near me, catching his arm. (It was Oxford.)

"Hey! What!"

"That—going off there—a black thing."

"I don't see it." Nor did he want to, I judged.

I guided his arm, extending it in the proper line. "Sight by that."

But I could not make him see it. He and I then diverged from the others, not much to his liking, and while we hastened after the nameless thing, I bethought me that I had changed my electric torch to these clothes. I hauled it from a side pocket, darted a cone of yellow ahead of us, cast an elliptic figure of yellow on the grass, but found no trace of the thing.

Oxford, however, saw an object ahead which made him give a yell. He stopped petrified, and I followed his look far before us. What we both then saw was too distant to be the thing I had observed nearby, unless it were indeed a fiend possessed of superhuman powers. He was crossing a patch of ground a hundred yards away where the moon streamed down unscathed by clouds; save for the quick, brief clearing, indeed, we should not have caught sight of him. Like the hopping, gliding thing on the lawn, he was black, or robed in black. Contrary to report, however, if this were Parson Lolly, his figure appeared not to be tall but distinctly short and squatty. Just then the fringe of a cloud partly obfuscated the moon, but still that space was clearer than all around it. While the figure glided toward the trees, it seemed to heave its shoulders and grow a foot, two feet, taller! Again it writhed itself into greater height, its long cloak billowing, and again! Just before gaining the covert of branches, it turned toward us a moment, twice the height of a man. And its head, if head it had, was only a pointed thing with unguessable features in the cavern of its hood. The moon was absolutely overcast when the figure, again wheeling about, went beneath the trees.

"Do we go after it?" I asked sardonically.

"We—we do not."

"Righto."

I heard a gurgle from Oxford's lips and guessed that his heart must be rotating in his throat. His shoulder to my touch was quivering, and while we went to rejoin the rest he staggered as if in drink, although certainly sober. But his nerves aren't the best, I shouldn't wonder, for there must be regular occasions when he quaffs and quaffs again.

They were a chastened, vaguely murmurous company we discovered almost beneath the arch of the ancient gate-house with its ivy swarming up and up, now standing lone, its walls on either side all shorn away. Only a spurt or two of a match they had to see by, until I came with my torch and they made way for me. The light on the weather-beaten stone was like the circle of an old medallion or mellowed painting: two women, one pallid and lifeless, the other, seated on the grass, supporting the lovely, unconscious head on her knees.

I supposed instantly that this was the young English-woman, Millicent Mertoun, who lay wan—the most beautiful creature, I believe, I have ever seen. Fine breeding, fine spirit were in her stricken face. Cold loveliness, indeed, with the life gone out of it; eyes set widely apart, closed beneath straight black eyebrows which were now lifted apeak with the intensity of strain that showed in the fine lines across her forehead and the slight drawing-back of her short upper lip, disclosing her large, evenly graduated teeth. The lashes that rested upon her cheeks were remarkably long, deep black, and it was their fragile, almost imperceptible stirring alone that betokened a possible reawakening to life. Her chin was softly rounded, and in the disorder of her abundant black hair a delicate ear was exposed. The suspension of life had withdrawn the blood from the full-contoured lips, left the cheeks pallid, but while I gazed at the face and the aristocratic little neck, twined about so by the tumbling length of masses of black hair, I had a whisper of what beauty the face might have when expression was restored to it, and the eyes, of unguessable depth and sweetness, were open.

Of the other woman's head I caught only the partly averted profile, while she bent over Miss Mertoun, with one hand clasping together at the throat the unconscious girl's loose gown, apparently a garment of negligée. She, of course, must be the American girl, for it was at the sound of her voice that Sean Cosgrove had torn across the lawn. There was dignity, I thought, in her head with its straitly fastened golden-brown hair, and a lovely tenderness in the solicitude of her pose.

She was in the midst of speech, relating the adventure which had brought her and her companion to that plight. She did not look up or turn her head when the light from my hand broke over her, and all the while she spoke her watchful gaze was for the features of the girl whose senses were benumbed. American speech it was, yet the words came from her lips with a chiselled precision, the tone tending toward viola depth.

"—blinding, yes, not blinding alone, but maddening. I got her into looser clothing—she wouldn't go to bed. She gave no sign of fainting, but the pain drove her into delirium more than once, and I almost sent for someone else to help me with her. Then the pain went down, and suddenly she went to sleep."

Someone, I think Cosgrove, took a step nearer. "No, keep away, please. Don't try to move her yet."

"But, Paula, how did you ever come—?"

The American girl precluded the end of Alberta Pendleton's question. "Of course I am coming to that. She went sound asleep, and I thought it better not to undress her; so I let her lie on the bed, and I curled up in the chair by the window. Millicent's wretched evening had left me tired out, too, and I don't remember anything more until when I woke up to find her awake again and wandering about. There was enough light from the globe by the mirror to see that she was terribly distressed, but it was not with pain this time. She was suffering from some—"

Paula Lebetwood hesitated for a moment, then recommenced. "I think she was walking in her sleep."

A note of surprise and pity came from all our mouths.

"Were her eyes open?" asked Mrs. Belvoir.

"Yes, with the darkest vagueness in them."

"Didn't she recognize you?"

"I don't know."

"What?"

"You see, it all happened so quickly. Only a couple of seconds after I had roused myself the clock in the Hall of the Moth commenced ringing midnight. Millicent stopped for a moment and put her hand to her heart, an odd thing, I thought. 'It's his music,' she said, and made for the door."

Renewed exclamations of surprise attested our close-held interest.

"She ran down the hall—"

"But, Paula, did you let her—?"

"She was too strong for me, or perhaps too quick. She twisted away from me when I tried to prevent her from leaving the room. She almost flew down the hall; I was afraid she would throw herself down the stairs, and I caught up with her just in time. We came down—"

"Did she make any sound?" burst in Pendleton.

"Yes, a wailing sound—if there were any words, I couldn't distinguish them. Didn't you hear her? Oh, I was wishing you would. I didn't dare to cry out, you know, since she was in that dangerous state."

"We heard, dear," said Alberta Pendleton. "But the sound kept changing, and we were undecided."

"She had a definite intention to go out, and out of the front entrance we went whether I would or not. And then, then, while we were far away on the lawn, we saw the—the—I can't name it."

"What was it like?" asked Pendleton, and I recall that all of us closed in a little further to hear.

"The head, I suppose you'd call it. It was—awful."

"What—where?"

"Didn't any of you see it?" she asked in much surprise, yet not for a second lifting her intent look from Millicent Mertoun's face. "It was just after that I noticed that foul reek of blood."

"Blood!" That was Eve Bartholomew's cry.

"Oh, haven't you noticed that either? The smell was so bad, I feared it would have some ghastly effect on Millicent. I hoped she wouldn't notice it, in her condition. And then—we were beyond the gate-house, coming back toward the mansion, when we saw—the head."

"Where, for God's sake?"

"About a hundred feet away from us. I heard something stirring first, something scuttling, you might say. Then we saw it. Ugh!… Straight out of hell, surely.…"

Pendleton's excitement was getting too much for him, and he broke through courtesy. "Why do you keep boggling it? Where was it? What did it do?"

"Crofts!" reprimanded Alberta.

Still with averted face, Paula Lebetwood tried to satisfy our fuming host. "Where? I don't know exactly where. Near the gate-house here, I suppose. It seemed thirty or forty yards away. It was enormous, about six feet high—oh, fully that. It hung in the air—there wasn't any body beneath. And it didn't do anything, just remained there long enough to be seen, half a second, perhaps, and disappeared with a sort of sigh. I thought I heard a sigh. It—well, it simply went out.… It was hideous."

"What did it look like, dear?" asked Alberta, more to anticipate her bluff husband than to satisfy curiosity, for her question was tremulous.

"Hideous—a great round head with red goggle eyes and a hole for a nose and broken teeth all grinning. It looked alive and staring—worse than any mask I've ever seen—an indecent thing.… Oh, don't think that it was hallucination—poor Millicent saw it too, though it came and went like the winking of an eye. It seemed to strike to her heart—and to mine, for that matter—and she could manage to walk only a few steps more—on my arm—through the archway before she weakened and collapsed, and I saw you all there outside the french window, and called."

She turned her head full toward us for the first time since Oxford and I had come from our private chase. Such was my position when she lifted her bent head that I, and only I, saw, on the yellow-lit ground revealed beyond, a small placard with uncouth letters thereon, large enough to be read in spite of their unshapeliness:

PARSON LOLLY SeNds REGaRDs
LooK OUT FOR PARSON LOLLY

A storm sprang in my mind, such a whirlwind of spirit as I believe I have never before experienced, when behind the quick, expectant face of this American girl, one so tender to her stricken friend, one so fearless, I saw that obscene sign. She was at first dazzled by the light in my hand, and her dark blue eyes show wonderfully bright and wild. Her gold hair then had a fine-spun beauty. And beside the old gate-tower lay the sneering message of one who affronted both manhood and womanhood. Anger at the marauder who made beauty his victim, shame for being duped, fear of being duped again, a craving to bring the rascal down—these and I know that not what other unleashed gales met in the cross-roads of my mind. The winds rose to raving, towered into hurricanes. My soul was dizzy, staggering. I was not rational at that moment—then the gales went down. I bit my lip hard, stepped around the two women there, picked up the sign (which had been printed with a smudgy pencil on a stiff folio sheet) and showed it to the rest.

"Parson Lolly!" exclaimed more than one.

Then Oxford, perhaps intending to be jocose, said:

"'Beware of Parson Lolly.' Beggar's a bit late, it seems to me."

"At least," said Crofts Pendleton thickly "it proves he's human—the devil!"

"*In some ways human*, perhaps," amended Maryvale.

"What else, then?"

"Less than human. Consider the birds of the air, my friends. They are, I suppose, less than human—yet—they—can—fly!"

I gave a stout shrug to rid myself of the disquiet compelled by such a suggestion.

Anxiety over Miss Mertoun's exposure to the midnight air prompted Alberta Pendleton, not for the first time, to urge taking her inside the Hall. But Miss Lebetwood shook her head in a determined manner, and with a gesture showed that she believed it was too far to carry her to the mansion.

"It's very mild out here now," she declared. "I know sleep-walking people. If she were to wake up while she's being taken, it might have some long-lasting ill effect. Alberta, please don't ask again. I want her to be in my arms when she opens her eyes. You good people don't need to stay. I—and Sean—can wait here with her alone."

But none of us would go. Then while we waited to see a greater sign of life than the restlessness of those long black lashes on the pallid cheek, down from the dark north came that ragged, hungry voice I had heard while alone earlier in the night, a cry that tore at our nerves and congealed our blood to ice-drops in our veins. A carnal, raving cry, thinning to a shriek that pierced the ear, swelling to a howl that loosened the knees.

Of that dire, abysmal wail of mad desire, an overtone must have found a counterpart in Cosgrove's spirit. Out of the past of his kind, that had seen things more clearly in the dusk than in the plain light of day, that had loved cries of battle and death more than joyful cries, some strain may have wrung the man's soul. Terribly to all of us, he raised his voice in answer to the inhuman call; I, at least, had no sense of body or of time and place while he burst into a black rain of words, a torrent of rancour, and defiance against the fiend of the pit, whose incarnate self he seemed to hear in the voice of the beast.

But a low call from Paula Lebetwood reduced him to a stunning silence. "I think she's coming to."

The unconscious girl's fingers fluttered briefly; her lips stirred; her whole body stirred a little. She turned once, twice, restlessly, and sank, with a little sigh, comfortably and trustingly into the American girl's embrace. The trace of a sneer had vanished from her face, and her breast moved with her breathing.

"She's sleeping now," said Alberta Pendleton, and stooped beside the pair on the grass.

Miss Lebetwood whispered, "Dearest, do you hear me? Do you know me? It's Paula.… Dearest, do you hear me?" She stroked the pale forehead free of its last furrow.

"Yes," came like a shadow of a word from the sleeping girl.

"Dearest, Paula wants you to come with her." Still she spoke, soothing, caressing, in the effort to woo her to awaken peacefully. And the eyes of Millicent Mertoun opened, revealing themselves to be of a deep blackness that rivalled her errant hair, opened to see only the smile of love on the face of the American girl bending over her; and the English girl smiled too.

"Your headache is all gone, isn't it, dearest?"

"Yes…but where…is this?"

"Don't be frightened, dear. It's the lawn by the gate-house. Now we're going inside."

"But how?… I don't understand…these people."

Miss Lebetwood kissed her cheek, leaned her forehead against it. "Never mind, dearest. Everyone is a friend, you know. Can you walk? Here, now."

The English girl was sitting up; she rubbed her eyes, and sent short, bewildered looks this way and that, far from comprehending her situation. Too many of the party were trying to explain everything to her, and she was beginning to look desperate and unhappy.

"Never mind the silly people," said Miss Lebetwood sensibly. "See— we're just a few steps away from the house—where we've been before, you know. Now we must go in. Sean, help me."

The Irishman and the women at last began to support the strengthless girl into the Hall. It must have been a full quarter of an hour since we had poured out from that vaulted chamber into the enigmatic night and had heard the call from the gate-house. Now the servants were roused, summoned by someone, and lanterns were rushing across the lawn in our direction. I had commenced to go with the party about Miss Mertoun, desirous of casting a light before their feet. But Pendleton called me back somewhat peremptorily.

"Bright enough from the Hall for 'em not to stumble by." Alone in the great mansion the Hall of the Moth sparkled forth, but the glare from its massive chandelier was a sure guiding light. "We need you here," added our host; "there's a good deal more of this needs looking at."

At a phrase from him the lanterns began to swing hither and thither about the lawn, and we men of the party passed across the drawbridge under the resounding gate-house arch.

"Is this usually lowered?" I asked.

"Usually. Can be raised for the sport of it. It's part of the main drive, you see. It must have been hereabout that they smelt—"

He had no need to say more.

"Great God, what an unholy stench!"

"It *is* blood!"

"Bottles of it."

Crofts Pendleton's voice shook. "I hope—it's not—anything serious."

Just then nothing could have struck us as amusing. Lord Ludlow interjected, "Remember, sir, that there is a missing man—"

"Oh, Lord, look there! My boot!"

Belvoir lifted a foot for inspection, while I turned the eye of the torch upon it. The leather was stained with a fluid dark and thick.

"My God!" observed Pendleton.

"It's jolly well begun to clot."

"Look out, you chaps, you'll mire yourselves."

"Show us the place, Bannerlee."

My torch exposed a patch of darkened grass only a foot or so each way. There was nothing else about nearby.

Pendleton, half aghast, kneeled on the edge of the patch and studied it.

"A lot of blood's been spilled here. It must have soaked down, a goodish bit of it, but there's quite a pool about the grass roots. This spot will have to be guarded tonight. Pity we've tramped about."

A thick voice lifted in excitement from the north of us.

"Oh, Mister Crofts, sir, do come here."

"What is it, Tenney? Let it stay, whatever it is."

"Small fear I'll touch it, sir. It's one of them old fightin' irons."

"A weapon, by heaven!" exclaimed Lord Ludlow.

"Has it blood on it?"

"All sticky dried, sir."

We were beside the quaking man-servant in a jiffy or two, staring curiously where lay a small battle-axe, with an inconsiderable curve of blade. It was a weapon of uncommon slightness. Both metal and wood were dark with the same viscous fluid, the handle being quite slobbered with it.

"From the armoury!" cried our host. "The foul devil's actually been inside the house! Don't touch it!"

"That weapon was on the wall at a quarter before eight," said Lord Ludlow. (Ah, I knew why he could say that!) "I was passing through to the library for my glasses." (There, to be sure, the old rascal prevaricated.)

"You don't say!"

"This looks like a serious crime," remarked his Lordship.

"Serious crime!" Pendleton snorted. "Ludlow, you surprise me. I thought it was child's play."

"I think that by a serious crime our noble friend means a particular crime—don't you, Ludlow? Isn't it the customary euphemism?" asked Belvoir.

"I mean murder, sir."

"Should have said so in the first place," growled Pendleton, and added, "No need to say it at all."

"It's jolly irregular, though," declared Oxford. "All that blood in one spot, and this gory thing over here."

"This was not done according to rule," rejoined his Lordship.

"It was not carried out as planned," declared Cosgrove, who had come out from the mansion again.

"And one, er, detail only needs to be filled in." That was Belvoir from somewhere in the darkness behind us. "The, er, *corpus delicti*."

"Gad, yes—scatter, now—search—all the way to Aidenn Water."

The cluster of lanterns spread into kaleidoscopic figures again, although the men seemed none too happy to leave the protection of one another. But they did not discover any further traces of the marauder or a vestige of a victim who might have furnished all that blood. My own light picked up the last find of the night, a round, battered object on the grass even further north than the blood-stained axe.

"A hat!"

"Can it be Sir Brooke's?"

Pendleton leaped ahead of us and snatched it from the ground, held it from him contemptuously.

"I doubt it."

"I can tell you certainly that it is not Sir Brooke's!"

One man, at least, jumped at the sound of a female voice among us. There was Eve Bartholomew, standing tall and tragic, clinging, I thought, to the last pinch of nerve she possessed.

"I couldn't help being interested, you know," she remarked ingenuously, and gave a little high-keyed laugh. "I just came from the Hall. But I can assure you that Sir Brooke has nothing to do with this affair. He would be mad to take any part in it. He would be mad to wear that rag of a disreputable hat."

"Yes, Mrs. Bartholomew," I agreed, "he would. I was about to say, before you identified the hat as not Sir Brooke's, that it belongs to me. I wore it down the slopes of Aidenn Vale."

"You did!"

"Yes—none too new when I set forth with it this morning, it has suffered a lifetime's wear and tear with me today. That is the history of the hat."

"But where did you see it last?" demanded Pendleton.

"I left it hanging in the entrance-hall. And I saw it on the rack as you and I came down the stairs before we went in to the Bidding Feast."

"By gad, I remember it too," he assented. "Then if—"

But he never finished that sentence, whose protases and apodoses might have filled an hour. Quick with surmise, we turned back to the house.

Millicent Mertoun and her retinue had by this time gone upstairs, but the Hall of the Moth was full of the women-servants of the house, arrayed in white as if risen from their graves in winding sheets. A small boy in a nightgown, scared half to death, was blubbering soulfully, as were some of the women. Blenkinson, the butler, the only man of them who had not got into clothes and gone forth, was quieting everyone with loud sibilance.

Pendleton confronted them somewhat nervously.

"There's been too much racket about nothing," he asserted. "Miss Mertoun walked a little in her sleep. That's really all that's happened. You're all very silly, you see, to take on so. Now get to bed."

But when they had departed he turned upon Eve Bartholomew with a face full of bale. "I can tell you one thing about Sir Brooke. If he doesn't show up tomorrow and clear things up a bit, he'll find no Bidding Feast when he gets here. I'll invite 'em to clear out. I'm not going to have my guests hounded and threatened."

Mrs. Bartholomew gasped. "Why, you can't say that Sir Brooke has any-thing—"

"I don't know," scowled Pendleton, "but I want him—here!"

We are truly blissful marriage celebrators.

….A thought had been germinating in my mind ever since the moment of my near-madness on the lawn, when the iniquity of Parson Lolly had so taken hold of me. When we were alone:

"Crofts, I want to prove I'm not crazy. Show me where you want me to sleep, and give me a book to write in. And keep it quiet, for heaven's sake."

"A book to write in?"

"I have many words within me craving to be penned. Give me a book to write in, and show me my room."

Well, this is the room, and these some of the words.

Now to tell of the many things that happened to me today before these many things.

CHAPTER 2

THE BULL

Yesterday at one o'clock in the afternoon.

About this time I was sitting on a damp sharp stone, looking about me and seeing nothing. I had walked for a long while and gotten nowhere. For there was persistent mist still in the uplands, and I had strayed into the thick of it and was hopelessly befogged, hungry, and a trifle anxious about the probable duration of my helplessness.

My thoughts just then were largely retrospect. I had set out from—well, I have forgotten the spelling of the place, but it's no matter.[1] The names in Wales have fascinating orthography and, to one not adept, rather unobvious pronunciations. I had set out from this place which must be anonymous in order to search for something that had not been seen for several centuries, the private oratory or shrine or cell of St. Tarw, a rather unbelievable name, or, in the American idiom, a bully one, whichever way you look at it, for a Welsh saint. It's one that anybody can say without arduous practice. The saint himself was a rather incredible individual. It happens that I know something of saints, they being a particular hobby of mine, and yet I was uncertain at that moment whether St. Tarw was a man or was a whisper on the faëry breeze of legend. But as it happened, in the course of researches in London, I found hints that, man or whisper, he had left or there had been left for him in what today is Radnorshire, a monument of stone in which he did his devotions, or had been believed to do them.

It was in the Book of Sylvan Armitage that I ran across the clue. The Book is a chronicle of the diversions of a sixteenth-century gentleman, and mine is a genuine first printing of 1598. It contains an allusion which I am confident refers to a performance of the "Merchant of Venice" at Blackfriars, which allusion would stagger the erudite who prate glibly of the "order of Shakespeare's plays," if they gave it a thought. But much more interesting to me is the reference to the devotional seat of St. Tarw.

---

1   Actually Llanbadarnfynydd, nine miles away, where I had put up before. My landlord had given me a lift half-way down in his Morris. (Author's note.)

Sylvan Armitage, progressing through Wales in 1594, visited the house of an Englishman residing in that lately war-distraught country. On one of their "long gaddynges and peregrinations afoot," for riding was not feasible among these broken mountains, they came upon a humble structure of "hewn stones, much dishevelled and marvellously coated by moss," says Sylvan Armitage. He adds that the "cella" had been built under a bank, and that this very fact was then threatening its existence. Small chance of success then for me.

So yesterday while I sat on my ungrateful seat with the mist wreathing about me, I half-abandoned the search before it had properly begun. For the dozenth time I took out the letter I had received the day before from my dear old friends, Jack and Mary Bonnet of Bristol. Their barque, recently returned from Australia, will leave the dry-dock in a day or so and take the sea again from Bristol next Monday. Would I join them in a "terror and pleasure" trip somewhere around Africa or the Scandinavian coast? Of course, I reflected, it would take me fully a week to wind up my affairs in preparation for such an ocean journey. I must drop the saint business. I looked at the fog, felt sick of saints, and almost decided I would go.

I had let down my burden, a soldier's knapsack and a fairly well-loaded one, to the grass beside my feet. I decided to eat my luncheon. I tucked the Bonnet letter away and took out my beef-sandwiches, milk in a thermos-flask, and walnut meats, a substantial meal in small compass. My long morning's tramp on the uplands had made me very hungry. It was not only the tramp, but the slipping and falling and crawling, for the yellow grass was long and trodden flat by cattle, making the side slopes very toilsome, and, in the mist, risky, for you sometimes did not know whether you might fall ten feet or a thousand.

I had been exploring Aidenn Forest, but I had early left the lowland area of trees. The uplands, miles of broad-topped hills in a range of horseshoe shape, were given over largely to cattle-grazing. There were long pastures of rolling and heaving slopes, like the gently-breathing ocean of midsummer. My meal over, I unfolded my contour-map of the Geographical Institute and pondered over it, trying by recollection and inference to determine just where I was. But I had not the remotest clue to slope or distance. I might have been at one extreme of the horseshoe or the other, or any spot betwixt. It was two o'clock.

Neither my literary nor my philosophic studies, which are supposed to chasten the mind to resignation, comforted my thoughts in the least, but suddenly I was aware of a change in the atmosphere. The mist seemed suffused with silver, then with gold. Soon the phantoms of fog had retracted far on either side in lofty, shifting, sun-rayed banks, and the air became clear about me. But I remained in doubt about my position.

For the mist had cleared only to the shoulders of the hills, and left the rolling heights a-sparkle like early morning; but the valleys and the great outer hills of Wales, girding Aidenn Forest, were blind to me. From the declining sun I could tell which way was west, but knowledge of that direction alone was no use. Was I on the western curve of the horseshoe or the opposite? Nor did it help to recall that my ascent of Aidenn Forest had been the north, where the two curves meet, the open part of the horseshoe being to the south. I was as confused as ever.

At least I could walk freely, keep to the smooth uplands without peril of falling down some gap or gully. I strode on in the grandeur of the sun, the mighty halo of mist extending a mile all around, a more gorgeous glory than bully St. Tarw or any other of the blessed men of earth ever wore. The towering wall of mist was warm with the light that occasionally melted through and dazzled the ragged hill-slope underneath; the cloud-caps wreathed and spired like golden smoke, and I went on proudly and merrily in my enormous prison. I felt like a god, exultant. I reached out my hands and lifted my face to the heavens. My loneliness apotheosized me. I laughed. I shouted, *ebriatus*. Never before have I experienced that sense of space and power, that vigour beyond muscle and sense, that reckless rapture!

Nearly an hour passed. Grasshoppers leapt to either side of my path with little soft comings to earth; the sound was like the first drops of rain. Black-game and grouse twice or thrice scampered and scudded from my feet, and suddenly out of the fog which had closed in on my left swept a great bevy of unknown birds with a thunder of wings. I judged then that I was not far from the brink of a steep pitch on the edge of the uplands. The mist which had glorified me was beginning to hem me more straitly and I bore away to the right, being wary of pitfalls.

Gradually, while I moved up and down the placid slopes and crossed wide expanses wherein I was an ephemeral topic for cows and shambling tattered ponies, an inexpressible sense told me precisely where I was on the lofty horseshoe of Aidenn Forest. Fragmentary half-submerged memories of my contour-map, of the dip of the slopes where I trod, of instructions proffered me by scraggy, wry-spoken yokels (with obligato of a pig screaming at a gate), of the arc described by the sun, of the bated breath of the breeze—all these united to fix my certainty. My feet just at that moment were ascending on the flattened grass of a small summit; Mynydd Tarw I knew it was, whose highest spot was considerably above two thousand feet. Mynydd Tarw, on the verge of the horseshoe's eastern bend, was where I had concluded the oratory of St. Tarw was most likely to be found.

I explored the hill and all about, but unfortunately it was creased and gorged by channels, tiny valleys. Trees and rank underbrush grew in these troughs, increasing in thickness down the declivity, and the banners of mist were tangled in the trees. The trunks were clammy, the fallen leaves dank, the earth too soft for good footing. My shoes sank over the ankles in leaves and loam. Bereft of my halo, I had little joy. And after an hour of climbing up and down, groping and grasping, of peering for traces of foundered or buried walls, I realized, with a shock that sickened me, that I was out of my reckoning in the lower fog again, and that I could not trace my way back. I could not even tell in which direction Mynydd Tarw lay.

I was almost frantic. It was now past mid-afternoon, less than two hours before sunset, and had I known the bee-line to my hostel in the difficultly-pronounced village, I could not have reached it before darkness had long covered Wales.

The valleys, immersed in mist below me, were a wilderness, and broad of expanse; once on the uplands again, however, I believed I could find Mynydd Tarw, and thence strike on the true way home. As for exploring the Vale of Aidenn Water itself, I had no reason to believe that man had ever built a habitation there. To regain the uplands was my anxious wish; but not even this was an easy feat. I was weary already, from physical exertion and strain of mind, but it should have been easy to keep my course upward, however slow my progress. Yet the yellow grass and the heather was flat and long, and whether still dry or drenched with fog, slippery and maddening to ascend upon. Moreover, I would find myself in channels torn and scarred by water, now streamless in summer season, but choked with thorny creepers and thick spear-like stalks in malign barriers.

But I persevered, although I found the mist had grown thicker above as day declined. Presently I recognized the sweet smell of new-cut hay in fields above me, and soon afterward kneeing myself to the sharp edge of a parapet of rock, I rejoiced to see the smoky round of the sun. There was a line of wild apple-trees along the rim of the uplands at this point. The crooked branches and straggling shoots of them made them all like black hats of witches wreathed with tattered ribbons, save for the one directly before me, through whose limbs half-despoiled of leaves the sun sent a wicked leering shine that made me singularly uneasy.

I had come into a region thickly populated with cattle. There were a score on the hillock to my right, and when I had gone thence over a bristling wire fence I found a hundred more filling the twilight plain with their shadows. There was not a sound from the widespread throng, but I had a feeling that each dispassionate bovine head was turned toward me, and I advanced with something of the shyness of a child crossing a drawing-room where he feels every eye cold and critical. A little the uncanny sense gripped me that I had happened upon some land undiscovered by Gulliver, where cows were people, and very superior people. There had been so few of them visible all day, now so many; I could not rid myself of the notion that I was an intruder.

(Just then the reasonable explanation did not occur to me that atmospheric conditions had much to do with the migrations of the beasts from place to place on the horseshoe.)

Across an unkempt stone wall which I whipped up laggard muscles to leap—I was going rapidly—sweet-fleshed sheep, of orthodox tan, the cross of Welsh mountain breed with black-faced "Shrops," were nudging one another in an anxious mass. I looked toward the sinking sun and discerned a black rift perhaps a mile distant: the Vale of Aidenn Water, with the prominences of the western arm of the horseshoe, Great Rhos, Esgair Nantau, and Vron Hill, nosing up to the sky even another mile beyond.

Then down on me came dark ruin with a rush.

I was aware appallingly of some vaster shadow blotting out the gorgeous disc which lay on the western hills, a shadow blatant, militant, perilous. A sting of fear in my breast goaded me to instant flight; I was plunging away all in an instant, every part of me in panic, without realization of what it was from which I fled.

Ten seconds of rushing flight, a frantic glance behind me, and my returning faculties told me what that fell form was, horned and pawed, with cavorting death-like head and eyes evilly a-gleam, the shape rampaging, the feet tremendous on the shaken ground. I knew too well those signs of the Hereford breed, the twining horns and the white face so startlingly suggestive of the skull beneath. It was a bull, the hugest bull on earth, insane with murderous passion.

Terror winged me in that course for life. Once I stumbled and rolled down a slope littered with small stones, but my speed was scarcely lessened. I must have regained my feet, for I drove myself through a patch of merciless nettles and awful thorns, yet was hardly sensible of being torn and stabbed. Not until long afterward did I feel the heavy bruise, like the mark of an iron palm, which my hard and firmly fastened pack had printed between my shoulder-blades, saving me a worse blow. Now my due training for the mile at the University, not so very long ago, and the desire for strict regimen then instilled in me, and my frequent jaunts on foot through broad countrysides, were in good stead. In the beginning of this breathless chase, I had had a wide margin of advantage, and now I was all but holding my own, when ahead of me I saw deliverance. For I had turned westward in flight across the leveller hilltop, and the brink of the Vale of Aidenn Water, with its slope looking a precipice all around and its hollow now a mammoth bowl of impenetrable fog, was less than a furlong away ahead.

Risk had to be taken to make safety sure. I chanced another ugly fall by a quick twist of my neck. I led by twenty yards. Gradually, therefore, I diminished my pace so that at the verge of the cliff only ten feet might separate us—and just before I would have leaped out into the turbid air, I used every remaining particle of strength in a sidewise lunge downward to the grass, letting the bull flash with unconquerable momentum over the edge.

But I myself was a vessel of momentum and could not by any frantic clutching and clawing soever keep myself from sliding over the brink and slipping from an abrupt decline to a sharper one, whence with horrified mind I felt myself go over the verge of nothingness! While I fell backward with eyes staring to the lurid sky, I saw the hulk of the bull shoot out from the summit of the cliff. Never have I seen a thing as black as the mass of the beast, with limbs winnowing in the air and head and vast nose outstretched. The black body would have crushed me to pulp had I not flung myself aside a moment before. I know that I must have been still in the air when the bull struck a thrust-out ledge far below the cliff—I had caught just an instant's glare of one eye, demoniac and hopeless—then the animal went bellowing and thumping down through the fog into unseen depths until one final crash and cry ended sound in ghastly silence.

CHAPTER 3

THE HOUSE

I don't suppose I was in the air a second, but there was time enough for me to rue my neglect of Jack Bonnet's invitation. Why hadn't I turned round and gone away from the Forest and let the oratory go hang?

I was aware soon afterward that I was still alive in a queer place under the shelter of the hilltop, a place all caved-in earth and half-buried squarish rock, like heavy tombstones thickly lichened, and resting, some of them, one upon the other. I was on my back with my head on a pillow of fungi; beneath the pillow, however, was a sufficiently flinty foundation. For a long time I remained supine, and listened with interest while my heart gradually resumed a normal rate. The upper tangle of the fog was just beyond and below me; yet when I looked at the dark brink above, I realized that never, never could I climb back at the spot where I had fallen. But I felt a great gladness.

I explored the place little more than was necessary to get my bearings. So upon regaining enough strength I commenced to creep along the face of the cliff, now and then dipping into the region of the mist and losing sight of the sky, which was growing desolate of light. At length I found a slope where the grass was short and turf firm, a sward. I went now at a pace between a walk and a run and congratulated myself on making headway, though the brow of the ravine was forbidding above me still. Then the bank became startlingly overgrown with trees, and the drizzle was thicker among them.

I slowed to a snail's pace, and that was well for me. All too soon my foot gave way on the left-hand edge of a mass of undergrowth quite impenetrable to sight. I struggled to take hold of something, did, in fact, grasp stems that yielded instantly to my weight, for they were frail and grew on a perpendicular face of earth. Once more I had the exquisitely dreadful sensation of falling whither I could not tell. My body ripped down through a mesh and tangle of shrubs that availed almost nothing to stay my descent. I accelerated.

Then my ribs struck a goodly branch with a knock that did indeed break my fall, but before I could twine an arm about this saviour, I had jounced to a lower branch, thence to the ground, this time with only a moderate jar.

I was on a narrow rocky path with the densely overgrown hill on one hand and the mist of the Vale—yawning space—on the other. I thought for a flash that I had invaded the home-ledge of some unrecorded ape or gorilla. For a creature cried out in my very face, a man coming up, as it were, out of the living rock of the path before me. He was fustian-clad, heavy-set, dark-featured, scowling frightfully, and my impression was that he was almost spent of breath. His mouth gaped in a rictus of strain and fear.

"Mawkerdjey—immilath acowal!" So they sounded, the words he spat in my face, the shout he shouted uninterpretable by my English ears in that cranny of Wales. But meaningless as was the shout to me, it remained clear in my auditive memory, as a scene sometimes is keenly limned in one's inattentive sight. And I was sure it was not Welsh. Nor was this because Radnorshire is a backsliding county where the ancient language has yielded to the new. The shape and stress of the cry were unlike what speech I have heard in the remoter areas where Welsh is still spoken.

In an instant the fellow had scuffled past me and was ascending in the fog, while yet I leaned on my hand with buzzing senses and jerky mind. I staggered to my feet and looked upward along the path. At the head of the rise a glimmer of sea-green sunset-light lingered, and the broad bulk of the man staggered against that semi-darkness, a diminishing silhouette. At length I saw him reach the top of the rise, throw up his hands in a sort of gesture of weary achievement, and disappear to the uplands beyond.

Excitedly, and full of profitless conjecture as to what might be his business upon the rolling solitudes of Aidenn Forest, I turned on my way down the zigzag path, being resolved to explore the Vale for shelter since now it was hopeless to make my way over the fells and crags to my Welsh tavern lodging that night. The outcry of the ape-like man was still distinct in my ears, an undecipherable shout, one, I knew, strange even in this region of strange tongues.

I had paused, arrested by a sound the like of which I have never known, a roaring sound, not the boom of cannon or the rage of water or the thunder of avalanche, all of which I have heard. It came from below and far away, a gentle roar; I thought it might be some superhuman voice. As a fact, while I listened, I became convinced that it was a voice of great power with something unique and quite baffling in its quality, one full capable of terrifying a man of unsteady nerves. Yet I was sure that in a different context I would recognize that quality as a natural thing. The muffled echoes of the voice rocked around the Vale; words I am sure there were, the same phrase or sentence repeated many times, but the utmost strain of ear and faculties did not enable me to distinguish the meaning of a syllable. Then the distant shout and its reflections ceased, and I heard only the still grasses. I went on, full of living fancies.

A new sound greeted me out of the darkness, the rippling song of a nightingale on my right beyond the brink. The trees in the depths of Aidenn Vale, then, must be near below. And presently finding almost level ground, I heard the chuckle of water, and discerned a lofty fall of dulled silver, indeed passed it so close that the rising spray touched my cheek. Thus I had found Aidenn Water, not far from its springs on the shoulder of Black Mixen at the upper end of the horseshoe.

Straining my sight in the clogged air, I could trace the black thread of the watercourse on my right hand. Beside it I trod, to the broken descant of amorous birds. And while I went the way of the stream south among the wilding trees, the dark mist paled. I raised my eyes; great Whimble hill loomed before me, and over its stern summit crept a chipped and gibbous moon, softly lustering. While the moon went up the sky, I trolled on southward in air grey and spectral under the frowning summits of Aidenn Vale.

The pathway left the stream for a gentle rise through the trees. Still I could hear Aidenn Water clamour down the Vale while it skipped along. Soon I emerged from the thick of the wood into an open space, the level summit of a vast mound, and with a certain freshening of surprise found myself approaching a lonely wall built by human strength.

A wall—no more—ruinous and desolate, toppled in many places from its original height.

Passing closer, I discovered the confounded and scattered remnant of other wasted walls, strewn like bones in the brightening glamour of the moon. And midway among them stood one tree of mighty stature, doubtless rendered even more towering by the witchery of mist and moonlight.

Sometimes acoustic conditions prevent one from hearing what goes on just round the corner only a few feet away. So, then, my path led me toward the south-west end of the ruin, and precisely at the standing angle of the stone I ran into another man. I did literally run into him, for he was soft and spongy, and my first feeling was that I had encountered a hot-water bottle strolling as leisurely as if on the Mall.

We recoiled from a position cheek by jowl. A light flashed in my eyes, and at the same instant I directed the glare of my pocket-torch, which I still possessed, into his eyes. Our speeches, too, crossed each other.

"Pardon! I didn't hear you, sir!"

"What are you doing here?"

It was not the greeting I had expected; in fact, I felt it quite discourteous. Moreover, he kept the spot-light of his dark-lantern playing on my features for some time, and his piercing eyes studied me critically. In return I gave his exterior a good scrutiny.

My light revealed a tall figure, appearing excessively, grotesquely tall because it was wearing a very high, narrow top-hat, almost a steeple-hat. The man was large and round as well as long. His face compared with the rest of his body was relatively narrow; I saw glittering eyes and a long, straight nose, eyebrows black like coals, and a mantling, pointed beard, also very thick and fiercely black. What gave me the creeps was that this beard did not grow quite straight, but was tilted a little to the left.

His clothing, I saw in this long dissection, was that of an elderly man, a black double-breasted frock-coat, not cutaway, and black trousers which descended to elastic-sided boots. And under the arm toward which the beard slanted was lodged an old, bulgy umbrella with a large metal handle. He quickly shifted this article into his right hand, grasping it toward the point so that it might be a weapon of considerable moment, his left hand holding the dark-lantern.

He was the first to break the silence. Smiling, he replaced the umbrella under his arm.

"Ah, pardon me, please. I see that you are on my side." His voice, now I noticed it, was rather deep, and yet rather young for one of his solemn appearance.

"I'm sure I'm not against you," I answered, and lowered my light out of his eyes. He followed suit.

"You are one of the natives of this region?" he asked, and with his question came the thought to me that he might be a foreigner, although his full, somewhat throaty voice was perfectly assimilated to the Anglican inflections. Those coat-skirts somehow gave him a little of a Continental aspect—and that umbrella! Didn't Schubert always carry an umbrella? or was I thinking of Paul Pry?

"I should say not," I responded. "I, too, am a stranger."

"Ah, you, *too*? What a pity!"

"Yes, am I not correct in believing that you—"

"Quite so, sir; my name, sir, is Septimus MacWilloughby, and I was taught not far from Birmingham. And now, sir, will you kindly tell me what you have been doing here?"

"Been doing? Doing? Why, nothing, in the sense you seem to mean. And have you any business with me? Isn't it rather—?"

"It is necessary."

"I lost my way in fog up there on the hilltops and came down into the Vale in the hope of finding some sort of shelter. I was just passing by this—"

"Yes, of course," said Mr. MacWilloughby, in what seemed to me a rather meditative tone. "Tell me, please: in your travelling today have you run across a very small grey spaniel, with ink-spots?"

I was reduced to repeating, "With ink-spots?"

"Yes, certainly: I repeat, a small grey spaniel, with ink-spots. The dog was not to blame if the bottle was too near the edge of the table. No, I see that you have not. Well then, by chance you may have seen a pair of Scandinavian ponies, both lame in the off foreleg?"

"I certainly have not."

"Dear me," sighed my interlocutor. He stabbed the ground with his umbrella, leaned upon it with both hands, large, red, bloated hands, nervously twitching fat fingers. "And finally, did you notice whether any snakes—"

I was growing exasperated, whether or not this *soi-disant* MacWilloughby was making merry at my expense.

"Don't you know," I asked harshly, "that there are no snakes in Radnorshire?"

"But these were from my menagerie. Dear me, my menagerie will be dreadfully depleted, I fear. You didn't—?"

"Look here," I exploded; "have you a Bull of Bashan on your list? If you have, your bull's dead—I can tell you so much. With the exception of a cave-man who was running up the path there, every animal I've seen has been indigenous."

"But snakes—from my menagerie," he protested mildly, ignoring my tone. He indicated with the umbrella and his free hand, for a pencil of moonlight from rifted clouds had caused us both to stow away our torches. "Snakes about so long."

"No, no!"

He shrugged disappointedly. "Well! If it must be. Then you will tell me, please, which of these hills"—he included them all with a sweep of the umbrella—"is called Kerry Hill?"

"Why, none of them. Kerry Hill is outside this county, thirty miles away."

"Oh, so far away? Then I must be leaving at once. I have a friend who lives in a little house on the top of that hill, and he will be anxious for me."

Whereupon Mr. MacWilloughby strode past me, but checked himself. "Stay—what was that you said about a cave-man?"

I was willing to humour him a little longer. "Oh, I met *him* right enough. He shouted some gibberish in my face and passed me going to the uplands."

"Oh? Now that is very good. You may think it inexcusable of me, sir, but I had the idea for a little while that you were that cave-man. I asked you those questions partly to hear a little of your language. Now, since you say Kerry Hill is so far, I really—"

He commenced to walk away, but I protested.

"I think it's time you answered a question or two of mine. I don't know what possesses you to climb into that wilderness, even if your whole menagerie is kicking its heels up there—they'll keep. But you can at least tell me what I'm likely to find further down the Vale. Shall I find anyone there?"

The stranger's face, in spite of its startling features, grew really pleasant with a smile. "I believe you will find someone further down. Yes, I believe you will find all you want."

"I'm not looking for any special number of people," I told him tartly. "I want a house—shelter—a place to stop overnight. Am I clear?"

Mr. MacWilloughby seemed to have lost interest in his surroundings. In answer to my question he murmured, "Yes, you are very likely to find a house," but his thought seemed to be running in other channels. He was biting the beard of his nether lip. Suddenly he drew himself up. "You might mention—if you decide to stop—to the master of the hostelry, that his many watch-dogs are causing me inconvenience. Secretly, you understand. All this you must tell him secretly. I enjoy the society of the menagerie, and of many kinds of dogs—the Russian wolf-hound, the Dalmatian—but I do not care for the two-legged kind he has out tonight. It is not a thing I like to mention, you understand—it is so delicate—but when one is actually precluded from stepping across a stile—" Hand and umbrella made an expressive gesture. "You catch my drift, I perceive."

"I'll be sure to tell him," I remarked sardonically.

"You will?" he exclaimed with a parade of pleasure. "Then in that case I shall not need protection against the rain."

His arm shot out, and I saw the umbrella fly up like a thick javelin through the air, to disappear beyond the wall beside which we stood.

"Another thing!" he cried, and I detected a real note of sincerity in his tempestuous voice. "Tell the golden-haired woman that I have warned her to beware of the blighter with the red face and the pot of money. She should dismiss him—utterly. I have seen what I have seen."

I emitted a dry "No doubt."

"Thank you, sir, for your great courtesy," said Mr. MacWilloughby. His lofty hat he removed with a flowing ease; he bent his back in an old-time inclination. Then in the fluctuating moonlight I saw not only black beard and brows, but as well a wriggling mass of black hair. He was smiling, but his smile now had a touch of wildness, even of ghoulishness. He set his hat upon his brows again.

"I shall not need even finger-nails if I meet another like you," he said.

He turned on his heel and continued his stately promenade toward the summit of the Vale. I watched him until the moon surrendered and the mist had him. Where was he going? To join that prehistoric man on the hill? And where in heaven's name had he come *from*?

Mad? Was he mad? No more mad than I. I realized, the moment he had projected his umbrella, that he was eminently sane. But he had overplayed his part a little—for his audience.

Continuing on my southward way, I soon passed the site of what had been the outer walls of this great castle, though now little remained save one block of hewn stone upon another here and there. Most of the material had probably been carried off to build some mansion of a later age.

I left the ruin, advancing down the Vale, whose bounds of lofty crag and hanger were darkly visible for a little while. But I could not leave behind me the thought of the huge man and his eccentric speeches. Only new surprises could reave that vision from me; and presently, passing a large, white-painted, wood-gate, I was startled to observe that although I was in a wilderness, it was an extraordinarily well-ordered wilderness. The trees along the path, ash and sycamore, I believed, stood at like distances from one another and were spaced regularly opposite. I seemed to be marching along a smooth avenue in a park; the remoter trees, too, although they were obscure as fleeing ghosts, appeared to flee away in serried ranks. The spaces in the glades looked clear of underbrush. I was glad to note these signs, if signs they were, of human tending, with their suggestion of human nearness, for even my refreshened strength was slipping away from me and the welts and strains of my body were clamouring again.

Quicker than I had expected, I was out of the toy wilderness into a clear space of thirty-odd yards (the dominant moon showed me this), and Aidenn Water was roaming close beside my path. A brook going to join the larger stream from some hill-recess on my left was crossed by an old stone bridge with urns at the ends of its stone balustrades, a ridiculously massive structure for so insignificant a watercourse. But a few seconds later I passed another object built with overplus of formality and ostentation, a semi-rustic house which could have been no more than a summer-house, quite unsuited for habitation but freaked and loaded with statuary and gewgaws.

"The eighteenth century!" I murmured. "What nightmares did they not have in the Age of Reason? Am I now to find a geometrical mansion of Georgian brick?"

I had entered a new zone of drizzle and mist when I had my first evidence of the house appertaining hereto. The fog thickened almost to the density of a wall, and when the well-ordered path ceased at the edge of the lawns, I blundered against a tree trunk, one of three standing alone in gloom and grandeur in the open space. I generously cursed the spirits, whose exhalation, as every Welsh peasant used to know, the mist is. By a flash of my torch I recognized the three tapering shapes as horizontal cypresses, and at once I felt relief, for I was sure that these none-too-hardy trees must be of a recent and venturesome planting. I was becoming convinced that human lives were not far from me.

A few steps more and I was standing on a pebble walk beneath the shorter northern wall of a definitely up-to-date structure. The stone may have been old stone, but it had been smoothed off within a generation, and the ivy had evidently been somewhat restricted in its rambling in order that the broadspread glass of this storey might not be effaced from the light. Why all this glass? A conservatory? I stepped across the walk, flashed my torch, peered in, saw a glimmering galaxy of flowers, sniffed and detected a hint of their thick odour, was satisfied. A conservatory it was, extending from end to end of this northern wall, with unlit, wide-paned windows from end to end save where a steep outer stair led up to a small roofless platform and door in the first storey; and I perceived a vague second storey, above which chimneys sprouted.

Now, I should not have lingered here more than a few seconds, had not there burst forth a chill sound that actually took me out of myself for a moment, a caterwauling from somewhere behind me and further toward the mountain wall of the ravine. It seemed impossible that such a desecration of silence could proceed from a single throat. It was a sobbing cry full of hunger, but there was positive anger and direness in it. It had a quality, too, of immitigable anguish, as though all the hopelessness of dumb beasts were its burden. Once the throbbing cry subsided into a gruff growl, and then, strangely enough, was the first time that I recognized its clamour as that of a cat. "But," I remembered thinking, "it must be a cat as big as a wolf." And while the last throes of the savage wailing echoed back from the hill, I looked up to the gloomy heights of the mansion, as if I expected each dark window to flare with inquiring light.

In puzzlement and lively eagerness to discover more about this mansion, I turned to the right and followed the walk to the corner of the conservatory, where it joined a drive that wound out of the right-hand darkness. I discovered that the side of the house extended a hundred feet or more parallel to the course of Aidenn Water. Visible, too, on the broad lawn at four or five rods' distance from the house was a tall, two-legged thing, fifty feet high by a rough judgment, an erection of twin towers with a passageway above and between, the whole standing lonely, dark and still.

The conservatory's narrow side ended in the jutting of a tower, quite black. Between this and the next tower, its counterpart, I caught dim glimpses of modern french windows, a pair of them, evidently belonging to the same large room. There was a formal entrance between the second tower and the third, but since it was unlit, I decided to go further in hopes of finding the main portal. Yet I had a view of what was behind the door, and again I paused, fascinated.

Inside the third tower, the projecting half of an octagon studded with little windows, I saw a taper burning low in an old candlestick fastened like a bracket on the wall, a thing of fantastic crooks and curlicues. The light was blue and brittle, for the wick was surfeited with grease. But I was able to see three men in the panelled hallway, two of them standing, or perhaps leaning, against the wall. Of these I perceived no more than their dark featureless forms, and a marked stiffness in their attitudes. On the opposite side of the hall from the candle, they were too vague to be any more particularized than as human forms. The third man, save for his little tuft of white hair, had been no more than a smudge either.

For he was bent over, his back toward me, *and he was picking the pockets of the other two men*! I can describe his actions in no better way. They, seemingly stupefied, made no motion to prevent!

I must say that the old, white-tufted fellow was not very adroit at his work. I stood absolutely spell-bound while I watched him paw about the clothing of the two others. The candle guttered with special vehemence, and the pilferer turned upward to it an anxious eye. Then he appeared to make a decision; standing full length, he crossed to the candle and lifted his lean fingers to snuff it. I was impressed by a sight of his narrow brown face, vulturine in contour, with the tall, furrowed brow of a student, the thin, pale lips of an ascetic, and the broken-off jaw of a fighter. The expression was whimsical and wily. The light glinted for an instant on a green eye, on white smiling teeth, and on the diamond stud in his shirt-front. Then the fingers smothered the feeble flame, and he was in the darkness with those dazed ones I suspected were his victims.

And I hastened around the fourth tower, larger than the rest, at the southern extremity of the mansion. What was I to do? Had I in fact witnessed the induction to a serious crime? Was it my duty to report what I had seen? It must depend on circumstances; perhaps the old tufted sinner was the proprietor himself. I must be cautious. I must be dissimulative.

Above all, I must not be surprised.

An electric chandelier sparkled in the large corner tower, revealing it to be part of the sumptuous library of the mansion, empty of persons. I found the entrance I sought in the middle of the south end of the building. The crunching drive made a great circle, leading to a square-arched, ivied entry. A barred lamp above the vestibule faintly revealed the arms of the house cut in stone at the apex of the arch, and surmounting this, as a sort of crest, was the rude but unmistakable image of a cat's head. I dimly perceived a feline nose with faintest trace of whisker running along it, and triangular ears. The mouth was grinning, not pleasantly.

Here was matter for vast surprise, but I must not *be* surprised!

I stepped underneath the arch, to the broad iron-bound black-door. Another pale light revealed the knocker, an iron piece in the shape of the paw of a cat. There was also the button of an electric bell. I grasped the paw and struck twice.

Almost immediately the door opened. "Come in," said a voice. "You've been—"

I must not be surprised! But I gaped, and gurgled, for all I know.

The sturdy square-set fellow in evening dress who had opened the door so suddenly and who now stood in the half-light was staring at me, beginning to look a little *distrait*.

"Oh, so you're not—" he commenced brusquely, and, changing his tone, recommenced, "But *are* you, or aren't—?"

"No, no," I managed to gasp. "I'm not—I don't think so."

I had known nothing of Aidenn Vale or of the ruins, mansions, or creatures in it. But I knew this man!

CHAPTER 4

THE BIDDING FEAST

"Pendleton!" I exclaimed, "the Honourable Crofts Pendleton!"

"Eh?"

"Hail, fellow well met! This *is* a lark!"

The man was nonplussed. It had always been, at least for me, one of his chief charms when we were in the same college, the haziness and obstruction of mind that were so strangely assorted with his solidity of physique. Now, eight years between, he was bulkier than ever and (I was willing to wager) yet more detached from reality in his mental operations.

He was scratching his fine mane of hair now, irresolute. And he really had reason to be confused while we confronted each other in the dimly-lit porch. For I presented such a scotched and scrambled appearance as never before, mould-mud-and-sweat-clotted, unrecognizable no doubt even to my most accustomed friends. Why should he not be startled when in this gear and guise I greeted him with burbling cheer?

He looked so dumbly helpless that I had to laugh.

"Man, man, do you mean to say that you don't remember me by my voice?"

"Your voice?" repeated Pendleton. "Yes, it sounds familiar" (he was lying), "but somehow I can't—"

I kept chuckling, and he looked hurt; so I said, "Of course you can't. I'm Bannerlee, Alfred Bannerlee."

The announcement drove him back a pace. "No!"

"Emphatically yes."

He was studying me intently now, quite rapt. "But how on earth did you find your way up the Vale? It must be full of stinking fog down there in New Aidenn."

"I came *down* the Vale!" I announced. "There's a thimbleful of mist up in the north, too."

"*Down* the Vale! You say you came down the Vale!" Then suddenly realization and recognition of me burst upon him for the first time, and he reached for my hand and gave it a good pumping, grasped my elbow, and took me inside. "My dear man, my dear fellow, you must have had a sickening time. Delighted to have you with us. By gad! How on earth did you ever find this nook in the woods?"

"I'm an antiquarian, you know, a nomad. I might better ask how you did the same," I rejoined. "And, er, are you the butler?"

"No. Of course not. I'm the host. Why, what do you mean?" He stared at me with the old uncertainty.

"You answered my knock with remarkable alacrity."

"Oh, I was just at the door, going to open it anyhow. I was on my way to my room when I heard you out there." He gestured toward the drive. "I imagined you'd want to be let right in."

"But, my dear Crofts, you didn't know who I was."

"Oh, yes, I did. That is, I thought I did. Oh, there's a fine state of confusion here. You see, we've been waiting for Sir Brooke Mortimer since before dinner. And as he's not sent word, we're still waiting for him."

"Oh?" I said.

"Yes," said he.

We were standing just inside the hall, which contained some of the finest screen panelling I have seen. I guessed, rightly, that it was Henry VIII. work. A multitude of little heads peered out from the wall beneath coats-of-arms, and the foliated edges of the wood were as delicate as lace. There was a settle standing on the left-hand side, where the ceiling sloped down sharply, evidently beneath a winding stair.

Pendleton seemed struck by a sudden thought. "You'd like to change, perhaps?"

"My dear man! If you'll fit me out! I shall perish otherwise. As I am, I'd rather not see people."

"Well—would you mind waiting here a moment? I'll fetch Blenkinson. Not long. There's a good fellow."

He was gone, and I sat me down on the restful settle with some gyrating thoughts to compose.

But before I had time to set one thought beside another, a new man in evening dress came breezing nonchalantly past me to the door, which he opened and peered out of, to close it in a moment with a small shiver. It had grown chilly out-of-doors during the latter hour of my odyssey. Turning, he beheld me in my recess.

"Hello," he exclaimed mildly. "So you *have* come. No news of him?"

He was, I now think, one of the most deceptive-appearing persons I have ever encountered, of a type emphatically British, but the extreme of his type. He was the nonpareil for unobtrusiveness and lack of distinction; without even the stamp of vulgarity, he was ordinary and unnoticeable to the last degree. I have never seen a man who appeared to possess so many properties of a vacuum. His age, perhaps, was somewhere about the third decade. He was of no particular height (actually about five feet seven) or weight (about ten stone ten), and his face was all that was commonplace. A pair of futilely brown moustaches divided it into upper and lower portions, in the superior of which pastel-grey eyes kept an unblinking but unobservant watch; below, his mouth and jaw were neither strong nor weak. His complexion was pale but not to excessive sallowness, and his brownish hair, rather thin, was faintly flecked with grey. His dinner coat fitted exceptionally well.

"Yes, I have come," I answered, "but I'm not sure I'm the 'you' you mean."

"Why, you're Hughes, the keeper, aren't you?"

"No, I'm just a friend of Pendleton's."

"Oh, is that so?"

He was not cloudy and remote like Crofts Pendleton; rather I thought I detected even a trace of the sardonic in his tone, and I must have flushed at the remembrance of my rough and woebegone attire.

"I don't look the part, I admit."

"Well, no, you don't." He held out his hand with a cordiality surprising to me. "Belvoir's my name—Ted Belvoir. It's B-e-l-v-o-i-r, you know."

"Bannerlee's mine. B-a-n-n—"

"Oh, that's all right. I spelled mine out on account of these Americans. They think it's funny to pronounce it 'Beaver!'"

"Americans!"

"Why, you must be quite a stranger here. Didn't you know—"

"I know nothing. I am indeed an utter stranger, save for being acquainted with Pendleton. You see that I'm rather the worse for wear; well, I've been running and scrambling and climbing all over Aidenn Forest today, and to cap the climax I fell into this Vale and blundered upon this house."

"All over Aidenn Forest?"

"Yes, I am an antiquary of sorts."

"Now, that's very interesting, very interesting. Why, you may have— have you seen anyone?" There was a glimmer of excitement in his pale eyes.

Now suddenly it occurred to me that reticence might be useful in this mansion whereof I knew so little and that little full of perplexity.

"Why, what sort of person?"

"Oh, a gentleman prowling at a loose end."

"I should say not," I assured him, "unless he was mightily transmogrified."

"Well, that delays us again."

"I suppose the man you mean is, er, Sir Brooke Mortimer."

"Yes." His eyes widened. "Now, how did you know that?"

"Pendleton told me before he went to fetch the butler."

"That's the man, that's the man. Irritating, isn't it? Hughes and some of the other servants have gone in search. That's why our host takes so long to get Blenkinson, who must be busy."

"You don't tell me the servants have gone out to scour for him!"

"He's such an irregular blighter, you know. May have tried to walk it from New Aidenn or even from somewhere else on the line. They're going to telephone down when the station-master comes for the evening train. You see, he wasn't due on any particular train, but they expected him to send word ahead. So they're in a pretty pass."

"What's the man look like?"

"Oh, a little, piddling sort of minnikin. Wearing a couple of pairs of glasses, most likely, and sure to be smoking an offensive cigar. Speaks with a lisp when he gets excited—sometimes when he isn't. You couldn't have seen him?"

"No," I avouched. "Neither today nor any other day." I had already resolved, by the by, to tell no stranger about the men I had seen. I wanted to be believed.

I refrained from asking why Sir Brooke's presence was so necessary for the comfort of all, but my new acquaintance evidently saw the question in my face, for he answered it in a manner to provoke my curiosity yet further. "He's going to propose the health of the bride, y'know."

A third personage came round from the other side of the stairs, and the blood in my veins gave a little leap when I recognized the white-haired man whose suspicious behaviour I had overlooked in the dim room with the tower windows. His gaze was inquiring, as if he had come to see whose the voices were, and when he saw my unaccustomed face, he gave a cluck, as if to say, "I know who *you* are," and demanded peremptorily:

"Are you the missing idiot?"

I said, "Perhaps."

His little dark eyes sparkled. "Then you're not—no, I see you're not. You haven't, by the way, seen a lost sheep of a knight outside?"

"No."

Somehow Belvoir had melted away upon the coming of this gentleman; now the old fellow, with his eyes pursuing the other down the hall out of my view, snapped, "So much the better. We have at least one crazy man here already."

"Indeed! What is his name?" I asked with much enjoyment, expecting to hear Belvoir identified, for I judged that no love was lost between these two.

"Cosgrove!"

"Oh! I haven't heard of him, I believe."

"Well, you will."

He was gone!

I listened to his waning footsteps down the hall for only a brace of seconds before I had made a hasty, rash decision. I would see, before anyone else, what was the state of affairs inside the room where I had witnessed this old fellow's dubious practices. I edged around the curve of the stair, saw him moving briskly away at the other end of the wainscoted and carpeted passage, which was quite broad enough to be called a good-sized gallery. There were two doors on the right, four on the left (counting one by the stair-foot, where the corridor broadened almost into a room), and one away at the far end, which last must lead into the conservatory. A collection of portraits, large and small, hung over and between the doors, although, since the hall was wholly enclosed by rooms, they must never be seen save by artificial light.

By the time I had comprehended so much, the old gentleman had disappeared through the farthest door at the left. An entrance behind the stairs I judged to lead into the library where the light was blazing, perhaps as a beacon for Sir Brooke. The room I sought must lie beyond the door facing the stair-foot. I felt like a burglarious person while I opened it and stole into darkness, taking out my electric-torch. And the moment afterward I felt like a fool.

The yellow cone of light played on walls hung with trophies and weapons of every age and sort. I saw the old candle-bracket by the window, and the closed doors leading to rooms on each side, as well as to the open. Standing where the "men" had been were two hollow suits of armour, complete in plate and chain.

So the old codger's only crime must have been a little harmless fussing about. Still, why had he chosen near-darkness when there was, as now I saw, an electric switch beside the door? Perhaps the switch was out of order; I had not the courage to try it and see. Almost, but not quite, I acquitted the white-haired gentleman of evil design.

I lost no time in returning to my station in the hall. I was on the settle, and had almost decided that Crofts Pendleton had forgotten me when he appeared apologetically, with the butler, carrying a loaded tray, at his heels.

"If it's compatible with bathing, I got Blenkinson to put some dishes together. Dinner's just over."

"My dear Crofts, you're too thoughtful."

"Very seldom, I assure you," he smiled.

"Certainly, I'd like to break the edge of appetite, anyhow."

"Then we'll go up to my room."

Blenkinson, with impeccable whiskers, looked as if he might be the Master of University College. With the tray, he followed us up the circular stairs, whose well reached into the dim heights of the second storey. A room on the right of the first landing was Pendleton's.

"Hullo, it's dark! I expected Ludlow had come up. He complained of feeling seedy."

The long corridor of this floor, which I later found to lead to the door of the landing of the outside stairs at the north end of the building, was invisible until Pendleton touched a button on the wall.

"Ludlow? Is he the tufted individual, hawk-like?"

"Why, yes. Have you seen him?"

"We have conversed slightly. He's downstairs."

"He must be feeling better," murmured Crofts. Yet somehow I distrusted that his Lordship had suffered even a little twinge.

Now Blenkinson withdrew discreetly as a Dean, after examining each dish on the tray and giving every cover an approving caress.

"May I ask a question?"

"Blaze away."

"Aren't things a little out of order here, tonight? Or are there no ladies present?"

"There are ladies, plenty of 'em. But what do you mean?"

"Why are the men prowling around the House? Where are the ladies? Don't they customarily leave the men at the board?"

"Oh, yes, usually." There was a light in his eyes that caused me to expect something quite illogical and characteristic. "But here it's the other way round."

"What?"

"Here the men leave the table to the ladies. It's the local custom."

It had come, the sublimely ridiculous. But still—I ventured: "Then most of your guests are Welsh folk?"

"Not one; all English and American. But 'When in Rome,' you know, Bannerlee. I like to pay tribute to the *mores* of the place. That's a word of Belvoir's; you know what I mean."

In anyone but Crofts Pendleton I should have held such deference to the manners of the parish or the borough or the shire to be a gesture of mock. But mockery was out of the question in that face of perfect guilelessness. So innocent and susceptible were those big features that I had a momentary impulse to tell him that there appeared to be "goings-on" in the House. But I forbore.

So, beginning to lay aside my reeking clothes, I asked him the nature of the party, and if it were in celebration of a particular occasion, and in so doing I met point-blank another of his vague notions, disassociated from the working of any ordinary mind.

"A very special occasion indeed," he declared. "We are having a wedding party—that is, there's going to be a wedding party; tonight it's a Bidding Feast."

"Bidding Feast?"

"Yes," said Crofts, evincing much pleasure in his revelation. "It accords with the folk custom. You look oddly. Haven't you heard of it?"

"Not sufficiently, I fear."

"It's very old, very old, to help the married-pair-to-be to set up house-keeping."

"Then I am amiss in not knowing something of it, having turned desultory antiquarian since we were last together. Tell me about it."

He seemed shy and apologetic. "Of course we don't go into all of it—the donations of bread and cheese and sugar and such, or promissory notes (they've been recognized as legal obligations in the courts, you know). We haven't had any of that, or selling cakes and ale for the enrichment of the couple. These are wealthy people. And we've dispensed with the 'inviter.'"

"Oh, you have?" I asked ironically. "What, perchance, is he?"

"A professional in the business exclusively. He tramps the country for several days ahead and bids the householders with a set of humorous doggerel verses, or printed ballad. I've several works describing it all in the library downstairs. It used to be a universal thing in Wales, but it's almost a dead-letter now." He looked as if he were about to sigh.

"And you say that you're reviving it for a couple who are not Welsh?"

"Welsh? Of course they're not Welsh. Paula Lebetwood's an American, and Sean Cosgrove—well, he's an Irishman."

"One hopes so. And how goes the Feast?"

"We're being terribly festive! Under the circumstances, you know...."

Here was the maddest, one might say the most pitiful, of Pendleton's fancies. A Welsh Bidding Feast for setting up a couple in housekeeping—only minus the Welsh folk, minus the donations, minus the cakes and ale, minus the "inviter," minus about everything, in fact, except the good intentions of the host! A ghost of a Bidding Feast.

"Surely, Crofts," I remarked, "if you are trying to revive the good old Welsh customs, you might suggest a bundling party."

He went red, but was too good-natured to take offence. "Nonsense, man. Don't mention it. Why, it's an immoral thing. Sermons used to be preached against it."

"But under the circumstances!" I repeated his phrase. "Morality is a question of local custom, isn't it? The *mores*, you know."

"*Mores?* Oh, you sound like Belvoir, who's been getting everybody in a stew." He overlooked his own introduction of the word.

"Well, I shan't propose it, my dear man. I know that I should be mobbed, without a Welshman in the Vale to protect me."

A flicker of movement crossed his features, and his voice was constrained, even grave. "Without a Welshman?—well, I don't know."

"You're aggrieved, Crofts. What's the matter?"

"This place is full of wild-eyed superstitions," he declared, beginning to pace the length of the room. "We have a few Welsh servants—they keep the place up while it's unoccupied—and they're agog with the Gwyllion and the Tylwyth Teg. They're stirring up the rest with tales of the haggish fairies and dwarfs and goblins that seem to infect this locality."

"Well," I laughed, yet with a pinch of unease in thinking of the near-apparition who had occurred on the ledge-path, "as long as nobody has met his own funeral and the dames and peers of elfin-land keep outside the walls—"

"But that's just it!" he cried vexatiously. "There's *been* an invasion. The women have made me put all their best jewellery in the strong-box, and still they're fretting."

I paused in the act of drying my back. "You don't mean—"

"The worst visitant of all is in our midst, and unless we dispose of him our nerves will be in tatters!" Then he lapsed into sudden contrition for his vehemence. "Of course I'm not such a fool as to believe any of it."

"The supernatural, you mean?"

"That's why I said I'm not so sure we haven't a Welshman in our midst. He must be at the bottom of it all. Confound it, somebody must be."

"Whom do you mean by 'he'?"

"Parson Lolly," answered Pendleton, with slightly bated breath, and I remember that I was impressed into silence for a moment.

"*Parson* Lolly?"

"So he is called."

"And who may the Parson be?"

"A legend, just a damned legend."

"And a Welshman too?"

"That's it!" he exclaimed with an eager gesture. "Don't you see it must be so, or else there's hell let loose in this valley? It must be a man, must be, must be! Only—" He checked himself.

"Well?"

"No man can do the things Parson Lolly is said to do."

I made a complete break in my toilet and scrutinized my friend, who was visibly shaken. He said, "It's no use trying to describe how it feels to be a host in the midst of such a hullabaloo. It's the very devil. And I can't *do* anything to stop it. Helplessness is a terrible thing."

"Now tell me some of this nonsense," I urged. "And first of all, why 'Parson'? It's creepy."

"It certainly is," he agreed. "That designation adds oddness, sinister, too, to the whole portrait of him."

"What else is there in his portrait?"

"He's old, several hundred years old at the most conservative estimate of the servants. His business is general mischief and bedevilment and, I surmise, thievery."

"What does he look like?"

"He has the face of a demon, red with hell-fire, and streaked with smoke. He has the likeness of a man otherwise, but he wears a great flowing robe of black; there's where the 'Parson' part comes in, I suppose. The robe is vaster than any prelate's of earth, though there again you have the sinister touch. He—he flies in it, Bannerlee, like an enormous crow! He's been seen flying away over the Bach Hill."

"How far is Bach Hill from here?"

"About two miles."

I resumed my dressing, and simulated a laugh, for it would not do to seem too much impressed with this fol-de-rol. Pendleton maintained his appearance of dead seriousness.

"I wonder if there's anything else. Oh, yes—his voice."

"Voice?" My question must have been sharp.

"It's a young voice and an old voice in one. He's been heard, Bannerlee." Pendleton licked his lips. "I've heard him myself."

"You must leave this, Crofts," I admonished, dimly aware that I was cribbing from literature. "You're letting your imagination make sport of you, of course; but, tell me, what's been the spring of all your troubles? What's actually happened here?"

His mood had shifted. "No, let's change the subject. This is no way to receive a guest, with omens and warnings."

"But, good heavens, you only make it worse when you stop at the warnings. I want to hear some of the facts."

"You really do?"

"This is absurd. Of course I do."

But Crofts' mind was then in an unwilling state as regarded retailing the misdeeds of the Parson. He became sketchy. At first there had been annoyances among the servants, the overturning of pots and skillets, the displacement of articles, some so thoroughly removed that they never would be found. For the past forty-eight hours these trifles had been throwing the kitchen into an uproar, but one more serious thing had occurred the previous evening in the presence of the guests who had already arrived. All Pendleton would tell me of this outrage was that it had to do with the smashing of the conservatory window, and that then the voice of the Parson had been heard by everyone.

"It makes me feel sometimes, for a minute or two, that there may be something in it," he muttered finally. "Why isn't it possible that someone has found a method of flying with a minimum of mechanical aid? It will happen sooner or later."

"When I see him taking off, I'll believe—not otherwise."

"That's the sensible thing to say—very sensible."

Now in the course of this long conversation I had disencumbered myself of my damp-heavy explorer's gear, had cavorted in the bath between the rooms of Pendleton and his wife, had donned his dressing-gown and shaved with his razor, had covered myself with one of his old business suits, now "uncomfortably snug" for his frame, but flappingly loose for mine. The food I had reserved until after the bath; although the things were now cool, I took half a cupful of coffee and sampled the leg of a duck. I resolved to confide one thing to Pendleton now; perhaps it would bring him some relief. So, swiftly explaining my movements in Aidenn Forest that day, I related my adventures with the man on the ledge-path, and hinted that he might be at the root of the mischief.

"What time was that?"

"Over two hours ago, I suppose."

He shook his head, wistfully. "No, I wish it was as simple as you suggest. But the Parson was making trouble among the servants only an hour before you came."

I thought of the menagerie-keeper, yet somehow he didn't fit into this situation.

"I'm sorry, Crofts. Still, you mustn't let such antics disturb you."

"I won't, I won't," he promised, but I thought his protest a little feverish.

While we went downstairs I gave him the best imitation I could of the stranger's cry on the ledge-path, and asked him if he believed it was Welsh.

"No," he said, with the gravity of conviction, "no, that's certainly not Welsh."

Bless his simple heart! I believe he knows no more Cumraeg than I.

We moved along the galley-passage, and nighed the third left-hand entrance.

Now, just as we were about to enter, while we heard the voices of festivity inside, he turned to me suddenly.

"I'm sending the boy to your village beyond the hills tomorrow morning—whatever-its-name-is—for your things. You're to be one of us, of course."

"My dear Crofts, I hate to intrude."

"No intrusion. And there are other equal strangers among us. Will you stay on for a couple of days?"

"I'd be delighted."

"Then I'll announce you as one of us."

We joined the Bidding Feast.

I motioned my host to precede me into the midst of the party. Now it so happened that we entered with none to observe us, for this door opened beneath an old musicians' gallery.

We had no sooner entered this shady spot than I placed my hand on Pendleton's sleeve and put finger to lips, and stood to take in the scene in silence. The head of a cat, with ears singularly set back, made a rest for the hand at the pillared foot of the winding balustrade to the gallery. It had given me a moment's shock at first, but now I set my fingers along that smooth nose and peered covertly from the concealment of the little staircase. The Bidding Feast, save for floral and evergreen festoons about the Hall, had all the look of two tables of ordinary auction bridge.

But I hardly did more than give a secret glance at the guests before surveying the extent and features of the Hall itself. Flat-ceilinged, its wooden roof supported by braced thirty-foot timbers, a room regular in its right-angularity, it nevertheless gave the impression of spaciousness. It was two storeys in height, full forty feet in length, and obviously of great age, perhaps a bulwark of war, for its ashlar masonry was undisguised by arras, woodwork, or plaster. Somehow, save for the chimney-piece in the wall beyond which the conservatory lay, a fireplace which was massive without being cumbrous, the appointments of the room seemed to me inept. All the Tudor furniture was gone, and in its stead was a collection of mahogany and walnut pieces from the lion-mask period—and later—looking frail and prettified in that ancient stronghold of defence. The woven-backed chairs, the spindly animal-legs of the tables with their claw-feet, the spider's web marqueterie decorations, were to my mind strongly out of keeping. The waxed floor was in part covered by old English "Turky" carpets. Altogether a medley of anachronisms was the Hall of the Moth, but its walls a-frown and towering chimney-place lent nevertheless a thrill of antique grandeur.

Two of the eight card-players I recognized, of course, Lord Ludlow and Belvoir, who were opposed to each other at the nearer table, where the deal had just been made. Lord Ludlow, who was facing me, lifted his cards from the table, arching his brows above the pince-nez which now clung to his sharp-wedged nose. Satisfaction gleamed from all quarters of his countenance.

"*You* haven't the right kind of face for cards," I thought; then a notion made me mutter, "Or, I wonder?" The old dissembler!

I was impressed by the vague familiarity of the back of Lord Ludlow's partner, and guessed her to be the hostess of the Bidding Feast. I had known Alberta Pendleton in the early days, and had seen that stately back preceding me up the aisle at her wedding. It had taken on added dignity, if anything, in the intervening years, and I expected, rightly, that her delicate beauty (Pendleton had been ungodly lucky) would have ripened into greater loveliness.

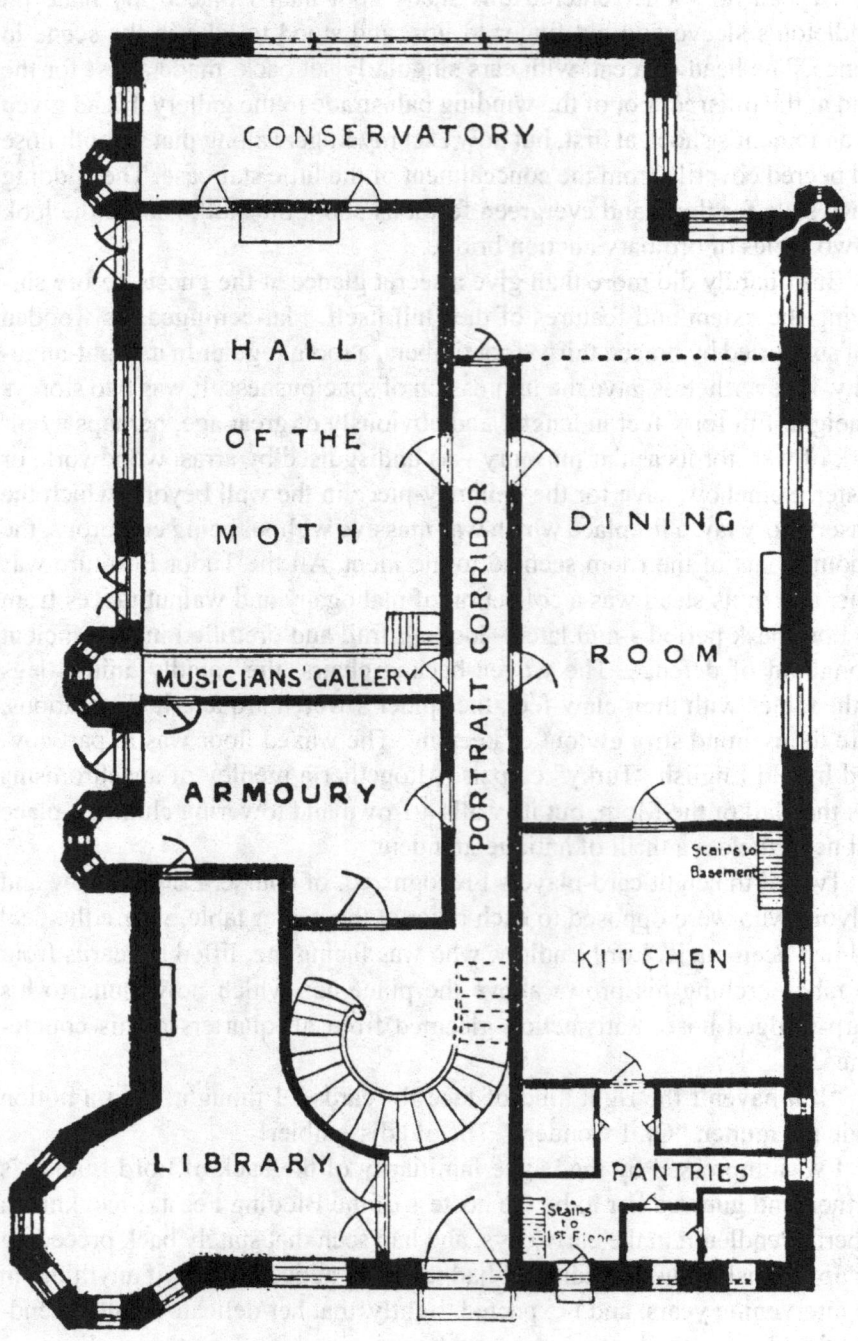

CONSERVATORY

HALL

OF THE

MOTH

MUSICIANS' GALLERY

ARMOURY

PORTRAIT CORRIDOR

DINING

ROOM

KITCHEN

Stairs to
Basement

LIBRARY

PANTRIES

Stairs
to
1st Floor

Belvoir, on her right, was opposite a woman I intuitively knew must be his wife, for she might have been his widow. It was not only that she looked older than she was, and gave that impression, for she was gowned in black relieved by grey, and that her cheek was pale, having a worn softness, or that her composed voice, rather full and sweet, seemed full of twilight memories; she had the half-experienced, half-expectant air which bereft females wear. And indeed I supposed it could hardly be otherwise for her, married as she was to a man who seemed without a trace of colour, without a morsel of flesh to him, or a drop of blood, the acme of innocuousness.

At the far table three men were playing with one woman, whose back was turned to me. Facing her, and me, sat a bright-eyed, youngish fellow with short black hair, a face almost crimson-red, and on his right and left respectively a dandified-looking chap with waxed moustaches, and a good solid individual of immobile swarthy countenance, the image of a substantial, dependable Englishman. This ponderous person was dealing with a regular, unhurried motion that recalled to me the grinding of the mills of God.

"A pretty kettle of fish!" I murmured to myself, and added to Crofts, "A variegated lot, old fellow! So many different tempers and purposeful minds reduced to the same dead level by the permutations of fifty-two pasteboard slips. Saddening, Crofts, saddening."

"All intimates, one way or another," he whispered. "Good friends, mind you, but you'll find them fighting half the time."

"They certainly look engrossed in the game."

"Ah, but that's a pretence. They keep up a very brave front, but any trifling disturbance would set them wild."

"You don't say so."

"I tell you, man, there's something foul and fearful in this damned Vale. I half regret—well, come on. You've got to meet them sometime. They've all heard about you."

CHAPTER 5

KINGMAKER

Forthwith commenced that three-legged race I have already described, in whose zigzag course I was presented to all these people in about two minutes.

While my mind was still in a haze, a small thing caught my eye and made me give a much larger thing a rapid, cursory, and at the same time careful survey. The small thing was still another image of a cat's head, this one in profile with jaws apart and bared teeth, the head forming a heraldic badge tucked into one spandril of the Hall fire-arch. The renewed sight of this insistent emblem had a bad effect on me. The leering head at the outer door, the sleek head at the foot of the balustrade, and this vindictive head brought the sharp, nerve-tearing cry of the outer darkness into my ears again.

"Crofts"—I must have spoken with asperity—"why the devil didn't your family choose some holier badge than a damned cat's head, with nothing funny or Cheshire-ish about it?"

"My family? Not my family."

"Oh, not—"

"Lord, no. Dirty thing, isn't it, that one? But not mine. Bought this place a couple of years ago. Look there, for a primitive genealogical sign."

I thought at first he was pointing to the badge and I leaned to examine it at closer quarters. The spandrils of the fire-arch had the usual long crinkled leaves of the early Tudors; on one lay the royal rose, on the other the badge of the head.

"No, no, not that—the mantel-tree itself."

Pendleton tapped the very old and thoroughly blackened beam of oak resting on the upraised hands and the heads of a pair of grotesque knee-bent dwarfs in lieu of corbels. And while I stared at it, somewhat at a loss to grasp his meaning, he passed his hand along its outer surface, saying, "If you can't see, feel."

This mantel-tree, obviously the original, though forming more than merely an incipient shelf, was unusually low for the period (if I knew anything of such) and I had to lean a bit to get my eyes flush to it. My fingers felt the slight roughness of lettering, and I deciphered, in French characters, the smoke-stained names "Arthur Kay" and "Biatryx Kay," which Pendleton assured me I read correctly.

"None of your ilk, you say?"

"Oh, no! Quite the most ancient family in these parts. Here before the House itself, before the castle."

"That ruin up the Vale?"

"No, I mean the castle this house is remnant of. That other—up the Vale—that was the Kays' too."

"And the head of the cat?"

He shrugged. "You ought to know more of these things than I, you grave-digger. It's part of their coat-of-arms. Look."

I had already taken in the entire fireplace. It was in harmony with the grey walls. The over-mantel, like the interior of the unlit chimney-place it-self, was composed of large stone blocks, very ancient, and the beam on which the names were cut formed a canopy from which it receded to the summit of the lofty chamber. The half-obliterate vestiges of what must have been a cross were visible in the centre of this curtain of rock, and on either side a shield with unrecognizable blurs for quarters. Only where Pendleton pointed I could see what might have been a feline profile.

As my host remarked, the subject of bearings lay more aptly in my spe-cial province than in his (which was, I remember, the excellence of sodium and its compounds). I was about to launch into a necessarily brief statement of what this device might signify, when Blenkinson entered and murmured something inaudible to his master.

"People at New Aidenn," remarked Pendleton with slight ellipsis. "Be back at once." This last was a promise, not an imperative.

He followed the servant out, and my exegesis was, as it happened, for-ever postponed. Gilbert Maryvale, whose partner, Oxford, had made the dec-laration, seeing me solitary, rose from his chair with the peculiar lightness that was so unexpected and came to my side.

He looked at me with inquiry in his very dark eyes while he settled him-self against the over-mantel. "Word from Sir Brooke?"

"I believe Pendleton's gone to 'phone the station-master at New Aidenn. We'll know, doubtless, in a minute or two."

"Yes, doubtless."

I thought I perceived a greater interest striving to suppress itself in him; I looked at him sharply. "Just why, Mr. Maryvale, are we all agog over this gentleman's absence?"

He was abashed for an instant, then, cocked an eye in humorous confes-sion, and spoke low. "Caught, I suppose. Well, Mr. Bannerlee, I don't think that, barring an exception or two"—he hitched a shoulder toward the nearer table where Mrs. Bartholomew was deliberating whether to play the ace or not—"I don't think we *are* particularly agog as a whole. One may have one reason, one another, but mine is that I believe Sir Brooke Mortimer is a good deal different from what he seems. And you may be sure that I'd not be telling you that if I weren't sure that his real purpose will be revealed—"

He said more, but I did not take in the sense of it. Eve Bartholomew, I noticed, played the ace, which was immediately trumped by Oxford; but that was a trifle. What had taken me out of mind for a moment was the striking similarity of his words to the thought in my own brain, that the people in Aidenn Vale were other than they seemed. This, great as was my attraction to it, was scarcely a topic to be pursued with my acquaintance of a few minutes, and my next contribution to talk turned the subject.

"I was about to ask Pendleton a question; may I victimize you?"

"Why, certainly—if I can—"

I lowered my voice to half its volume. "I am sure that you can. This, according to our host, is a genuine old Welsh Bidding Feast. But as far as I could discover, most of the attributes are missing, and especially the most essential one of all."

"What's that?"

"The bride in prospect. I am quite certain she is not, er, here."

He laughed with his eyes, throwing back his head quite gleefully. "You may be sure she's not. Of course, our good Cosgrove's American betrothed—did Pendleton tell you she's American?—isn't in sight just now. The fact is, Miss Mertoun—Oxford's her cousin—has been headachy all evening, and Miss Lebetwood has been staying with her since she went to her room."

Crofts Pendleton had returned; he was beside us on the heels of my latest speech, and his face revealed excitement somewhat chastened by alarm.

"Shall I tell 'em all at once?"

"But what's to tell?" asked Maryvale.

"He wasn't on the night train, but the station-keeper thinks someone like him came up in the afternoon. How he—supposing it was he—missed getting in the motor—there Wheeler was waiting for him especially—unless he wanted the walk—he *would*—well, shall I?"

"It will raise nobody's spirits," said Maryvale. "But suppose you do."

"Hughes and the men are back from below the bridge," muttered Crofts. "They've seen nothing of him either." He clapped his hands for attention.

I kept my eyes on Crofts while he made his statement, but out of the tail of one I noticed that Maryvale was scanning the inhabitants of the Hall, as if to catch the effect upon each. The effect was strong. When my eye took in the room, everyone had laid down his cards and was looking at the blank countenance across the table. There was hardly a word spoken; no one asked a question. Then Eve Bartholomew took up her hand once more.

"Sir Brooke is a sensible man," she announced. "He has probably returned to New Aidenn to put up for the night. And there are men looking for him if he is lost. Let's go on playing."

By her determination, which at the time I divined to be only a courageous sham, she drew the widely surmising minds in the room back to a focus on bridge. A few minutes later Maryvale, with a courteous but irresistible gesture, waved Pendleton into his place at the table opposite Charlton Oxford, and my host picked up the newly-dealt cards with perturbed countenance. Maryvale rested a foot on the fire-dogs—they were of much later date than the fireplace itself, their brass enriched with blue and white enamel—and took from the mantel-shelf a long-stemmed clay pipe, a veritable churchwarden. This he carefully packed with a shaggy sort of tobacco and smoked with deep-drawn pleasure, having offered me an excellent cigar, which I declined in memory and anticipation of flight from bulls.

Presently, since Eve Bartholomew had given the fumes several looks askance, and sniffed, Maryvale with a smile led me to the nearest of two entrances of french windows, opened it, and stepped outside. I followed, descending a step or two to the drive beyond which lay the lawn. The air was mild again and the fog had become only a mystery in the trees.

"Too chilly for you?"

"By no means."

"We'll stroll."

At that moment we were beside the little jutting tower between the Hall of the Moth and the glassed conservatory, with a small rockery just across the drive. I noted that the scent of flowers at that spot was remarkably strong, almost as the heady reek of the interior must be. I asked Maryvale if he did not notice it too.

"Ah, yes. But that's because there's no glass in that window. They're burning some oil-heating business inside until the glazier comes."

"Why, what's happened?"

"You've not heard?"

"I think Crofts—he wasn't at all explicit."

"Nor could he be. It was only a matter of a crash of a splintering window, and a shout by a most hollow and bewildering voice. Then, I must admit, there were other shouts from some of us, and one or two of the ladies were not above screaming. And nothing was discovered save the fragments of glass."

"What did the voice seem to say?"

"It was clear enough. It shouted some rigmarole about Parson Lolly. 'Parson Lolly's here,' or 'Look out for Parson Lolly,' or something of the kind."

"What do you make of it? It worries Crofts severely."

"Do you wonder? No, I don't profess to make anything of it myself. We must wait until we have more evidence."

"Which may be most unpleasant."

"Oh, as for being afraid…"

We paused, I remember, by one of the large french windows looking into the Hall of the Moth. At the table nearest us Cosgrove carefully noted down the score. He picked up the pack, shuffled deliberately, dealt. The cards flew bewilderingly from his hand like a flock of humming-birds released from a cage; they swirled and gleamed in the light. Yet Cosgrove's arms were motionless; only his right hand and wrist moved as swift as the eye could conveniently follow.

"Cosgrove," murmured Maryvale; "what a man!"

"What do you mean?"

My companion's surprise was thoroughly ingenuous. "You don't know about Sean Cosgrove?"

"I don't know much about any Irishman."

"Irishman or not, he's a rarity—a sort of hardness next to positive stolidity, yet with plenty of *savoir faire*—caution in thought and preparation, and then a sure swiftness like that dealing of the cards; add to it a consecration to an idea so whimsical and quaint that heaven must laugh, and heaven must speed him."

"What idea may that be?"

"It's one of those secrets everyone knows—Ireland redeemed."

My "oh" was certainly disappointed.

Maryvale looked for some time at the red face of him before he chose to enlighten me further. "Many wild young Irishmen have burned and blazed for Ireland free, but never one I've known had the genius of imagination of this man." He added in a low-toned parenthesis, "Barring the Marquess of Killarney, I've no doubt he's the wealthiest Irishman in the realm."

"That's enough distinction for one Hibernian."

"Seldom known in his race, surely. And he saves his money, looking always to the gleam of his great goal."

"Well enough, Mr. Maryvale—but you speak as if he had some special vision."

"A Free State is nothing compared to the bright morning in mind."

"Ah, an anarchist!"

Maryvale chuckled. "That was certainly an unlucky dive of logic, my friend. No, Mr. Bannerlee, Sean Cosgrove aspires to restore the ancient dynasties of Munster and Leinster!"

"But—well, how will he find the lines? They're extinct, aren't they?"

"I should hesitate to say categorically where Cosgrove is planning to discover them."

"But how will he set about it?"

"Well, if I tell you baldly, you'll think he's utterly mad. He's going to advertise in the *Times*."

A vast vacuum of seconds must have gone by, while I looked again intently at the huge face so solemn over its slips of pasteboard, before I ventured, "And what do you think of him yourself, then?"

"Let me explain what I meant when I said that Cosgrove will advertise in the *Times* to find the true rulers of Munster and Leinster. He will not advertise there alone; he will put the inquiry in every little rag and sheet. He will send men among the peasants on the land to ask. He will receive answers, will he not, Mr. Bannerlee?"

"Of every sort."

"Of every sort, as you say. The genealogist will ridicule, the republican will sneer or snarl, the crank will present his ready-made conclusions, the peasant will tell the tale his grandmother's grandmother crooned to her and she to him. And Sean Cosgrove will receive every answer for the sake of the good that may be in it. He is ready to examine every contention of the genealogist, to sift the fables rigorously, to get at the root of every wild story, to criticize every legend—and in the end he will find his man, or find his truth! Let us go in."

We reopened the french windows, entered the Hall of the Moth.

I looked at him, who had so suddenly, yet so unaffectedly, made almost an intimate of me in the brief hour of acquaintance, tried to appraise the pent brows and the fugitive, almost wistful eyes of Gilbert Maryvale, the "complete man of business." Those eyes, what were they seeking, or what had they discovered? They saw deeps, I knew, soundings surely unsuspected by these more or less ordinary people, by that old vulture with white plumage, Ludlow—or Belvoir the nonentity—or, certainly, this fancy man Charlton Oxford—or our unimaginative host, Crofts Pendleton—or Sean Cosgrove himself, who from Maryvale's account must represent the quintessence of insurgency and holy tradition.

These "ordinary people," I had called them. But were they, any of them, ordinary? My total impression of that company at the Bidding Feast had become one of masks and shadows. Such obvious contradiction as seemed to exist in the case of Maryvale and such duplicity as Ludlow's might have their subtler likenesses in everyone. Mrs. Belvoir, with her melodious voice, might be a volcano which had never gone up in flame and ruin; this dapper Charlton Oxford might be a leading light of the Society for the Cherishing of Atheism. Crofts Pendleton had assured me that their air of studious interest while rapt in the complexities of cards was a dissembling of fear, but I wondered if it might not be a dissembling of something else as well, something which I could not then grasp intuitively. But I felt its existence, just as a man in a pitch-dark room may be, they say, aware of another presence.

Maryvale, catching me look first at him, then at the absorbed contestants, drew a mistaken deduction.

"No, Mr. Bannerlee, no sign of any of them wanting to give me my place back again. There's a riveting fascination in cards if you're keyed right." I believe he looked a bit ashamed of his cross-bred metaphor. "One of the many forms in which chance plays pranks upon us. All, all thralled."

"Some more and some less, however."

"Oh, of course, but my point was that no one escapes the lure. Even the unlikeliest—"

"Mr. Cosgrove, that would be, I have—"

"I think not, I really am sure not. Oh, no."

"What? You don't mean his Lordship?"

Maryvale took his pipe in his hand, smiling, waved it. "You do not know us, Mr. Bannerlee. We are really quite a surprising company, we friends of Cosgrove, and his, er, enemies. Now who, beside the respected Mr. Charlton Oxford here, seems to you to personify most thoroughly the spirit of conformity, the one cut out most neatly for a player of auction bridge?"

I needed not to hesitate one whit, but with a nudge indicated Belvoir. "He seems made to fit into any background."

Maryvale laughed long and with absolute silence. "Yes, yes," he whispered, "a family man, I grant you, with legitimate children, a householder in suburbia—so far so good. That's irony *in excelso*. But for deep down conformity of spirit, like the thousand and one of his neighbours in Golders Green, ye gods! Why, man, he's the most radical wight in England—a stick of dynamite!"

"He!"

"Haven't you read his 'Bypaths'?"

"His! Good God!"

Then from the farther table came a cackle from Ludlow: "Well, I say it *is* so!… Saint Paul knew as much psychology as any of your puffed-up pedagogues."

Alberta Pendleton (who was his partner) said promptly, "Did you play the deuce?" Our hostess is more tactful than her husband.

Belvoir gave a thin Italian sort of snicker. "He's trying to," he said.

I just made out the low, luscious voice of Mrs. Belvoir: "Ted, that wasn't good. Half a crown, please."

"The family penalty for a pun," explained Maryvale.

Ludlow gave a sudden sneeze, a whooping big sneeze, which must have disturbed the cards on the table. "I beg—" he said, and sneezed again.

My face being turned toward Maryvale, and Ludlow's back being toward me, I had no more than an imperfect glimpse out of the tail of my eye at what happened next. Our noble friend drew his handkerchief out of his breast-pocket with a bit of a flourish, and something white and smaller came out along with it. At that precise instant Ludlow was preoccupied with a third sneeze which took him unawares and made his plumed head bob down to the green board. There was consternation at his table, amusement at the other, but I was the only one who saw the object fly off to the left, poise for the cleaving of an instant in flight, and glide and swoop gracefully down to the floor beside the long-case clock in the corner. There it lay, a slightly crumpled slip of notepaper, scrawled upon.

I gave some small exclamation, crossed in front of Maryvale, picked up the morsel. It was certainly not my intention to scrutinize the writing, but it was impossible in the act of recovery not to see some words. All that made the least imprint in my consciousness were the two concluding lines:

"…you leave it in the mail—you know where; I'll come and get it."

Not even the signature gave me any impression; but it, I must confess, looked like an intentional enigma.

A step or two across the floor would have taken me and the slip to the discomposed Ludlow, but in my way was a large reddish hand, attached to a long arm, and the arm hung on the shoulder of an Irishman whose naturally red face was filling with unaccustomed blood.

"Mine, sir," said the bridegroom-to-be.

I shook my head. "No, Mr. Cosgrove, you must be mistaken. I saw—"

"No doubt. Mine, I said."

"But I saw it come out of the pocket of Lord Ludlow."

"No doubt." Cosgrove swung about in his chair with a ruddy scowl. "And I'll trouble his Lordship to explain how a piece of my private correspondence arrived in his pocket, and will he please tell me what use he thought to make of it?"

Our minds play us pranks. The quarrel itself should have engrossed me, but an absurd irrelevant detail about Cosgrove seized my attention. This was the first time that I had seen the back of his head. His black hair, I have stated, was short cut, and at the rear the recent clipping had left a broad streak of white between his splay ears, so that a person seeing him from behind for the first time, far from supposing him the wealthiest bachelor in Ireland, might take him for a yokel just come from his potato patch, rawly scissored for the fair, to complete with other yokels for the favour of rustic beauties.

Then my glance shifted to Lord Ludlow, who also had swung about in his chair, stiff and upright, his small bright green eyes sparkling, his face full of indignation, like an affronted gerfalcon's.

"What do you mean, sir? I have no interest in your correspondence, I am sure."

"Leave your pretences, shame on you, sir!" said Cosgrove (to whom I had in impotence surrendered the slip). "This is a private communication. I repeat, what presumption—"

"You're mad," scoffed Lord Ludlow. "I know nothing about your communications. I don't carry them about—"

Quite half-wittedly I interjected a hasty, "But my dear Ludlow, I saw it fall when your handkerchief—"

This was mere idiocy, diverting the wrath of the god to my own shoulders. The thin man turned spryly upon me. "If you will kindly confine yourself to your own business, Mr. Bannerlee, without excursions into the fantastic."

"Mr. Bannerlee is right, I have no doubt," asserted Sean Cosgrove with ponderous emphasis; "and he is prying into no one's business when he tells the lawful truth."

"Fiddle-dee-dee!" cackled Ludlow.

* * * *

Explicit! Here, with the hurly-burly of the quarrel is completed the exposition; what admired disorder ensued in the next fifteen minutes I described at the outset of my half-the-night's scribbling.[2]

What has it meant? What does it portend? I am sure now that the intangible feeling impressed upon me in the Hall was one of hostility, not the sort divulged by semi-secret looks and half-heard imprecations, but a congeries of criss-crossed feuds hidden completely by the thick veneer of social amenity.

Well! Sleep we must in spite of thunder. I have written as often I used to, feverishly, with absorption, but never with such a theme! What will tomorrow bring? What shall I have to relate tomorrow midnight? Nothing dull, I hope; I trust nothing grievous.

(Eve Bartholomew, whom I thought I heard prowling an hour ago, left a slip of paper under the door: "Money! I've known Sir Brooke to forget it before."

Poor devil of a woman?)

---

2   All this is more than four times as much as I wrote that night, but I did set down something more than five thousand words. (Author's note.)

CHAPTER 6

STRAIN

October 3. 9.15 P.M.

I awoke, late in the morning, of course, very much refreshed. For a moment or two I was puzzled by my situation; then the tenseness and terror of the preceding night stung me. I knew that brooding over those wild events would lead to no good—of this and other matters I had already made up my mind. I kicked off the bedclothes and ventured out of my door. It was a minute or two past ten, and on my secret march in last night's borrowed dressing-robe down to Pendleton's room for a bath, I found no sign of any other guest.

Half an hour later, in the dinner-room across the corridor from the Hall of the Moth, I sought breakfast. On the threshold, his back toward me, I found Ludlow vehement, making warlike gestures at someone inside.

He looked unnaturally thin and bent, Ludlow, attired in a suit of cottage tweed, a smoky grey, a thing surely inherited from some plethoric uncle, for it hung on his Lordship like a bag and at the same time was too short in particulars. His trousers were certainly not intended to show all that length of woollen sock, and his wrists shot out from his sleeves like a conjurer's whenever, as now, he straightened his arms. His Oxford collar, cut off too soon, exposed a lean craning neck.

Belvoir was seated at the table. He was on the point of remarking in his blandest voice:

"And you know, my dear Ludlow, the notion of obscenity is certainly modern."

"No such thing," sputtered Lord Ludlow. "Your opinions are atrocious, sir, and your books are vile. You should be boiled in oil for your opinions, sir—and for your books you should, er, er—be parboiled!"

"And you, my good sir, should be embalmed," rejoined Belvoir with equanimity. "You *are* embalmed, by Jove! A good job, too. That will explain everything."

"Thank you, sir!"

"Not at all. My good sir, have you ever descended to fundamentals from that altitude of sublime cerebration that you seem to be soaring in whenever I expound my lowly beliefs?"

"Fundamentals? What do you mean by fundamentals?"

"I mean facts."

"You mean a perversion of the facts, sir!"

Belvoir had caught sight of my grinning face over Ludlow's shoulder, and for my benefit, I believe, he carried on a spirited rejoinder. "My books, upon which you have delivered so restrained a stricture, are little more than depositories of facts, my good sir. When I assert that modesty is a purely conventional matter, I am not spinning a yarn from an arm-chair. When I remark that modern marriage—all marriage—is the outcome of hardened tribal customs, I am not foining in intellectual darkness. When I comment on the different conceptions of chastity, instancing the preparation for marriage of Babylonian girls in the temples of the priests—"

Ludlow had been standing still as death during these words, but I could see that his cleaver-like brownish cheek had been taking on a very amiable purple hue. The mention of Babylon fired him.

"Babylon! Filth! Pah!"

"Quite so, if you are viciously entangled in the nets of your own particular hidebound, Tory—"

"You're a fool, sir, and the sooner you—"

"But how beautiful to the Babylonian woman—"

"Rubbish! In the first place, you haven't any—"

"Even you, Ludlow, if you had happened to be a priest in Baby—"

"Outrageous, sir! What right—"

"Why will a Brahmin wash—"

"I am not a Brahmin either, or a—"

"Or take the case of murder. With us it is a crime, but in—"

"Poppycock! Would you do a murder, sir, to show your immunity to so-called custom?"

"I'm too kind-hearted," murmured Belvoir.

"And yet you recommend us to throw overboard everything we have saved from the past—to cast convention to the winds—to wallow in a sty of the senses—to debauch—"

After a few purple seconds, like a puny Jeremiah, lifting spindle arms out of his sleeves while he raised his fists, he turned and stalked forth in a billow of smoke-grey tweed, kicking a porridge-bowl along the floor. Beholding me, he snapped "Good morning" while he went past.

"Lord Ludlow doesn't stomach new ideas very readily. His digestion was formed during the supremacy of the late lamented V.R."

Belvoir spoke from the floor, wherefrom he smilingly recovered the por-ridge-bowl. I then saw that other dishes, and silver, lay scattered.

The "stick of dynamite" explained, "The good Ludlow *will* jump incon-tinent to his feet when he wants to bully someone, regardless of whether his tray's on his lap or not. He *will* eat his breakfast off a tray."

"Good lord!"

"Oh, small harm. I did not press my argument until he had emptied every dish. As you see, neither ham nor egg hath left a stain."

I helped him recover the *disiecta membra*. While we collected the crock-ery from the carpet, Belvoir murmured, "Poor Ludlow! Too many spinning-mills—I'm afraid some of them are going on in his brain."

"Spinning-mills!"

"Yes, didn't you know? Our noble friend is chairman of a good few busi-nesses in cloth—from Ulster to the Outer Hebrides."

"But really, Mr. Belvoir, I'm surprised to find you carrying on any aca-demic controversy this morning."

"Eh?" His features held a vague look of trouble.

I had set about loading a goodly plate at the sideboard. "Well, it strikes me that you were having a row about the wrong thing."

"The wrong thing?"

"Gad, man, hasn't anything happened here to set tongues wagging, that you must bicker with the noble Lord about folkways and the comparative conceptions of chastity?"

"Why, you don't mean—"

"Great Scott, is everyone in the House as indifferent as you two? Am I the only one who remembers there was a massacre last night?"

"Well," hesitated he, "I suppose that those signs and evidences—at night—"

"You mean, now it's good broad morning sunlight, everyone has calmed?"

"Considerably, Mr. Bannerlee. Even Miss Mertoun, who saw that horror, wanted to go out of doors this morning, but Miss Lebetwood forbade it."

"Miss Mertoun!" I looked up astonished from sausage and bacon and steaming coffee.

"Last night, you know, we supposed that she would have to remain in bed half a week. But a blue morning sky re-creates the world, and people. Besides, a couple of the most painful enigmas are considerably lightened. What do you lack? Milk?"

"Yes."

"You won't find any, I'm afraid. The milkman's man—we've had it over the 'phone—is in the throes of a nervous breakdown."

"Doesn't Crofts keep a cow of his own?"

"He does, but the beast has failed ignobly. Well, as I was saying, last evening's troubles are mostly dissipated."

"Which?"

"Sir Brooke, for one. Pendleton has had a note from him in the morning post."

"He's not coming?"

"Well, what should you say? The note consisted of three words: 'Wait for me.' What should you say?"

"What does Pendleton say?"

Belvoir laughed. "Poor chap, he's almost off his chump still, as you may guess. Governing a household threatened with theft and no one knows what else is out of his line. He's in high dudgeon over it—wants to know how long he's supposed to wait, why he should be expected to wait at all, and so forth. *He*, if you like, hasn't forgotten last night."

"What I can't see is, why this gentleman's absence should paralyze the proceedings."

Belvoir winked. "We can't have the Feast proper unless the bride's health is drunk, and Sir Brooke is assigned to proposing the toast."

A few seconds went by while I absorbed this statement. "No one else could propose it, of course?"

Belvoir grinned. "Well, opinions differ. Crofts says anybody can, but Cosgrove solemnly insists that no one else *shall*!"

"What difference—?"

"You'll have to ask Cosgrove; but he won't tell you the answer, the real answer, that is. He's put his foot down, though. No, Sir Brooke means no Bidding Feast; that's flat."

"How long do you suppose the festivities can be postponed?"

"A day, says Pendleton. Then if he had his way, the marriage would take place, Brooke or no."

"The marriage! With all that ugliness and horror unexplained?"

Belvoir shrugged. "What would you have? The fact is that the blood is not so significant as we thought. Pendleton would have sent for the police today, I dare say, in spite of his stand last night, but the source of the blood has been found, or rather missed."

"The source?"

"A possible or probable source. A sucking-pig with all necessary qualifications is gone from the sties. Pendleton seems to believe that a poacher may have slaughtered it, or that someone has indulged in a ritualistic blood orgy, or that—but we can't make out what he thinks, if he knows himself. Come outside, Mr. Bannerlee, and see for yourself how the exhibits have lost their grisliness in daylight."

We met Pendleton at the foot of the stairs. His greeting to me was effusive yet a trifle strained. He had been going up to call me; hadn't expected that after my long—here he looked at Belvoir, bethought himself, and stammered—well, he hadn't expected me to be up so soon. The boy Toby, he said, had at nine o'clock been sent on his bicycle through New Aidenn to the ineffable village, to fetch my bag from the inn, and incidentally to re-inquire about the reported appearance of Sir Brooke at New Aidenn station. Most of the guests, however, believed the identification had been mistaken. As a fact, Sir Brooke was quite irresponsible enough to stay overnight and not 'phone. But since the message— Were we going out? He'd come, too.

On the lawn beyond the mighty gate-house—and herefrom in the day-time we could see the narrow glitter of Aidenn Water beyond the tennis-court some distance up the bank—on the lawn the blood-pool, now a dry clot, and the hatchet with helve and blade both stained, were fenced off with guards of chicken-wire.

"And don't you think these are serious testimony?"

"To what? to what?" Pendleton inquired. "What can we make of Parson—"

"You have swallowed this Parson Lolly, hook, line, and sinker. Now I—"

"You and Oxford weren't so chirpy last evening," observed our host.

I was indignant. "Well! Did I seem to be in the same condition of nerves—"

"You saw the same thing."

"But, Crofts, man, it surely can be explained somehow without—"

He was impatient. "Yes, of course, everything can be explained. Things have been happening, oh, quite explainable things, all of them—only not one of them *has* been explained. But what I object to is giving them an explanation that's pure conjecture. You evidently think there's been murder here. You seem to believe that's human blood. How do you know it isn't pig's blood?"

"Why not try to get someone here who can tell?"

"Someone *is* coming," snapped Pendleton.

"Oh, you have sent—"

"No; more guests arriving, that's all. Late comers."

"Like Sir Brooke?"

"No, not like Sir Brooke. Sir Brooke promised to come yesterday; these weren't expected until today."

"And one of them will be able to tell—"

"Doctor Aire should be able to tell," said Pendleton wearily. "Come on over to the court, and let's forget this."

I acceded gladly enough. Belvoir begged off on the score of writing letters, and Cosgrove, that moment hailing us from the library window, came through the armoury door in baggy knickers and an Irish edition of a sportsman's coat (black and astonishingly high in the collar).

While Cosgrove, Pendleton, and I moved along northward and surveyed the meagre walls of the glazed conservatory, we could tell from the mere vestiges that that large room and the storey of three bed-chambers ranged above it were later engraftings to the house. The tinting of the stones was bolder, undarkened, and brick had been used to some extent north of the tower that marked the limit of the original wall.

An odd thing, that conservatory window fractured by the Parson in his latest escapade. Brilliant purple clematis framed the lower expanses of conservatory glass. Beneath a small birch-tree opposite the great burst-in window we paused for a moment in order that I might see the damaged section. Again the blooms within sent out a heady breath. The gap in the glass was extremely irregular in shape, a good five feet in its tallest dimension, half that in its widest. Today, said Pendleton, the glazier from New Aidenn, already come for a preliminary examination, would bring his paraphernalia and close up the place.

"That's quite an opening unprotected."

"Oh, no fear," said Crofts, "the door from the conservatory into the corridor had been double-locked and bolted from the corridor side. Always is, anyhow, unless someone wants to go in to make music."

"Make music?"

"Yes, the piano's there, you know."

"And how do you account for the shape of the smash? It looks as if someone walking on air had stepped through the glass."

"Someone flying?" muttered Cosgrove, running his finger along the edge of the broken pane.

Pendleton made a movement of annoyance. "Oh, I don't try to explain it. I leave that to you, sleuth-hound. That description of yours sounds very probable to me."

"Our poor, dear host," I murmured pityingly. "Forgive me for harping on the ungrateful chord of mystery."

From beyond the thick-clumped shrubs to the north and toward Aidenn Water came a staccato of handclapping and a few bright tones of voices in the fresh, vibrant sunlight. The sounds reminded Pendleton of our objective.

"Come along to the tennis. That must be Paula playing."

"Isn't it a bit late in the year for tennis?"

"I suppose so, but Paula would play it in Iceland."

"She is good then, I take it?"

"Very good. She'd give you a run, Bannerlee."

"Oh, Lord, I'm no use any more. What sort of court have you, Crofts?"

"Hard. Too much rain here for anything else."

While we went our way, I was all alert for signs of the billowing and swelling marauder of last night, and I thought ruefully how a fictional detective finds clues even in bent grass-blades. I kept my eyes wide. We crossed the lawn and passed near the cypress trees where the black-robed creature had disappeared. Surreptitiously I looked for footprints; nothing was distinguishable.

Before reaching the track leading to the pretentious bridge over the tributary stream, we swung left through the bushes and soon came to a knoll full of scaly-red, twisted strawberry trees.

"These are aliens in England," explained Cosgrove to me, while we wound our way upward through the plantation. "But in my country they are natives. I like nothing better than to loiter among them; they almost make me think I am in old Muckross again. There is one reason why I like your Highglen estate, friend Crofts."

We found a pleasant clearing there, where we could lie, having a view both of the lawns and of the tennis. The strawberry trees extend thickly beyond the knoll and around the court, which is only a few yards away from Aidenn Water where it comes straight down the middle of the Vale before making quite a detour toward the western escarpment. A doubles match was in progress, and the knot of spectators was too intent on the exchanges to notice us.

"There's Paula," indicated Crofts. "Look at that shot! She's master of us all with the racquet."

A white-skirted player had given a leap, a *whang* was to be heard even from our vantage-point, and another patter of applause. I thought the Irishman looked satisfied.

"I approve of the excellence of women in games," he said.

We reclined at our ease and had a good view of Miss Lebetwood and her partner grinding down their opponents. Cosgrove, it developed, had never played tennis, nor did he any other game—now. In his "youth," he told us, he had been a good Rugger player, I think he called himself a "dangerous partisan"; "murderous" I thought might be the fitter word while I gazed at his countenance full of heavy seriousness and wondered when this young man considered his "youth" to have ended.

He swept his arm toward the enclosure where the players darted and skipped. "As for this juvenile pastime, my part in it has been confined to holding the fish-net."

I gave an astonished "Fish-net!"

"Yes, on the stream bank."

Crofts Pendleton rolled over so that he might address me. "We lose a good few balls here."

"Well, these tangled strawberry trees might swallow any number."

"There's more in it than that. It seems almost uncanny sometimes how many are never recovered."

Cosgrove said, "The number of missing balls is extraordinary."

"Yes, and wild shots often go into Aidenn Water. We usually have someone on the bank with the net to recapture them floating down!"

"That must be a grateful task."

"It is like all other labours of love," rejoined Crofts, "a joy to the doer, a wonder to the Philistine."

I looked sharply at my friend; little nippy speeches like that were not like him.

Our talk drifted away from the games. I mentioned that ruin farther up the Vale, which I was eager to see by daylight. Cosgrove had some wild tale about it which he told with sonorous impressiveness—only, while I watched the lithe leaps of Paula Lebetwood and witnessed the accuracy of her shots, the gist of the history escaped me. At this moment all I can recall of it is that the word "treachery" kept coming in. Even if I was distracted from appreciation, Cosgrove seemed to derive a pure pleasure from hearing himself pour forth. But Crofts Pendleton did not dote on the tale; instead this account, doubtless half fact, half legend, seemed to remind him of present broils.

During an exchange of courts, I let my gaze alight on Mynydd Tarw, that northern hill above the ruin, whereon Aidenn Water begins at Shepherd's Well. My glance roved down the western line of hills, Black Mixen, Great Rhos, Esgair Nantau, and Vron Hill, the last directly opposite us across the Water.

"Do you see it?" Crofts said suddenly.

"What?" I asked, rolling over with a start.

"The tumulus on Vron Hill. Some old josser lying up there with a ton of stones on his chest."

"No, I don't see it."

"Neither do I. Funny thing about it, it lies just over the shoulder of the Hill from where we are. At sunset, though, it looks quite grand up there, if you can see it."

"Somehow I've noticed that," I remarked gravely.

"What do you mean?"

"Things look better if you can see them."

Crofts brushed aside my feeble attempt at leg-pulling. "Seriously, though, Bannerlee, you should have a try at it this evening—from your window, or from outside on the balcony. I'm no good at old stones and that kind of thing, but I do get a thrill when I think of that codger up there sleeping it off. He chose a breezy place to wait for Judgment."

"I will have a look," I promised. "I can't see, though, why this antique gentleman selected that Hill in preference to any one of several others hereabout." I indicated with my arm. "Why, that one, for instance, or that one, must be a couple of hundred feet higher. Don't you think so?" I put it to Cosgrove, but he hesitated to commit himself, and Crofts said that I had better ask Miss Lebetwood, if I were too lazy to consult an ordnance map.

"She's hot stuff at all that, really—very useful."

I saw Cosgrove give his head a doleful wag.

"Her brother—American army officer—killed," explained our host. "Before he sailed for France she made him teach her all he knew, apparently. She and he would pore over the maps and plans together, I understand."

"Yes," came in Cosgrove with his voice like the great slow tramp of oxen, "she has too many of these unwomanly things in her head, I misdoubt. Photography—"

"Topography, you mean," contradicted Crofts, surprised out of his jaded condition into smothered laughter by the Irishman's blunder. "Topography, not photography."

"I said photography, and I'll stick to it," replied Cosgrove with never a smile. "And topography as well. Do you call them fit studies for a woman?"

"They, and others like them, are the very things that make you ache for her," said Pendleton with what I considered remarkable penetration. "They form part of the wonder of her, the quality that makes it hard for you to realize just what a prize you've captured. Come man, frankly, what would you give to have her for your wife two days from now if she didn't have intellect as well as a treasury of golden hair and emotions which permit a strange susceptibility to such as you?"

I looked curiously at Cosgrove, to see how he would take the challenge. He took it stolidly, with never a sign on his rufous countenance; only after a while his eyebrows lifted sharply, as if he considered the possibility of truth in his friend's words.

For my part, I soon was too absorbed in the dart and dip of the tennis ball to notice much more of the talk. Pendleton kept trying to tell me more about Miss Lebetwood, how she loved climbing, how on earlier visits she had taken the unpromising lad Toby in hand and uncovered surprising intelligence in him. It all had something to do with photography—or was it topography?—no matter. She had even brought down some apparatus—or was it maps?—and given it to him. Cosgrove kept still now, while our host rambled on, evidently glad of any topic he could talk of without unpleasant associations.

Suddenly the game was over, and everyone concerned trooped toward the House. Pendleton was hailed by somebody and had to join the returning party, though I think he would have been glad to remain out of sight of his country home just then. I was well content to stay with Cosgrove, for the man rather fascinated me; his mind seemed to be full of admirable inconsistencies.

We strolled southward where Aidenn Water makes that monstrous sweep to the west beyond the towered gate, and further where the stream swings sharply eastward again under the very toes of the bounding hills. There stood the bridge, a crossing of one arch: ill-hewn, moss-grown moor stone with a two-foot parapet, quite immeasurably old and quite quaint, with an immemorial ash-tree overlooking it from this side. The water stole peacefully underneath. I expressed surprise that it would bear any considerable weight, and Cosgrove with an air of commenting on the irrelevant remarked that he did not suppose it was ever expected to bear any greater weight than Pendleton's motor or a tradesman's team and wagon.

"Look at it, I say, look at it. They build no bridges like that today."

We remained several minutes there beside the water-crossing, which was indeed picturesque, then turned toward the half-hidden House in some haste, for the sky had gradually been overcast and now there was a premonition of showers in the nip of the wind.

We hastened through the main portal of the House, beneath the stone head of the cat, just in time to escape a flicker and dash of rain.

There at the foot of the stair-well was Pendleton again, with a long, sour face.

I suppressed a desire to laugh.

"Well?"

"That damned, diseased pest!"

"What! Not the Parson once more!"

Cosgrove cannoned an incredulous "No!"

With the suddenness of a conjurer our host thrust before our noses a second cardboard placard scrawled across with uncouth printing mingled of capitals and small letters, now composing a message of more sinister purport:

LooK ouT FOR PARSON LOLLY

He MEAns BUSINeSS

"Ah, yes," I murmured with perhaps a little too much surface effort at nonchalance. "Parson Lolly means business now. He was only trifling last night."

"He was interrupted last night—be sure of that," intoned Cosgrove.

"Damned lucky for us, then."

Pendleton was unsteady with righteous embarrassment and rage when Cosgrove interrogated him. "Where was this thing found?—who found it?—when—"

"Harmony—one of the housemaids—the vixen," snapped Pendleton, and seemed unable to make headway.

"Why is the good Harmony held in such opprobrium?" I inquired.

"I swear she's lying—the minx—or she put it there herself."

"Where?"

"In your room, Sean, lying in the middle of the floor."

Perhaps Pendleton had been saving that item for rather a stiff jolt at the last. I happened to be looking at Cosgrove and saw his eyebrows jerk upward prodigiously, as if they were going to fly off his forehead, and the eyes beneath them bulged and stared like glass.

"In my room? When was this?"

"She just came down from doing the beds—says she found it there not five minutes ago."

"Hem," said Cosgrove, his features settling into a study.

"Come, come," urged Pendleton, making a nervous movement of impatience. "Tell us—when were you in your room last?"

"A little after nine, I think," answered Cosgrove, solemnly scratching his black-thatched head behind the left ear, his look scowling and intent upon the floor, his brow cleft by one heavy wrinkle. "I saw the boy riding the bicycle out of the barn; that would be nine, you said. I heard Lord Ludlow quarrelling with the man Soames for bringing him the wrong color of towel, a quarter of an hour later—fully. And I came out in the corridor in time to see Soames disappear down the stair."

"After a quarter past nine," said Pendleton. "That leaves over two hours—unless Harmony—"

"It couldn't have been there and you not see it?" I asked.

"In the centre of the floor? Mr. Bannerlee!"

"Are you implying that it was left there last night?"

"I withdraw the suggestion, Crofts," I said, "although—"

"There are enough 'if's and 'although's' in this to—to stock a political editor," grumbled our host.

"Has the placard any mark, any peculiarity—"

"For identification, you mean?" Pendleton turned the cardboard over between his fingers, dubiously. "It's like last night's—cut round the edges with scissors or a knife—might have been part of the bottom of a box of sweets." His voice was despairing. "I suppose enough board for twenty foul things like this comes into this house every week. And in all Wales—"

"Our search—supposing we go about a search—will hardly be as broad as that," said Cosgrove, and I was struck, as many times before, by the lack of lightness in his voice. He meant just that: that if the placard were investigated, the whole country need not be drawn into the matter.

Our host turned to the Irishman: "Search won't do any good; that's certain sure. But I'll have the servants up this afternoon. (Bannerlee, you be with me while I question 'em and tell me what you think of their candour—you've no prejudices, you know.) Sean, what do you think of it? Are you alarmed?"

Cosgrove laughed contemptuously.

"But it's directed to you this time."

"It's casual, casual. What could anyone—what could this meddler have against me?"

"It was left in your room."

"By chance," insisted Cosgrove. "There could have been no malice toward me in it."

"But, by gad, what shall I tell the people here?"

"Nothing—and swear the woman Harmony to whisper never a word."

"Yes, of course, I've sworn her on the Bible until she was blue-scared, the jade. But this thing?"

Cosgrove reached out and took the placard. He tore it across, placed the pieces together and tore it again, and repeatedly, and handed the bits back to Crofts.

"Make a small fire in the Hall."

It impressed me as a really brave thing, and I believe that Crofts felt the same admiration for him who dismissed such a message, apparently out of the air, from man or superman or sub-man.

"Here goes, then."

"Has the boy come back with my bag?"

"Not for at least another hour, I'm afraid. He has a long hilly road to ride—down through New Aidenn and all the way around by the south skirts of Aidenn Forest."

"Sir Brooke?"

"Not a nail of him. But the others have come."

I echoed, "Others? Guests?"

"Doctor Aire and the two young, very young Americans."

"And what says the Doctor to the blood on the lawn?" asked Cosgrove.

"He took some of it up for microscopy. He can tell if it's probably human or not. He's more than a little interested."

We had entered the Hall of the Moth from the portrait corridor, and through the plenteous windows saw a swift rain pouring down.

"The evidence is getting wet."

"Canvas spread over," Crofts assured us. "And *this* evidence now gets carbonized."

We watched the fragments of cardboard smoulder, flare, and become consumed in the fireplace where raindrops spattered down the chimney, until only ashes were left, and a tiny spire of smoke. Cosgrove disintegrated the ash with the poker.

"*That's* a blessing," said Crofts, taking out his watch. "Luncheon-bell in ten minutes. Between now and then I shall smoke not less than three cigarettes."

CHAPTER 7

COURT OF INQUIRY

We ate beneath a sprinkling of electric lights and my mind was glum with foreboding.

As usual, Ludlow made himself manifest. His sneer in a shrill staccato was apparently directed against Doctor Stephen Aire, a new arrival. Him I had not yet met, the table being already seated when I came down from revising my toilet in my lofty bed-chamber.

"—and the wrigglings and windings of the new psychology, the *new* psychology, forsooth!"

A diatribe by Lord Ludlow I already considered to be in the nature of a treat, and I leaned forward to see how the challenge would be received by Doctor Aire, who was seated at the same side of the table as I. All that was visible of him, of course, was head and shoulders, extraordinarily broad and square shoulders in rough purplish tweed, and a shocking small and yellowy-looking head with tight-stretched skin, a balt spot like a tonsure in a ring of sparse grey hair, and short pepper-and-salt moustache. His eyes (I could see, for he sat only two away from me) were small and bright and seemed to be twinkling amusement.

"The new psychology, sir—"

"No, Ludlow," clicked the doctor, his thin bloodless lips curved sharply upward at the ends, "not the *new* psychology, of course. *Why, Saint Paul knew as much psychology as anyone living* today*!*"

At this iteration of his own words of the night before his Lordship stared, swallowed, and collapsed into silence. A small but delighted squeak produced by a morsel of a girl at the other end gave away the secret of prearrangement, and a laugh murmured about the table.

Now, I was not the only one who particularly noticed this very young lady, "Lib" (short for Liberty!) Dale. While I took in her appearance, I became almost intuitively aware of another gaze making an angle with mine. Cosgrove was staring at her, so enigmatically that I removed my glance from her to him, just as she turned her blue eyes upon me with a quick little movement of her head. Vastly *interested*, totally engrossed, seemed Sean Cosgrove just then, but the quality of his interest was untellable. In the judgment of a second, I guessed his to be a look of, almost, aversion; he seemed fascinated, yet scandalized. Then the fleeting expression was gone, and he leaned back, turned to his neighbour.

Now I was aware that another beside myself was intent on Cosgrove!

Pendleton sat in sole occupancy of the head of the board. The ends of the table, however, were broad enough to seat two of our numerous party, and Alberta Pendleton shared the foot with a youth of sturdy appearance. Bob Cullen completed the American group among us. His alert eyes had the odd habit of blinking owlishly at whiles; he possessed also a pug nose, a good, clean-cut mouth, and a jaw meatless and determined. Between the mode of his smooth black hair and that of "Lib" Dale's there was, as far as I could see, little to tell. He was very shy. His contributions to conversation, such as I had happened to overheard, had been "That's right," and "Yes, Ma'am," addressed with schoolboy gruffness to Alberta Pendleton, who smiled on him with aunt-like approbation. He has attended for a year, I understand, one of the great American universities.

He, then, was staring at Cosgrove, while the Irishman's regard rested in trouble on the boyish features of "Lib" Dale. The American youth's face went unwontedly white, and his eyes, now wide open, glared. There was nothing puzzled in his expression, only resentment and a vague awe, as if he knew he confronted a better man than he.

Then Cosgrove shifted, and the drama of three seconds, which has taken three pages to describe, was over.

Chairs scraped; we rose to our several heights. "Lib" and Bob were distinctly the shortest among us, and Doctor Aire was not much taller. But the physician, standing up, was the strangest creature in the room—a clockwork man.

That broad-shouldered body in the tweed-suiting was boiler-shaped, and the long, gaunt arms and short, stodgy legs, seemed casual appendages joined at convenient locations. Atop this mechanical contrivance his head stuck like an absurd plaster carving on a pedestal. I could not but feel a queasy, half-repugnant sensation when, on my being introduced to him, his yellowy, almost Chinese-looking face was close to mine, and I saw only the blue shadows where his eyes had retreated and the narrow-lipped mouth nigh to white in its bloodlessness.

I looked about to be presented to the pair of young Americans; they had already skipped out of the room.

"Since it's still raining and we're tired of the things we've been doing anyhow, we're going to get Doctor Aire to tell us about the old magic in this neighbourhood," said Alberta.

"That will be frightfully jolly," I remarked, surprised at the bizarre field of knowledge evidently studied by the physician.

"I'm afraid it will be, as you say, 'frightfully jolly,'" remarked Doctor Aire, with his smile at the very ends of his mouth. "I'm not sure the subject—in view of events—"

"Why not the new magic instead?" asked Crofts.

Doctor Aire turned his head sharply; I almost expected to hear a ratchet click. "What's that?"

"The stuff in old Watts' attic, I mean. We've found a conjurer's outfit there, Doctor. Why not give 'em a show? That performance of yours at Coventry was as good as any professional's."

"Oh, we'll settle that in the Hall," smiled Alberta. "Come along, Mr. Bannerlee."

"But I want him here," objected Crofts. "We're going to examine the servants."

"You really want me?" I exclaimed. "But I don't know your servants—haven't seen but four of 'em yet."

"That's just it," he explained. "I want someone to be here who can get a good unprejudiced impression of how they behave."

"Well, if I can assist—"

"But have you asked Mr. Bannerlee if he *wants* to stay and listen to the silly—"

Crofts besought me. "Oh, come, Bannerlee, you know as much as Doctor Aire does about magic—you with your antiquities."

"On the contrary, it is one of the fields where I have done very little spading, but—"

"There, see," smiled Alberta.

"But I was going to say that this interrogation of yours sounds particularly interesting. I'll stay, if you don't mind, Alberta."

"Of course not," laughed Pendleton's good-natured wife. "I only tried to protect you. Crofts is a fearfully long-winded inquisitor."

"I think I am the best judge—" began he, but the door closed, cutting short his speech and her laugh.

There were thirteen servants in the room when the tale was made. The dessert dishes from luncheon had not been removed. Crofts sat at the head of the board; I was inconspicuous in the curtained recess of the window where Belvoir had sat at breakfast-time.

From this vantage-point I had my first glimpse of the grounds immediately east of the House. I saw an unexpected lawn with lovely flower-patches extending to the kitchen-gardens. On both sides were topless and toppled walls much gnawed by time, clearly a portion of the ancient, much vaster edifice of which Highglen House is a survival. A group of well-preserved square stone buildings about thirty yards away on my right were, of course, the stables and garage.

The half-dozen women-servants and two elderly men-servants, besides the magisterial Blenkinson, were in chairs along the inner side of the room, while the other men stood with marked differences of composure before the screens that guarded the entrance to the pantries and the kitchen. The number of "below-stairs" folk would have been much greater, of course, had not the Pendletons requested their guests not to bring personal servants. Thus we men all valeted ourselves, and for the ladies the staff of maids had to "go round."

Pendleton began bluntly: "It's about this foolishness of Parson Lolly."

Blenkinson lifted the lid of one eye, the better to observe the master of the House. "And did you mean to say, sir, if I may make so bold, that any of *us* have anything to do with the honfortunate affair?"

"Everything, everything!" said Crofts, and to allay a hum of dismay and dignity offended, hastily added, "Oh, don't misunderstand, please. I mean just this: this Parson Lolly—this ridiculous Parson Lolly—of course, we don't believe in any such nonsense. What I want to do is to get from each one of you, if you can pull yourselves together and give plain, straightforward statements—I want to find the origin of this folk-tale—this fairy-story—from each one of you—that is—do you see?"

"Can't say as we do—speakin' for me at least," drawled a gaunt tawny-faced man in a leather coat and vest and corduroy riding-breeches, a cartridge-belt hanging over his arm. His voice had the pleasant modulation of this countryside, with a little chirruppy uptilt at the end of each phrase.

"Hughes, I expected—you see, of course, that it's that common talk of you—all of you—and such as you, that spreads such wild, romantic, and unfounded legends through the countryside. Now, a man four hundred years old—which of you has seen such a man?"

"If I may hinterpose," came in Blenkinson again, "I might remind you, sir, that most of us are not of Welsh extraction. These foolish stories don't 'ave much credit with us from London and other parts, you may be sure."

This speech was approved by vigorous nods on the part of several, while three or four, the darker-faced and smaller ones, glowered for a bit, particularly two of the women, strikingly handsome and strikingly alike. Old Finlay the gardener smiled with sublime sarcasm, such as to elicit a question from Pendleton.

"I was thinkin' as how they was all flummoxed and flabbergasted last night. It tickle me—that it do. They fules!" The ancient slapped his knee and burst into a silent guffaw. "Why, they tales—"

"One moment, Finlay," said Pendleton; "we must go through this in an orderly way."

"Sir," Blenkinson cautioned.

"Oh, yes, yes, of course—what you say is very true—forgotten about it." Pendleton scratched his head, saw light suddenly. "Why, of course, er—most of you are English, not British—"

"What's that, sir?"

"Not Welsh—same thing. I suppose, then—there won't be much—well, let's see how much we do know. I'll take you in turn."

He spoke to the men standing by the screen. "Wheeler, Tenney, Morgan—any of you had any, er, experiences in the stables? Wheeler?"

"No, sir," answered a young, rubicund fellow with a swollen and discoloured cheek and blue-ringed eye. (He drove the Pendleton car.) "Nothing but when we were called out last night."

"Where did you get that eye?"

"Fell over pitchfork, sir, and hit the side of a stall."

"Tenney, you?"

"No, sir." He who answered was a tired-looking man, whose eyelids were most of the time let down. The two words, his total contribution to the inquiry, were drawn out to the length of polysyllables.

"Morgan, you're a Welshman from around this district. You must have a lot of these old wives' tales simmering inside that head of yours."

The man, a swart, square-bearded little man, speaking with the sing-song of local accent, answered that he had heard tell of Parson Lolly "out of the cradle."

"I've no doubt—ignorant folly," commented Pendleton. "Well, what is all this nonsense?"

"You mean about Parson Lolly, sir?"

"Yes, what about him?"

"Well, sir, they do say he be the biggest of the farises and he be out of sight of any man for age."

"Farises?"

"He means the fairies, sir," interpreted one of the women, a mite of a person sitting on the edge of her chair, with a wisp of tartan colour at the throat of her black lady's maid's uniform.

"Eh? Oh, Ardelia, thanks," exclaimed Pendleton, while the stableman Morgan mumbled something about the propriety of a "not Welshly person's" keeping still, and one of the two handsome women gave her small fellow-servant an unsisterly look and said, "Hop-o'-my-thumb!"

"Go on, Morgan," bade Pendleton, quieting a general stir.

The ensuing account was full of omens and transformation, of black calves and fairy ovens, of wizard marks, sucking pigs, "low winds," and horses ridden by the "goblin trot" in stables at night.

"Great Scott, man! Do you believe all this?"

The "London servants" and those from other parts tittered.

Morgan seemed to be weighing his words. "Well, that be hard to say, sir."

"What's hard about it? Don't you know what believing is?"

"Right well I do, sir, but—"

The small Ardelia woman with the fleck of colour at her collar bobbed forward. "If he can't say it, I'll say it for him. Sometimes he does believe, and sometimes he doesn't. Now, Saul Morgan, say if 'tisn't so."

The stableman gave her a critical glare, but assented. "That's nigh the way of it, as Miss Lacy says, sir."

"Well!" snorted the interlocutor. "Sometimes you do and sometimes you don't! And what causes these changes of front?"

"I beg your pardon, sir?"

"What makes you believe—"

"Well, sir, sometimes it's right dark outside, you understand, and things or somethin' you can't see—well, they—"

"What, the things you can't see?"

"Yes, sir. They have a way of surely creepin' in your blood, if you understand what I mean, sir."

"Yes," said Pendleton, settling back, and, I thought, shivering a little, "I suppose I do."

Morgan, on account of his complete and ingenuous exegesis of the lore of Parson Lolly, the object of much ironic commiseration from the "Londoners," pulled out a florid handkerchief and wiped the beads from his brow. He stole a half-ashamed glance at the diminutive Ardelia Lacy, whose wide disapproving eyes made him squirm and shrink.

Pendleton turned to the women ranged along the wall, whose examination was shorter. Harmony, Em, and Jael, minxes with buxom bodies and good fresh faces, were "not Welshly people," and had no traditions of Parson Lolly in their mental make-up, but they evidently had some respect for him born of the stories of indigenous servants. Harmony's troubled look showed, to be sure, that she was remembering painfully to keep the secret of the new announcement of the Parson, but by none save Crofts and me was her embarrassment marked. Ardelia Lacy, minute and prim, personal maid of Alberta Pendleton, was also a "Londoner."

The two dark-featured, vivacious women, were the "Clays," Rosa and Ruth, cook and housekeeper, nieces, it appeared, of Hughes. Rosa Clay it was who had shown a little animosity toward the "foreign" Ardelia, indicating possibly a rivalry in respect to the favour of Morgan the stableman. They knew of no doings of Parson Lolly prior to the arrival of the guests for the Bidding Feast.

There remained three men-servants grouped in chairs about the foot of the table: Blenkinson the staid, Soames, footman, with mutton-chops and unction, and old Finlay the gardener with his irrepressible silent guffaws.

And in the background against the screen loomed the figure of the man in out-of-doors clothing and cartridge-belt, the gamekeeper. Crofts looked at Soames and Blenkinson reflectively, but passed them as already examined. He raised his eyes.

"How about you, Hughes?"

"*What* about me, sir?" Again the keeper's voice betrayed his kinship of race with Morgan.

"You, too, have this mythology of the Parson pat, like Morgan?"

"Well, sir, I hardly think Morgan had it 'pat,' as you say," answered the man, turning the eyes in his motionless head toward the stableman, who muttered something unintelligible. "I don't think he was very well taught, sir—things mixed up, or something, and things that didn't belong there, you might say. Now, as it was always told me—I come from down Powys-way, sir—"

"You surprise me, Hughes, a man of your age and sense. Now, what about this? While the House was empty and you and the rest were caretaking, what signs were of Parson Lolly then? I don't mean larks and pigeons—I mean real evidence lying around, or real activity."

"Nothing, sir."

"Not anywhere in the preserve? Not in the whole estate?"

"No, sir. Nothing used to happen until you brought down the folk that are here now."

"I see, I see. And you know nothing of the cause of the disturbances of the last few days?"

There was an ominous pause, while Hughes seemed to be considering his words. The room grew a little tenser; Pendleton looked up in surprise.

"What! You do!"

"Well, sir, I might say so; it's connected with what I've heard about Parson Lolly. But it's an old story, sir—tells about the great lord who built the castle that was here."

"Ha! It does? About Sir Pharamond Kay?"

"It's sure to, sir."

"Sir Pharamond—hm—built this castle—exactly—well, come on, man; what is this?"

Contrasted with Morgan's, that was a thoroughly intelligible tale the tall keeper recited in his voice with the mellow burr and up-ended sentences. Under those conditions of semi-darkness and suspense in the old, black-beamed chamber, it made a thoroughly moving story. And to one who knew the rigours and alarums of feudatory existence, who realized the ingrown awe of their masters felt by peasants with a long tradition of ancestral servitude to imperious Lords Marchers, it was quite obvious what a foothold in fact this tale of enchantments must have had. For from his youth, or ever that most ancient castle up the Vale was destroyed, Sir Pharamond Kay had been a wizard, and between him and Parson Lolly, then presumably a magnus in the prime of his powers, existed a rivalry shrewd and unflagging!

Wizards, to be sure, are not born but made, and Sir Pharamond went through complicated and profound measures to acquire his occult influence. This was before he had achieved his turbulent lordship, and his father ruled all Aidenn Forest with mailed fist. Sir Pharamond first unbaptized himself by three times spewing out water from the Holy Well. Then he stitched up his own lips with three stitches and for a certain space fasted and remained dumb. When he had unsealed his mouth again, he went by himself to a lonely room and did certain rites with a Bible, a fire, and a circle drawn with blood upon the floor, whereafter the Bible was ashes and Sir Pharamond, as he well deserved, was a true and certified wizard.

All this while Parson Lolly, whose sphere of influence included Aidenn Forest, had been watching the career of the ambitious necromancer with baleful interest, and now the older magician believed that he must try conclusions with the usurper or be shorn of his potency in this region. In the guise of a skipping hare he invaded the castle, and having come into the presence of its lord, suddenly assumed his wizard shape and challenged Sir Pharamond to a contest for supremacy. This took place at the Four Stones (monuments of an eldern time still standing lonely in a field-corner some miles beyond the mouth of the Vale) and the Lord of Aidenn proved to have an Evil Eye so strong the Parson was put to rout. In the form of a buzzard he fled to the desolate summit of Black Mixen at the top of Aidenn Forest. But Sir Pharamond, having assumed the shape of a small caterpillar, clung with all his legs between the shoulders of the bird and reconfronted his rival when he alighted where The Riggles are now. Those enormous scratches are the marks of his buzzard-claws.

Then when the Parson strove with powers enforced by the deadly fear he was in, the tide of battle turned. On that solitary hilltop, moreover, the elemental influences were on the side of the older magician. With a dart of his beak the Parson sank a deep wound in the cheek of Sir Pharamond, destroying the efficacy of his Evil Eye. Then it was the Lord of Aidenn's time to flee, and he escaped to the innermost black sanctuary of his castle.

But Parson Lolly overthrew the castle, whose skeleton of clay slate chunks lies wasting up the Vale to this day.

Thenceforth, although Sir Pharamond lived on, his magic was only the shadow of what it had been, and he lived in perpetual dread of Parson Lolly. He built him a new castle where the mill had stood, and where Highglen House stands today. But he never found content within his re-erected halls. The menace of the Parson hung over his days and nights. Whenever in his woeful heart he meditated regaining his former ascendancy, from the cheek of his portrait on the wall blood would run and in his own cheek he would feel overwhelming pain, as when the Parson had driven his buzzard-beak into the flesh.

"One moment!" interjected Crofts. "Do you mean the painting in the corridor?"

"No, sir; it's that little one way up on the wall of the Hall of the Moth as I mean."

"Ah!" My host licked somewhat dry lips. "Go on."

"There's not so much more to it, sir, I expect. The Parson finally *would* make an end of Sir Pharamond. He sent Sir Pharamond's own corpse-candle for Sir Pharamond to see."

"Corpse-candle!"

"A dimmery light, sir—it floats in the air. It's a sure sign of a death in these parts. And the Tolaeth sounded, too; so Sir Pharamond knew then that it was all up with him."

"The Tolaeth—I don't think I know what that means," said Crofts. The Welsh folk stirred just a little.

The keeper's voice fell, I do not think by design. "The rappin's, sir, that come just before a person dies. Tappin', sir, like—"

Our hearts were in our throats while he finished the speech in a sudden gasp—"like that."

For from the other side of the corridor wall, high toward the ceiling, had sounded three sharp knocks.

And again, before a breath was taken in the room, three knocks again—and again.

"It's the Three Thumps." Morgan's voice was that of a strangling man.

"Coffin-making," muttered one of the Clay sisters, her eyes lightless.

I saw Crofts' glance flit about the room, taking in the whole group. I, too, had thought of collusion, but the number of servants was complete; none had slipped out while the keeper's story was in progress.

Crofts remained irresolute for only a few seconds before he jumped up and sprang to the door, flung it open and glared down the corridor.

"Empty," he said, and I could not tell whether satisfaction or distress was uppermost in his voice. Then the silence for a bit was blank and appalling. He returned to the table. "Get on with your story, Hughes. We'll find out about this fol-de-rol later."

"Well, sir, the Lord of Aidenn was sure to fight the Parson again when the signs had come. He still tried to get back his magic power, and the blood stood out on the picture and the pain came in his cheek. But he knew that it was life-and-death, and he kept repeating his spells and made a man of wax against the Parson. But just as he was going to drive a bodkin through the man of wax, the pain of his old wound made him stagger, and everyone heard the Parson laughing though they couldn't see him, and the portrait fell down from the wall—and Sir Pharamond was dead!"

All of us, I believe, drew a long, grateful breath. Crofts sat quietly, seeming to cogitate.

At length he said, "Look here, Hughes. That's a priceless fairy-tale, but what makes you think it may have any connection with what's going on here?"

The keeper hunched a shoulder toward the corridor wall. "You've just heard that, sir. And if there *is* a Parson Lolly, sir—"

Crofts leapt in the breach to nullify this dangerous beginning. "We'll not discuss such a preposterous supposition."

"They do say, sir," appended Hughes, "that blood will come on the face of the picture when the time comes for Highglen House to be destroyed."

"Destroyed?"

"Yes, sir. By Parson Lolly."

There was no denying that Hughes had scored several palpable hits, besides the unaccountable business of the knocking on the wall, and Crofts was glad to dismiss him, so to speak, from the witness-box.

I, seated in the embrasure of the window a little way behind Pendleton, had an unobstructed view of the upper iron-bound door leading into the portrait-corridor. While, then, I happened to glance at the substantial iron handle of the door, for it had no knob, the roots of my hair stirred and a thrill shot down my spine.

For, very slowly, the black bar was turning while something outside softly pressed downward on the handle.

The fascination that took hold of me then was almost hypnotic. I forgot the room, the people there, the cracked fleering voice of the old gardener; all that existed for me then was the slowly descending bar. To call attention to the thing never so much as occurred to me. Nothing occurred to me. When the bolt of the lock had been drawn back, the door began to open with imperceptible motion—an inch—two inches—and was at rest. The handle gradually returned to its horizontal position. It seemed as if I had taken only one breath during those four or five minutes.

Crofts' questioning went on, and little by little I came out from the spell of the door, which remained ajar. The questioning went on, with some secret listener outside in the passage. Still I held silence, for, clouded with excitement as was my mind in those minutes, the notion of danger did not possess me. I kept my eyes on the motionless door, dreading that it might open further, distinctly unwilling to see what it might disclose—and the questioning went on.

Pendleton was learning nothing from Finlay; I was vaguely aware that the old gardener was fencing with the over-anxious Crofts.

Then a thing occurred to relieve the tension: from the kitchen entry came sound of hurried movement, of a dish falling to the floor, and presently was visible the tousled head of a boy peering around the edge of the screen, a head surprised into a gape by sight of the assemblage.

"Come in, Toby," said Crofts. "We're—"

"I just got back, sir, with Mr. Bannerlee's bag and all. Oh, sir," cried the head, bringing its body into the room, "the Water's swellin' awfully from the rain—"

His hair was quite tangential, and his shoes and clothing bore marks of the storm. An ulster dangled both ends from his shoulders. He was breathing hard with exertion added to stress of spirit.

Pendleton began to explain to him: "We are trying to clear up this business of—"

"I waited under ellum, till the rain stopped," persisted the excited lad. "It went under old bridge with a roar and a roar. I misdoubt—"

The exciting thought of the door softly released and pushed ajar had grown weaker in my mind upon the entrance of Toby. But again my eyes chanced to light upon the portal, and again my blood rushed pell-mell through a throbbing temple. For, unless my senses were false, the door trembled a little, as if uncertain whether to open farther or to shut. The secret watcher's hand must be upon it still!

In a daze I arose and came out of my retirement in the window-place.

"Crofts," I said.… "Crofts."

So hushed was my voice that he spun around in his chair with open mouth, and the servants' chorus gave a slight gasp.

I tried to open a path through my throat for words to issue.

"Crofts… here's something—someone, I mean—watching us."

"How? What on earth do you mean? What's the matter with you?"

I extended my arm toward where showed a long narrow slit of blackness between jamb and door-edge.

"There."

"How do you know?"

My courage was small, but I summoned more to add to what I had. "I saw the door opened from the passageway. I tell you this inquiry has been overheard."

I strode toward the door, while from behind me came the scrape of Crofts rising to his feet, and the rustle of the servants. Open that door I would, if the fourfold centenarian himself were waiting outside to do me mischief. But I believed, and would not have been sorry to discover, that the unknown visitant had by this time fled, and with this hope upholding me I gripped the handle-piece and jerked the portal open.

But no! A man stood in the corridor.

CHAPTER 8

WAGER OF BATTEL

Gilbert Maryvale!

"Oh, you!" exclaimed Pendleton, and appeared completely contented at once.

"Isn't it awful?" asked Maryvale. "Isn't it awful?"

Pendleton and I stared speechless at him; in me, at least, the old surprise had given place to new astonishment twice as strong. What was the matter with this man? The only light in the long windowless corridor came from a translucent electric globe far at the foot of the stairs, but even in the vaguely illuminated passage I realized that something had happened to Maryvale.

"I saw the boy coming by the drive, and I thought he might—there might be some news of Sir Brooke at last. The doctor is telling some powerful things. I've been in and out of there twice. I always—I thought I'd better get away…came to see if the boy had…"

"One question, Mr. Maryvale," I said quickly. "Were you in the corridor a while ago tapping the wall with something?"

"Why, yes, with my friend Crofts' cane." He turned to our host. "But I assure you I did not harm the cane."

"The cane be hanged," responded Crofts. "But why in thunder did you do it?"

An expression vanished from Maryvale's eyes almost before it deepened there, a softness, a look of meekness, a chastened look; I thought it a revelation of painful things kept subdued.

"Something suggested to me that there might be a secret passage in one of the walls of the corridor. I was trying, high up—"

Our host made a disgusted sound. "One thing you may depend upon, Gilbert, no matter what happens. In this extant portion of the castle there are no secret passages. There's not so much as a priest's hole or a trap-door or a double wall to a cupboard. There's one bogie laid, anyhow. You may as well know that you made fools of us in there. Where the devil did you go afterward?"

"I'm sorry if I annoyed you. I just went back into the Hall of the Moth. But Doctor Aire—I didn't care for the hobby of Doctor Aire. So I returned again to hear if there was anything about Sir Brooke."

The servants, of course, had clustered around the door with quite natural and honourable inquisitiveness. Pendleton turned on them.

"You may go—and mind, don't talk about this all afternoon. The subject is closed." Ah, trustful Crofts!

So out of the dining-hall they filed to their aloof world of below-stairs: Ruth and Rosa Clay of lustrous person, Ardelia Lacy (giving the Welsh stableman a look in passing that was obviously a piece of her mind, though its crushing significance was hardly clear from the evidence), the maids, Jael, Em, and Harmony. Morgan and his fellow stablemen, Tenney and Wheeler, got out next, and the tall keeper gravely followed them behind the screen. Soames and Blenkinson both had hard work getting rid of old Finlay, who seemed to think that the occasion demanded more of his japes, and who finally thrust his head out from behind the screen for one last comprehensive wink at me.

Pendleton turned to the boy, who had set about his somewhat unorthodox task of clearing the dessert dishes.

"Did you inquire about Sir Brooke, Toby?"

"Yes, sir, I did," answered the lad, looking white over a load of china and glass ware on a tray.

"No news, I dare say."

"Oh, yes, sir, as a fact there was, sir."

"Eh? Who told you?"

"It was the station-master at New Aidenn, sir. He was very angry, sir, when I told him that you didn't believe he had seen Sir Brooke. He said to tell you, sir, that he was certain-sure. Those were the words I was to tell you, sir."

"Did he take a ticket from him?"

"He can't exactly remember, sir, but he's sure he saw him somewhere in the crowd. He must have taken his ticket, sir."

"Bosh!" exclaimed Pendleton. "Why, I have a letter from Sir—"

Toby continued in his unruffled style. "And he said he remembered Sir Brooke very well from other times he was here, sir. A thinnish, middle-sized gentleman, with a bang of mouse-coloured hair over his eye, and double glasses, and his silk bow tie tilted toward his ear. He remembered him quite well, you see, sir."

"It seems," said I, putting in my oar for the first time, "that *you* remember remarkably well, Toby."

The boy gazed at me as if I were a sport of nature, a phenomenon of dubiety amazing. "Why, he made me repeat what he said until I had it by heart, sir. He was very angry, Mr. Pendleton."

Pendleton was in a brown study, until I plucked his sleeve and whispered. "Thinking won't help. Let's get out of here, or the boy will have something to regale the servants with."

But Toby now proffered a request. "Please, sir, will it be all right if I take a picture of the servants tonight? Miss Lebetwood gave me her old flash-light camera when she came down this time, sir, and I want to use it."

(Photography—not topography!)

"Why, hm, yes, I suppose so. Are the servants for it?"

"Some are afraid of the flash, sir, but I'll show 'em how it works."

"Go ahead, then, after dinner. Don't blow up the place."

"Thank you, sir. I won't, sir. Miss Lebetwood will help me, sir."

Maryvale was still standing in the corridor when we came out.

Crofts relieved his pent-up bitterness. "What a man! He sends me a letter, very explanatory, containing three words: 'Wait for me.' He arrives at New Aidenn station last evening, but doesn't deign to make use of the car I sent to meet the train; he even avoids speaking to the chauffeur, to mention that he intends to walk. He then strolls off somewhere, apparently to lie low until it pleases him to disclose himself. He'll be lucky if he finds the house occupied when he makes his appearance."

"But he may have got lost, of course."

"I had men out searching. Every foot of the Vale was beaten last night."

"Still, your men may have missed him."

"Well, then," Crofts declared with fine sarcasm, "suppose the gentleman did get lost and have to sleep in the nasty, damp Vale and get sniffles. Where's he been all today? Climbing about up there where you were yesterday?"

"Ah, now you are asking reasonably. I can't imagine. What is it, Mr. Maryvale?"

For Maryvale had suddenly grasped my arm. Now he released it, and ignored my question.

I could not gauge the look on the face of the "man of business"; it appeared to have volcanic possibilities, yet subterranean still. To regain the trivial and commonplace, I sounded Crofts on the matter that had irritated me ever since I had seen the unstartling words in the letter of dispute last night.

"By the way, Crofts, I may have to be sending out a message or two if I remain here long—"

"Of course you'll remain—"

"Where's the mail for posting?"

"Why, just hand whatever you have to one of the servants. If you need stationery—"

"But isn't there a particular place—"

"Oh, yes, if it's more convenient—there's a rack for outgoing mail under the staircase. It hangs above the end of the settle."

"Thank you."

Maryvale was busy fingering the lower part of the wide gilt frame of one of the portraits, a full length representation of a man in cuirass and metal thigh-plates, holding his helmet in one hand, leaning with the other arm upon a convenient pedestal; his narrow face looked like that of a newly-elected thane of Hell.

"*That's* Sir Pharamond Kay," Pendleton remarked, "first builder of the castle this House is remnant of."

"Yes…yes," Maryvale murmured to himself, concluding his investigation of the frame. "The gilding is valuable at any rate."

Pendleton and I reciprocated glances of bewilderment, but Maryvale seemed disinclined to explain himself further. He was even unwilling to precede us back into the Hall of the Moth, which he had deserted a little while before, and wherein the entire rest of the company were still listening to Doctor Aire. Alberta Pendleton received us with her charming smile, and we took places beside her at the foot of the room, and that other, smaller, bewitched or accursed portrait of Sir Pharamond glared down on me from the wall.

The rain having ceased long before, and the clouds being a little broken, the sun was, so to speak, red in the face from trying to dry the lawn. The french windows were opened, through the northern one we caught glimpses of the glassman from New Aidenn making whole the damaged conservatory window. But there was no tendency toward seeking the out-of-doors. Most of the party were quite sated with the open-air sports afforded in Aidenn Vale.

Doctor Aire, moreover, would have demanded attention under any circumstances. Apart from the fascination of his subject, there was authority in the clipped, methodical manner of his speech. Just now he was telling of the last case of Appeal of Murder, that relic of early ages whereby one acquitted of a death-crime could be compelled to defend himself anew by the might of his body. As late as 1819, it appeared, one Thornton, when acquitted, and when the dead girl's brother had made Appeal of Murder against him, had thrown down in challenge to "wager of battel"—this we were in time to hear—a gauntlet as strange as the occasion, without either fingers or thumbs, made of white tanned skin, ornamented with sewn tracery and silk fringes, crossed by a narrow band of red leather with leather tags and thongs for fastening.

Cosgrove was listening. But of a sudden it seemed to me that his attention was curiously directed beyond Doctor Aire, beyond the vicissitudes of the accused and acquitted Thornton, who had needed to go on trial again with only the prowess of his body to defend himself.

"Listening, surely," I told myself, and asked myself, "*For what?*"

Doctor Aire's recital went on, encyclopedically.

"Lord Ellenborough had to admit that the procedure was competent, although there had not been a whisper of the Appeal throughout the kingdom for forty years. But the curious crowd was disappointed when the appellant withdrew; so there was no gladiatorial exhibition for the chief justice to preside over. It is extremely unlikely that Mary Ashford's brother had ever intended to carry his Appeal into force, he being a slighter man of body than the appellee—and for that reason Thornton had probably been emboldened to make the brave show he did with his extraordinary gauntlet of white tanned leather."

In the half-darkness underneath the musicians' gallery were a pair of listeners who had been within neither the range of my vision nor the scope of my thought. Now one of them, the young American, Bob Cullen, became in an instant the cynosure of the company.

For the youth, scarcely more than a lad, rose from his seat beside Lib Dale, and the exclamation that came from his lips twisted every neck in the Hall.

"So *that* was it!" The expression of ire on those young, unformed features was almost comical.

Despite a hurried, "Bob, don't be sil," from Lib, the youth advanced a couple of steps toward Cosgrove, leaving no doubt against whom his wrath was directed. He raised his shaking arm and pointed at the Irishman, he opened his mouth and was attempting articulate words, but only one word issued, a smothered one:

"You—you—"

Cosgrove's face was a thing to watch, while the parade of emotions passed across it. Mere surprise vanished with the first turn of his head along with the rest of the heads. His eyes widened, but for a few seconds were blank with absolute stupefaction, and when enlightenment finally appeared to come within him, the resentment expressed in his lowering brows and glowing eyes seemed to be mingled with a sense of shame, or else there was no meaning in the sidewise shift of those eyes and in those irresolute lips. He swallowed, and his head made a small, sharp jerk in the act. A muscle twitched in his cheek. Bob Cullen was still saying, "You—you—" and Lib Dale was whispering dire things to him.

That other, admirable, American tried to deal with the frenzied youth. Paula Lebetwood said, "Bob, you're making a child of yourself. Remember where you are."

"What's the trouble?" asked Ludlow in a matter-of-fact tone.

"Ask him—ask him, that's all!" cried Bob Cullen bitterly, and then, as is the wont of youths who believe themselves wronged, commenced himself to explain. "He thought—you thought, Mr. Cosgrove"—("*Mr.*" Cosgrove; much revealed by that "Mr.")—"you thought that because you were bigger and stronger than I was, that you could get away with talking the way you did. Well, you needn't think that it was because I was afraid of you—"

I noticed that Lib Dale was actually twisting her young compatriot's arm in an endeavour to gain his attention, but he held on through pain, white and red by turns.

"I'm ready any time you are, Mr. Cosgrove, and don't you forget it. I'll show you, Mr. Cosgrove. I'll fight you a duel or a wager of battle or any-thing—"

"My dear boy," slipped in Doctor Aire, who took the interruption of his narrative in very good humour, "the wager of battle is null and void. That was the whole upshot of my story, if you had only the patience—"

"I don't care if it's null and void or not. Mr. Cosgrove, if you're a man—"

Paula Lebetwood had taken hold of the half-hysterical youth's other arm; she placed a firm hand across his mouth, effectually stifling what further wild challenge he might have uttered on the spot. Lib sank down flushed and pouting, her blue eyes flinging defiance to all of us. Cosgrove, who had not uttered a word, had a face like a man's in an apoplexy, and his head was lower between his shoulders than it was accustomed to be.

The youngster Bob Cullen was still standing there like a bulldog in the centre of the ring, anger adding a degree of dignity to his stature. Ten, twenty, seconds may have gone by, and still he confronted the Irishman, whose only recognition of his challenge had been a turn of his head and that slow dark flame in his face.

"Well?" demanded Bob Cullen.

Still the Irishman preserved a silence of stone.

"Oh, Bob, you sorehead," cried Lib Dale, grinding her heel into the car-pet. "Of all the id—"

"But Bob, dear," pleaded Miss Lebetwood, "what Sean said to Lib was long, long ago in the spring, and she's forgotten all about it, and so should you, you silly kid."

The voice of Cosgrove came thundering, overwhelming. "Woman," he said, and a quite perceptible thrill passed over us, for he spoke to his intended wife, and "woman" as he said it then sounded the most brutal word he could use—"woman, no need for you to defend me. The code of this young upstart is not my code, by the heavens—nor is yours my code. Stand aside."

"Sean!"

"Stand aside—did you hear?"

"But Sean—"

"While the light is in me, I shall offer it to you, woman, and to all others I find in need of grace—even if it gall your young upstart there."

Paula Lebetwood had tottered a step backward, with an expression of the utmost pain and loss upon her face. Suddenly her face was hidden in her hands, and her shoulders heaved with swift gusts of feeling. Then she lifted her face tearless and hot-eyed and defiant beneath golden hair turning to riot.

"Sean, how unmanly, how cowardly! Oh, if you knew how I despise you now. Oh, I need air—air!"

She turned from us abruptly, then paused. Her bosom moved in a long, slow breathing, and she turned her head to look at her lover, whose gaze did not meet hers. A veil of anger seemed to fall from her features, and the fire softened in her eyes. But this was no melting mood. Instead, a serene aloofness reigned in her face, and she seemed like one who studied Cosgrove from some region above, studied him with sympathy and compassion. For a space of time—perhaps a minute—there was this silence. Then, as if she had shown enough that she was not embittered by passion, she departed swiftly.

Through the passage of the french windows she strode, out to the lawn, and across, to be lost to sight in shrubs alongside the gate-house.

So, splitting into new faction and fresh enmity at every hour, the Bidding Feast at last witnessed the discord of the lovers themselves.

Cosgrove's rebuke of his betrothed had stunned us, and her answering rebuke had left us wild and speechless. None stirred to follow Miss Lebetwood. In me, at least, the strife of feeling was comparable to the mad stress of the night before, when the first message of Parson Lolly had been found. I knew a delirium of bewilderment, a very horror, in the instants following those outbursts.

Cosgrove's face, now so blotted with blood, took fantastic dimensions, seemed twice its size. The room appeared an enormous room, and the people pigmy people. Sir Pharamond's portrait leered and sneered. Every proportion was indecently distorted, and time, like space, was bereft of its comfortable conventions. The seconds seemed to stagger past.

Then Pendleton, no longer held by Alberta, rose so hastily that his chair banged backward against the stair-post of the little gallery. "Yes, by gad! Let's all get some air. This room is stuffy as blazes. That's what puts us all at sixes and sevens."

"I really think," observed Eve Bartholomew, "that it's the absence of Sir Brooke that gets so on our nerves."

"Let's declare a truce—no, let's make peace," smiled Alberta Pendleton. "Sean, you and Bob haven't any ill-will, have you?"

Since his betrothed's condemnation of him, no petty enmity could very well find hold in Cosgrove's soul. His defeat told in his dejected head and drooped lids. He didn't answer Alberta.

But Bob Cullen, whose excitement had flagged, was suddenly overwhelmed by his former audacity. "I—I suppose you folks must think—you must think—"

"That's all right, Bob," soothed Alberta; "you just lost your temper for a minute, that was all. Anybody is likely to do that."

"He let Mr. Cosgrove get his goat," put in Lib Dale in a *sotto voce obbligato*; she was still much displeased with her compatriot.

"I'm—I'm sorry—I apologize," said Bob.

"As for me," said Cosgrove suddenly, "I do more than apologize; I make anew."

"Why, Sean, how—what can you mean?" gasped Alberta, for the Irishman now stood on his feet looking around the Hall without explaining his remark.

"Yes, it will do," muttered Cosgrove. "God can come from there"; and he gestured toward the musicians' gallery.

"G-g-god?" stammered Pendleton.

"God the Creator," responded Sean Cosgrove, and he appended a few words as inconsequential as any Crofts himself could have used: "I've seen the book in your library."

"But what do you mean, man?" cried Pendleton. "I never heard—"

"Tonight," said Cosgrove, "in this Hall we shall rehearse the play of 'Noah's Flood.'"

"'Noah's Flood!'" came a gasp from most of us.

"Animal crackers," mumbled Bob Cullen obscurely.

"What's 'Noah's Flood?'" asked Pendleton. "I've never seen any book of that name—"

"It is inside a book of another name," answered Cosgrove; "one you have never opened, I dare say. Here, at five o'clock, we shall have tea; is it not so? Then I shall unfold—"

"It's an old mystery-play," said Alberta. "Crofts, I'm surprised."

"But won't there be, er, costumes, and so forth?"

"For me, at least, no costume," declared Cosgrove. "Man, made in the image of God, shall need no gaudery. I should scorn to deck and disguise myself to play my God."

"You don't mean that you're to appear in the, er, in the—"

"In the altogether?" finished Eve Bartholomew in a thin quasi-hysterical tone. "Oh, Mr. Cosgrove—"

"No doubt," Doctor Aire put in sardonically, "Sean is thinking of the mediaeval way of playing Adam and Eve with a screen up to their necks."

"Leave it to me," said Cosgrove.

"But won't all this furniture have to be shifted?" inquired Pendleton nervously.

"Leave it to me."

"Alone—how will you do it?"

"With my God-given arms."

"But shouldn't the servants—"

"I will do everything that must be done. But first," and here I thought Cosgrove became a little wistful, "let us go outside and breathe the God-given air. Leave all to me; assemble here at five o'clock."

He marched out, his face, with a look of grim regret and determination, turned toward the place in the shrubbery where Paula Lebetwood had disappeared. The last we saw of him, he had followed her out of sight.

The company began to disband.

CHAPTER 9

THE BONE

He might hardly have been in the Hall of the Moth all afternoon, had my impressions been evidence—so quiet he had kept, relapsed out of the main light of the room into the shadow between the beetling chimney-mantel and the old long-case clock. Perhaps the indefatigable quaffing of whiskey-and-sodas, which industry is surely his favourite, had proved soporific in that dusky alcove, whence only his crossed feet had appeared, shod sparklingly, spatted sprucely. But now Charlton Oxford, glazed to a hair, waxed to a needle, was standing in the aperture of the opened french windows, and his look, whatever his legs might be, was steady.

His eyes were fixed upon the gap in the lawn shrubs where Sean Cosgrove had disappeared. Surely that was an unguarded moment; his speech, although low, was vehement, since it was addressed to a man now far out of sight and hearing:

"Your code, hey? Your damned code." He wiped the back of his fist savagely across his mouth; the heartiness of his baleful speech may have given him the satisfaction of deep drink.

I, who alone had heard, tiptoed close behind him, and like the tempter spoke softly over his shoulder.

"And what may your code be, Mr. Oxford?"

Frightened, he swung, caught his heel on the carpet edge and thudded heavily against the corner of the age-blackened mantel, face bleached and eyes popping.

"Oh, it's you, Mr. Bannerlee," he exclaimed with much relief, and attempted to pass his alarm off in jest.

"Yes, and really, what did you mean? I'm interested."

"What's my code, you say? Ha, ha, Mr. Bannerlee, 's too long, sir, to put it in so many words, if you know what I mean.... But there's *one* thing"—for emphasis he dug a flabby forefinger into my ribs—"*one* thing I'd never do that our fine CCosgrove wouldn't have the decency, the *decency*, sir, if y'understand—and the common sense, too, damme, if it comes to that, you know—'s much common sense in it as anything else...y'understand..."

"And what article and section of your pandect could Mr. Cosgrove learn from?"

Oxford steadied himself, and over his face came a phase of profundity. He gave me a knowing look, and his voice sank to a sibylline tone: "Never take another man's woman—never meddle with 'em!"

"But a woman unprotected, eh?" I felt like asking, yet refrained, for someone else was nighing us, one at whose approach Oxford appeared to feel distressed. The fancy man evaporated into the afternoon sunlight down the lawn, and Maryvale, who I think had been standing alone in the centre of the room, was at my elbow.

That changed look was stronger than ever about him; there seemed a gaunt and haggard spirit in his eyes.

"Mr. Bannerlee, you must have heard terrible tales today."

"Surely none that deserve such a violent—"

"Oh, yes, yes—some dreadful things have happened in this countryside. Cosgrove tells me that this morning he related to you the fall of the old castle, and in there"—he gestured toward the dining-hall—"what awful things you must have listened to."

I smothered a laugh that was half-breathless, for there was real distress in him. "Mr. Maryvale, you exaggerate—"

He laid his hand heavily on my arm, and his fingers took hold. "But there is one story more terrible still!"

"Indeed, indeed?"

"Yes, indeed. There are legends of this Vale—none more appalling. Did they tell you—but they could not—of the Lord Aidenn's arm that would not die?"

"The arm that would not die?"

"You know the man's picture, for you examined it in the gallery. And there"—he motioned toward the portrait—"is the other representation of that orgulous, cruel man."

I stared again at the pitiless, thin face with a slight and enjoyable stir of nervousness.

"It is a dreadful legend," averred Maryvale. "They never found—" He turned his head, saw something, and ceased.

For now came a new interruption, and one that I was right glad of, since Maryvale just then was too remote and metempirical for comfort. Of his grisly story of the arm of Sir Pharamond Kay, whatever the fable was, I had no dread; but in the baffling Maryvale himself now was something unapproachable that moved a mild antipathy in me.

The interruption came in the form of a small, hoydenish, vivid-lipped creature called Lib Dale. The last to remain in the Hall, save those who had spoken with me, she and Bob Cullen had been engaged beneath the musicians' gallery in a tense-toned division of ideas. Even while Maryvale had been drawing near me, I caught a glimpse from the heel of my eye of Bob shuffling his feet in loathness to depart at the hest of Lib. At length, apparently in disgrace, he had passed limply through the farther entrance into the corridor. "Go out and soak your head," was Lib's parting tenderness, which I overheard. Then, spying me with Maryvale, the startling little thing came to interrupt. The man of business had checked himself in the midst of his sentence; he seemed to withdraw into some inner chamber of himself; a darkness enveloped the peaked soul in his eyes. He was gone, and I was left alone to encounter the sprightly bit of femininity.

"How do you do?" she asked. "Shake. You're you and I'm me. We know each other's names, or else they shouldn't let us out."

"No, they shouldn't," I retorted feebly, without knowing what I said, save that it was idiotic.

"Well, don't shed tears about it. Don't be so vulgarly emotional. Can't you dig me up a real live saint, Mr. Bannerlee—something I can take home maybe and show the folks?"

"I should think that the legends of this countryside—"

"Or a legend, if it's handier. I've never seen a genuine legend, Mr. Bannerlee. Lead me to it. Hasn't my education been neglected?"

I uttered a faint denial.

"Oh, yes, it has," she chortled. "For instance, I get my English all gummed up. But that's your fault."

"Of course."

"Now don't be sil. You don't know what I mean. For instance. Have you noticed how all the books you English writers write about we Amurricans have us saying 'I guess' this and 'I reckon' that about every once or twice in so often? Now, over where I come from nobody talks that way so that you could notice it, but over here in your delightful little island we have to pull that kind of stuff once in a while or the natives wouldn't know where we're from. Savvy?"

"Oh, quite."

She had perched on the back of a carved gilt couch with upholstery in rose *Brocade de Lyons*.

"And now how about getting busy on that saint proposition? One out of the Old Testament or anything. Warm puppies! Won't I have the kids at home goggle-eyed? I should snicker."

"Saints in the Old Testament are few. And I'm afraid—"

"Not so rough, not so rough! What do you mean, you're afraid? How will this sound in your biography, that you refused a maiden's prayer? I'll have to take you in hand; you ought to be trained." She reached down and gave a tug at a gravitating stocking. "No, from your face I see it's hopeless. Well, what are you going to do to keep the ennui away?"

"I had an idea," I remarked hopefully.

"Quick, quick! Don't keep me in starvation."

"In connection with the method of making up the quarrel suggested by the good Cosgrove—"

"Yes, yes, I follow you there—everything except the 'good'—"

"Since the good Cosgrove says that the text of our play of pacification is in the library, I was thinking of having a look at it and refreshing my memory."

"I can follow you there, too; only no refreshments here, thanks—'Noah's Flood' is all news to me as a big, throbbing drammer. Sounds sort of frisky, I mean riskay, putting all those animals to bed. Who wrote it?"

"The authors of the mystery-plays are unknown."

"Something fishy there, I'll bet. Come on, show me this sensation."

She grabbed a hand of mine and dragged me through the room of weapons into the spacious library, a room of irregular shape, since the curve of the staircase well rounded one wall and the huge jut of the south-west corner tower made a pocket-like projection almost equal to a separate room. A monumental mahogany break-front bookcase occupied the principal straight wall of the room, and other glass-covered stacks of shelves lined the shorter and the semicircular wall and the spaces between the windows. Altogether there must have been three thousand books.

"Gee whiz, Croftsy must be some reader," said Lib. "I was never here before, and I've got a brainstorm already."

I smiled, wryly, no doubt. "I believe that the library, like the portraits and the symbol of the cat and the legends of Aidenn Forest, came to Crofts with the building. In fact, though I haven't looked these over, I imagine many of them are of a sort unlikely to interest our host."

Indeed, the major portion of the collection were volumes which could stir the interest only of the antiquarian and the erudite student of literature. Few, I am sure, bore the twentieth-century imprint. Included were old books of all assortments of inconvenient sizes from folio to duodecimo, and although in their glass prisons, whence no doubt they were taken and dusted quarterly, they looked spick and span, still they had a lonesome air, as if longing to be handled for love.

I mused. "Now where shall we look for one particular volume in all this?"

"Are you putting that as a question, Marshal?" asked Lib. "That's not fair. I'm in the enemy's country here; don't know the landmarks."

"We might look over the ones of reasonable size first. The thing's a reprint. Early English Text, I dare say."

"I don't get you, Admiral, but am game to follow you in a leaky boat to the death. I gathered that this Flood has an alias."

"Er—"

"Doesn't go under its own name, I mean."

"That is correct."

"That's right, you mean. Well, well, Duke, can this be it?"

She had opened one of the doors of the mahogany case and reached high from the basis of one toe. The volume she persuaded to fall down and which she caught was actually a bound issue of the Early English Text Society and contained the Digby and Coventry Plays.

"By all that's wonderful! How did your eyes pick out that title so quickly?"

"Never looked at the title—way up there. What do you think I am, Senator, a telescope? Say! I just took a slant along the shelves."

"A slant—along the shelves?"

"Right. I thought that maybe the 'good' Cosgrove had been taking a peep at the crucial volume lately and maybe hadn't put it back quite even. Savvy? Now, let's have a look."

But she wrinkled both nose and forehead from the first sight of "Processus Noe cum filiis," and fluttered the pages very much askance.

"I don't get this stuff at all. What language is this?"

"English."

"Why, it's worse than Amurrican."

"It's really Middle English, you know."

"No, I don't. See here, what does a choice morsel like this signify?" She read, in a manner unknown to linguists, the following lines:

> *"Ye men that has wifis whyls they ar' yong,*
> *If luf youre lifis chastice thare tong:*
> *Me thynk my heart ryfis both levyr and long*
> *To se sich stryfis wedmen emong.*
> *That looks as if it might mean something."*

"Yes, Noah was very wroth with his wife."

"His wife? His missus?"

"She was a scold, and Noah, as the gloss of Professor Pollard says, bids husbands chastise their wives' tongues early."

"Not so hot, not so hot," remarked Lib, apparently in disparagement. "Where do all the other folks come in?"

"Oh, there'll be parts for everyone. Noah's family was large, and there were plenty of animals to go round.... He beats her a bit later on," I added hopefully.

She clapped the covers to. "This is too rough for me. It's not ladylike. I'm not crazy about—say, what goes on in there?"

Somebody was making a stir in the armoury, whence issued an occasional scrabbling sound. Lib poked her head cautiously around the doorpost.

"Why, Doctor, what would you seem to be doing this elegant afternoon?"

Doctor Aire was standing with a cutlass in one hand and a claymore in the other. He lifted his gaze from the floor in surprise and gave an affable welcome.

"Oh, hello. I had no idea anyone else was indoors."

"We've been giving Noah the once over," said Lib. "What's the idea of all the weapons?"

"Well, you see that early battle-axe lying so well protected out there, if it was chosen for the commission of crime, has one or two peculiar things about it. It amused me to find whether—but no, you'd better guess for yourself. I understand that the subject is taboo just now, and a very good thing."

Lib stamped with animation. "That's not a bit nice. This is such a dull afternoon, and now you won't even tell us your secrets."

"Well, there's one," smiled the Doctor with a sort of saturnine indulgence. "Feel the weight of these." He handed over to her the pair of weapons. "Take a look over the lot." He made a sweeping motion to indicate the walls crowded with arms. "Then think of the axe that lies out there inclosed by chicken-wire. Then draw your own conclusions."

Lib poised the cutlas and claymore and returned them. "Doctor, you're a whiz. Any more funny little wrinkles?"

"Take your time," said the doctor. "Examine them all."

"You give me too much credit," she declared. "Come on; what have you found out?"

Doctor Aire gave a slight shrug, one shoulder lifting higher than the other. It was a mannerism I had observed before. "Miss Lib, you have all the brains necessary for this extremely simple point, which I have practically given away already."

"Well, you're a teaser. I'm not a little girl any more, you know. I don't *like* being teased."

"You must think it out for yourself," insisted the Doctor, still smiling.

"Well, I won't; so there! You're perfectly horrid!"

"Perfection in any wise is seldom gained. I am honoured," he murmured, but Lib, tossing her head and departing to the lawn, in affected dudgeon, probably did not hear the conclusion of his courtesy.

We laughed together while he replaced the weapons to their props and fastenings upon the wall.

I looked about the chamber, up the walls crowded with weapons to the very shadows of the ceiling. Save for the two full-armoured figures of sheet and mail, most of the equipment I supposed to be Elizabethan or later, although the Doctor was sure to be a better judge than I. One gigantic harquebuse à croc with its support attached dominated the broad wall between the armoury and the Hall of the Moth; all around it were muskets, calivers, petronels, dags and tacks, and a couple of blunderbusses, besides firearms whose names I did not know. The short wall opposite was full of cutting and crushing weapons; hence had come the two with which the Doctor had been experimenting. Between two sets of lances standing upright for a frame, the eye was mazed in an intricate pattern of partisans, maces, falchions, hangers, axes, poniards, and, one might believe, every other size and shape of sticker and slasher and pounder.

"I suppose you alluded to the heft of the axe we found last night out there? Its weight is certainly inconsiderable."

"Yes," agreed the Doctor with a drawl, "it appears to have been about the lightest object on the wall. Why did he take that—that hatchet? I'm inclined to think that it was made for a plaything, not a real working instrument. Odd, its selection, very odd."

"I don't see why you emphasize the point."

"Well, look here, where it was taken from, about shoulder height. Now, assuming naturally that the man who took it wanted it for business purposes, why didn't he take this axe here, something less than a yard further up? There's real power in this fellow. Or was the intruder fumbling around in the dark in a room he wasn't acquainted with? And then the blood."

"Ah, yes; I have been waiting with interest to hear your decision there."

"No decision is possible immediately, if you ask me where it came from. I have no kit with me, of course. I accept for the time Pendleton's assurance that it belongs to the missing pig, slaughtered in we don't know what ritualistic manner. But the position of the blood on the weapon is what annoys me. You recall it?"

"The handle was slobbered with it."

"And only a few spots on the blade. That would assure us the killing was done with the axe, even if the weapon weren't so inefficient. Ah!" He lifted his hands in an attitude of dismay, a stiffish caryatid-like pose. "Pendleton's right. No good comes of talking of these things. They'll unravel. I'm going to get cleaned up for the rehearsal at five, Mr. Bannerlee. I've been discussing transplantings with old Finlay the gardener, and my hands have tested some extra fine dirt."

I saw the Doctor swing his body out of the armoury with the regularity of an automaton, his trunk stiff and upright, his narrow legs working like scissors; I heard the Doctor enter on the winding stair.

Then, alone in the armoury, into which the first faint smoke of dusk was creeping, among so many instruments of death, where the intruder of the night before had stolen while the mockery of cards was in progress in the Hall, and where he might steal again—there, then, I was not at ease. I had flickers of apprehension, and the room seemed musty, close. Both mentally and bodily I felt cabined, confined. More than half an hour remaining before we were due in the Hall, I resolved upon taking a light breather up the Vale, to stir my sluggard blood and puff away my fancies.

No one appeared on the lawn or in the environs of the House. As I faced north up the Vale a fairish breeze met me face to face, and I realized that the storm was still in the atmosphere. The airy armies high above the hills were marshalling once more. A little while later the sun, not far above the ridge, was flecked with cloud, and the smouldering embers of the beechen hangers were, one might say, extinguished to black ashes.

By the time the glories of colour were lost on the hillsides, I had reached the clearing beyond which lurked the cottage of the sisters Delambre. This stood in a gorge-like recess, where flowed the small stream with the ridiculous bridge which I had noted when first I journeyed down the Vale. Good, full inspirations of the untainted air had restored physical tone, and my thoughts, too, were less troubled, perplexed. I was free of most of the jangling discord of the day, of Belvoir with his eternal harping on morals as accidental products, of Ludlow in his vigilance to combat offensive ideas, of Lib and Bob and their little bickerings, of Cosgrove and all the enmities that had heaped around him: Bob's and the Baron's and Charlton Oxford's, and—almost—the abrupt flaming of the Irishman and his bride-to-be. That single incident must have impressed the houseful of us as rudely as a dozen ordinary quarrels of man to man.

Of the taste of this unpleasantness I could not wholly rid myself, nor of another thing, which strengthened in the diminishing of light. This was the witching time of day—and I could not get away from Parson Lolly.

Well I understood Morgan the stableman when he said that there were whiles when the "otherness" took hold of one. Having crossed the clearing, I stood near the cottage of the French sisters, who, though nothing concerning their characters had been told me, I conceived must be eccentrics, women so distant from their nativity, if not in mere statute miles, certainly in their lives and surroundings. While I looked at the cottage, a rugged thing of stone, scarcely two stories high, with roof of hewn stone tiles, as is common hereabout, I thought it had a deserted and disappointed appearance. It was far too early, indeed, for even tired farm-women to be abed; yet no light glimmered through window or cranny. I approached; I even knocked. No response.

Puzzled, disturbed, I retraced my path.

So feeling, I came in view of Highglen House, all dark and still on the edge of sunset. I passed beneath the clustered cypress trees; I traversed the northern span of the lawn and passed the conservatory with its mended panes.

I stepped on the driveway where it passed the Hall of the Moth, intending to advance to the front entrance and ring the bell there, having enough hold on reality, in spite of my fuming blood, to recall that my own shaving things had been in my bag recently fetched by Toby, and that with hot water I could quickly remove the stubble of the day, before the first reading of "Noah's Flood" in the Hall of the Moth. At the moment of my setting foot on the drive, I remember, the faintest sound of speech wandered to me from somewhere beyond the gate-house. I could not distinguish any voices, but there seemed to be both men and women in the party, doubtless returning from beside Aidenn Water.

Then I chanced to look inside the Hall of the Moth.

Now, now, now is the time when I need to hold each sense and faculty to accurate account. For what I saw then, what then I took to be hallucination, now I know too well was something real, something serious, and something totally inexplicable to all who have heard of it.

Through the cleft between the eminences of Esgair Nantau and Vron Hill a single dart from the sun still leaped, lustering the twilight about the house. A fragment of that glimmer, about the size of a top-hat but rudely circular in shape, played and smouldered mild, high on the bare stone of the inner wall of the room. Except for this wavering spot, dusk had taken possession of the empty Hall, wherein even the masses of the furniture were invisible to me.

The chanciest glance took in the gloom of the chamber, but before I had looked elsewhere, my eyes perceived yet one other thing distinguishable in the obscurity, and all the blood in me leaped. To indicate definitely the position of the object, I should say that to the best of my affrighted recollection it was just beyond the couch which Lib Dale had mounted earlier in the afternoon during her talk with me, although the couch itself, like the rest of the furniture, was now absorbed in the pool of darkness.

In the air perhaps a foot above the imagined position of the back of the couch, with no visible means of suspension or support, was what I can describe only as a clean white bone.

CHAPTER 10

THE LAUGH

A white bone, six inches long, the broadened knobs at each end a little darker than the rest—horizontal, perfectly still.

Perhaps I had gazed at this thing in fascination for twenty or thirty seconds before it stirred at all. Then the faintest swinging motion seemed to occur, on a horizontal plane, and suddenly—now my heart was going mad—it rose a couple of feet as if jerked by a string, and remained motionless once more, until the swinging recommenced, one end and then the other moving slightly toward me and away.

The comforting tones of voices had died; it might have been that I and that apparition were alone in the Vale, a man and a white irrational bone. I was of no mind to linger there until the thing should leap up again and drive me into an apoplexy. And all the while the basis of reason in me was firm, and there was a voice bidding me quit my folly, for there could be no bone in the unsupporting air of the Hall. Yet I did not enter the chamber and get within the same walls as the apparition; instead I abandoned the place to its ghostly visitant, hastened around to the front entrance of the House and rang the bell, although the door itself was unlatched.

I wanted hot water for shaving.

Soames, answering the ring, I met at the foot of the winding staircase. My voice, I believe, was controlled out of its excitement when I ordered the water, which he promised to bring at once.

It was with a doubtful, distracted mind that I entered my room and caused a tiny apex of flame to glow on the fresh candles standing at either side of my writing-table. For a breath of open air, I swung the casement window inward. The breeze, forerunner of storm, brushed past outside, but no more than writhed the candle-flames.

I looked out.

As I have stated, my window gives on what I suppose I must call the balcony, though part of the ancient battlement stands there in lieu of a balustrade, remnant of an age before even this room was built and when the top of the wall was no higher than the window-sill. Odd that the old parapet with its indentations remained when this lofty course of rooms was made. This wall above the second storey cut off my view of the lawn, save where a gap of the crenellation permitted me to look almost straight down to the drive. Directly below me I now saw nothing, and far beyond the gate-house towers, rising to the level of the roof of the mansion, was only the dusky dark expanse to Aidenn Water. But about the twin-legged gate-house itself the afterglow lingered in a tiny pool.

I suddenly remembered Crofts' admonition to have a look at the tomb on Vron Hill, and my promise that I would. With an athletic effort I squeezed through my window and stood on the roof outside. To my disappointment, the sky beyond the Hill was darkened with clouds whose purple came near to black. The tumulus was indistinguishable against them.

I moved to the edge of the parapet and leaned over one of the cops of the crenelled wall for a better look about.

It appeared that two or three people were gathered by the winch that works the drawbridge and were having great glee in their endeavours. Rusty metal shrilled, a little cloud of laughter burst upward, and the huge bridge descended. There came a thump when the platform settled into place. Then amid a new little cloud of laughter, the winch set to work again, and the bridge commenced to rise.

My attention was diverted by something at my feet, the merest trifle lying at the base of one of the merlons: a twisted strand which might have been part of a piece of light rope. It was about the length of my finger-joint, far from fresh, one end newly abraded, the other decayed. It was, as I said, a trifle, but it was curious. I could not think then, nor can I now, how it got there; and certainly the fresh abrasion was not more than a couple of days old. I had a notion of showing it to Crofts for an opinion, but when I considered what the energetic response of our much-tried host might be when asked to account for a fragment of half-rotten rope, I changed my mind. But I tucked away the strand for future reference.

One last look up and down the empty lawn, and I slipped back into my room.

I recalled my shaving, which now must be rapid if I were to be ready in time for the reading of the play. A few preliminary preparations made, I ran into an unprecedented number of mishaps.

I seemed to have an unsteady fit. Soames had not yet come with the hot water, and I was in a hurry; my watch said a quarter to five. I made a beginning, however, ridding myself of my coat and shirt and addressing myself to the oak chest whereinto I had transferred my things from my bag during the ten-minute interval before luncheon. But at once I realized the unsuitability of sixteenth-century appointments for purposes of personal convenience, for the upper drawer was jammed or stuck. I hauled, jerked, and jogged sidewise. Suddenly, *bang!* came out the drawer, but the handle had parted from it, and I, handle in hand, staggered back, crash! into a stool in the corner of the room. When I separated myself from the stool, and we were both on our legs again, I recollected that I had tossed my shaving utensils into the drawer of the writing-table, as being readier to hand.

Then indeed I had a brainstorm, an eagerness for haste being added to my disquiet of mind. Soames might be there with the water at any moment, and I not ready. Clutching razor and strop, I looked in vain for a proper place to attach the strop; my dissatisfaction with the old room as a place for personal embellishment was not diminished at all when I finally chose one of the curlicues of the candle-bracket on the north wall for a hook. Like the similar one in the armoury, this was very old, and like the bureau drawer, it seemed malevolent to thwart me. Holding the strop firmly while my razor executed loops and pirouettes, I was aghast a moment later, so suddenly did the fastening of the bracket give way under the strength of my hold upon the strop. *Squeak!* went the old, damp-rotted iron, the candle-holder on its pivot drooped crazily, and I was staring at the thin red cut beside the finger-nail where the razor-edge had nicked me. This capped the climax.

It was comedy, no doubt. For me, nevertheless, it was a bad half-minute. I smashed the bracket back to uprightness; one blow sufficed, since there had been no fissure in the metal itself. But my finger could not be cured so cavalierly. And shaving now was out of the question before five o'clock! Of such trivialities are wrought either contentment or black spirits.

I chucked away strop and razor and went to the door, wondering what had become of Soames, and shaking off the drops of fresh blood from the index-finger of my left hand.

I heard someone coming up the stairs, and at the same time a peculiar sound of rending rose from the Hall beneath the threshold where I stood, followed by the loud slam of a door.

I said to myself, "There must be someone in the Hall now," but the next instant thought, and all else, was reft from me.

For from some part of the house someone was laughing. No—to avoid error from the first—I thought then, and at the present hour this all who heard are willing to swear: the laughter came from no human throat. Yet is Parson Lolly not human? And if he—but this shows the inconsistency of our fear. Yes, I will swear it was no human sound that roared and re-echoed through the House, gleeing and gurgling, curdling the blood of us who were within the walls. So huge was the uproar that the place of its source could not be told, and it went on and on unendurably for immeasurable seconds, to change to silence with a sudden gulp.

I dashed to the window for a quick look, and could see nothing in the darkness, but discovered a glow spreading from immediately below me. The chandelier in the Hall must be lighted now. Then flinging my coat on,

I rushed out of the room, impelled by a sense of dread and danger, and an anxiety to get where people were. I met Soames, hot-water can in hand, at the head of the stairs underneath the solitary electric bulb. He was green, a mildewed colour, startled into stone.

I sprang down the stairs without a word, and he, galvanized, followed with a gasp:

"Gord, sir, is that *him*?" He meant the Parson.

On the landing of the first floor stood Lib Dale, her fingers nervously fluttering about her face.

"What's the matter? What's happened?"

"Something drastic," I said, while we went speeding together down to the entrance vestibule. Soames, still carrying the water, brought up a thumping rear.

"Oh, wouldn't it be awful if someone's kicked—I mean, if someone's been knocked off?"

"Knocked off?"

"I mean if an individual has been assassinated," she explained haughtily, and then for an instant her impertinent little face went to chalk.

We were standing indecisive in the passage. Hardly a minute had passed since the end of the laughter. A scream suddenly sounded from the lawn beyond the Hall of the Moth, a cry of agony which might have seemed terrible had not it been for that astounding laugh which had preceded it. In its awful context the scream was pitifully thin and feeble, but it was human, certainly.

"That's on the lawn."

"Yes, Governor," choked Lib, following me at a half-run through the gallery-door of the Hall, through the nearest french windows, and so to the drive.

Beside the small tower near the mended conservatory window something dark was stretched, with three or four people about it. While Lib and I were still thirty feet away, we could tell in the widespread light of the Hall chandelier that a body lay there.

"It's a corpse," cried Lib. "Oh, my God, is it Bobby?" She rushed forward.

I turned to Soames. "Round up the others, quickly."

"Yyes, sir"; he went back with the ineffable water.

I remember that just as I came up from the lower french doors of the Hall, Belvoir, crossing the lawn from the direction of Aidenn Water, arrived at the other side of the group by the small tower.

He looked down with a curious, contemplative expression. "This," he said, "must be the body we missed last night." It was not a flippant speech; it seemed to fit the occasion.

The body lying here, half on the ground, half on the step to the french window, with Miss Lebetwood kneeling on one side, Doctor Aire on the other, was Sean Cosgrove's. Supine he had fallen, or had been turned, his face bereft of its solidity, a flabby thing, his eyes closed, and the edge of a bloody wound showing beneath his left ear, a wound that apparently had a continuance behind.

With knit brow Doctor Aire let down Cosgrove's wrist and shook his head. His thin lips stirred; he muttered:

"It's no use."

Miss Lebetwood rose in a paroxysm of pain; she warded off Alberta Pendleton. In the scattered glow, with hair dishevelled and eyes afire, she looked like a prophetess of old, pulsing with authority. With a gesture she put us aside; it was as if she were putting us out of her thoughts. From us she went, and disappeared in the vacancy of the lawn.

Pendleton, smitten by a thought, cried "The weapon!" and dashed into the Hall. We saw him go to the armoury door and saw the room brighten with electricity. Then the Doctor and I made the same decision.

"Don't touch the body," cautioned the Doctor, and he and I together followed our host into the room of weapons, among which he was wildly ranging in a mad search.

"Nothing's been disturbed here," observed Doctor Aire.

But Crofts, deaf, continued in his frenzy, drawing every old rickety sword from its sheath, tearing every weapon from its peg or stud, rubbing his fingers along the cutting parts.

"Not there, Crofts, not there!" I cried, taking him by the arm, since speech had no effect.

"Which of these did it?" he demanded.

"None," answered Doctor Aire decisively. "You can see at a glance—"

"But one of them must have a stain. There couldn't have been time to wipe it dry."

"None are stained," returned the Doctor. "Come with me."

He and I had nearly to drag Crofts out to the lawn, to the spot beyond the gate-house towers where the small axe had lain covered from the storm.

"But that's a puny thing!"

"Yes," said the Doctor, "but even a bullet may do damage, and the puny axe may have been in the hand of one of prodigious strength. A light weapon and a heavy blow; it may have broken the weapon, of course."

"It will hardly be here, in that case," I suggested.

We were beside the chicken-wire. There stood Miss Lebetwood, her white hands clenched against her dark dress.

Her voice was cold, toneless. "I've been waiting here, wondering how long—"

"No matter, Miss," said the doctor, "we're here—that's what matters."

I lit a match which managed to keep alive in the stir of air. The canvas, held down by heavy stones, was in place. Crofts yanked the sheet away. We gasped.

There lay the small axe, undisturbed. The Doctor stooped and touched the blood-slobbered handle.

"It's dry, absolutely. Well, I'm whipped. I'd have sworn—"

We were hastening back to the House almost while the words were in his mouth. Now there must have been a dozen guests and servants clustered about the body. I turned to Crofts.

"Who found him there? Was anything seen? Where was he killed?"

He was too distracted to pay attention. He was running his fingers through his mane and whispering little phrases to himself.

A woman with trembling hands held out some white thing.

"Look," said Eve Bartholomew. "See what I found when I came by the end of the House—down there by the large tower." She pointed toward the corner round which lay the main entrance.

"Another—another!" I exclaimed, and Crofts snarled, "It was time for another, damn his black heart! What does this one say?"

We read:

LOok OuT foR THe CATS CLAW

PARSON LOLLY

"The Cat's Claw! What's that?"

"How do you expect me to tell?"

"Again we find this damned thing—too late!"

"There's fresh blood on it!" exclaimed Crofts, taking the placard from my hand.

"Of course there is, you fool. Look at my finger."

"How did you do that?"

"Razor."

Alberta was looking over her husband's shoulder. "Where did you find it, Eve?"

"Right at the corner of the House. It was on the grass, with the writing downward."

"Now," said I, "if there's one thing about this atrocious deed that I can swear to, it is that there was nothing at that spot ten minutes ago. I rounded the corner to enter the House so as to fetch one of the men-servants by ringing the door-bell. The grass had nothing on it."

"I was over by the gate-house," said Bob Cullen, "but I wasn't pulling the winch. I was waiting for Lib to come out again. I was watching the end of the House all the time until the lights flared up in the Hall. I'll take my oath, I will, that nobody went round the corner after Mr. Bannerlee."

Doctor Aire objected. "But after the chandelier was lit—when that part of the House and the lawn outside the windows was bright—you might have overlooked some shadow slipping along the wall further south."

Yet this explanation satisfied me no more than it seemed to quell Bob himself.

"Look here," Crofts suddenly roared. "Perhaps *he*—" He flung out an arm toward the dead man.

"What do you mean?"

"He—himself—"

"This placard was his doing, you think? Impossible!"

"Why not? There was no one else here. That one in his room this morning: he took *it* mighty calmly."

"Sean was not a child, or a fool," said Miss Lebetwood coldly.

"Who lit the chandelier?" I asked.

"Ah!" murmured the Doctor, and raised one shoulder higher than the other.

"Did anyone see him before—this?"

Miss Lebetwood spoke. "I was the first to see him, Mr. Bannerlee. He was kneeling, I thought, on the step outside the window—but he must have been—falling...."

"Paula—don't tell it, dearest," cried Miss Mertoun.

"There's nothing to tell," said Paula Lebetwood, still brave, still vibrant, commanding. "I am not going to break down, Millicent dear. I—have told of myself.... That was all. He lifted his hand from the stone, as if he wanted to reach his head—but he fell forward. That's all."

"But that unholy bawling laughter—"

"It was from—somewhere else. It wasn't very loud out here, but it was what made me look towards the House. Then I saw—him—while the laugh was still going on. But I didn't scream until—afterward, when he fell."

"The lights were on at the time, of course," observed Doctor Aire.

"They had been on for a minute or so, I think," said Miss Lebetwood. "But I had paid no particular attention when they were lit."

"The fact is," said the Doctor, "we don't know where he was when he was struck. He must have been nearby—couldn't have gone far with a bludgeoning like that."

"Blenkinson, you there?" asked Crofts.

"I am, sir."

"Have you 'phoned Superintendent Salt at New Aidenn?"

"I 'ave, sir. 'E's coming, and looking out for hall suspicious characters on the south road."

"All right, then."

"Hadn't the women better go?" asked Ludlow practically.

"Go in, everybody," said Crofts.

"Must *he* be left?"

Doctor Aire said, "Put something under the back of his head and cover his body with something. I'll stand guard here. He can't be moved until the police arrive."

"God!"

A bellowing leaped upon us out of the north, a roar that instead of tailing away mounted higher and higher upon itself. The wind, which had been bustling, seemed to disintegrate while the darkness of sound swept through the Vale. Resonant, tremendous, devastating, the sheer undifferentiated noise bore down on us, oppressed us with its weight. Brimming the hills, it actually made the ground tremble. It was nothing like thunder, but as if something buried alive beneath the earth had awakened and vociferated horribly. Several of the women stopped their ears, and there was an awfulness in seeing their mouths open in screams when the sound was wholly lost in the roar up the Vale. It was as if they had all gone dumb and raving. Even when it had ceased at climax, the echoes of the roar bruited from crag to crag made the Vale alive with sound. And when the final reverberations had sunk to peace, we gaped at each other silenced for a little while, even the body of the man forgotten in the overwhelmingness of sound. When we spoke, it was in whispers.

"Could that be—thunder?"

"Thunder—like that?"

"It was like Judgment."

"What was it, then?"

"I can tell you what it was," I said.

They were round me in a moment, greedy.

"An earthquake?" asked Doctor Aire.

"A landslide—almost an avalanche—on one of the north-most hills."

"But what could have caused it?"

"There may have been a condition of incipient instability, waiting for rain, perhaps."

"For rain—what rain?" interposed Pendleton.

In answer to him a vast sheet of purple lightning pictured all the north of the Vale. It vanished, sweeping us into an instantaneous blacker darkness, but again it glared, and again, while unmistakable thunders rang. In that dazzling fulgour the nearby features of the scene were revealed to us as in bright noontide, but above the Black Mixen, above Mynydd Tarw, above the other northern peaks, hung a great tower reaching into illimitable night like a waterfall from heaven. Again the lightning blazed, and we beheld the hanging shafts, like sun-pillars among clouds, save that these were black—or like aerial waterspouts soaring above the earth. And this stupendous cliff of water was visibly moving toward us, down the Vale!

Crofts Pendleton turned from the terrific sight, with a bitter-happy look. He gestured toward the north. In the effulgence and clamour of the storm he stood like a valiant pygmy.

"By God," he shouted, "there's one direction cut off—for the fiend who did this!"

"Particularly if the zigzag path has been blocked by the landslide," added Belvoir.

"Praise God, the police are coming by the south road. There's no missing him if he tries to leave the Vale tonight!"

"Sir Brooke!" cried Eve Bartholomew suddenly. "Sir Brooke! Where is he?"

"We should all like to know," said Crofts.

These speeches had been shouts. Now the Doctor made a megaphone of his hands in order to be heard. In a blaze of lightning lasting several seconds we saw him hunch his shoulder and head toward the top of the Vale, whence the rain, white rain now, and horrible, was pushing back towards us. "This will be on us in a minute. We can't leave this poor fellow's remains here, regulations or no. We must get the location and position of the body down in writing at once. I'll take responsibility."

Crofts and I stooped to lift by the shoulders and feet respectively. During our brief act of carrying the corpse into the Hall and composing it on the couch, the wind suddenly rose into a mighty strife, and heavy plashing drops of rain came sousing on the windows. The gale was mad with leaves from the dishevelled autumn trees, which came knocking on the panes, clung there for moments like silhouettes, and were whirled on to their fate.

Crofts stood beside the useless and ironic tea-service, agaze at the streaming windows. His lips were moving, but I heard no speech from them.

I moved over beside him. "Who is Superintendent Salt?"

"The best man for detective work in Radnorshire, and the Chief Constable knows it, they say. Lucky for us Salt lives in New Aidenn. But he'll never get here tonight—not in this deluge."

Something dashed against the window-pane, and from us came a stifled cry. Handsome Ruth Clay, who had come in to remove the tea things, was standing with her fist jammed halfway into her mouth, her frightened eyes staring to the stormy night.

"What's the matter?"

"See, see! The Bird!"

I followed her look, just in time to see some small dark object blown before the wind and lost in the howling murk. "It came up against the window. I saw it."

"And what of it?"

"It's the Corpse-bird, sir. It means a death!"

"What!"

"Oh, I saw it, sir—no feathers it had—only like the down of other birds' wings—and eyes like balls of fire!"

"Nonsense, woman. Besides, this Corpse-bird, as you call it, should have come before. The damage is done already."

"Yes, sir, there's poor Mr. Cosgrove's body lying there, sir. But the Bird means another death."

CHAPTER 11

SUPERINTENDENT SALT

October 4. 2.35 P.M.

Yet the two men from New Aidenn had come up the Vale through that ruinous rain and wind. From the corner library window I myself had dimly seen them plodding up the leaf-stained drive against the blast, and had been at the cat-head entrance when Blenkinson admitted them, grotesquely dishevelled by the storm. The very tall one, whose hat was gone and who carried a bulgy black instrument-case, was Doctor Niblett, Coroner as well. Superintendent Salt, a man of more pulp, and built on the underslung plan, wore a necklet of grizzly beard and had short curly hair, like a Roman Emperor's. I at once christened him Peggotty, "a hairy man with a good-natured face."

Quite a little lake had sluiced and oozed from their coats and shoes before Pendleton came rushing downstairs from his wife's room.

"You got here?"

"I expect so," answered Superintendent Salt in the indecisive way that I have learned is universal with native Radnorites. "I had my neighbour the Coroner come along, Doctor Niblett here."

"Oh, yes: glad you did. We've met, haven't we, Doctor? Gad, you look war-shot, both of you. Is the storm so bad?"

"We've tramped it from beyond the bridge or thereabouts."

"Tramped it!"

"Half the bridge was down, Mr. Pendleton. We were forced to leave the car on t'other side and make a dash over afoot. The way it looked, Mr. Pendleton, with the water risin' so, I doubt you've any bridge at all there by now. The stream's fair ragin'. And you say there's been a killin' here or something? A guest of yours, maybe? Shockin'."

"What a day!" cried Crofts fervently. "This way, gentlemen." But in the midst of the portrait-corridor, he paused. "This is murder, and a damned mysterious murder. There's been a landslide up the Vale, and that path must be blocked. Did you pass anyone going south as you came along?"

Peggotty, or perhaps I had better let his name go as Salt, responded, "We did not, and we have a witness who was by the bridge since before five o'clock to show that nobody had been across either way."

"What kind of a witness?"

"Reliable. The Coroner and I have known him for these a-many years." From aloft Doctor Niblett nodded grave agreement. "Road-mender, he is. Shelterin' under a tree from the rain. Had been at work just beyond the bridge, so he couldn't have missed seein'."

Elation seemed to make a dark glow in Pendleton's soul. "Then he's trapped, the dog! That is, if you—did you tell this witness to watch—?"

"I think," said Superintendent Salt, "that we might be havin' a look at the body."

"Er, yes. Yes, of course—I was taking you. I'll order a good fire lit at once to help you dry."

I followed Crofts with the overshadowing Coroner and the plump Superintendent into the Hall of the Moth. Doctor Aire and Lord Ludlow were waiting there; the body of Sean Cosgrove lay on the couch with the *Brocade de Lyons* upholstering, and across it was stretched a decorative leather skin plucked down from the wall.

Introductions were curt. Doctor Aire pulled off the cover, revealing the corpse. The limbs had been adjusted carefully. *Rigor mortis*, of course, had not yet supervened, and the features, save for the laxity of the jaw, had much the expression I should have expected to see in untroubled sleep. First Doctor Niblett bent for his swift, searching preliminary examination, turning the dead man's head in his long, large-jointed fingers. The Superintendent followed in more deliberate manner, while Niblett went gratefully to the climbing fire.

It appeared that Salt is not one of those master-minds who require a vacuum in order to get results. He actually began to function in our presence! For at length, rising ponderously from his knees, upon which he had been scrutinizing the soles of the dead man's shoes, he said, "See here, where's the weapon?"

Crofts shrugged his shoulders, having a bit of a flea in his ear, and Doctor Aire answered, "We haven't the slightest idea. There's a pretty muddle about weapons. We've weapons to burn, but none of them appears to be connected with the case."

"We'll go into that later, then. You haven't disturbed the contents of his clothing, I see."

"Certainly not."

Methodically Salt removed what Cosgrove carried on him when he died, turning out each pocket when empty and examining the inside. Besides the loose coins, watch and chain, and wallet, there were a number of hand-written and printed sheets in several pockets.

Ludlow singled out one slip from the heap and called Salt's attention to it. "This thing," he said, "was the subject of some acrimony on the part of the deceased last night. He accused me, in fact, of pilfering it."

"What's that?"

"Perhaps," continued the wily Ludlow, "I had picked the sheet up somewhere, absent-mindedly, I suppose, and forgotten about it. It was rather a tense day. But Mr. Cosgrove saw fit to declare that I had rifled his correspondence—he claimed it as his, at any rate. Can you make any more of it than I?"

"What do you make of it?" asked Salt, who had been reading it the while.

I fancied a little spite in his Lordship's tone. "In the light of events, nothing. Suppose you show it to my friends here. One of them may suggest some interpretation that will throw light."

Crofts was obviously bursting to get a look at the screed, and I myself was glad of the opportunity to see what else it contained besides the singular remark about "the mail." It commenced without indication to whom addressed:

Dear Sir,
    I suppose that I shall see you before long, and we may discuss the topic conveniently.
    I must inform you, however, that my principals leave me no option in the matter. I hope you will realize your untenable and actually perilous position; we do not want your brains scattered about. On the evening of my arrival, I shall expect a communication from you, stating whether you will be amenable. Suppose you leave it in the mail—you know where; I'll come and get it.

I studied the signature for some time before I made it out: "Lochinvar."

"And you say that you have no idea what this means?" asked Salt.

"I wish I did!" responded Lord Ludlow; then, looking sorry he had spoken with such feeling, he added, "I mean that if I did, I might see some reason for Mr. Cosgrove's bursting into a tirade against me."

"Oh, yes?" remarked the Superintendent dryly, and turned to Crofts. "I suppose you couldn't tell when this was delivered?"

"Not while he was here," returned Crofts promptly. "The only delivery is at eleven, and I sort the mail myself. Cosgrove never got any."

"Well, I suppose we must show it to the others in the house and see if anyone recognizes the hand." Salt stood pondering a moment, then braced with decision. "And now I think that I've heard enough puzzling odds and ends about this crime. I want somebody to tell the story of it right straight through, so I'll get the tit-bits in their proper places."

This was clearly for Crofts, and I did not envy him. I remember that the rest of us were going to depart when Salt retained us with a gesture. So we were part of the audience while our host, with much nervousness and with some little assistance from the rest of us, told who were in the House, and what, in the main, had happened until the time Blenkinson had rung up the New Aidenn police station at five-twenty-two.

Only once did the Superintendent put in a word. Crofts had been setting forth as well as he could our bodily dispositions after we had left the Hall of the Moth. "So none of us could have been near him, and there's no trace of anyone else. And there you are, Superintendent."

"Oh—ah—um," remarked Salt, his eyes moving about the walls. "Secret passages?"

"None," snapped Crofts.

"Go on, sir, please. This is very interestin'."

When our host had finished, Salt emitted a noise both gruff and complacent.

"A pretty job," he observed. He cast a look about the room, as if the atmosphere of the Hall of the Moth impressed him for the first time, and he gave a conscious shiver. I saw his eyebrows twitch for a moment when his glance fell on the iniquitous portrait of Sir Pharamond on high. "A pretty job and will take a lot of doin', I expect."

"Do you want to see the rest of us now?" asked Crofts. "The party is waiting in the conservatory." He indicated the door with a nod.

The Superintendent regarded the corpse with lack-lustre eye, and pulled his beard reflectively. "Nno, not tonight, if you please. Not now, thanks. I'll take 'em all in the morning. As a plain fact, there's too much blood-and-thunder in the atmosphere tonight. Keeps people from thinkin' straight. And we can't catch the murderer tonight, anyhow." He paused a moment, blinking thoughtfully again; he was given to these interludes of cogitation. "But see here; we may clear this matter up." He showed the "Lochinvar" letter. "I'll just pass this round and see if anyone twigs the writin'."

"This way, then," ushered Crofts. He preceded us into the conservatory with its great windows, where the company was sitting in little breathless groups of twos and threes.

Only Maryvale lingered alone, beyond the grand piano, his fingers sometimes very lightly pressing the keys in chords of some neutral mode, neither major nor minor.

Salt explained that he intended to ask but one question just then, alleging anxiety lest anyone should be overwrought in the situation of time, circumstance, and weather. He gave an uneasy look at Maryvale, whose chords seemed to deepen the sombreness of the rain-beleaguered room. The "Lochinvar" letter went the rounds, until it reached Eve Bartholomew beneath a large potted plant whose leaves were like donkeys' ears. She gave a pleased cry, then a gasp.

"Sir Brooke wrote this!… But what does it mean!"

"Never mind what it means, Ma'am," said Salt. "And who's Sir Brooke? Not here, is he?"

"Don't you remember?" Crofts asked. "He's the missing—"

"Idiot," murmured Ludlow, and went on to say: "I haven't known our infirm absentee as long as this good lady, and his writing is unfamiliar to me, but it surprises me greatly that he signs himself 'Lochinvar.' Curiously unfit I should say. Madam, was that one of his baptismal names?"

Mrs. Bartholomew bridled. "I have no doubt Sir Brooke had good reason to sign himself any way he thought proper."

"I have no doubt either," acquiesced Ludlow, and added the remark, "Don Quixote."

"Haven't eaten yet?" Salt asked.

Our host said, "Hardly!"

"Suggest you do, then, and everybody try to get some rest. All doors locked, windows latched. No danger now, of course—only never give temptation."

"This way, then, if you're for food," bade Crofts, and led the way into the dining-room, where he himself was to make a wretched job of eating.

The conservatory emptied slowly. A few people followed Crofts; perhaps two-thirds of men make for the stairs and the cold comfort of their bedrooms. At the bottom of the well I drew Miss Lebetwood apart from Mrs. Belvoir. Then, I confess, I felt ashamed, and spoke awkwardly.

"Miss Lebetwood, forgive me if I—that is, I hope you won't mind—if you don't want to answer—"

Her voice was quite controlled. "Yes, what's the matter, Mr. Bannerlee?"

"It may not have anything to do with this awful—"

"What do you want to know, Mr. Bannerlee?"

"You remember telling how Miss Mertoun—before she wandered out last night—how she said something about its being 'his music'? Well—"

Paula Lebetwood winced and said, "You want to know what that meant?"

"It's rather stuck in my mind, you see—and I thought—"

"You're not a detective, are you, Mr. Bannerlee?"

"Why—no—I—"

"Your name is Bannerlee, isn't it?"

"Certainly, Miss Lebetwood."

"Forgive me; it was rude. But I am so tired—and your question—"

"Please don't—"

She interrupted, but her hesitation had become as great as mine, and there was certain displeasure in her tone. "Excuse me, I beg you, but I—don't—think I want to tell you, Mr. Bannerlee. I can hardly call it my—secret, you know."

"Pray excuse *me* for asking. But you may be called on to tell tomorrow. It will be painful, I'm afraid."

"Oh, I hope I won't have to. Really—really, it has nothing to do with—"

She fled up the stairs, and I, full of musing, went into the dinner-room and tried to eat. But it was no use then. I excused myself from the group about the table (pale, they were, as if Death itself had taken a seat at the board) and slowly proceeded to my second-storey room.

I wrote in this diary, and while I wrote I heard slight sounds below. Not until a long time later, when hunger had at last made itself felt and I hoped to burgle the larder, and stole down near midnight—not until then did I realize the full import of those sounds. While I passed through the corridor to reach the dining-room door and thence the kitchen, the far entrance of the Hall opened, and an unusual glare of light burst forth. Doctor Aire stood on the threshold. He wore a cook's white apron tied beneath his arms and pinned to his trousers below the knees. He was rubbing his fingers on the edge of it. Using the instruments of the tall, wordless Coroner, he had just performed the superfluous but required necropsy upon the body of Sean Cosgrove.

"The blow on the neck did it; nothing else the matter. He had a whale of a constitution."

Aire, too, was hungry. But it almost robbed me of my appetite again to see him eating with those gruesome fingers.

As the Superintendent foresaw, it was well that the *post-mortem* was quickly done. After all, we were cut off from escape. The bridge was wholly gone; so we had already learned by telephone. Burial of the murdered man somewhere in the Vale might yet be necessary. The King-maker entombed alone, uncoffined, far removed from the odour of sanctity!

Aire, Salt, and I came up together at half-past eleven. Poor Crofts had been troubled enough about finding places for the two officials overnight. On the first floor the rooms were filled: the Belvoirs, Oxford, and Miss Lebetwood take up the left portion of the storey not part of the upper reaches of the Hall, and on the other side the Pendletons, the Aires, Bob Cullen, Ludlow, and Miss Mertoun have rooms. Above these the only habitable chambers are those of Maryvale, Mrs. Bartholomew, and Lib at the south end, and mine up the passage. Between my room and Lib's are two chambers filled with stores of oddments anything up to a century old. The great rooms across the passage from me are also depositories and magazines of much that has been undisturbed since long before Crofts bought Highglen House.

I knew that our host took Salt and Niblett over the House in a sort of preliminary inspection about ten o'clock, for they arrived finally at my antique domicile. Crofts, thoughtless oaf, had given me no warning, and I was nearly caught in the exercise of pen and ink. I contrived, however, to thrust my writing-book underneath the table and to snatch a piece of notepaper. I was inditing a letter when the Superintendent looked in.

Then they stood in the doorway and discussed sleeping-quarters.

"Disadvantages every way," complained Crofts, "whether you try the ground floor, the first, or the second—but of course I forgot—there's no place available on the first."

"The first floor will do us very well," said Salt.

"Eh? What do you mean? You surely don't mean—"

"Mr. Cosgrove's room? Yes. Dr. Niblett and I will divide the sleepin' there and beside the corpse."

Cosgrove had occupied the east-projecting room furthest north in the older body of the House. Miss Mertoun's, beyond it, is above the newly-built conservatory, and since, as I may have said, the conservatory does not extend the entire width of the house, Cosgrove's room juts out, making a notched corner at that end of the mansion.

"But surely—"

"I'm leavin' my superstitions out with my boots tonight," observed Salt solemnly.

"But why not carry the body up there? I'll have a bed made—"

Crofts gave it up after a while, though I am sure that not for a king's ransom would he himself last night have occupied the narrow chamber that had been the Irishman's. The voices became faint down the passage; the last I heard was Salt's diminishing assurance.

"I took the liberty of usin' your telephone. I gave the Chief Constable a stiff surprise. There are two of the county police—"

CHAPTER 12

NOAH'S FLOOD

Same day. 8.30 P.M.

And now we know that the Chief Constable has left the direct handling of the case to Salt, under a discreet supervision from afar. Wise of the Constable, since he had no hope of reaching the storm-bound house!

By chance at the bottom landing I met Millicent Mertoun. I thought her more lovely than ever, though the terrors of the day before had altered her cheeks to something like the hue of wax. But her inexpressible dark eyes glowed with undimmed fascination. She smiled, courageously, I imagined.

"It's terrible, isn't it, Mr. Bannerlee, to have to eat when everything is so awful? But I'm hungry, really. I couldn't take a bite last night."

I sympathized.

"Have you heard anyone speak of finding a scarab, quite a small scarab?"

"I've just come down myself this morning, you see; so, of course— But perhaps I can help you look for it. Whereabouts do you think you lost it?"

"It's not mine—it's Paula's. She won't tell anybody about it, of course, because it's so unimportant compared with... She's troubled about it, though. It's an heirloom, I believe, from someone of her family who was in Egypt."

"I shall have a look for it, I assure you."

"I'm afraid it's no use looking, thanks, unless someone's just happened to pick it up. It was a tiny scarab, set in a ring, and it probably came loose outdoors."

"Outdoors!"

"Yes, she didn't notice it was gone until after—after—"

"I see. Well, Miss Mertoun, I'll let you know in case anyone mentions such a thing."

"Oh, thank you. But don't say I told you."

The straggling procession into the breakfast-room was not merely a subdued but even a sorry lot. Dismay and hunger both had been at work on most of us. Few, I believe, had slept. I myself had, but it was a sleep tossed and pulled by past and future. Food, however, worked its customary melioration, and when at ten o'clock we were summoned to meet Salt in the conservatory, scarcely anyone looked the worse for the mental battering of the day before. I suppose Crofts Pendleton was actually the hardest hit.

It transpired that Salt had already been about the grounds, rain-infested as they were. Insulated in rubber, he had examined the site of Cosgrove's death, seen the canvas-covered axe, and made a tour of the immediate environs of the house. Already, too, he had concluded an intensive search in Cosgrove's room and among his belongings, and to that room the unlucky Irishman's body had lately been conveyed, which relieved some of the gloom in the Hall of the Moth. Now, with the Coroner of few words seated beside him, the Superintendent stood watchfully in the sinus of the piano while we filed into the undertakers' Elysium. The servants were already standing hangdog along the wall.

"I'll have to interview each of you separately, ladies and gentlemen," Salt announced. "But I must really get acquainted a bit with you first, and have your names down. So, if you please, I'll just ask each of you in turn to tell who you are and what brought you—I mean what association you've had with Mr. Pendleton here."

At this moment Blenkinson took the centre of the stage without a cue. "If I may hinterpose, sir, I 'ave in my pocket a very comprehensive document, I may call it, which will simplify your task considerably."

"What's that, for God's sake?" exclaimed Crofts.

I am sure that the butler never had so many heads looking at him before, but with the coolest air he produced from his tail-pocket a sheaf of papers, and smoothed them lovingly.

Blenkinson was balancing a pince-nez on the bridge of his nose. "With your permission, sir, I will read. Hm! Hrrum!" He teed off and began.

It proved that the butler the evening before had assumed the rôles of despot and inquisitor in the world below stairs, and had then been my serious rival for honours in composition. Blenkinson read loudly in a high, thin voice, a woeful torture to the ear, his eyes behind the pince-nez bulging whenever he licked his thumb to turn the page. The screed he unfolded to the gaping company began with a preamble and concluded with a peroration, and must have been a couple of thousand words long. It was a vindication of the servants' hall against base suspicion in the matter of the late demise of Sean Cosgrove.

The evidence was in a sort of interlocking system. From the time Crofts had dismissed his court of inquiry after luncheon, until the hideous laugh that emanated from we don't know where, the whole baker's dozen of servants were accounted for and quite removed, I should say, from the province of investigation.

The boy Toby had been outside the kitchen entry peeling potatoes and onions all afternoon, on promise, vain, as it proved, of being let off at night for semi-bucolic revelry in New Aidenn. With him for half the time were Jael and Em, the maids, who according to the condensed economy of the house always joined in the "parin's and dishin's." When released from knives and vegetable-baskets, they resorted to the room of their companion Harmony, whom they awoke from snores, and the trio proceeded to improve the afternoon with gossip. Rosa and Ruth Clay could testify to the earlier snoring of Harmony; under the eye of Blenkinson they had then prepared tea, had early wheeled the tea-table, minus tea and hot water, into the Hall, and had gone to the stables for a bit of genteel chat with Morgan. From then until the catastrophe they vouched for him, as well as for the other stablemen, who were moving about, momently in and out of sight, over one hundred feet from the place of Cosgrove's death. The jealous eye of Ardelia Lacy, too, herself seen in and seeing from Alberta Pendleton's window, corroborated the Clays; she had come down and was sipping tea in the kitchen at the moment of the attack upon Cosgrove. Soames polishing silver until he answered my ring, and old Finlay pottering about in the flower-beds, were amply vindicated. Even Hughes the keeper was accounted for in Blenkinson's compendium, for there was plenty of evidence that he had been in his room mending a refractory gun for three solid hours.

That gives a faint idea of the method of Blenkinson's "document"; it does not begin to do justice to the detail and close-meshed cogency of it. The servants, severally and individually, are out of the investigation. For my part, I never for a moment considered the implication of any of them could be other than mad.

Blenkinson, however, had done more. He had unearthed one or two bits of evidence that may be valuable. Of these I shall relate one, leaving the other until the problem occurred of checking Cosgrove's whereabouts after he followed Miss Lebetwood from the Hall of the Moth.

Very early indeed yesterday morning Jael, polishing the kettle, sat at the window by the door leading from the kitchen along the passage to the servants' rooms. In her carefreeness she was singing a measure, when her eye caught movement in the kitchen-garden near the chicken yard. A strange man, "shaped like a lump," was prowling there. She opened the window, shouted warning to the stables; the invader uttered a short heathenish exclamation and ran away toward the head of the Vale. The men later found his footmarks in a carrot-bed.

Strange to say, there had been no inclination on the part of the servants to assign the attributes of Parson Lolly to this interloper. Perhaps the fact that he left footprints robs him of the distinction. Instantly, however, I recognized in him the gorilla-man I had encountered in the twilight when entering the Vale for the first time. Probably Jael saw him seeking breakfast.

Blenkinson concluded with a peroration the essence of eloquence, pleased with himself as an old stager applauded on his return at sixty in the part of Romeo. For our lively buzz showed that the butler had stimulated us out of our moroseness, made us forget ourselves, even in that rainy, melancholy morning.

"Priceless," I heard Belvoir chuckle, and our harassed host unbent so far as to smile, whereas Lib Dale forgot the solemnity of the occasion in open chortling. Lord Ludlow muttered something about "probably a stickit minister." As for the servants, they seemed to be in a stupor of admiration.

Whatever Salt may have thought of Blenkinson's taking evidence behind his back he kept it to himself. Reaching over, he grasped the document about to disappear into the coat-tail pocket once more, and placed it in his own inner pocket instead.

"Very interestin'," he remarked. "Now I'm fully informed on that subject. I could pick out every one of you," he said to the servants, "when Mr. Blenkinson here alluded to you. You're all excused for the present." He turned to the guests. "But I'm not clear yet about all of you ladies and gentlemen. You first, Mr. Pendleton, though. How long, now, have you owned this place? I seem to recall it's about two years."

"It is, just."

"And did you know Mr. Watts that was here before you?"

"No, Superintendent, I did not. The House was an unsold portion of old Watts' estate. It must have been five years after his death that I negotiated for it.... Wish to God I hadn't heard of it," he appended under his breath.

"That was all my fault, old fellow," consoled Alberta Pendleton.

"This furniture and the pictures, now, eh?"

"Everything came with the House. Library of books, tooled-leather style—storerooms full of odd stuff, costumes and furniture, crocks mostly—but we did find a fine Buhl bureau buried among some stacks of Victorian newspapers, and dragged it out. There was a little of everything in the attics. He must have been a prime scholar and collector, old Watts."

"A little of everything, you say? What do you mean, Mr. Pendleton?"

"Cheese-parings and candle-ends: trash, you know. Some unusual pieces though. Old Watts must have rowed for his college, or with some club, when he was a youngster. There were oars and other boating paraphernalia in one of the rooms—so much of it we expected to find a shell entombed. I ran across equipment there for a parlour magician—quite elaborate. We were hoping Doctor Aire would give us a show with it only yesterday. And—well, I'll take you through the lot, if you like."

"Yes, please." Salt addressed Alberta. "*You* hadn't known Mr. Watts? You spoke just now—your fault, you said—"

"Oh, no; I meant that Crofts bought the place because I preferred it to any other we inspected. It was so out-of-the-way." She drew the silk scarf about her shoulders closer, as if she were cold. "But that makes it all the more horrible now."

"Who were the solicitors?"

Crofts told him.

"And by the way, Mr. Pendleton, what is your line of business? You, er, are in business, aren't you?"

"Yes," answered our host briefly. "Drugs. Manchester."

I knew that after this preliminary survey, the Superintendent would interview us separately on the events of the fatal afternoon.

He chose to commence with Maryvale. Salt held the door open for the man of business to pass through, entered himself, and carefully closed the door. It was with a kind of misgiving that I watched them disappear, for now began the really crucial part of the investigation, the ascertainment of precise times and places, the attrition of fact against fact, and the weighing of hypotheses. And I was not at all sure that I fancied Salt, any more than I had last night in the beat of the rain.

The rain continued. The servants had gone, of course, and now the taciturn Coroner departed to catch up sleep in Crofts' room; so we were an intimate group once more. But the blight of cheerlessness had fallen on us again, and mystery reached its wings of fear about us. The mutter and hiss of rain sometimes redoubled at the vast windows, sometimes sank to a whisper, and those windows from their very size, seemed to admit a darker darkness. Hardly a word was spoken, and that not always heeded.

It was a quarter of an hour before Salt appeared with Maryvale. The official tugged at his border of beard with somewhat dubious expression. It was not hard to imagine that Maryvale had proved an unsatisfactory answerer, now that this strange, detached fit was upon him. Salt nodded to Alberta Pendleton, who passed through the doorway. Maryvale without a word took the piano-seat she had vacated, and began softly to play his sequences of brooding, atonic chords.

The inquiry progressed behind the closed door. Some of us Salt detained only a couple of minutes, persons who could merely verify, but not add to the information already at his disposal; others were with him twenty minutes or more. Among these I was.

"I don't think—ah, yes, now I seem to remember. You're the gentleman who had a nasty fall or something. Well now, do you mind tellin' me how you happened to get here, and if you know anything about this case?"

I suppose that I was able to tell him more than anyone else. I decided then to give my information without stint, since it was not the sort of thing that could possibly benefit mankind by concealment, and it might even speed

Salt on the track of his theory. I recounted every incident I have here set down: the search for St. Tarw's devotional site, the bull, the gorilla-man, the menagerie-keeper, the winking window, his Lordship in the armoury, and whatever else did not merely coincide with other evidence. I did *not*, however, allude to this diary. Salt, by the way, did me the great honour of hearkening without gasp or demur to my story of the tall, bulgy man with the Paul Pry-Schubert umbrella.

In the end he reverted to the matter of the saint's oratory. "This ruin or something you were lookin' for, now. Maybe I could give you a feeler for findin' it."

I said that he was very kind, that when I set forth from London the task had seemed dubious, and now the death of Cosgrove had driven my hobby well-nigh out of my mind.

"You'll soon get over that, I expect," he encouraged heartily. "Now, I'm none of your experts on old stones or old codgers, of course, and I never did hear of the party you mention, but when I was a boy I had a good share of climbin'—aye, and of fallin'—in Aidenn Forest. I can mind once runnin' across something that sounds like your whatnot. By gummy, sir, if I don't think I could guide you there yet!"

And forthwith he gave me a series of directions, which he insisted I take down. However interested I should have been in these two days ago, now among grimmer things the project of finding the oratory seems trivial, seems superfluous. But I jotted down what he told me, thanked him, and returned to the conservatory.

The spark of speech had been fanned into life during my absence. They were talking of the events of the day before—what else could they?—but they had happened upon a particular and engrossing phase. No longer, as all last evening, did they repeat to each other what they themselves had done; they had been over that so many times, all to no purpose. When, like me, each had given his account of the afternoon, it was evident that none of them could possibly have been concerned in the death of Cosgrove, or even could have seen the manner of it.

Where, as a fact, had they been after the moment of the Irishman's disappearance through the shrubs among which Paula Lebetwood had fled? Well, no one had remained long in the House. The Pendletons and the Belvoirs, together with Mrs. Bartholomew, had formed a party for a walk and had gone south. Avoiding the road, they had made their way through park-like portions of the estate all the way to the bridge, to marvel at the volume of Aidenn Water there. Far in the distance beyond the bridge, they had seen the road-mender working his long hours. Ludlow and Miss Mertoun had struck off for a stroll where Aidenn Water makes considerable of a bend beneath the western hills. Bob Cullen, feeling wretched after his dismissal by Lib, had gone alone the opposite way, kicking a disgusted trail in the turf past the stables and on beyond to where the steeply-wooded slope of Whimble Hill commenced. After her departure in dudgeon from the armoury (and from Doctor Aire and me) Lib had gone outside to look vainly about the grounds for Bob, then had come in to find Miss Lebetwood, but had encountered me on the stairs instead. Dr. Aire, having washed his hands free of gardener's loam, immediately went out, chanced upon Maryvale in the tiny grove of cypress trees, and sauntered up the Vale with him. The men turned off the path to approach the eighteenth-century summer-house, upon whose rotting steps they sat for a half an hour. Incidentally, they saw me wandering toward the deserted farm of the sisters Delambre, and saw me returning therefrom.

Oxford had spent the most peaceful afternoon of all: seating himself in the shade of the gate-house to smoke a cigarette, he had gone to sleep in good earnest. Awakened by a sound, he discovered Miss Mertoun, Ludlow, and Belvoir amusing themselves by turning the winch of the drawbridge. Belvoir, having left his wife and the others below for a brisk walk back along the stream, had met Miss Mertoun and his Lordship, and had suggested the pastime. By now Bob Cullen had made a broad circuit of the House, and stood aloof somewhat churlishly, refusing to be beguiled by the action of the drawbridge.

My report of my own doings, told at breakfast, and including as it needs must the impossible bone, had met a polite but agnostic reception. The table had lapsed into nervous silence. Ludlow, tapping his pince-nez on one knee crossed over the other, stared out the eastern window with a crinkly smile.

"The mystic bone!" he murmured ironically. (The epithet has stuck.)

"What are you suggesting, Lord Ludlow?" I asked brusquely, for my feathers were perhaps a little ruffled.

"I should say you needed to have your sight examined."

"It has been, recently, and pronounced excellent."

"Then why not consult our friend Doctor Aire, professionally? He has had something to do with mental cases."

I was going to retort when Alberta's even tones admonished me "not to notice his nonsense or he'd get vain"; so I let it go at that.

As for Miss Lebetwood's hour before the tragedy, she had soon relaxed her pace among the strawberry trees, and the wave of anger had ebbed away. She found herself nearby the tennis court. Feeling, she said, very much ashamed of her lack of self-control, she postponed returning to the House as long as possible, and began to search industriously for some of the lost tennis balls. She failed to recover a single one, and at length, noticing that the planted grove was becoming thick with twilight, and glancing at her wristwatch, she realized that she must hasten back to the House unless she were to miss tea, and appear more ungracious than ever. She did not, of course, know of the plan to rehearse "Noah's Flood," for neither Cosgrove nor anyone else had she seen. Aire had spied her just emerging from the thickets to the lawn. From the time of her outburst against him, she was not to see her betrothed again until, when half-way across the lawn a few rods above the gate-house, she saw him kneeling, as she thought, and dying, as it proved, beside the small tower.

All this, certainly, was threadbare to tell by this morning; backward and forward the courses had been traced until there was disgust at the *resultlessness* of it all. But now I returned from Salt to find a new problem had arisen in the company. Miss Lebetwood (who with Millicent Mertoun was now engaging in the last of Salt's private conferences) had said that since Cosgrove had not found her by the tennis court, it was extremely unlikely that he had ever looked for her at all; and once she had uttered these words, every person in the conservatory was acutely aware what a *non sequitur* yawning lies in the seemingly harmless assumption that because a man stares hard and plunges into some bushes he is of necessity searching for something beyond those bushes. Well then, what *had* Cosgrove been doing, and where, from leaving the Hall until receiving his death-blow by the tower?

In vain we attempted to make out for him an itinerary which would account for the afternoon. All that the united company could supply was one fact sandwiched between two uncertainties, and even that fact had been offered by the servants' hall. I may record the items thus:

First uncertainty: Doctor Aire, who left me alone in the armoury a good quarter of an hour after Cosgrove departed from the Hall, says that before seeing Maryvale, he caught a glimpse of what may have been a human face among some dogwood shrubs a little to the right of the cypress grove. But whether it was Cosgrove's face, or that of an intruder, or "the prodigious Parson's" (who is so familiar that he seems no intruder), or whether it was no face at all, Aire refuses to commit himself. He seems rather inclined to believe himself the victim of an illusion. The scientific mind, I suppose. (Query—Could *this* have been the gorilla-man? If so, we have the first evidence to substantiate any definite person's presence about the time and place of Cosgrove's death.)

Fact, from Wheeler, the youthful chauffeur, via Blenkinson's document: Cosgrove beckoned to Wheeler from behind a corner of the garage at about ten minutes past four. Answering the signal, Wheeler had been conducted to a place out of sight among the decaying stonework. (Stables and garage occupy part, but not all the site of the ruined south-east portion of the castle.) "I want no one to overhear us," said the Irishman, "and I want you to keep eternally silent about what I am going to say." For emphasis he placed a pound note in Wheeler's hand. "There will be five more for you at the end of my stay here if you do what I bid you and hold your tongue." Wheeler swore eternal fidelity, and Cosgrove gave his orders. "It's almost nothing I want. Tonight there will be a foolish entertainment in the House, and everyone will have the costume of an animal. The costumes, I know, are in the store-rooms on the second floor. Now, I have a friend who must enter the House to me without anyone being the wiser. He can come in during the mummery if he has the appearance of an animal, and I want you to see that he finds his costume. You know my room?" Wheeler said he did not, and Cosgrove explained that he occupied the room next the inner conservatory wall. "The tower there juts out corresponding to the one on the other side between the Hall of the Moth and the conservatory. At a quarter past nine I shall drop the costume from the tower window; it will be an extra progeny for the elephant, or some such vanity. I want you to be on hand from the time I mentioned until my friend comes a little later, and I want you to see that he gets into the costume and into the Hall, where the performance begins about ten. My friend will also come beneath my window, but I shall no longer be in my room; so you must be there to meet him." Wheeler guaranteed satisfaction, and was sure that he and Cosgrove had not been seen during this colloquy. (Nor had they been, but they had been heard. Morgan, overhauling a saddle in a harness-closet just beyond the wall, could verify the tones of the men's voices, but had distinguished none of the sense. In vain, later, he tried to wrest Wheeler's secret from him.)

Second uncertainty: Belvoir believes, but is not prepared to swear, that just as he and Miss Mertoun and the Baron approached the gate-house from the direction of Aidenn Water, he saw Cosgrove on the lawn. Two things make Belvoir doubt if he actually did see the Irishman or not. First, he was talking about and thinking about something else at the time, and the sight was no more than a surface impression, so to speak, on his mind. Further-more, he may have been tricked by the twilight, for the huge shadow of the gate-house reached across the lawn just there, even ascending the wall of the House part way. If he saw the Irishman in the shadow, the image must have been extremely vague, for not only is the distance considerable from where the three were walking, but Cosgrove, it must be borne in mind, was wear-ing a black coat and dark blue breeches. Belvoir is extremely uneasy on the prongs of his dilemma. (Those with him saw nothing.) Asked what position Cosgrove was in, he answers curiously enough that if he saw the Irishman at all, he had lifted the canvas cover part way and was regarding the unexplain-able battle-axe.

But I came past soon afterwards, between then and the time Belvoir and his party reached the tower—and there was no Cosgrove staring at a battle-axe then! What does Belvoir's evidence imply, if it is evidence? Did the axe leap up and smite him while he gazed, and was he lying there unnoticed by me when I returned from the cottage of the sisters Delambre? And that "friend" of Cosgrove's, who was to come at a little after a quarter past nine—did he arrive so soon? Precious little he could have done to harm the Irishman at the appointed time. If only Wheeler had kept the tryst in the storm, instead of forgetting it completely in the horror of the night until Blenkinson nagged it into his memory again! Was this "friend" the same whose indeterminate face Doctor Aire had perhaps seen, perhaps not? To ask these questions is to realize how vain they are! Yet if we are to know the obscure, impalpable limbo of truth that lies behind this man's death, must we not know the answers?

The click of the door-lock startled us in the midst of almost lively discussion. Paula Lebetwood and her friend re-entered the conservatory, and Salt stood on the threshold with a thin sheet of bluish paper in his hand. The American girl was paler than before, and, I thought, exercising great self-restraint. While she took her seat beside me, I could see the tremors pass along her throat with each breath. But her eyes were staring at the Superintendent, and my glance followed hers.

Salt said, "This paper, I expect, is Mr. Cosgrove's Will and Testament." He held it up for us to grasp at; it was a single translucent page, a tiny thing to dictate the disposal of great riches. "With Miss Lebetwood's permission—I mean by her request—I'm goin' to read it to you."

"One moment," darted in his Lordship as Salt was about to begin without taking breath: "don't you know that it is highly irregular to read a copy of a Will until all the legatees—"

"You'll see why, sir, in a minute. Besides, this is sure to be the original of the Will, and all the heirs happen to be present!"

"Eh?"

"There's not much to it, you might say, sir. And Miss Lebetwood particularly wants there to be no misunderstanding."

Forthwith, in that zone of awe, he read the instrument, dated two months ago. It contained fewer than two hundred words. I do not know which to admire most, the clear-cut terseness of it, or the hard cynical sense of its incidental comments, such as, "my body to be buried as soon as possible after my death and as near as practicable to the place of my death, with the least emolument to lawyers, priests, and undertakers." And withal, according to those of us who have scanned the law most thoroughly, the Will is adamant to any who may attempt to break it.

As for its sense, it devises Cosgrove's entire fortune to Miss Lebetwood "for her own absolute use and benefit without exception, limitation, reservation or condition, forever." Cosgrove's brother, mentioned as having self-denied a share in the estate, is made sole executor. Rather pathetic, those words:

"IRELAND DELIVERED is the cross in whose sign I would conquer; but should I die, without me I know the good work can never go on. Therefore to her who is, or is to be, my dearest helpmeet and sharer of these the Lord's bounties, best fit to use them wisely, I bequeath all my worldly goods."

Salt gave us a few breaths to absorb the shock of this overpowering disclosure. I was almost clean stupefied, but I confess that a feeling of despondency came over me at that moment. It was not, of course, that I grudged Paula Lebetwood the fortune *for herself*. But I had supposed, in what brief moments I had thought of it, that Cosgrove's money would have gone to fight Cosgrove's good fight, even though a losing one. The lines of that fine poem recurred to me:

"They went forth to battle but they always fell:
Their eyes were set above the sullen shields."

No, that had not been this Irishman's philosophy; the great cause must wait now for the next great man.

The women had instantly begun to crowd about Miss Lebetwood with exclamations of surprise and pleasure, a flutter of congratulation which must have been an ordeal for the American girl.

Salt extracted from a side pocket an envelope whose flap he loosened with a pencil. He made the round of the room so that each of us could see what was inside. "Paper-ash, this is sure to be. It was all there was in Mr. Cosgrove's grate. Not a word legible, but one or two blank bits didn't get burned, as you see.... Now, there's no paper like that anywhere in the house; Mr. Pendleton will go surety for it. It's different paper from the 'Lochinvar' bit. I was wonderin' if any of you ladies and gentlemen had some like it— could explain the note, perhaps."

But not even Eve Bartholomew could help the Superintendent now.

Salt turned to Crofts. "It couldn't have been in the post, you say?"

Crofts answered doggedly, "Cosgrove never got any mail."

"For a man who never got any mail, he had a tidy bit of mysterious correspondence. Well, I see I shall have to wait a bit before I find what little secret was here." He looked at his large silver watch. "Thank you very much, all. I don't think I'll need to trouble any of you again soon; so I'll just take this opportunity to give you a suggestion, and maybe a bit o' reassurance. There are a good many folks we haven't located that must have somethin' to do with this case. You all know about Sir Brooke—Mortimer, I think it is; well, I'm telegraphin' for full particulars of him from wherever he came from, and havin' a look-out made for him. There are two men Mr. Bannerlee ran across the night he came that I want to find, and also it seems that those Frenchwomen, the Delambres, aren't on their patch of land. Through one of these outside channels, we'll come upon a solution. And that means simply routine police work. However, if I were you, I'd not go about separately very far from the House, and just for precaution's sake you might lock your doors and windows. No alarm, you understand—only you'll feel safer. Doctor Niblett will hold the inquest as soon as possible. I shall probably be here a good bit for the next few days, and I trust, with the kind permission of Mr. Pendleton, that you will not end your visits until I am certain-sure you can't assist me."

"Only too glad, Superintendent to have them all stay until you've cornered the brute," said Crofts between his teeth. Then, becoming expansive, he looked about with a satisfied air. "Well, I'm beginning to think this won't be a Scotland Yard case after all. And it's one of those outsiders surely. Crazy to think it could be any of us."

Suddenly a strange voice was in the room. "And I, Mr. Pendleton, believe in the possible implication of everyone here, including myself." Paula Lebetwood said the words, unlike any speech we had heard from her lips, a terribly controlled utterance, toneless, as if some insentient thing had spoken. She stood up. The tremor of her throat was still.

"Of yourself, dearest?" cried Miss Mertoun. "How awful to say such a thing!"

"Of yourself!" echoed half a dozen voices.

She was looking straight ahead, sightlessly. "Isn't it too clear for words? Can't you understand how *I* feel?—how I have felt all these weeks? It rests on me, don't you see? How can I ever touch a cent that was his until his killer has paid for his death? Oh, I've felt it ever since he told me—told me he was going to make his Will—" Her eyes darkened, and the first tinge of feeling came into her voice: bitterness. "I was a fool. I should have told him—then."

Miss Mertoun came over, leaned her cheek against Paula's, recalling to me that first scene by the tower on the lawn. "Paula, *dearest*." Gently she pressed the American girl back into her seat, soothed her with soft little speeches, almost made her smile.

Suddenly Mrs. Bartholomew lifted her head, an expression of penetrative power on her face, as if she were probing beyond the realm of sense. She made a quick outreaching gesture with her hands, withdrew them, clasped them in her lap. She began to speak once, but checked herself. Then:

"I have the eeriest feeling, but it is strong, so *strong*!"

"What feeling do you mean?" asked Alberta Pendleton with bated breath.

Eve Bartholomew's eyes were shining wide. "That Sir Brooke is *here*, *now*, among us!"

She stirred us. We pitied her then, in silence. Whatever he had been to her, or she to him—

She turned to the window close beside her. "This flood may end tomorrow, but it's the act of Providence all the same!"

"Oh, come, Mrs. Bartholomew," protested Belvoir's soft voice. "It's deuced inconvenient; no two ways about that. We may have to take spades and bury our poor friend here on the spot if it keeps up."

"That was his wish, wasn't it?" she retorted. "I say this sundering flood has been our one blessing. How shall the guilty escape now, if he is not one of us? And if he *is* one of us—" Her eyes beneath that lustrous black hair shone like gems in a mine. "If he *is*, he will betray himself before the flood goes down!"

"Bravo!" exclaimed Lord Ludlow. "Madam, I applaud you. You have feeling, and I respect you for it."

Miss Lebetwood raised her voice to the man across the room. "That sounds like an indictment of me, sir."

"Never!"

The American went on. "I suppose I seem to have no grief, no feeling. I am passionless; oh, yes! I tell you I am devoted to only one thing, the finding of the murderer. My task commences today, this hour, now. I see by the look on all your faces, and one of them still may be a murderer's face, that you are shocked. No, I have sorrow; I am not hard-hearted, save for a purpose. I have sorrow—you will never know how much—but I must get it behind me."

The easy tones of Superintendent Salt intervened. "Miss, I wouldn't feel so. Everyone is heartily takin' your part. Why you should think otherwise I don't know. And have no doubt of one thing: we shall get at the heart of this mystery soon."

"We must," said Eve Bartholomew. "The innocent suffer as well as the guilty."

"I am now going to make a careful inspection of the House," said Salt. "I got the lay of the land before turnin' in last night, but now, ladies and gentlemen, I shall take the liberty of lookin' through your rooms. Mr. Pendleton, I particularly want to see those store-places Mr. Cosgrove evidently had a fancy for, and the cellars. Plenty of cellars, of course?"

"Plenty. And a sub-cellar no one's been in since before we bought the property."

"Have you any idea what's down there?"

"How should I know? Nothing, I suppose. And anyhow, the trap-covers are locked with padlocks and sealed with an inch of dust."

"Ah, well," said Salt good-naturedly, "I don't think I'll make you sweep 'em off and unlock 'em. Only take me where they are."

Again while he and Pendleton made their way from the conservatory, I was assailed with doubt concerning the confident Salt. Was he to fumble the case after all? For it seemed to me in trying to resolve an enigma so baffling, no opening ought to be ignored. And the Superintendent was, to say the least, eclectic, when he chose not to enter the sub-cellars.

A hand was laid on my shoulder. I looked up, and was held by those eyes with their unsearchable gleam, Maryvale's.

"How will they ever solve this riddle and set this wrong aright, if they forget the spanning and roofing of the waters, and the deathless arm?"

"I do not understand you, Mr. Maryvale."

"What were Sir Pharamond's words? 'Let traitors beware!' Mr. Bannerlee, remember, sir, that they never found the arm of Sir Pharamond—and his tomb in old Aidenn Church attests it."

"What on earth do you mean?"

"Oh, Gilbert has a theory all his own," laughed Belvoir in a friendly manner. "It has absolute novelty to recommend it, and artistic value. It's the artistic side that appeals to you, isn't it, Gilbert?"

"Truth appeals to me as well."

"Well, really—truth!"

"What is your theory, Mr. Maryvale?" I asked with an attempt to disregard the twinges of apprehension that I felt in his presence.

"I have no theory: I have the key."

"Gilbert means that the corporeal, material, substantial right arm of Sir Pharamond Kay, builder of the castle which now is Highglen House, has risen from its cerements and laid a certain party low. Isn't that about it, Gilbert?"

"It is all you need to know."

"But what's that about the proof being in Old Aidenn Church?"

Belvoir gave a sly chuckle. "Go there some afternoon and have a look for yourself, Mr. Bannerlee. Old Aidenn is only three miles beyond New Aidenn, and both of 'em happen to be as old as Doomsday."

"It's as sound, anyhow, as Crofts' idea that a murderer couldn't escape from Aidenn Vale," remarked Aire.

For my part, I looked first at Maryvale's stooped retreating bulk, and then at the other two men, who solemnly looked at me. We did not speak, but the same thought must have been in all of us. The servants might understandably be shy of strange forms in the dark, but what was to become of *us*, if we began gravely to discuss wee grey-bearded men with voices like honey, or pixies perched on toadstools?

Young Bob Cullen had strayed to the window, was watching the raindrops, now meandering slowly, now darting down the pane.

"Talk about Noah's Flood," he growled.

"Forty days he had of it," mused Lib Dale. "If this keeps up forty minutes more, I'll be dotty. Oh, look!"

The whole conservatory thrilled with light. A golden-green path lay shimmering across the lawn. It had ceased to rain.

CHAPTER 13

THE WEAPON

Suddenly, and very softly, Superintendent Salt was among us once more. I knew of his presence only when I heard him speak.

"My Lord, one more question, if you please. The man—Soames I believe his name is—who has just conducted me to the cellars says you gave him a letter to post last evening."

"I did—confound him! I handed it to him and expressed a wish that if the storm should cease as suddenly as it commenced, it might reach New Aidenn in time to go out in this morning's post. Of course, when the downpour showed no sign of abating, I had it back."

"I presumed so, my Lord. In that case, I shall have to see the letter, with your permission."

"And that you certainly shall not!"

Salt was like the everlasting hills. "Only the envelope, my Lord. The superscription is all I need to see."

After a long ten-seconds' hesitation Lord Herbert drew a letter from his breast-pocket and held it close to the Superintendent's face. Salt peered.

"Hm. Is that it? Seems to be. Stamp uncancelled. To the Bangor and Newcastle Corporation, eh? 12 Gate Street, London, E. C. Very innocent, I'm sure, my Lord. Thank you."

I saw the quick purple flash into the Baron's face when Salt read aloud the words intended only for his eye. "I consider this an impertinence, sir."

"To be called things is all in my day's work, my Lord," responded Salt, and turning to Pendleton, he said, "You ought to open a little Post Office here."

"What on earth for?"

"For surreptitious mail."

"Bangor and Newcastle Corporation," I could not help repeating puzzledly, half-aloud, I fear. "What on earth connection can there be between little Bangor with its agriculture and Druid Circle, and the coal and battleships of Newcastle-on-Tyne?"

Ludlow said nothing, but I observed in his eye and in the hook of his bloodless lip a sublime contempt for my ignorance.

But at that moment everyone save me was looking toward the door leading to the Hall of the Moth, which had opened sufficiently to admit first the head and then the rest of Blenkinson. Again the look of transcendence appeared natural, even casual on his person. Spiritual transcendence, that is, for bodily he was in great bedragglement, as if he had wallowed in the rain just before it ended.

"Mr. Salt, I beg to report that the weapon 'as been found. I 'ave left it where I and Finlay discovered it, almost—"

I think the feeling of elation that visited me was shared by nearly everyone in the conservatory. I saw faces brightening. But Salt's did not.

The Superintendent gave one leap toward Blenkinson, cutting him dead off in the midst of his glory.

"Mr. Blenkinson, your admirable researches—invaluable assistance—indispensable services—fill me with alarm. Please be more discreet. Inform me in private of your discoveries, and let *me* be the judge whether they are to be shared by these ladies and gentlemen. For, mind you, *technically*, every person here is under suspicion—and that goes for you, too, Mr. Blenkinson. You may, or may not, be revealin' something valuable to the murderer himself."

Under this withering sardonic fire the smug efficiency of the butler had fallen ingloriously. "I'm—'gulp'—very sorry, sir, but—'gulp'—the fact is, I was so helated—'gulp'—that I—"

"Quite," agreed Salt; "quite. And now, Mr. Blenkinson, if you please, lead the way to this weapon, whatever it is." He thrust the butler before him through the door into the Hall, and looked back upon the threshold. "Kindly do not let your curiosity to see Mr. Blenkinson's find tempt you to follow us, any of you. Thank you." The door closed.

The weapon found! Tongues were wagging anew. I thought of the difference between Salt's previous assurance to us that the solution was to be sought among the many missing persons, and his recent proclamation that no one in the House was exempt as a possible murderer. Then in the midst of the babble came a still voice close behind me. I turned; Doctor Aire was leaning over the piano, his abbreviated form easily sheltering underneath the lifted cover.

"Mr. Bannerlee, how about a stroll up the Vale, now it promises fair weather? Mr. Salt has admonished us to go in pairs."

"Up the Vale—now? You must be emulating Noah himself, Doctor! The waters haven't yet descended from Ararat."

"I want to get rid of this cursed miasma of flowers. It's like some noxious emanation. My head aches with odours."

"But surely it's out of the question. Why, after this downpour, the Vale's certain to be swampland all the way up to Water-break-its-neck."

The yellowy doctor shook his head, smiling. "Strange, but you're wrong. You should really dig into the lore of this region, Mr. Bannerlee. The Welsh name of our locality, I have read, is Maesyfed."

"Oh? Meaning?"

"The absorbent field, probably. For the thirsty soil does wonders after rain; in summer even Aidenn Water sinks underground for long distances and leaves its channel dry."

"Well, I'm in favour of getting out of here if it can be done."

"It can; I know from previous visits. We'll give the sun and soil a couple of hours to restore dry footing."

"Well enough. I'll meet you in the library."

Salt re-entered just then and took Aire away with a few whispered words. I wandered into the dinner-room where stragglers were sitting at belated luncheon, for since yesterday's disaster the schedule of meals seems to have fallen into anarchy. I did not stay long at the board, however; perhaps the fumes of the conservatory had stopped the pangs of appetite. I excused myself and crossed to the armoury, intending first to glance over the array of the library shelves in the hope of discovering something of interest, then to go to my room and set down some of the multitudinous details of last night and today.

But I never got as far as the library. I heard a strenuous young voice through its door ajar:

"Ah, g'wan. You make me laugh—*you*. When they put a lily in your hand, you'll deserve the Good Boy's Epitaph."

"What's that?" demanded Bob suspiciously.

"'He loved his grandmother.'"

"You think you're funny, don't you? Well, I wasn't crazy about this Cosgrove. I would have been ready to do him in. He was no good for Paula, even if he did have all that coin. He was a fast worker, that's what he was. I guess you ought to know. He was a dirty bum."

"'Swine' is what you say in this country."

"I said I'd have polished him off, and I meant it. Wouldn't you?"

"Hush up, Bobby. Keep that stuff under your hat. You don't want somebody to overhear you talking crazy, do you?"

"Well, wouldn't you?"

Lib lowered her voice and spoke rapidly. "Yes, I would, for a brick like Paula. My God, what a man Cosgrove was! And she fell for him!" Then, "Change the subject, change the subject! To hear you talk like that would give an alligator nervous prostration. Suppose a few of those detectives were in the armoury."

There was a spell of silence, sharply broken by Lib. "Leggo my hand! What do you think this is, a golf links?"

"You tol' me to change the subject," said Bob with deep grievance.

"Don't be sil. Say, I think there *is* somebody in there. Look quick."

But I had fled into the corridor and, laughing heartily within, was half-way up the stairs.

In my room I immersed myself in that task of writing which has become almost my principal interest. I quite lost track of time while I wrote of Salt's arrival last evening and the rest of it. With a start I recalled Aire, looked at my watch, and leaped down the stairs. It was nearly four.

The short, spindly-legged man was waiting, and with a touch of annoyance I saw that Maryvale was consulting some book in a corner of the library, a book which he put down upon my arrival as if he expected to accompany us.

"Gilbert has consented to come along."

"Oh? Glad."

The sky was unblemished with cloud when we set out for that supposedly uneventful walk in the bracing hill-air, but the sun had sloped nearly to the high horizon of the ridge, and the light already had in it a subtle infiltration of yellow. Some jewels still glittered on the lawn, but the turf was surprisingly firm and pleasant to the tread.

We struck under the shade of the cypresses; through the systematic "wilderness" of planted trees we strode, toward the pretentious bridge, past the mouldering eighteenth-century summer-house, a thing quite dismantled and defeated and gutted out. Once I had fancied it as a possible hiding-place for mysterious visitants, but now I rejected it utterly. The old smooth lawns there were now ragged stretches of rough grass, still heavy with the rain where they lay beneath any trees, and sluggish lake-like ponds were the remains of once sparkling basins.

Aire paused where a grey fallen statue and its pedestal lay beside one of these sad meres, a place where the trees had hunched their shoulders together to make an extra twilight shade.

"About here, they say, a former occupant of the mansion, the one who built that summer-house, was found."

"How found?"

"Dead, Mr. Bannerlee, with his head neatly shorn away from the rest of him. That was nearly two hundred years ago." He grunted. "The chap *ought* to have been killed for putting up that thing."

"Good heavens! Who had done it?"

"I wish I could tell you. He was never discovered. I don't think the victim was a very popular gentleman; so there may have been connivance in keeping the secret locked away. A baffling affair it must have been for the Salts of that day. The time-and-space problem was mystifying then as now it is in Cosgrove's death."

I looked curiously at the little man with the broad shoulders. "Doctor, you certainly hit upon the strangest tales. Where could you have found that recorded?"

"On a special pasted-in leaf of an old family Bible. Quite a fascinating library Crofts owns without comprehending it."

"This is accursed ground," said Maryvale. "It reeks with lawless bloodshed."

We left the park with its sickly poetry and bore to the right by a field-path toward the prosaic potato-patch of the sisters Delambre, where the scarecrow bore almost too great a likeness to Baron Ludlow in his tweeds to be laid to coincidence. It was here that the brook later spanned by the absurd bridge came down from the indentation of the hill. We followed the narrow channel, where the rain-swollen stream now leaped against its banks, to where the deserted cottage stood in an oak-clump. The morsel of a stone-roofed house gave only a shy peep from its covert; it was like a doll's house, dwarfed by overshadowing branches.

"Do you think it possible that these women were concerned either last night or the night before? What were they like?"

"Cranky Frenchwomen. I've seen them on previous visits," answered Aire. "They always gave me the impression of being a couple of—well, I might say unfrocked nuns, if you understand."

"Sounds rather ambiguous, Doctor," I remarked.

I was suddenly put in mind of a tale I had heard in another spot of demon-haunted Wales, and I told it with some gusto. There two sisters had lived together and managed a small farm with the aid of one man. They were unfamiliar people and the country-folk were turned askance to them. The pair would vanish at a particular time of day, and their hats would be hanging in their bedrooms upon the looking-glass. One afternoon the farmhand hid under their bed to find out their secret. He saw them take off their caps and hang them on the glass, whereupon they themselves immediately turned to cats, and ran to the dairy and began lapping the cream.

A somewhat dubious look upon Aire's face as he gazed at Maryvale during my recital was, I fear, lost on me, for it gave me a thrilling pleasure to apply this tale to the sisters Delambre, particularly since in that grimalkin of appalling voice they had a fit companion for many an impious Sabbath.

"And by the way," I concluded, "the beast spared us its caterwauling last night."

"Last night, but not tonight," said Maryvale. "It will be hungrier than ever tonight. We shall hear it, unless—"

"Unless what?"

"We shall see," he parried.

"It's a vicious beast, if ever there was one," said Aire, looking in one of the cottage windows. "It's twice the size you'd believe it could attain. There's never been any other cat in the Vale whose nine lives were worth sixpence when this animal discovered its presence."

"And the birds," added Maryvale. "The nightingales that once loved this valley so—scarcely one is left."

Returning toward Aidenn Water at a point somewhat further north, we heard from beyond a gnarl of blackberry bushes the sound of footsteps and voices which proved to be those of Salt, wearing rubber boots, and of Hughes the keeper. They were making their way up the stream by the principal path, and I noticed that Hughes bore an axe of considerable heft.

Salt greeted us while we fell into step. "Sensible to get out of doors."

"But you're not here for your health, I fancy," said Aire.

"I am not. Mr. Hughes here and I are going to devote the last hour of daylight to satisfyin' ourselves about traces of the assassin on the other side of the Vale. We've scoured north, south, east, and west on this side of the stream, and never a footprint of him or anybody else. Mr. Pendleton seemed a bit anxious we shouldn't overlook the chance, and it is a chance."

"What is that axe for?" suddenly demanded Maryvale.

"To chop down a tree, sir," answered Hughes. "I know where I can make one fall across the Water. It's the only way to get over."

"I thought as much," I said. "What, just, is the state of things down at the bridge?"

"There isn't a trace of it left, sir," Salt informed me. "Sometime last night the stone ends were undermined by the current. There are men on the other side, though, riggin' up a makeshift, and tomorrow, maybe, if the stream goes down reasonably, we can get out of here, and get Mr. Cosgrove's body out, too."

Hughes pointed to the north, where the zigzag path down the mountain had been obliterated by the landslip. "Men from Penybont beyond the Forest are coming from the other side to clear that up tomorrow, too."

"Well, someone must have been moving heaven and earth!"

"Yes, sir; Mr. Pendleton was quite busy on the 'phone this afternoon."

"That telephone is not the least of our miracles," I observed. "I should have expected the line to be smashed to smithereens by the storm."

"Our wires run underground, sir," said the keeper.

"What!"

"Yes, sir, all the way to New Aidenn. There was too much trouble with it the other way; so Mr. Pendleton had it changed. Now nothing ever interferes with it."

I remembered something. "To bring into this discussion an element sadly wanting—"

"What's that?"

"Disclosures. Tell me, Superintendent, does the pall of official secrecy still cover the weapon discovered by the astute Blenkinson?"

"Not much use trying to keep anything secret hereabout," said Salt with a smile, which made me wonder what recent discoveries actually reposed undivulged beneath that sodden hat and those iron-grey curly locks. "The lid is off that little matter."

"It *is* the weapon? What had Blenkinson found?"

"A piece of angular slate, well shaped for holdin', provided with an almost sharp edge. Queer, isn't it? Here's a chap—I mean the guilty party—helped himself to what he wanted out of the armoury the night before; now, when he's in a killin' mood, he fetches along a stone. Plenty of rock like it in the Vale, of course. Seems likely, though, that it was picked up from that gimcrack rockery old Finlay wants to get rid of—just opposite the tower where Cosgrove was found."

"You're sure it's the instrument?" I asked.

Salt looked at Aire, who said, "The Superintendent called in Doctor Niblett and me for our opinions on that point. The Coroner and I agree that in the hands of a vigorous person, who must have approached Cosgrove secretly from behind, the stone might well have done the damage."

"But where was it lying?" I asked, with incredulity sounding in my tone. "How could we have missed it?"

"It wasn't lyin' anywhere," answered Salt. "That's a feature about it. It was embedded, sir, almost buried among the flowers outside the central windows of the Hall. If the rain hadn't played hob with the beds, and the man Finlay with Mr. Blenkinson hadn't been assessin' the damage, it might have remained there unnoticed for a tidy while."

"By Jove, though, that's a far-fetched hiding-place."

Salt raised his brows. "Is it? I think it was a clever one, sir. One second he strikes the blow, the next he hurls the weapon straight down into the loam. Inside half a minute he may be anywhere, and nothin' to connect him with the crime. Just a little more energy, and the earth would have fallen in about the edges and covered the stone completely. But as it was it must have taken strength, gigantic strength."

"It must have taken superhuman strength, Mr. Salt. Why, there had been rain, but it blew a bit easterly then, and those beds couldn't have got much of it. It was nothing like last night's inundation. The ground must have been hard."

"On the contrary, the ground was exceedingly soft. Remember what it said in Mr. Blenkinson's document, sir. Finlay had been waterin' those very beds, and waterin' 'em plenty after four o'clock."

"Were there any marks on this stone?" asked Maryvale. "Any signs such as I understand often guide the police in their search?"

"No, sir, none. And—"

"I thought so."

Ignoring this somewhat cryptic remark, Salt explained: "Unpolished stone isn't a good medium for takin' impressions. I'll stake my little finger, though, it was the stone that finished Mr. Cosgrove."

"Here we turn off, sir," advised Hughes.

We had been in sight of Aidenn Water much of the time, its cheerful flow increased to boiling spate. Through a partly cleared copse of larch, we could see it now, laughing with white teeth and greedy gurgle along a sort of rapids. The particular tree Hughes intended to chop was visible, already leaning half across the flood.

Somewhat to my discomfiture, Aire announced that he intended to accompany the pair across the stream. "Don't mind, do you, Bannerlee? I want to be in at the death of Pendleton's theory. Or will you two come along with us? Any objection, Superintendent?"

"More the merrier," said Salt.

But I cared nothing for the death of any theory compared with my eagerness to get farther north and see the great ruin beneath the hills again. Maryvale had no love for the thought of crossing above the churlish Water on a tree-trunk, and said so. We left the three proceeding to the bank of the stream, but I confess it was with a pang of premonition that I paced beside the man of business and heard the sound of the lusty axe grow fainter and fainter.

CHAPTER 14

THE FIENDISH CAT OF THE SISTERS DELAMBRE

For half an hour we walked on almost in silence, making the tritest remarks about our surroundings, particularly those peaks which shut in the valley ahead of us, from Great Rhos on the left across Black Mixen to Mynydd Tarw on our right. We now saw only a broken secant of the sun, and most of our light was reflected from the golden tops of the hills. Maryvale for some reason maintained an unusually sharp look-out, glancing restlessly every way among the glades.

Almost before I was aware, we had reached the outer of those dejected and scattered walls for so many centuries lying the prey of the elements and the spoil of house-builders and church-builders from down the Vale and beyond.

Some of these still remained high enough to show the embrasures where the upper windows had been, tall, slender apertures, one of them far on the other side even now perfect in the stonework of transom and mullions and semi-rounded arch. It was indeed the ruin of a knightly house, once spacious and splendid. The fallen walls seemed to have been struck or hurled outward by some terrific force or inward convulsion, as if behemoth had stirred and heaved himself from beneath the floor.

Flanking the walls to the left, where I had come past two nights ago and encountered the menagerie-keeper, I peered inside, over a chin-high portion, and gave an exclamation of surprise. The thick walls had indeed been hurled down from within. The vast flat slabs of the floor, what few of them remained, were tossed in disorder, and the earth on which they lay was piled in fantastic heaps alongside deep, irregular trenches—all grass-grown now, of course. A few bushes and one enormous beech tree found livelihood inside the wall.

For a couple of minutes Maryvale had been standing quiet behind me, peering this way and that in the twilight, as if he looked for some particular object.

"This gutted carcass makes me fancy things," I laughed. "Come, Maryvale, sweep the spider-webs out of my mind by flourishing vigorously the broom of truth. In other words, relate to me something about this place, and pity on your life if it's the old story of 'deflor'd by Glindur.'"

"Why, haven't you heard?"

"If I did it went in one ear and out the other. Say on."

I braced my hands on the broken top of the wall and leaped up, making my seat there. Maryvale joined me with very little effort, and we sat there kicking our heels schoolboy-like.

Again I saw him look about very intently, under the beeches, through the gaps between the stones, across the scrub growth between us and Aidenn Water a quarter of a mile distant.

"What are you looking for, Maryvale?"

"Sathanas."

"This place is too thinly populated, my friend. Come, what of this ancient hold? Bring on your heroes and cravens, your demigods and dastards."

"Gwrn darw—the pile of contention," muttered Maryvale, and he launched on the story.

I had expected another farrago of myth and tradition, perhaps larded with the same episodes that Hughes had spellbound us with in the dinner-room yesterday morning. Instead it was a fairly plausible story from some wholly different source, this account of the first historical building in Aidenn Vale. I enjoyed listening to the narrative; Maryvale enjoyed telling it. Gusto was the keynote of his voice, with its rapid utterance and changes of inflection. He made drama of it, and a valiant man of Sir Pharamond.

"Why, Maryvale, where did you learn all this?"

"This is history," he affirmed solemnly.

Moreover, he was beginning to peer about again, turning more than once in his speech to stare beneath the branches of the trees. That feeling of repugnance to Maryvale which I had before experienced returned hazily, and of a sudden I realized how lonely this place was, how close to us the hills were, and how dark and steep. I might instantly have urged our return had not my own roving glance caught a black object protruding from a bush inside the wall.

I broke in. "Look! Here's evidence the world's a madhouse!"

Down inside the wall I slipped, crossed to the bush, and triumphantly held high the black umbrella.

"He was real, Maryvale! He was no nightmare!"

While I unfastened the loop and opened the umbrella, Maryvale dropped from his seat and came beside me. He asked me what this was, where it came from, and whom I had met here, all in a breath.

"This is a clue, man!" I exclaimed. "Perhaps it has some manufacturer's mark—what's the matter?"

I could no more have released my arm from Maryvale's grip than from the strongest vise. But in a moment his hand relaxed, and then I caught sight of what he was looking at so hard.

On the northern wall, twice the height of that whereupon we had been sitting, crept something darker than the hills against which its form was obscure. Softly, swiftly, the form slunk along the stones, then gave a leap to the arched summit of that one perfect window and stood still, its head lifted, its form now stark against the sky—the form of an enormous cat, lean and lithe and tigerish.

Maryvale was breathing loudly. I gave him a swift look; his face was working, and with his eyes set on the cat of the sisters Delambre, he drew from a hip pocket the last thing on earth I should have imagined him to carry, a large revolver, one of the sort called in America, I believe, a six-shooter.

But the hideous expression of his face was more alarming still.

Here was a combination of circumstances I did not envisage hopefully: the lonely spot, the great cat, the man apparently unbalanced by the sight of the beast, and the revolver. I had only the umbrella.

Not a little afraid, I sought safety in valour. I reached out my hand.

"May I see that, Mr. Maryvale?"

He let me have the weapon without demur, and while I examined the deadly thing, I saw out of the corner of my eye that his attention was still riveted on the shape of the cat. I hesitated to break into that almost hypnotic absorption.

Perhaps a minute passed. I had put down the umbrella.

Then from the gloaming woods that fringed the mountain foot welled a sound like a bright bubble bursting into a hundred bubbles, a sound like the spray of a sweet fountain—the song of a nightingale from the deep solitudes of Black Mixen.

"The nightingale of Water-break-its-neck," I thought, for I had heard someone speak of this lonely music-maker.

The form of the cat stiffened; gradually it sank to a crouching posture, as if its prey were near at hand. Then tail and head went up, and its jaws were sharp against the sky, and the valley bristled with its starved and destructive yowl.

Maryvale was a man transformed from trance to action. Spasmodically he felt his pocket for the pistol, then recollected me. His voice was jumbled with the cry of the beast.

"Give me that gun."

"Wouldn't it be better—"

His utterance was quickly controlled to a whisper. "Give me that gun. I am going to perform a humane act. I came here for this."

"But, Mr. Maryvale—"

"Don't you understand?" he burst out. "I will free the soul of a ghoul from its tenement!" He grabbed the pistol from my hand.

"For God's sake—!"

"I am the best shot in the Midlands with one of these." He raised the weapon with a marksman's care and confidence.

The animal, surprised by our voices, had reared its head in our direction, and now, instead of making off, scrambled down from the window arch and came loping toward us, growling, as if it actually contemplated an attack. Its fur on end swelled it to twice its size. Maryvale shifted his aim quickly, and the clustering hills resounded with the echo of his shot.

But the cat, unhurt, sprang toward us spitting and snarling, with eyes that flashed. I realized when I saw those intensely flaming eyes that green, not red, must be the colour of hell-fire.

Again the revolver blazed, with no effect save to cause the beast to give a high leap toward Maryvale, full length upright, all fours spread wide and clawing, mouth hissing. Maryvale shot point-blank in the face of the animal, and the beast was enveloped in a fiery cloud, but it dropped to earth on all fours, fled unscathed past us, and disappeared beneath a bush.

Maryvale lifted his hands to the dark and empty sky. "Too strong—too strong—the infernal magic of this place."

I took a step toward the man, grasped the weapon, tugged to get it from him, cried, "What did you expect? You've loaded this pistol with blank cartridges."

"Blanks?" he shouted. "Never a bit."

Twenty feet away a straggling thin branch of a rowan tree came over the western wall and was ebony against the sky, having at the end some finger-clumps of leaves. Maryvale took quick aim, eyes protruding grotesquely, and fired; the branch trembled and one of the leaf stems fell away. Twice again the pistol rang out; the branch itself suddenly hung down, all but severed by the final bullet.

Maryvale laughed wildly with tempestuous eyes. "I should have known it was impossible. You cannot kill the soul of Parson Lolly with lead."

He threw away the weapon, went lunging along the wall. I followed, took him by the shoulder.

"Maryvale—"

But he thrust me off, violently, and began to run. I fell with my knee against a stone, and when I arose my chagrin was great, for apart from the pain my leg had gone almost dead, and I could scarcely hobble. Maryvale had found a gap between the stones, leaped through, and charged down the Vale. When I had managed to drag myself out from the enclosure, he was beyond sight and hearing. I shouted his name many times; no answer came back.

I knew that lamed as I was I must get down the Vale as soon as possible, for there was no telling what the man might do in this demented state. He might even have another gun.

The cat the incarnation of Parson Lolly! Then the realization leaped on me. What would they say, those in the House, when they were told that none of the three bullets had done the beast any harm!

So stunned I was by this lightning-stroke that without knowing what I did or being aware of my injured knee, I walked on with my brain in a storm of confusion. When, some time later, I was rid of the shock, but still wondering, I had gone half a mile and my knee was almost painless.

I commenced to run.

Ten minutes late I encountered Doctor Aire, who fell in beside me while I gasped what had happened.

"I was a fool," he panted. "Fool to leave him alone with you. He was excited—upset—I saw—that when you were telling—that story down by the cottage. You'll have to—go on alone. I can't—keep up."

He dropped behind, and the last thing I heard him say was, "I couldn't foresee—a miracle."

Talking winded me. I was spent when I reached the summer-house, and could scarcely walk to the mansion.

Alone in the Hall of the Moth I found Mrs. Belvoir sitting, rather pointlessly, it seemed.

"Maryvale—here?"

"Yes, Mr. Bannerlee."

"Where?"

"Upstairs. They all followed him when he came in. He is in his room."

"Was he violent? Why did they go after him?"

"Not exactly violent, no. But I don't think it's worth while following him any more."

I checked my foot on the threshold. "What do you mean, Mrs. Belvoir?"

"A personality balanced on a knife-edge is never safe. Poor Gilbert was too rash when he tempted the Influences in this valley. His mind is gone, for certain."

"Influences?"

"Of course there are Influences. I can feel them myself. Gilbert is only the first to give in."

I left this placid lady and made what speed I could up the stairs. In the passage outside Maryvale's room on the second floor, the Coroner and the rest of the men were standing.

"Is he in there?"

"He is," answered Crofts.

"Why don't you go in to him?"

"Because—well, because—"

"Because we all want to stay healthy," said Bob Cullen.

I learned what had happened. People in the Hall had seen Maryvale stagger across the lawn, in their alarm had heard him enter the armoury and disturb the weapons there. When some of the men looked into the room, Maryvale had departed, and a sword was missing. They heard him clamber up the stairs. Consulting in perplexity for a few moments, they decided to follow. The curious thing about this part of the affair is that in those doubtful moments Maryvale had not at once entered his room at the head of the second flight of stairs, but for some reason had hastened along the passage on that upper floor. For while the pursuers were on the second flight, Maryvale came rushing back, invisible (because of the curve in the staircase), and secured himself in his chamber. Knocking and calling evoked no response, save once. Then Maryvale flung wide the door, in his hand the drawn sword—a thin two-edged one like a Toledo blade.

"I'll kill anyone who comes in here," he said. "Leave me to do my work."

"Which," remarked Ludlow, when Crofts had finished this account, "I for one am going to accede to, as a reasonable request."

We agreed it was best to take turns standing guard. Belvoir, on account of his being particularly a friend of Maryvale's, offered to be the first on duty. We left him there, smoking his pipe, leaning against the doorpost, his ear to the door.

What "work" could Maryvale be doing?

Poor Crofts, a host with a dead man and a madman in his house! I passed him on the bottom step, gnawing a knuckle, apparently making quite a meal.

"Bad luck, old man."

He regarded me listlessly. "I had a 'phone call this afternoon from the Post Office. Harry Heatheringham has wired for full particulars."

"Ye Gods! Who is Harry Heatheringham?"

"Oh, I supposed you knew. One of the really high-powered detectives. Happens to be a friend of mine."

"Scotland Yard?"

"No, he prefers the country air. He's a Worcester man. I wonder what Salt would say."

"Ask him; he can't arrest you for it. By the way, how does the great man from Worcester happen to be so prompt in sniffing out this case?"

Crofts became nervous, as he always does when he has something to conceal. "He—he—we're, er, in what you might call communication. Dash it all, I wish the fellow would keep his promises!"

Salt came in, just before dinner, not a merry meal. He heartily approved Harry Heatheringham.

"Do you know, sir, I wouldn't be sorry to see him on the ground."

"I'm damned if I know why he isn't!" remarked Crofts, and fled to the telephone, to dictate a lengthy wire.

It transpired that the Superintendent and his aides had found not the slightest trace of recent human presence across Aidenn Water. They did not even find a new puzzle; they found nothing.

But after dinner Salt made a more fruitful inspection of the rooms on the second floor, except Maryvale's. He had been curious to discover why the demented man had gone down the passage before shutting himself in. He found why.

"There was a box of paints and a palette and easel, and some brushes, in the store-room next to you, Mr. Bannerlee. Mr. Maryvale must have known about 'em, of course."

"Some canvases on stretchers, too, weren't there?" added Crofts. "All here before my time. Seems to me I've heard old Watts used to dabble in paints."

"They're all missin' now, sir," said Salt. "That's what he was after."

"Paints!" exclaimed Belvoir. "Yes, that explains it, indeed."

"What do you mean, sir?"

"Gilbert Maryvale has been a very unhappy man," said Belvoir slowly. "He has been chained to a big business that would have gone to pieces without him. He has made lots of money, but always wanted to be a painter. You see, Mr. Superintendent, he had an exquisitely sensitive spirit, for all his dealing in bills and notes."

"I'm tryin' to see," said Salt.

"Well, he will never look in the flabby faces of a Board of Directors again. He has begun to paint."

* * * *

Is all the heart-crushing suspense in the world packed into this little Vale? Beyond the hills, I know, men and women are peacefully sleeping, and farther beyond, in the Glamorgan collieries, perhaps the night-shift is working with never a hint of the nameless dread that keeps us wakeful.

If I live through the night, I shall get out on the uplands early in the morning. I know a trick or two of throwing a hitch from tree to tree. With a stout rope I can climb one of these wooded hillsides, even if it prove vertical! Then I shall *breathe*!

3.50 A.M.

I have just awakened with a grim and unalterable thought. Confound Doctor Stephen Ashmill Aire for his subtle hints and theories. If what he suggested this afternoon is true, that there is some hidden means of access to the lawn, what awful consequences are thrust into mind! Yes, if he is right, the murderer may be one of those people who came rushing in from all directions while we stood about Cosgrove's body. I hesitate to write their names, but it may be Belvoir or Bob Cullen or Maryvale, for instance, or even one of the women, if in her fury her arm became iron.

And that fiendish cat that has driven Maryvale mad and that his bullets could not harm!

Worse and worse!

I shall now dress in tramping kit and doze until dawn.[3]

---

3   I have postponed until now a note which should have been inserted some pages ago, but which would then have interrupted the narrative. References to *the song of the nightingale* in this chapter and elsewhere in this diary demonstrate, as I think, the innocent romanticism of Mr. Bannerlee. Neither he nor Mr. Maryvale appears to have possessed a rudimentary knowledge of birds. Nightingales, to be sure, visit Radnorshire, and the old ones do not leave until autumn, but of course their descant ceases in *June*, when the task of feeding the young becomes absorbing. Unquestionably, the bird these gentlemen listened to was the song-thrush, which (as is well known) *resumes* its singing in October, when the now-silent nightingale has departed from the land. (V. MARKHAM.)

CHAPTER 15

THE RAINBOW

October 5. 10.18 P.M.

I slipped on my rough shoes, thus completing my toilet, scribbled a note for Crofts, and passed out of the door. From the top of the stairs came a soft recurrent sound. Bob Cullen had insisted on sentinelling outside Maryvale's apartment during the night; now the guardsman slept industriously, his head reclining in the angle of the doorpost, the rest of him curled up, his jaws alarmingly open.

Not disturbing him, I descended to the first storey, where I placed my note under Crofts' door, and continued down. My previous night's experience had taught me how to find the food supply readily, and I stocked my pockets with concentrated nutriment. Letting myself out by the front entrance, I turned to the left and directed my steps toward the kitchen demesne betwixt House and stables.

I was in luck. Twenty yards of fairly stout clothes-line were mine for the taking.

With the rope bent over my arm, I hastened past the dinner-room windows toward the cypresses that marked the first point on any journey up the Vale. Then I stopped dead.

For a woman was standing by the far corner of the conservatory, half-turned from me, looking at an object which she held in her hand.

With her other hand she made a slight gesture to someone around the corner, and the next moment I beat a swift retreat to the shelter of a rank of low birch trees. A man in his shirt sleeves dashed out from the behind the House, running like mad. He was a man I had never seen before!

With great galloping strides, his arms working like pistons, his knees rising incredibly high, he rushed straight for the clump of cypresses; there he turned as sharply as his momentum would permit and sped back to his starting point out of my view.

He had come and gone so quickly that I had little chance to take in his appearance. Decidedly, however, he was a long, lank man, and there was a touch of red about his face in hair and beard. But any attempt to mark him closely was defeated by mere astonishment at his presence, and wonder, in the name of reason, at what he was doing.

I quickly balanced the courses open to me. Should I reveal myself and challenge these unknowns? Or return secretly to the house and awake Crofts and Salt? Or continue my journey?

This last was what I did, for the cloaked woman happened to turn her head in my direction, and I saw that she was one of the Clays. Unless the Clays are to be relied on, no one is. As for my curiosity, which was more than a little, I smothered it. If the many perplexing incidents in the Vale have not by this time chastened the inquisitiveness of each one of us, we are difficult to school.

I went safe in the hiding of the birches until I reached the unshorn grass of the summer-house park; the blades were loaded with dew. While I crossed toward the regular path, I caught sight of the unknown racing again in my direction, and was half-alarmed for fear that he had espied me and was on my trail. Once more, however, he turned beneath the cypresses and fled back full tilt.

I had much to ponder on while I marched through the bleak and clammy dawn, and pondering made the miles seem shorter. I thought of Maryvale, who had walked here with me yesterday, of his dark sayings and the blight upon his spirit—of Doctor Aire, whose theorisings strike a vague discomfort into my mind. He, by the way, has taken full responsibility for the sudden madness of Maryvale. He blames himself for relating the story of the man found decapitated near the summer-house. That account, together with my yarn a little later about the witch sisters and the subsequent failure of Maryvale to destroy the cat, turned the balance of the unfortunate man's intellect, which had previously given token of a disposition towards instability. The incredible fact that three bullets did not injure the beast Aire says he cannot account for; yet I suspect him, somehow, of keeping close counsel on the point.

But even with these matters to turn over and over in a tussle of thought, constantly I kept wondering about the pair on the lawn, the man from nowhere practising his uncouth capers, the woman so intent on what she held in her hand.

I came to the spot where Salt and the others had parted from Maryvale and me the evening before, and now I turned aside too, for my determination was to cross the stream by the fallen tree and to assault the eastern wall of the Vale. There was no trouble in clambering along the improvised bridge; I leaped to the ground and in ten minutes reached the steep base of Great Rhos, prepared for an hour's battle with the densely-wooded slope.

Finally, wet to the waist as if I had waded a stream, I emerged on the brow of the hill where the heatherstems lay wriggling like the hair of a thousand Medusas. I walked rapidly, waiting for the sun to break through and dry me, and when it came soon afterward, I sat under a whinberry bush by a bank of rare Welsh poppies and ate a few dried figs and a piece of nut-bread for breakfast. From Shepherd's Well nearby I took a long draught.

The day promised to be glaring hot and abundantly clear on the uplands, and doubtless steaming in the Vale. I passed on to find some brink for reconnaissance. Among the hilltops, what a difference a few feet may make in the prospect!

I found a place on the edge of the sheer flank of the north of the Forest where the wide plains and fastnesses for miles about were revealed in shimmering prospect. I reclined and rested here for long, dried out thoroughly, and had luncheon: two legs of chicken, a chunk of unsweetened chocolate, and an orange which had wonderfully escaped crushing in my ascent. While I ate, I looked at the cloud-flecked hills spread all about in lovely confusion with fantastic writhen crests and crowns of Silurian rock. They were scraped and clawed by rivers channelling: Ithon and Clywedog and Wye gliding down their shady courses with here and there among them a glimpse of hill-hung woodlands, or church tower peeping over castle rise, or drowsy village looking unchanged for centuries. Surely from Aidenn Forest one could see the better half of Wales.

Of a sudden I slapped my thigh. "I'll do it!"

My large-scale map of the Forest was in my pocket, as was a map of greater scope, showing Wales and the western counties, from which I could transfer the angles and make a fairly good job of it. I would draw sighting lines on the Forest sheet, so as to identify those magnificent and anonymous hills that showed crags and colours from twenty, thirty, forty miles away.

I was at the northern end of the Forest. Should I work here? No, the sun had not yet driven the vapour from the remotest peaks of which I wished to find the names. Besides, there was no shelter near, and I saw some cool-looking groves on Whimble. I headed south for Whimble.

Wryneck and woodlark sometimes came curiously past while I worked on my maps under disadvantages, without table or board; I had to fold one sheet for a straight-edge if I wished to make a mark on the other. Sighting was difficult without a firm plane surface. But I had enthusiasm, and patience. I fixed lines pointing to mountains that, when I had found their names, for the first time seemed real to me, Cader Idris, the Brecon Beacons, many others—as the tracing I include here will remind me when I look through these pages in later years.

I still had some cheese in my pocket. I ate it for tea.

Then out of the sultry day came a sudden dash of rain along the hilltops, blotting out my mountains, and hedging in my horizon to the profiles of the nearby slopes. I realized that the copse of trees I occupied abutted the field where I had fled from the bull. Fair shelter must be near.

I made short work of hastening across the field and climbing down, this time, to the long broad ledge upon which I had fallen on the other occasion. There I found refuge from the weather, snugly ensconced on a lichenous seat of stone where the slaty rock was hollowed out underneath the eyelid of the hill. In my dim cubicle I laughed at the storm that was sending down its battery of rain.

For the first time in the day, I bethought myself of smoking. I had out pipe and tobacco, filled my pipe, and struck a match. It flamed and died. I realized in an instant what a tragedy my carelessness had caused.

That was my last match.

I would certainly have cursed myself in the limited number of languages at my command, had not something I had seen in that moment's flare of the match caused me to catch my breath.

The little recess of the rocks where I had taken refuge was filled with bracken and some coarse grass. The brief light had shown me that at the rear of the cave, if I may call it so, the sparser growth had been crushed down, thoroughly flattened—and the impress was that of a human form. Someone had used this place of late as his sleeping quarters!

I must have sat there stunned for several minutes before I stirred, or even began to think. When I had gathered my wits, it was not hard determining to get out of the place at once. Was this sleeper the man who had shed Cosgrove's blood? For all that had been discovered, he might be. But whoever he was, I had no wish to encounter him alone, and he might at that very moment be hurrying this way to escape the rain.

The rain, to be sure, had almost ceased, a fact which did not alter my determination to be quit of the ledge with all speed. Half a minute later I was out of the shelter and clambering up the bank, with my face set toward Mynydd Tarw's gorsy slopes. And now I watched the curving limits of the hills with half-apprehensive keenness, expecting at any moment to see the black dot of the unknown head rise into sight.

The shower had all but ceased; through a fine spray of rain the sun came glinting. I looked across the Vale, over Great Rhos. Ahead of me among the waste of hills beyond Aidenn Forest the land was black with storm for leagues, save where one great monument of light rested thirty miles away on Pen Plinlimon-fawr. On that bleak mountain-top the zone of splendour shone like a spot of hell touched by some ray of heaven.

I had the impulse then to look the opposite way. Yes, as I had surmised, to the south-east the meadows of Herefordshire were steeped in sun. And through the gauzy air with its wandering vapour-drops I saw a rainbow's glittering bridge from wooded slope to wooded slope across the mown hayfields, an arch beneath which the distant Malvern Hills lifted their profile against the sky.

I remembered then the great freedom and elation I had felt when on the uplands only two days ago, and wished that among these wonders that seemed spread for my eyes alone I might regain that long ebullient rapture. But I could not. Why could I not?

There I was with pipe and tobacco, perishing for a match!

Unless the cave-dweller whom I wished not to meet were near, there was no other smoking creature within miles.

But stay! I suddenly remembered the men from Penybont, repairing the one sole path to the uplands. If they had succeeded in establishing a new trackway, there was my best route back to Highglen House, toward which I must be tending, since the hour was nearer five than four. And one of them must have a match. If only they had not given over work for the day!

I had still a little distance to go north along the edge of Mynydd Tarw before reaching the top of the path. Signs of the landslide were not apparent here; yet I had made but one of the hairpin bends when I saw a broad scar and scoop where both earth and rock had torn asunder from the hill. Not until I was half-way to the floor of the Vale did the course of the landslide obliterate the zigzag path. The workers had not dug all the earth and stone away, but had made a substantial walking-surface some feet above the original one. And going a little further down, I saw to my joy that the men had not yet departed. They were not working, indeed, but standing about some object on the ground at the foot of the hill—and I had a premonition like a sword-cut what that object was.

It was the ill-clad, coatless body of the gorilla-man.

Not a quarter of an hour before, the men who had worked to the very bottom of the path, where the wreckage of the avalanche tailed away, had seen protruding from the earth a long and hairy arm and purplish hand. A large stone weighted down the body when it was found, and it appeared from the position of the corpse, and particularly from the writhen expression of the features, that the stranger had not been stricken instantly to death. Instead, he may even have been some way up the path when he had seen the hillside falling, and may have fled and nearly escaped. The groping arm upthrust seemed an indication that had not the heavy stone pinned him under, he might have struggled to the air, instead of being buried alive.

"Did any of you know him?" I asked, looking down at the face with its long, uncouth jaw and narrow temples.

"No, sir. He must have been a foreigner in these parts."

"This is a bit sickening." I certainly needed a pipe now. "Who has a match?"

They were quite as doleful as I. "Sorry, sir, our matches was all wet in the rain just now. Our coats was lyin' up beyond, and the shower got to 'em before we did. Matches are fair ruined."

I looked down at the ill-clad body. "By thunder, if I wouldn't rob a dead man for a match now. Were there any on him?"

"Not a one, sir." The men seemed to regard the idea as a thing of abhorrence, and I had to laugh my question away as a grim joke.

A couple of miles southward on the way home, I met the two workmen who had gone to Highglen House for a shutter on which to transport the body. Salt was with them, and all three regarded me oddly, which was natural, for I was carrying, besides the clothes-rope, the umbrella which I had left in the ruin last night.

"Decided not to hang yourself?" asked Salt, his eye on the rope.

I handed him the umbrella, which he received with puzzled brow. "Item," I said, "to prove the objective of the menagerie-keeper."

"Quite," he responded. "Have you seen what we're goin' after?"

"I have. He was the first of the men I encountered that night."

"I guessed so. Well, this party's out of it *al*together—time and distance, you know, time and distance."

"I suppose that's so. Time and distance, the two greatest villains that ever feazed the detective force. The landslide certainly did not occur more than fifteen minutes after Cosgrove's death."

"And this man was in it, was he?"

"What do you mean? Of course he was."

"Not just buried there afterward, maybe?"

"I should say not. By the way, Superintendent, don't go without letting me have a match."

"Not afraid of the dark, I hope?" Salt looked significantly up among the trees, where the light was thickening.

"No, not exactly, but I'm famished for a smoke."

"Smokin' is not one of my virtues," he responded. "I'm sorry, sir; you'll have to wait until you get to the House."

I was angry, yes poisonously angry with Salt. It takes all kinds of lunatics to make up a world, but is there any lunatic as irritating as the man who doesn't smoke?

I returned to the House, having all the while the awareness that forms were following and eyes watching me in the shadowy walks. To tell the merciless truth, these episodes of the Unforthcoming Match had chagrined me so that my nerves were teetering, and I had the uncomfortable sense that if I were to step from the centre of the path or make any untoward movement, something disagreeable might happen. I felt like a prisoner, and even when I had emerged upon the lawn, I did not like the way the black windows of the House stared at me.

"Great heavens," I thought, "am I coming under the thumbs of the Influences, as Mrs. Belvoir called them?"

The Vale was dim when I reached the House. I knew that I should surely find a match-holder on the mantel in the Hall of the Moth. I did, but some other smoker had abstracted the last match! I hope heaven's ears were closed at that moment.

CHAPTER 16

PARCHMENT—AND PAPER

There was, of course, a match-holder in the library. I looked into the room of weapons: although the light shone beyond the library door ajar, no sound came from inside. I thought the risk worth taking, and stepped in, rope and all, hoping (in my grimed condition) not to discover anyone.

The quiet of the room was deceptive. There were a lot of people there. Belvoir and Mrs. Belvoir were close together at the table with its red velvet cover, reading from the same book, which could not have been very fine sport for him, since he required about one-half the time she did to peruse a page. In the embrasure of the corner tower, Lord Ludlow was sitting with his back to the window and his volume held before his face so that no light from the chandelier might possibly fall upon what he read. This position he maintained the entire time I was in the room. In a secluded nook Lib and Bob were standing before a glass-covered case full of dark and mysterious tomes.

Belvoir looked up, while his wife began the page he had finished. "Hello! Where have you been?"

"On top of the Forest—all over it: a breather. What's happened?"

"Man killed by the falling hill the other evening."

"Yes; I've seen him. I met Salt going up there. But down here—what about Maryvale?"

"Quiet all day. He's working hard—too busy to eat—fact. (Finished it yet, my dear? Don't hurry.)"

"Is he really painting?"

Belvoir shrugged. "Wish I knew. This morning, through the door, he said he was, and warned us against interfering with him. Aire's standing by at present."

"But have you thought—the materials. Oil pigments need to be prepared. You can't pick them up on instant's notice after a number of years, or decades, and find them suitable."

"Salt showed us that yesterday's dash was far from being Gilbert's first visit to the store-room. He had pottered there quite a bit, and some colours he left behind in his frantic haste are fit for immediate use."

"He has painted before, then?"

"Yes, but not in this generation. Long ago."

"Pity. Did he say what he is working on?"

"No—no details. There's another development, though. Did Salt tell you?"

"Not a thing."

"You remember Sir Brooke?"

"Do I?"

"Well, that same useful road-mender who kept the vigil in the car last evening was interviewed in person by Salt about noon today."

"But how—"

"Oh, they've rigged up a practicable bridge for one person at a time down where the old one stood. Salt crossed it unscathed. (Very well, my dear. Carry on. I'll catch up with you.)"

"Yes?"

"Two nights ago the road-mender saw Sir Brooke as sure as taxes, crossing the bridge and proceeding up the road toward the House. (I agree with you, my dear. It's infernally dull. But Carlyle was a great man.)"

"Great Scott! We're closing in on him."

"I wish they'd leave off tracing that old boy," said a peevish young feminine voice from the corner. "He's old enough to take care of himself. I wish somebody'd trace my tennis balls."

"Why," I smiled, "what's happened to them?"

"The usual death," said Lib. "Bob knocked both of 'em into the Water this afternoon and presto vanisho! Now we can't play any more until somebody goes into town and pries a few loose from the corner store."

"Gee, he's got nerve, that butler," urged Bob, turning his plus-foured self toward me, and more toward the light, so that his somewhat pug-like countenance showed the full measure of affronted innocence. "You know what he said, Mr. Bannerlee? He said that it served us right because we played tennis so soon after Mr. Cosgrove died—Cosgrove!"

"It served you right because you thought my side of the court was in the next county," Lib snapped. "Now what can we do, except read?"

"There are worse things," I offered mildly.

"That's what we're looking for over there—a good book," exclaimed the youth.

"Well, these are just a little too rich for your taste, I fancy," I remarked. I scanned the titles behind the glass; I had not examined this case before. The shelves were not quite comfortably filled with bound volumes of learned periodicals and manuscripts in expensive leather covers, all having their titles impressed in bright gilt.

"Hullo, now there's a thing."

"What?" asked both juveniles at once, alert for something, even literature, to break the monotony of their existence.

I pointed to a cover with the words "MS. Elis Gruffydd" stamped upon it. "Evidently a copy of part of a historical manuscript I once read. If I remember rightly, it contains a passage about this house."

"Gee whiz, it does?"

"You're a wonder," declared Lib, with her nose pressed against the glass. "Why, we had that one down and gave it the once over. It was all Welsh to us."

"Oh, I mean in translation," I hastily amended. "Don't credit me with any knowledge of Cumraeg."

"What kind of a rag?"

"The Welsh language," I explained. "But I should think you'd find better hunting on those shelves over there."

"Those? They look sort of dull."

"I realize that the volumes are not provided with art-jackets in three colours depicting the discovery of slaughtered bodies and the rescue of lovely women, but behind those drab covers reside the works of Jane Austen, Scott, and the Brontës, Thackeray, Dickens—and Wilkie Collins!"

"Christopher! Seems to me I've read something quite hot by Wilkie Collins. Thanks, Mr. Bannerlee, I'll take a look."

Alone, then, at the case in the obscure corner, I opened the glass doors and ran my eye over the titles at close range. "Old Watts," as everyone styles him, had been something of a bibliophile, and I saw what I believed to be a number of absolute rarities, quite thrown away on Crofts, of course. I had reached my hand up to a dark corner, where a couple of volumes were lying on their sides, when an exclamation from my lips brought Lib back from Wilkie Collins at once.

"That was a strong one. What's the matter? See a snake up there?"

"No, but I found a mighty startling book," I answered, looking around and noticing with relief that probably only Lib had heard my exclamation. Bob and the Belvoirs had departed, and Lord Ludlow was holding his page so close to his face that I supposed him insensible to external stimuli.

"What's the big kick here?" she asked, looking at the little old book I had plucked from the shelf and whose age-tawny pages I was scrabbling through.

"If Crofts knew what a hoard he has in this library! Why, two or three of these quartos must be worth their weight in diamonds."

"Boy! What a chance! I'd sneak a couple away; only they all look worth a thin dime to me. What's this one you're palpitating about?"

"This is the volume responsible for my being here, Miss Dale. 'The Book of Sylvan Armitage,' imprint 1598. What do you think of that!"

She was holding the quarto to the light, screwing up her face while her eyes roved across the page. Something flickered to the floor. I stooped and picked it up: a flake of moss.

"That's funny," I said. "Some servant nodded when he dusted here. Well, how do you like it?"

"Too many f's. I get all tangled up reading."

"Those aren't f's; they're s's. You'll get used to them soon. Poor Cosgrove would have revelled in this."

"Oh, Cosgrove. Funny things he revelled in." Suddenly she snapped the quarto closed, and gave a careful look toward the harmless Ludlow, whose book was still held defiantly against the light, shutting out the universe. She lowered her voice. "Say, Mr. Bannerlee, remember the day I came down here, the way Cosgrove was watching me, like a fish?"

Before I could put in a restraining word, she began a hasty whispered account of events occurring some months ago, when Cosgrove, already engaged to Paula Lebetwood, met Lib for the first time at Coventry. Unquestionably, the orthodox Irishman had been shocked at the daring dress, behaviour, and speech of this insouciant American minx. Mingled with his disapproval, however, was a strong spell of attraction which caused him to be constantly hanging about in her presence. I believe that just as the element of unexpectedness in Miss Lebetwood's broadly capable character was in a large measure responsible for his desire for her, why here in this alert, sharp wasp of a girl, was also something Cosgrove had not experienced before, something tantalizing that would not let him be at peace. His attentions to Lib, so I gathered from her story, had grown more obnoxious as the days went by, and reached their climax one evening when by her bad luck he happened to find her alone at the far end of one of the gardens.

I had some difficulty at this point in following the extraordinary language of Miss Dale, especially since her speech now became spiced with a good many terms expressive of emotion. But it is clear enough that Cosgrove, detaining her in spite of her unambiguous complaints, entered into a long exhortation over her, more like a fanatical Puritan than a son of the Church. At first Lib had been bewildered, then frightened, for mingled with the Irishman's obloquy was a strain which at first she could not comprehend at all, but soon realized was an appeal to "make his banner her banner," an invitation of no uncertain tenour to "ride by his side through the high places of the world." The union of repulsion and fascination under which he must have laboured, as shown in this outburst, was identical with what I had observed on his face at the luncheon table.

"And that's the kind of a bozo Cosgrove was," perorated Lib. "That's the blighter (isn't that what you say?) that everybody around here thinks was lily-white. That's the Eringobragh that Paula's eating her heart out on account of his death!"

"Do you think so?"

"Do I? Don't I! Say, I know Paula. She's the best kid on this little ol' earth. Bannerlee, my boy, just because I like to talk like a fool half the time and can't get back on the rails the rest, don't get me wrong. I love Paula: I have ever since when I was dressed in a towel and she used to keep me from breaking my neck a dozen times every day. What I mean is, I know Paula. She hasn't been natural for months, not since she got engaged to this devil. She was a darn good sport and peppy all day long, not one of these heavy thinkers. But ever since this Cosgrove got so big on the horizon, she's been worrying for him—you know—the 'King in Ireland' stuff—or worrying *about* him—the dog! And since somebody polished him off with that rock, instead of feeling better, she's acting so quiet and intense I'm scared to death. Honestly, I've been crazy-scared. Last night she just sat and thought. I hardly slept last night. I heard you going downstairs awfully early this A.M."

"I wish I could help. But you see it's so peculiarly and emphatically a situation where I can do nothing."

"I know it, I know it," she acquiesced mournfully. "Gee, though, I wish she'd fall in love with you or something like that. I wish she'd take her mind off that Irishman. To think, he got so fresh with me, and then he went and bounced one off Mr. Oxford's jaw."

"What?"

"Sure; didn't you know? He got sort of green-eyed about Oxey. Maybe he had a right to; I don't know. I mean I don't know about Oxey; he did seem to be around a lot of the time. Paula wouldn't look at him, of course. Then Cosgrove hung one on Oxey's jaw, and we thought we'd seen the last of him. But Oxey shows up here last week smooth as ever—hadn't given up hope, I guess."

"I must tidy myself a bit for dinner. I wish I could help you, Lib. You mustn't worry."

"I suppose I'm making things out worse than they are." She took up the Book of Sylvan Armitage. "I'll plunge into this exciting narrative, and try to make some head or tail out of it." And just as I was going out of the door, she called with a flash of her usual impudence: "What's that you're smuggling under your coat?"

"My shoulders," I laughed.

"You must have the hump, then," she rejoined, and when I was at the stair-foot, I heard her cry, "Oh, look what I've found!" but I did not return to learn of her discovery.

Nor did I immediately ascend to my room. In truth, one reason why I left the library was that I had heard voices in the portrait-corridor: one tone was

Crofts', the other a strange, high-keyed speech I had never heard before. To learn whose voice this was I had retreated from Lib and her find.

I stole to the front entrance, opened the door with the cat-head knocker, peeped out. A dozen yards away my host was saying good-bye to the red-headed, red-bearded young man I had seen cavorting on the lawn at early day-break. The stranger now wore a blue suit of provincial tailoring and sported a huge yellow flower in his buttonhole. A moment later they parted, Crofts with a wave of the hand, the youth with a respectful salute. The owner of Highglen House then walked around past the library in the direction of the Hall of the Moth.

I noiselessly gained the lawn and followed the youth, who wandered with an air of negligence across the grounds by a shrubbery path which soon was lost in the grove beneath Whimble. Among the trees I ventured to draw closer to him, and was nearly discovered in consequence. For when I slipped around a stout oak to creep upon him, I caught him lying or rather rolling on the other side, convulsed with silent mirth! I marched backward on tiptoes, collided with a tree, and returned to the House.

After a plunge in the bath which Aire has kindly invited me to share, and after such improvement of my dress as my tramping kit afforded, I knocked on Crofts' door and had the secret out of him. He was waging a pitched battle with some shirt-studs, and would have told me anything in return for my relief.

"That red-haired chap? Foggins' new man. He came 'sweetheartin'' this afternoon, and I had a little talk with him."

"But who is Foggins, and how does his new man come to be here at break of day? How does he come to be here at all?"

"Oh, they've slung a footbridge over the Water down below. Finished late last night. Foggins sells us our milk. What do you mean by 'break of day?'"

"I saw this milk carrier dashing like a red streak across the lawn when I set out this morning."

"You did! So did I."

"You!"

"I heard him coming round the House past Alberta's room, while I lay awake at some ungodly early hour. I looked out, saw he was carrying a pair of spiked shoes in one hand, the milk can in the other. That looked queer. So I got into a pair of slippers and my dressing-gown and went to the upper end of the passage on this floor, intending to go out of the door and down the outside flight of steps to find what was up. But I saw everything through the glass. Rosa Clay—"

"Ah, Rosa!"

"You see (I got all this from the young chap himself just now) since this house-party began Rosa and Ardelia have been a little huffy over this man Morgan. Ardelia seems to bear away the prize; so for spite Rosa has begun to walk out a bit with this young fellow—seems a good enough young fellow."

"And why the athletic exhibition?"

"The way of a man with a maid—showing his prowess. Prides himself on being something of a runner, says he possesses a number of cups and medals won at fairs and such by fleetness of foot. In fact, this afternoon he showed me his card of membership in the Brecon and Radnor Young Men Mercurys."

"Ah, now I know what she had in her hand!"

He gaped; this was new to him. "What do you mean?"

"She was holding his stop-watch on him."

"Curious. His voice reminded me of something, too."

I remembered the laughter-spasm of the youth beneath the tree, but fore-bore just then to plague my host with new vexation.

The dinner-gong rang. While we passed down the stairs, I recalled our words of last evening on this flight of steps.

"Tell me, Crofts, has the great Harry Heatheringham of Worcester wired you his solution of these riddles?"

"He has not, but unless the fool who took my 'phoned telegram at the Post Office bungled it in transmission he has the facts."

"I look forward to seeing him."

"So do I. Good Lord, the night you dropped in on us, Bannerlee, I thought this was Lost Man's Vale. Sir Brooke omitted to appear, as you know; but I had already been waiting three days for Heatheringham!"

"Three days!"

"Since the Parson Lolly trouble had become serious. I had sent word for him to come as a guest; he had accepted. And until yesterday's wire, I haven't heard another word from him."

It was rather low of me, but I could not resist the second temptation to prod Crofts a little. I said:

"I hope you don't mind my pointing out that you haven't a particle of proof that wire came from Heatheringham at all, or that your message actually reached him, or that he's alive. How can you tell that you haven't been betraying secrets to some unknown enemy, or at least to some shrewd newspaper reporter?"

My host seemed to shrink to about half his size.

Tonight's dinner was the first orderly meal since Cosgrove's death. It was good to see people eating again with the suggestion of appetite. Even Miss Lebetwood had come down and had lost her tense, restrained look of earlier hours. Opposite me, Lib, most fresh and radiant, more genuinely girl-ish than I can remember her before, smiled on me mystifyingly.

The men had reverted to the English fashion of remaining behind the ladies. When we rose from the table I buttonholed Salt.

"Superintendent, does your censorship permit a letter to go out of the Vale once in a while?"

"Now you're jokin' me, sir. What is it this time?"

"No, seriously," I showed him an envelope containing a note I had scratched off in my room. "I want to send this to Balzing tonight for my own copy of Sylvan Armitage. That's an old book I've discovered in the library here."

"Bless my soul! And you want another copy? One for each eye?"

"Quite so; for comparison."

"Of course, Mr. Bannerlee. Carry on."

No sooner had we joined the women in the Hall, where a fire was lighted against the chill of evening, than Lib darted toward me, took my hand, led me to a small shaky-legged walnut cabinet, one of the objects which decorate but most inadequately furnish the room. An ornamental ebony box rested on the cabinet, and lifting the box cover, Lib revealed the Book of Sylvan Armitage.

"Prepare for a great shock," she said, slyly glancing about to ensure we were not observed. "You should have waited a minute before you skipped out of the library. Aren't I clever? I'll bet your copy at Balzing hasn't one of these gadgets."

While she spoke she had opened the cover of the quarto, a cover which looked to be unusually thick. The slim pink fingers of her left hand were prying, then disappeared beneath the edge of the book, and I saw that the apparent thickness of the cover was due to the fact that a pocket of paper had been pasted to the board with cunning, but with no special secrecy. From the receptacle she drew two folded pages, one age-stained, the other much younger, even rather new.

"See that!" she bade in a Gargantuan whisper, thrusting before my face the yellowed sheet, which was calf-skin. "Read that!"

"But it's in Welsh, and the parchment looks at least two centuries old."

"Oh, absolutely—but this goes with it." She handed me the other piece, and stood beaming, her smile including and enlivening every feature of her already brisk countenance. I could not help smiling back, and it was several seconds before I could turn my glance to the white sheet of ordinary folio paper, whose close script was legible enough.

"It doesn't mean such a much to a low-brow like me," I heard her say. "But if that's not some modern shark's translation of what's written on the skin of the fatted calf, I'll eat the calf-skin. What about it?"

I would have needed only a comparison of the proper names in the first few lines of each writing to assure me that it was so, had it not been the obvious conclusion, on the face of it. Lib had discovered an unpublished document, or part of a document, connected with Highglen House.

Two minutes later I had informed the company of the circumstances, and the Hall was as still as a vacuum. When I realized that all these people were listening to hear me read from the paper I held in my hand, my undisciplined hand shook. It is horrible to be nervous, and have to betray it.

I shrugged my shoulders and kept my hand as steady as possible. Here goes:

"'...in some fear of being ill-received in Cwm Melin, for the lord there had the name of an intemperate man, one savage to strangeness when the humour was upon him. But mammering was more harm than use in the pass to which I had come, and save in that stronghold I had no surety of shelter from the snow, the town of New Aidenn lying some uncertain number of miles beyond the Cwm. Increasing storm and cold compelled me to seek kind reception within the castle, avouching truly that I was a person who had lost his way in those wilds and stood in danger of the elements. Being admitted within the gate and taken before my lord, I was excellently welcomed. The man himself sat alone before the blazing hearth in a room called the Hall of the Moth, with weapons and machines and all the abiliments of war heaped in the corners. He was none of your pouncing and mincing followers of court, but sprawled like a great bulchin in his chair, with ragged Abram-coloured beard, immense mouth, and eyes like yellow flames. He bawled for sewer and cup-bearer, and a table was straight fetched, and a feast-dish set thereon, with a manchet and good sherris wine a-plenty. I fell to my refreshment, nor did it escape my notice that my lord was somewhat in his cups, which caused him to be exceeding merry and boastful. He vaunted long about himself and his own great valour and prowess, exulting mightily in his late triumph over Roger, Earl of Gwrtheyrnion, which was truly an achievement which will redound in the history of time. Much he said that is known among men, and presently fell to speech of Sir Pharamond, fourth lord of that name, who builded this castle on the mill-site, after his house close under the valleytop had tumbled to its fall through the perfidy of the false steward David, a most foul and dastardly act, published far and wide among men. Very gleefully and asperly did my lord relate how they had skummed the countryside for the scroyle, and how they had meted out his fearful fate. Now my lord waxed more strange and withal crafty in his words, saying that which is not of common report, relating how above the newly builded battlements Sir Pharamond had made a tier of chambers, so that rumour whispered he was mad—but lord Pharamond only smiled, and called the windows of those chambers his eyes for descrying treachery. And ever afterward, said my noble host, the builder of the castle on the mill-site was untroubled by plotters against his peace. Now when I was emboldened to ask my lord to make this thing clear, he said no word but seized a flambeau up into his hand and beckoned me to follow. He led me through the kitchens and down into a cavern that was there, with a standing pool of water in the midst. This, said my lord, is the drowning-pit of my ancestor, for it was his merry mood to fling his disobedient folk into the water with his own hand, not binding them, but pressing them back into the pit while they essayed to come ashore. Thirty he had once drowned in a single afternoon. For the rest, were he werry, he could shuffle them off with no more trouble than snuffing a night-light. Now do you see, said my lord, but in such cunning wise that I knew some deceit lurked behind his words. Nor would he say more, but departed from the vault, leaving me constrained to follow him or remain in darkness, though wishful to examine the cavern—yet full of thanks, on the other hand, that he had not practised upon me the custom of his ancestor.

"'Again in the Hall of the Moth my lord laughed immoderately before the fire, saying that for that gear he himself was proof against all traitordom, for he kept there a cat that was never tamed, more sure than forty watch-dogs, more trusty than twenty men-of-war, since that it leaped to the attack without a snarl or a struggle, full silently and suddenly, until it had achieved the kill, and it failed not to lay his enemy low. Beware, said my lord, of gib my cat's claw, and how you hear the purring of the cat, for its purr is more dangerous than the innumerable growl of hounds upon a hunting. The purring of gib my cat means death. I dared to ask that I might be shown this beast, provided it purred not at me. My lord, who had drunk much more wine since we had come from the cavern of the drowning-pit, bade me thickly go seek the beast for myself, and upon asking where, he bade me look beneath the perfidious tree, but beware lest it purr or I was doomed. So I said no more of it, discerning that while he grew the more merry he grew the more savage, and might well be goading me on to my destruction. At length my lord having fallen into a stupor, he was borne to his bed, and I conducted to mine, among those upper rooms which rose above the battlements. I slept sound, awakened but once, as I thought, by a long belch of laughter from some unknown part of the castle. Again sleep visited me, and in the morning, when the snow had ceased, a party of my lord's men being at point of breaking away to New Aidenn, I made one of their company and reached my destination in soundness, the afternoon being that of the fourteenth day of January, 1523.'"[4]

"Well," avouched Mrs. Bartholomew, almost before I had completed the last sentence, "now we know the ancestry of that frightful animal."

"The cat of the Delambres, you mean?" asked Belvoir.

"Yes. No wonder the Frenchwomen left it behind and Mr. Maryvale's bullets couldn't kill it."

"The cat's claw, eh?" mused Belvoir. "'Beware of the cat's claw.' Funny, Superintendent, that the Lord of Aidenn and Parson Lolly should use the same words."

"I wish someone would tell me," said I, "what is a perfidious tree."

"I should like to know, too," Alberta declared, "and what's more, why anybody should keep a cat under one."

"I wish Mr. Maryvale *had* annihilated that fiendish cat," said Mrs. Bartholomew. "It gives me a shiver whenever I think of it somewhere up there, maybe waiting for one of us."

Pendleton looked towards Miss Lebetwood and lowered his voice. "Why, you don't mean to say that you think the beast had anything to do with Cosgrove's death?"

"Cats don't usually hit people with stones," contributed Bob.

"Nonsense," called Ludlow sharply. "Fiendish cat, flying Parson, perfidious tree, deathless arm, mystic bone, and all balderdash!"

"Very well, my Lord," said Salt, who appeared ready to indulge in a little crossing of swords, "explain this tragedy without the balderdash."

"Explain it *with*!" retorted his Lordship.

The documents had been passing from hand to hand. "My Lord, I'll have a look at that manuscript, if you've finished," said Salt. "No, I mean the English-written one."

"I haven't it."

"But I thought—"

"I did have it a moment ago. I gave it to—er—"

"You laid it down on the mantelpiece. I saw you," said Alberta.

"Ah, yes; so I did. But it's not there."

Salt raised his voice. "Who has the English manuscript?"

No response, until a gasp from Bob. "Look, isn't that it?—in the fire!"

---

4   It may be necessary, in view of the occurrence later in the evening when Mr. Bannerlee read this paper by an unknown hand, to state that the translation here included is both correct and substantially the same as that which he read. (V. MARKHAM.)

Something ashen and fluffy was smouldering on top of the log, something that turned from grey to translucent pink when the flame brightened. Salt reached the fireplace in a leap, bent down, scrutinized the fragment.

"That's it, sure enough." He ever so carefully attempted to remove the crinkled piece, which vanished at the first touch of the fire-shovel.

Crofts extended the parchment in mollifying wise. "At any rate," he said, "we have the original here. No trouble having a new translation made."

Salt swelled like a small balloon, and his jaw was tight. "No, thank you, Mr. Pendleton. I'm not having any."

I heard Aire's suppressed exclamation behind me: "Of course not!"

"What do you mean?" I demanded, turning to the dark, outlandish face that came only to my shoulder.

"Why, Salt wants the manuscript because he wants the man who wrote it: someone, probably, who has lived here or been here before, knew the book, knew the Welsh language, and, particularly, whose penmanship is that of the paper."

Crofts, crestfallen, was still urging the original parchment. "At any rate, Superintendent, take charge of this. The burning must have been an accident; perhaps the sheet fell in the fire. And you can have another trans—"

Salt took, or rather snatched, the sheep-skin from Crofts, as much as to say, "Better this than nothing," and he did say, "I don't want *any* translation; I want that particular one."

"That's right," murmured Aire. "Whoever wrote that paper is Parson Lolly!"

CHAPTER 17

LANCELOT'S ULTIMATUM

October 6. 11.25 A.M.

Was he, I wondered, in the room at all? So far, since eight o'clock, I had not been able to detect the slightest sound from within the chamber. For longer and longer periods I listened with my ear to the door, all senses alert. I thought of knocking, but refrained, for Aire had counselled against it. But that inhuman stillness inside the room!

Suddenly footsteps resounded crossing the floor, no secret footsteps, but blatant and decisive ones. I had hardly time to draw back a little from the entrance when the door opened and Maryvale stood on the threshold.

I was shocked, for with the exception of two days' bristle he looked so much himself. When he saw me, he tossed his head back in a laugh that had the natural ring.

"Ah, you, Mr. Bannerlee. I wondered which of the gentlemen was protecting me this morning."

Yes, he seemed quite the same as when I had first met him and we paced the walk outside the Hall of the Moth. Quiet and courteous, sane and substantial, he smiled on my embarrassment.

"Aren't you coming in? You've had a long wait."

I was trying to meet his cheerful eye and to think at the same time. "I should rather expect you'd wish to come out."

"No, thank you; I have been out."

"You have? No one told me."

"Of course not," he said with his fluent ease of manner. "Last night my oils weren't quite right, and I looked for some common varnish in the stable supply room."

"Well," I laughed, "I should think you'd have thought of food before varnish."

"True, I have not been eating very heartily. Some carrots and raw cabbage from the kitchen garden was all I could obtain. The darkness rather hindered me."

"But I heard nothing of this. Who let you out?"

"Let me out? My dear sir, I go out when I choose, by the window!"

"But you couldn't have climbed down the wall."

"Mr. Bannerlee, we seldom know our latent powers. What I set myself to do, I do. It is a great deal easier than you suppose when the windows have cornices and the ivy is reasonably firm."

"But climbing back?"

"You have observed the ladder, of course. For the present, I find it obviates much of the difficulty. Later—" His voice trailed out, and he changed the subject with a renewed invitation to enter. "I am glad it is you who are the first to see my work. I think you will know how to evaluate it."

Perhaps I was not prudent, but I was bitterly curious to see what was the product Maryvale had taken extraordinary measures to create. I stepped inside, noted the broad, slant-shouldered room to be in order, saw lying across a chair the thin sword, a mere rapier, with which the man had threatened to make a ghost of any who interrupted him. A stout walking-stick would have smashed the blade to splinters in a twinkling. The bed had not been slept in, or on. The only litter in the room was near the casement, where easel and canvas stood and rags and brushes were scattered on the floor.

"The pigments are not dry yet, of course," said Maryvale. "Still, the work is done."

Maryvale's canvas was about four feet each way, and save for an irregular space in the centre, every inch had been drawn and coloured with minute care. Almost it might be said that the one derogatory criticism was that overloaded detail diminished the interest of the principal subject. For the picture was no mere daub of good intentions. Though even my inexpert eye saw deficiencies in technique, they were faults due to a long unpractised hand—they were nothing. Once on a time, indeed, Maryvale must have studied his art to advantage, for now in spite of imperfect materials at his command, and in spite of long unacquaintance with the medium, the power of his idea overrode the difficulties, and the magnificent though intentionally uncompleted painting drove its impression home.

Only, as I have said, the background and lesser adjuncts demanded a greater share of interest than usual. A peculiar circumstance abetted this fact. The central figure had no face.

The scene was above a valley so deep that its bottom was lost in darkness, where the whole middle air was drenched with rain to the colour of smoke, through which the sun, westering and low, sent a shaft of dripping light. Higher, against a black and sullen mountain-side, the thunder-heads were gathered in inky monochrome, and down the sky wriggled a huge worm of lightning, so dazzling that it affected the eye with torture keen as that which a loud shrill sound inflicts upon the ear. And round about, outside the clouds and within them, flickered the suggestions of menacing shapes, skinny arms, abysmal eyes, demonic smiles.

In the centre, a solitary figure hung in the track of the storm, not upright, not poised as if for swooping flight, but horizontal in the turgid air, resting with four limbs widespread, like some unholy ghost brooding over the nether gulfs of hell—Parson Lolly. The pitch-black cloak flapped restless in the tempest, and from the indistinguishable murk below came up the scarlet gleams from unknown forges.

Parson Lolly's neck was twisted upward and the face turned toward the beholder, save that there was no face. Examining closely, I saw that not the faintest lines had been drawn for one, that Maryvale had simply ceased at that place in his design. The sinister suggestion was enforced by the bulk of the decapitated figure against the livid storm, by the hands with their hint of feline claws, by the shadows cast downward by those hands, like the doom of pestilence scattered down the gulf.

The artist stood by the window, his back to the light, but I could see the high glint of satisfaction in his eye.

"You *do* approve, I can tell."

"Maryvale, this is—well, it's beyond anything I expected. Where did you study?"

"Two years with Coselli in Milan. But that was long ago; I could not have done this then."

"What are you going to do about the face?"

"I doubt that I shall ever finish it," he said, looking at his handiwork. "No." He shook his head and his eyes contracted to points of light. "It may be the only picture I shall ever paint—"

"Surely not!" I cried with much feeling. "You have the incommunicable gift."

But Maryvale was far aloof. His voice had changed into that distant tone that suggested withdrawal beyond the sphere of ordinary mortals. And when he spoke, I became as cold as ice.

"I know now why Cosgrove passed away, with all the embroilments and hubbub he used to cause."

I responded with a sense of rigid self-control: "You aren't, er, implying he terminated his own existence?"

"He was killed so that I could paint. When all this excitement and investigation is over, that is what they will find. I think it is well his life is ended."

"Come now, Mr. Maryvale, without cavil or casuistry, tell me who performed this beneficial murder."

"Someone, I do not know who, of the house of Kay."

Same day. 4.30 P.M.

For some reason the Superintendent appeared highly gratified and very lenient toward the universe. Alberta Pendleton, though perhaps no more curious than the rest of the table, was the only one who ventured to find out why. Wheedling, she persisted from the fish to the fruit, and at length wore out Salt's defences by attrition.

The table grew still while the Superintendent opened a wallet capable of holding a couple of folios and very carefully withdrew a piece of notepaper which he held by a sheath of blotter fastened with a clip.

"Take it by the corner, *if* you please, and mind it don't catch fire. That was a neat trick somebody played on me last evening, but I'll thank you not to repeat it," he admonished a trifle grimly, opening the note and handing it to Mrs. Bartholomew, whose eyes grew twice their size within two seconds while they were fixed on the writing.

"What does it say?" chorused half a dozen voices, but Mrs. Bartholomew could only give a huge swallow and an audible sigh, and handed the paper to Maryvale without looking at him.

"Read it to us," besought Crofts, who sat at the far end of the table and whose turn would not come for at least a couple of minutes.

Maryvale complied:

"Sir,—
Will no plain speech cause you or your principals to understand that the die is cast and the snowball is rolling downhill!"

A long low whistle broke from the reader's lips.

"Go on!" (from Crofts.)

"Oh, Mr. Maryvale, that's not fair!"

"Don't stop, please."

"For God's sake, go on!"

"I will go on," said the man of business. "'My deeds be on my head!'"

After that perhaps prophetic sentence the silence seemed to sway and swirl. Alberta asked in a small voice, "Is that all?"

"No, there is another paragraph, equally concise:

'I have acquainted Mr. Oxford sufficiently with the particulars, and I do not see that there is any need for you and me to discuss the situation. It remains simply for you to take what measures you consider best, or to accept the inevitable. You cannot stem the tide.'"

About twenty-four startled eyes suddenly turned full glare on Charlton Oxford.

"No signature?" asked Aire.

"Yes, the message is signed 'Lancelot,' and a postscript adds, 'These notes and their method of delivery are an unnecessary risk. I suggest that your answer be the last, since on my side the question is past debate.' That *is* the end."

Oxford sat between Miss Mertoun and Lib Dale, on my side of the board. Lib promptly struck a finger into his waistcoat, so that he squirmed, while the English girl looked at her cousin with wide wonder, or a clever imitation of it, in her fine black eyes.

"What in thunder have *you* got to do with this mess?" demanded Pendleton.

"Yes, Oxey, old sport," appended Lib, "what's all this secret stuff? Are you a great man and we didn't know it all the time?"

But Oxford, his eyes very uncomfortable, made no answer than to shrug his modish shoulders, and Salt came to his rescue.

"Don't press Mr. Oxford, if you please. He is bound in confidence to me."

"This, I believe, is an admissible question," said Aire. "Is the note a recent discovery of yours?"

"Found it an hour ago."

"But surely you couldn't have overlooked it in your previous search in Mr. Cosgrove's room."

"Right you are. But I didn't discover this in Mr. Cosgrove's room."

"Oh?"

"No. It had been delivered."

"Delivered? What the devil do you mean?" asked Crofts.

"It was put where Sir Brooke told Mr. Cosgrove to leave it."

"In the mail!" I exclaimed, a great dawn rising in my brain. "Wait a moment, Superintendent. I'll tell you where you found that paper!"

"Gumme, if you haven't guessed it or something."

"In the armoury!"

"Right."

"In the armoury?" Crofts echoed dully, his brow scowling down.

How clear the recollection was: the armoury in misty bluish light, the three vague shapes of men, the one with the white tuft and shirt-front picking the pockets of the other two, the narrow face at the candle before the room was turned to darkness. Unsuccessful that search must have been; Cosgrove must have "posted" this letter afterward. But what was Lord Ludlow's part in this muddle? Surely he played an extra hand, perhaps a lone hand. I looked at his guileless countenance and would have given a guinea to know what was going on behind it.

I shifted my attention to Salt again. "But there must have been some disturbance, Superintendent. I don't believe that even you—"

"Cleanin'," acknowledged Salt. "Miss Carmody—Jael, that is—was dustin' about. No question she shook it loose, for it was lyin' on the floor under the newer suit of armour when I passed through at twelve o'clock."

"But I don't see—why, the mail is—" commenced Mrs. Bartholomew diffidently.

"The coat of mail, the coat of mail," growled Bob Cullen.

"That's it," said Salt. "You see, Mr. Pendleton, you had a little Post Office here after all. This note was tucked away between the chain-mail and the cuirass. Couldn't have been a better hidin'-place, as long as there were no children in the house to pick things to pieces."

The ladies had passed from the room, and we were on the point of following, when Salt recalled us with a casual remark. "Well, I'm poppin' off now, gentlemen."

"Eh!" exclaimed Crofts. "I thought Dr. Niblett—"

"We're off together, sir. The Coroner's conductin' the bodies, and I'm conductin' the Coroner."

"For heaven's sake, send us some newspapers to read," I urged.

"I will, I will." Salt cast his eye somewhat sardonically about the circle. "Any more small commissions from any of you gentlemen?"

We clustered at the doorway where the melancholy caravan set out in charge of Dr. Niblett. The bodies of Cosgrove and of the unknown, stitched in sheets and laid along improvised stretchers, were to be carried by motor as far as the temporary bridge, across which they must be borne by hand. The undertaker's van was waiting across the Water to convey them to the mortuary, where tomorrow they will be "viewed" by the Coroner's juries impanelled to sit on the bodies.

They were gone.

CHAPTER 18

GRISLY PLANTING

With the departure of the dead men from the House, the mansion seemed to me for the nonce most lonely.

I drifted away from the others, into the vacant Hall of the Moth, slouched down in one of the flimsy chairs. My mind was rather wistful for the deceased Cosgrove, wanting him back, but not quite sure whether I preferred him to return alive or dead.

Voices of persons passing in the armoury came to me.

Belvoir's: "Why, Galton proved that long ago. It stands to reason—"

Lib's: "Shoot that man!"

A pause in the universe. Then the lightest sound of feet tripping down the stairs, the flutter of a white skirt in the corridor, and an apparition crossed the door. At unexpected sight of me, the apparition became motionless in a pretty sort of confusion, while I staggered to my modest height.

"Oh, Mr. Bannerlee! I didn't expect to find you here. That horrid old man!"

"Why, er—good heavens, Miss Lebetwood, what do you mean?"

"Blenkinson."

"What, the Master of University College!"

"Why, no—"

"That's only my ambition for him, you know. When the post is vacant, I intend to put up his name for it. But what's the wretch done?"

"He scolded me!"

"The impudent—"

"Or he would have if he dared. That's the same thing, isn't it?"

"But what, specifically?"

"Well, you see, I was coming out of Millicent's room. She was going to have a game with me this afternoon, but told me she felt too tired after all."

"With the last ball disposed of by Bob Cullen?"

"The last I'd let that precious pair have, that was. I had sense to keep a few for myself. Well, I was awfully sorry Millicent wasn't up to it, and I would have gone back to my own room and changed out of these clothes. But when I came into the passage, Blenkinson was stepping along as large as life and as still as a—as a cat. When he saw me he stopped about six feet away and just let down his jaw and stared."

"Very bad form."

"I said, 'What's wrong, Blenkinson?' pretty nippily, I guess, and he gave a sort of groan and said, 'They are taking Mr. Cosgrove's remains to the mortuary, Miss.' I didn't say anything; so he groaned again."

"Really, you mustn't concern yourself with the foibles of a foolish old servant. Anyone with an ounce of sense would know you mean for the best."

"*Mean* for the best!" The sweet grave eyes dimmed a little. "I'm *doing* for the best! Each day since this happened I've been alone for hours, thinking, thinking, thinking. I know more about Sean than anyone else here, and I go over every particle of knowledge I possess, to discover if it can have any bearing on his death. Oh, I've thought so hard that my head hurts—and emotions like this tear you up even if you're too busy thinking to pay attention to how you feel. Don't you see, Mr. Bannerlee, I mustn't be a weeping-willow sort of person; I've got to get some relief once in a while. I've got to get the air into my lungs and the blood into my brain, if I'm to do any good. I'm doing more for Sean by swinging a racquet than I would if I bedewed his brow with tears."

"You're right, by George! Did you tell this to Blenkinson?"

"To that old woman!"

A silence came. I watched her; her eyes wandered restlessly from object to object within the room. She turned suddenly toward the window and looked at the glorious day, and as quickly turned to me again. "Oh, this is too good to be wasted! I must play. I've got to have someone to beat, Mr. Bannerlee; may I beat you?"

The youth and verve of this girl, her strength of spirit, and the unspoken appeal in her clear blue eyes, were almost too much for me. There was a directness about her, like the passage of an arrow to its mark, unusual in women, I believe, when combined with such softness and allurement as is hers. I had a very noble impulse to take that straight and slender body in my arms, and to bestow a needful comfort of kisses on lips and cheeks and on that cruel golden hair.

As with most such good impulses, this one changed into something inferior: I bowed politely. "I'll do my best," I said. "Give me ten minutes. I'll borrow what I need from Crofts, as usual."

"Will you? Oh, thank you so much!" (To be thanked, so earnestly, by a *dea certe*!) "I warn you, I'll beat you. I hope you can give me a battle."

Such was my hope, too, when we stepped on the concrete court a quarter of an hour later.

I should have been routed had I not been able to deliver a smashing serve which landed in the proper court about one time in three. These serves were almost always clean aces, and after one of them I was startled to hear applause from the little knoll which overlooked the court some distance away. There was Lib.

"Hotto servo, old sportsman!" she called. "Glad there's somebody Paula'll let play with her old tennis balls."

It was due to happen sooner or later, of course, but it was rather humiliating immediately afterward to have a wild shot from my racquet fly many yards over the enclosure.

"Bravo," called Miss Dale, and laughed and laughed. "Hotto smasho!"

"Sorry," I called, rushing across; "I'll get it."

"Try," laughed the lonely spectator on the hill. "Serves you right, Paula. The great big brute of a man!"

"I think it went into the stream," said Miss Lebetwood. "You'll have to run."

"Oh, I'll save it right enough; plenty of time to intercept it," I answered, turning my rush toward Aidenn Water, which, owing to a convolution of its course, was some forty yards above the end of the court and about twice that distance from the side-line.

I kept a careful watch; no ball came down.

"It must be among the strawberry trees after all," I said, and we commenced a search through the planted grove which had been so grateful to the dead Irishman, while Lib favoured us with audible quips at our discomfiture.

"Just the same, I believe it went into the water," said Miss Lebetwood at the outset of our hunt.

"Well, I'm sure it didn't," I contradicted. "How could it have? I got over there in plenty of time—"

"Well then, find it here."

But the ball was not to be found.

We resumed the match. I served doubles.

"Don't lose your nerve," called Lib. "I've mortgaged my—say, folks, there's a rumpus up at the House. Jiminy, I'll bet something's happened!"

Miss Lebetwood and I looked at each other.

"What is it, Libkins?" she asked sharply. "What do you see?"

"Slews of people—millions of 'em—running around the House. Say, there's Doctor Aire going like a pump-handle. Say, I'm going to see what this is."

I looked at Miss Lebetwood, and we broke into a run, following Lib.

Although we arrived almost the last of the crowd, Finlay, the venerable gardener, was still positively drooling with excitement. To him the credit must go for having inadvertently put a term to more than one of our galling problems.

Crofts rather fancies carrying on old Watts' custom of experiment with unusual trees and shrubs. For the sake of their jewel-like red berries, he had a couple of Guelder Rose plants, almost full-grown, ready to be put in the soil, when Cosgrove's death set all things awry. Today they could not be kept out of the ground any longer. One of the small trees was to be placed at the turn of the drive around the front of the House, about fifty feet from the library tower.

At the appointed site Finlay had merrily tossed up the soil from a considerable cavity while Miss Lebetwood and I played our game. There had come a jab of the spade which appeared to make the earth settle somewhat. Again the gardener pressed the spade with his heel; the earth seemed to give way. Alarmed, for he knew that there were no drains passing beneath this lawn, Finlay got out of the pit he had digged, reached down and poked experimentally with his tool. Of a sudden, the bottom of the hole sank something like a yard, and a chunk of antique subterranean masonry, broken off, was revealed, with sluggish black water visible through the gap. But something else was showing there, too, besides the mass of soil which had fallen through the collapsed roof of the waterway:

A face, with lips, nose, eyelids, cheeks distended into a simple green sphere—and a hand, its palm covered with thickened, white, and sodden skin.

Sir Brooke Mortimer was found.

I was far too late, of course, to hear what had been said by those first around the hole. I learned afterwards. Crofts Pendleton, barring some natural repugnance to the body in process of dissolution, had seemed to take a sullen joy in the discovery.

"Here's your murderer!" he had even cried.

"No, no! Never!" Eve Bartholomew murmured, gave a slight shriek, and fainted dead away, to be carried by stalwart persons into the Hall.

"I wonder," said Belvoir.

"Of course not," declared Miss Lebetwood, and challenged Doctor Aire: "Isn't that so?"

"Yes," he answered; "he's been dead at least as long as Sean."

The Guelder Rose plant, which must have a new hole dug for it now, lay alongside the cavity with its branches bound up and its root encased in a bag. Beside the rose lay the body of the unfortunate Knight, drawn from the mysterious water-channel. I should not have recognized it, had it been the corpse of some friend of mine.

Mastering the disgust that welled in me, I bent over the drawn face, with its nostrils dilated and eyes forced forward from their sockets. The dead lips were parted and the blackened tip of the tongue protruded between the teeth.

I arose, looked down into the eyes of the physician. "Strangled?"

He shook his head slightly. "By water only. The tongue's a *post-mortem* result. Look at his fingers."

The fingers of the huge hands resting across the chest were covered with slime, save for two or three, the ends of which appeared excoriated.

"He was drowned in this subterranean waterway. God knows how he got in, but you can see that his fingers clutched at the oozy walls and in some places must have pressed through the slime to the stone itself. There's a mark on his forehead, too, not quite so easily accounted for. No connection with cause of death, however."

"This *is* Sir Brooke, of course?" I asked. "It might be anyone, for all the humanity left in the lineaments."

"I'm sure it is from the description of the clothing alone," declared the Doctor, "but we can satisfy ourselves without delay."

He plucked the arms from across the chest, then unbuttoned the coat. Across the waistcoat extended a black band affixed to a pince-nez with double lenses. Aire held these up with a significant look, then reached into the inside pocket and withdrew the dead man's wallet. This was conclusive, for inside it was stamped the name in gilt: Crowell Brooke Mortimer. But the flutter of voices that came was not for this discovery.

From between coat and waistcoat two objects had been dislodged, objects which rolled out upon the lawn: a couple of water-logged tennis balls.

I picked one up. The cloth was rotted, and slipped off with a scrape of the finger. "Well," I said, "now we know how Sir Brooke lost his way."

Same day. 9.55 P.M.

In half an hour Salt was among us once more, and half an hour later he had come upon the entrance to the underground channel, an arch of stone masonry veiled by an overhanging branch of alder and almost wholly submerged in the stream. It lies, as we expected to find, at the part of Aidenn Water nearest the tennis court, and a fair current sweeps beneath it. This curious tunnel appears to extend several hundred feet, and does not end where the Knight's body was found. The corpse had been detained by a partial stoppage caused by the collapse of some of the masonry. But we have not discovered where the channel rejoins the main stream. If I am at all a judge of facial expressions, Salt is a disappointed man. Evidently this gruesome factor casts some elaborate equation of his out of all computation. It struck me at dinner that Aire, too, looked a bit frustrated.

Talk in the Hall of the Moth after dinner was equally divided between pity for Sir Brooke (and for Mrs. Bartholomew, who was absent) and amazement at the lopped and disordered accounts given of our mystery in the London papers which Salt had brought with him as he had promised. I rather enjoyed hearing Ludlow pitch into the gentlemen of the press, for whom it is obvious he has no love—and for those for whom he has no love he has no mercy.

Maryvale came up, and for once I did not feel uneasy at the sight of him. He was smiling broadly, I thought a little too broadly after what had occurred this afternoon. I recalled, however, that Aire was now taking precautions to insulate Maryvale from contact with any atrocities which may present themselves—and then flashed through my mind almost the very words which the man of business was about to say.

"You don't think so cheaply of my warnings now, Mr. Bannerlee. Now you must realize what was meant by the spanning and roofing of the waters."

"Fully."

"No, sir!—not fully. There is much for you yet to know. But all this agitation, this ebullition in the newspapers, this official scrutiny, will lead to nothing."

"You refer to what you told me this morning?"

"As I said, this man Cosgrove was removed because he stood in my way and in the way of my art."

I thrust in sharply. "Did you remove him yourself?"

"No," answered Maryvale, "but I have done worse deeds."

3 o'clock in the morning.

I have heard a curious thing. A few minutes ago I woke with a start and lay wondering what had roused me. Then the cry of the cat throbbed from the upper Vale again. The howl rose and fell endlessly, as it seemed, until, while it mounted to a new pitch of despair, it broke off. There has not been the faintest murmur since.

CHAPTER 19

THE DEATHLESS ARM

October 7. 11.15 A.M.

A Spartan is among us.

Not only did Eve Bartholomew appear this morning at breakfast at the early hour Salt had suggested, but she seemed almost in brighter mood than before, and I can understand how the discovery of Sir Brooke, for better or worse, may have taken a burden from her mind. Still, she is brave, though she spoke with a rather wan utterance, addressing me, who had the fortune to consume porridge next her in the window.

"I had expected it," she said. "Of course I never could have hinted such a thing before, but I realized that sooner or later such a man as Sir Brooke must fall foul of one of his many enemies."

I uttered some vague sound.

"Mark my words, Mr. Bannerlee, the villain will be brought to vengeance for that blow! I understand how Miss Lebetwood feels—why, Blenkinson, what's the matter?"

"Nnothing, Ma'am. I beg your pardon," said the butler, who had been fussily arranging the window-shade, and took flight.

"What did he do?" I asked quickly.

"He made the most extraordinary grimace I have ever seen. I hope the man is not subject to, er—anything."

"I think not," I answered drily, guessing well the cause of the facial disturbance. "But you were saying, Mrs. Bartholomew?"

"I have something that would do the poor man good. I must speak to him later. Er, what *was* I saying?"

"That you understood how Miss Leb—"

"I do, indeed! I admire that young woman, and I intend to follow her example. Until the murderer of Sir Brooke is found, I shall not rest!"

But this was nothing to what was in store later. An hour afterward Salt had us all in the conservatory, very much on tenterhooks. When he had surveyed us with calm and taken the roll mentally, he made a little speech.

"Since you'll all be goin' to New Aidenn for the inquest this afternoon, I thought I might give you a few hints. The fact is, we want as little as possible to come out. I have those orders from higher up. The Coroner's business is to ascertain the cause of death, if he can; the rest is my business. I know Dr. Niblett will play the game accordin' to my rules, and he won't try to carry the question any deeper than that the deceased came by his death by means of the stone that Mr. Blenkinson luckily discovered. But there's no tellin' what some busybody juryman or other may want to know; so I want to warn you there's one subject you must be shy of—that's this 'King in Ireland' topic. There's enough hullabaloo in the Emerald Isle right now without spreadin' that."

"Still," said Alberta, "I don't see how we are quite going to tell whether a question will lead—"

"I'm comin' to that, now. I'm goin' to share some facts with you. This that I'm tellin' you is the result of special information from Miss Lebetwood, Mrs. Bartholomew, and Lord Ludlow, added to a few small discoveries of my own. Now, remember, I want you to keep this budget of facts in mind and not show by a word or a sign that you know anything about it. That's the only reason there is for this assembly. Anybody behind that door, Mr. Pendleton?"

Crofts flung open the studded portal, revealing emptiness in the corridor.

"Servants sometimes like to wait behind doors, just in case anyone should ring for 'em," observed Salt. "You might keep an ear open in that direction, sir. Now, here's the way of it."

From what we heard in the next half-hour, what a change comes over the picture of Sir Brooke! I had heard of him as capricious, cantankerous, unsure-footed, gentle-hearted, weak-eyed, sick: the image of ineptitude. Yet what was he but the emissary of the powers behind the powers that be!— no fool at all, but the super-confidential spokesman of an Office powerful and discreet! I had heard of him as a guest like the others, save that he was to "propose the bride's health." Now we envisage him as coming to meet Cosgrove plenipotentially under the guise of the Bidding Feast! There had been earlier meetings here between these men. Indeed, while the revelation increased in scope, I began to wonder if the whole idea of the Feast was not shrewdly put upon Crofts by Cosgrove's suggestion, so that there might be an out-of-the-way corner for the final tryst between the representatives of the United Kingdom and of the Kingdom of Ireland about to be reborn.

"It may relieve Lord Ludlow's mind," said Salt, "if I clear up his connection with the affair at once. That Bangor and Newcastle address, sir," he went on, looking at me, "seemed to give you a turn the other day, but it was really rather enlightenin', you know."

"I must be very stupid—"

"Not a bit of it—only you should have studied your geography just a little more thorough. So should I, for that matter; I didn't guess the connection either. You see, both those places are in Ireland."

"Ireland!" came several gasps as one.

"Fact. Two little towns near Belfast, nearer twenty than thirty miles apart, I shouldn't wonder."

"What goes on in those places?" asked Aire. "I've been in Bangor, County Down. It has no industries to speak of."

"Yes, in the main those are seasonable towns; both on the coast, I believe. But Lord Ludlow and the other principals have projected a tolerable business in the linen-weavin' line to give employment to every inhabitant the winter through; so there'll be flourishin' manufactories in both a year or two from now. And that properly explains Lord Ludlow's interest: day by day here he was tryin' to find what was goin' to happen to his pet lamb."

"I don't see what you were in a sweat about," said Crofts, turning to Ludlow. "Cosgrove wouldn't have matured his plans in a generation."

"That's where you're sure to be wrong, sir," contradicted Salt. "The truth is, nobody except Sir Brooke could have had an idea how near Cosgrove's coup was to takin' place. One or two more parties to sound, a little time to work out the final details and give the final orders—and the fat would have been in the fire! Why, the papers say Ireland's half-mad today as it is."

"Where do you come in?" asked Crofts belligerently, fixing his eye on Oxford this time, and that well-nurtured gentleman lost countenance, but Salt made answer.

"Mr. Oxford has been pretty close to Mr. Cosgrove all along, as you'll recall," he said to our host. "He may have excited Mr. Cosgrove once or twice, but that was in another connection altogether." Although guardedly, the Superintendent gave a swift look toward Miss Lebetwood. I intercepted it. "Another connection altogether. I think perhaps that it was due to Mr. Oxford keepin' such a good watch on Mr. Cosgrove and his servant that Sir Brooke made up his mind to come down here when he did and have the cards laid plain on the table."

"This servant, who was he?" put in the insatiable Crofts. "Cosgrove never brought a servant to any house of mine before."

"He's in the mortuary, too, now."

"What, the gorilla-man!" I exclaimed.

It was so. I comprehended many things in an instant, and Salt's re-enforcement of them came tumbling after. The creature I had met near the top of Mynydd Tarw, who had dwelt in the cleft of the hill, had been an Irishman, Cosgrove's servant. That was an Irish yell he had yelled plump in my face, some adjuration to bid a demon begone, for he must have taken me for a fiend of the mist when I fell in his path. The unaccountable burned paper in Cosgrove's grate was a message from this man; he it was whom Cosgrove had intended to smuggle into the House as an "extra progeny for the elephant."

I recollected our meeting, how he had seemed to be straining, staggering, spent with haste, even before he had encountered me and found a new cause for flight. The presumption was strong that he had lately met with some alarming experience. What could that have been? Had he seen the black-bearded unknown, the menagerie-keeper? There was nothing in that person's colloquy with me to suggest it.

More likely the gorilla-man had run across Sir Brooke. Still, in the mere encounter there could have been no cause for terror; neither was anything to the other, and the Knight was hardly a figure to inspire awe. What was more probable than a meeting on the Water bank above the tennis court? One man was skulking secretly; the other had lost his way. Possibly there had been a collision, or perhaps the prowler had only seen the shape of Sir Brooke taking form in the fog, then suddenly falling in the Water at a fatal mis-step. That abrupt fall, perhaps one choking cry, no more, before the instant total disappearance of the body beneath the tunnel arch (of which the gorilla-man could have no knowledge)—these account sufficiently for the fear in Cosgrove's servant, spurring him hillward. This, I believe—and it is Salt's belief as well as mine—is the true story.

"Maybe it's not quite cricket to criticize Cosgrove, now he's gone," said Crofts in an unusually reflective manner. "I do think that he might have shot straighter, you know. I don't see what he was driving at when he brought this ruffianly man of his down here in secret, to lurk about, perhaps to thieve, and above all, to be brought among us in disguise that evening. What was the point of that, I'd like to know!"

"No doubt about it," declared Salt. "Mr. Cosgrove, havin' no idea what had happened to Sir Brooke the night before, expected him surely to be here by the time the Noah thing commenced."

"What's that to do with it?"

"Why, Mr. Cosgrove was particularly anxious to bring the pair of 'em together, I expect."

Crofts looked at Salt as at one suddenly seized with dementia. "To bring them together? Why should he want to do that?"

"To show he meant business, Mr. Pendleton."

Aire asked quickly, "Who was this wild man?"

"Ah, I was wonderin' who'd ask me," said Salt. "Please don't mention it, ladies and gentlemen, but the man killed by the landslide was sure to be Toban First, the royal King of Ireland!"

Same day. 10.10 P.M.

A couple of snubbed and highly aggrieved juries brought in verdicts of "Wilful Murder" and "Misadventure" respectively, as they were told to, and within half an hour of my entering the mortuary, I was in the street again. For a few minutes I was busy resisting the minions of the press, who buzzed about all of us but secured small plenishments of honey. I surmise that the likelihood of exposure to blandishing newsgatherers was the principal reason why Blenkinson, finder of the stone, was the only servant brought from the Vale to give testimony.

Alberta suggested that instead of returning to the House immediately the party should spend the afternoon in motors. Everyone gladly acceded to this means of relief from the oppressive atmosphere of the Vale; everyone, that is, save Aire, who, having given his evidence in the second inquest, had withdrawn to prepare for the third, which will be held in a day or so. At the last moment, since we made too large a crowd to be packed loosely into the pair of available cars, I, too, seceded from the group, alleging quite truly that since the afternoon was fine, tramping and exploring would do me perfectly.

Time-wracked New Aidenn lies in the shadow of its huge castle mound whose fortress no longer stands atop, and the vestiges of old city walls are far out in the fields where the cows find succulent grazing. In ordinary circumstances these vestiges of greatness and evidences of decay would have kindled my ardour in the antiquarian way, but now I was resolved upon two queerer visits.

I found Aire with Sir Brooke in a side chamber of the mortuary itself. There was a faint scent of balsam in the room, which was fitted with some of the appurtenances of a laboratory, and Aire, in a white smock, had a slip of glass and a pipette in his hand. Sir Brooke lay on a table at the far end of the room, mercifully covered with a sheet.

"Ceremonies over?"

"They are, and no one the wiser. Your duties finished?"

"Oh, this isn't duty, exactly. I could shunt it if I wished. Only chance, you know, has made me the responsible medical witness in all three deaths; so I have assumed the mantle of whoever corresponds to a divisional police surgeon in the country. I'm well paid—curiosity, and all that sort of thing."

"Well, has curiosity received any communicable reward?"

"Prophecy fulfilled, at any rate. As I said, this man was drowned— drowned and nothing else."

"But didn't you say something about a bruise on the forehead? Mrs. Bartholomew won't give you peace until that's explained."

"No, I mentioned a mark, not a bruise. Peculiar thing, you know—no contusion, just scraping and scratching of the skin above the left eye. In itself nothing unusual, but there was a long wood splinter stuck there; that's the oddest feature of the death."

"What's it like?"

Aire took from a rack on the wall an envelope, and from it extracted a thin fragment, about an inch long, dark brown in colour, and feeling like rock.

"Why, this isn't—"

"It requires microscopy to show that it's wood at all."

"I'd never believe it, surely."

"It's almost petrified. That happens, extremely rarely, when certain kinds of wood are immersed in running water for long periods. The organic substance is replaced by precipitated mineral matter."

"Well, it doesn't strike me as being of such vast importance."

"One wonders, for instance, what's kept it submerged and stationary."

At the door of departure I laughed. "A question indeed. But I must be off."

"Sounds as if you had plans for the afternoon."

"I have. I am going to take a walk—Belvoir's hint, you remember."

"I can't say I do."

"A walk into the past. By the way, you had a letter this morning. May I ask if it was in reference to the blood-test?"

"It was, indeed. And pig's blood you found that night for a certainty. The test reaction of the blood I sent with anti-human sera was negative."

"There's some comfort in that, but it leaves the problem no less vexed than before."

"More vexed, if you ask me. If it had been the vital fluid of a man, we'd have some notion of what we're looking for. As it is, even the nature of the problem is vague."

"Cannibal," I said. "Well, I must be going; these roads are new to me. When I return to New Aidenn, I expect a bit of interesting mail myself."

"Oh, yes?"

"Yes; I've sent for my copy of the Book of Sylvan Armitage—not that the missing portion of the manuscript is in it. I've thumbed the volume too much to have overlooked anything of that sort. Well, cheerio."

"Cheerio." Aire returned to his far from cheery work while I set my footsteps out of town and eastward.

On every side around the graceful slopes of hills intercepted one another in a little-changing prospect while I trod the highway across green Radnor Plain. I passed the prehistoric Four Stones in their black-grey stoicism, passed Doomsday parks, passed old cottages with slate-shingled roofs. Above an avenue of oaks the square tower of St. Stephen's in Old Aidenn had been gradually mounting the sky ahead of me, and in due time I diverged from the road and climbed the oak avenue to the village.

What would I find beneath that Norman tower? Hints of symbolic meanings of the "deathless arm" were rife in mind. Are the descendants of Sir

Pharamond Kay living yet? Perhaps—and the suggestion caused me to bate my breath—one of us guests in Highglen House actually belongs to the family of Kay. This supposition had not occurred to me before as a live idea. Now it had force. It was, too, an hypothesis that offered scope and direction for investigating, and in a subject where I was more or less at home. Perhaps (a big perhaps) I might play a large part yet in the untwining of these twisted skeins.

I will not say that I was growing excited while I procured the church key from its custodian in one of the handful of straggling houses remaining of the mediæval town: I had, in fact, been excited and eager all during my walk across the monotonous plain. I entered the churchyard by the lych-gate; the place was overcrowded with crumbling stones among the red-barked yews. The men and women with shears, who trimmed the grass along the graves of dear ones, looked at me, I thought, with more than ordinary interest; there must have been marks of eagerness in my face. I unlocked the wire-screen outer door, found the portal within the vestibule unfastened, and entered the little church.

The empty air smelled sweet and sanctified. The hour was clouded, and I wished that some of the oil lamps hanging from the low roof might be lit, for the interior was rather cavernous in the absence of sun. Searching, I seemed fated to encounter everything but the thing I sought. These were features with a reputation: the rood screen of fan tracery and leaf-flower-and-grape carvings, that unique organ-case dating back to the Gothic period, the window of St. Catherine's Wheel—but I spent not a second apiece on them, looking with greater interest at the tombstones in the floor, at the memorial tablets between the windows, and at the 'scutcheons painted on the wall with colours still bright.

A flash of lightning drove the darkness from even the remotest corners of the church, and my heart gave a leap. That instant I had seen a long, bulky object in a recess of the chapel on my left.

It was the tomb of Sir Pharamond, stained and gnawed by centuries. The effigies of the lord of Aidenn and his lady rested there in stone, with small beasts recumbent at their feet. I lit a match to examine the face and figure of the man. The crown of the head was clean gone, and a fragment of the chin had fallen away, but it was impossible not to recognize the sharp, malignant features, the keen lips, the close-set eyes as being those of the paintings in Highglen House.

The left arm of the effigy lay across the breast, the mailed fist clasping a broken sword. The right arm was missing.

At first I thought that, like the pieces of the head, it had been a prey to time, but careful examination by the light of a second match proved the carving to be complete: the chain mail ended neat at the shoulder. No right arm had ever been there.

In haste I stooped and lit a third match to read what might be decipherable of the inscription, but another lightning flash disclosed the words still distinct on the side of the tomb, and I read while it thundered:

> **Let Trecchours be Ware**
> **My Right Arme Shall Not Dye**
> **For soo I have Ordeyned**

These were all the words upon the monument.

CHAPTER 20

THE RECRUDESCENCE OF PARSON LOLLY

I chanced upon an alternative road, with more variety in its prospects, to take me back to the mouth of the Vale, omitting New Aidenn entirely and saving a third of my journey. Even on this short-cut southward, I found daylight part drawn into evening when I reached the top of the vast hill called the Smatcher, shaped like a loaf of bread, and began to descend through its larches to the entrance of the Vale. Gleams of sun walked from peak to peak while violet dusk deepened along the skirts of the hills. On the highway below me I perceived a human figure trudging toward the branch road to the House.

I straightway recognized that sawed-off, machine-like form, and the peculiar drawing-up of the shoulder with each step. Doctor Aire was preceding me through the twilight.

I hailed him and joined him. "I thought the others might pick you up."

"Not returned yet, I dare say. Didn't call for me, at any rate. So I'm getting my fortnightly exercise." He looked up at me quizzically. "You found everything satisfactory?"

"Damnably the reverse. Why, there never was a right arm on that effigy. Do you know, Doctor, I believe Maryvale has the mission in life of plaguing me!"

"Not you alone, let me assure you. Other persons are agog over his cryptic remarks. I, for instance."

"You? Oh, no."

"Yes. You didn't hear what he told the Pendletons and me this morning at breakfast? He said that Parson Lolly is dead."

"Parson Lolly dead! That was fudge."

"On the contrary, he assured us with perfect gravity that the Parson died last night."

"He was pulling your leg."

"Not a bit of it. I know Maryvale that well, anyhow."

"Give it your own name, then; I'd call it empty talk."

Aire twitched around at me in a surprised way. "Never," he declared. "Sure, Bannerlee, you must realize by this time that there's always something behind what Maryvale says. He doesn't merely vaporize."

We were approaching the temporary bridge. "I wish you'd tell me exactly what you think of Maryvale, Doctor. I confess that to me there's something uncanny about the man. If he's mad, he ought not to be loose among us, and if not—"

"If not?" Aire cocked his head to hear.

"—if not, he's up to some subtle game."

"Oho, you think so?"

"What else, for heaven's sake?"

He waited to cross the bridge before he answered. "No, that's not my reading of Maryvale. I look on him as a man wrestling with an idea, the idea of Parson Lolly."

"And still I don't get hold of your meaning."

"It's this way. Gilbert Maryvale has come to Aidenn Vale before. Each time, certainly, a tradition of the countryside, a popular half-belief, has been mentioned, more often discussed with some fullness. It is, to say the minimum, a fable of much piquancy, a legend above the average in interest, this tradition of the goblin-parson—is it not?"

"Granted, granted."

"Haven't you often wished that fairy-tales were true? Maryvale has almost convinced himself to believe in Parson Lolly. His mind hasn't conquered the idea, seems to be more or less at the mercy of it. But sometimes he rebels. Now and then he can see the absurdity as well as you or I; he can even laugh at the Parson. But again he will fall into perplexity, confusion, shame, fear over the idea. And he is capable, under suggestion or after shock, of getting into the throes, quite possessed with the reality of the unreal, virtually a maniac if you like that word. At these times he makes the supreme surrender one is capable of making to ideas."

"What is that?"

"Why, he *acts* on them. Remember his carrying that revolver up the Vale."

"Thanks, I remember well enough." We went on in silence a little way, and then I said quickly, "But that doesn't explain everything. Madmen are consistent; that's why they're mad. But Maryvale tells me that someone of the house of Kay did this murder, and sends me over to Old Aidenn to find out about that missing arm, and—"

"Of course he is not consistent; that's why he is *not* mad, as you persist in thinking. He is very much mixed, but his ideas don't fit into a complete system. I shall be sorry when they do, and I think the sooner he leaves the Vale the better."

"Why don't you suggest it?"

"I have, to Salt. However, the Superintendent doesn't want our group to be dissolved for a few days yet. I'd have Maryvale out of here in a jiffy, though, if I felt his mental condition were critical, not simply fluctuating, for there's not the remotest possibility of his being implicated in Cosgrove's death."

"Let me see, where was he, just?"

"Sitting with me on the steps of the summer-house the whole time during which the murder could have happened. But if he is shielded from any further mental concussion, I suppose there's no harm in his staying on here a while longer. Besides, you know, he will have it that the Parson is dead."

In the thickening gloom I could make out no expression on the face of the man keeping step beside me. I spoke cautiously.

"I take it, then, Doctor, that you don't think Maryvale may have a hand in the manifestations of the Parson?"

He laughed. "Rather not! How could he?"

"I wish I could tell you. But in any case I suppose—I devoutly hope, anyhow—that the manifestations are over, and the explanations will be in order henceforth."

"I second you willingly."

We went on. I stumbled against a stone in the roadway. "Doctor, you've heard about the man I encountered the night I came here; I mean the one with the umbrella."

"Yes, Salt asked my opinion about that chap."

"What opinion could you have?"

"Question of sanity again."

"What do you think?"

"Hopelessly sane, I should say. You didn't take him for crazed, did you?"

"No; I suppose his talk was fabricated."

"From Salt's account, I judged it was—most of it, anyhow."

"Which part do you exempt?"

"Well, wasn't there an urgent warning about calling off the dogs, and a reference to golden-haired woman? Believe me, Bannerlee, this Mac-what-ever-his-name-was meant what he said just then."

"Perhaps. But what I wanted to tell you, Doctor, was that I can't help connecting Maryvale with that man. The physical differences in their appearance aren't so great that they couldn't be one and the same, what with a false beard stuck on crooked, and the rest of it. It's unlikely, of course, but still—"

"Tut! It's impossible."

"You don't know. You weren't here that night."

"Trust Salt. He has ascertained beyond a shade of doubt that Maryvale and the rest of the party were in the House the whole evening. The only possibility is that one of the servants *might* have gone out looking that way, and you know how likely that is."

I gave a shrug to dismiss the whole question as insoluble. "I thank my stars I wasn't born a detective."

"Curious how dark the House is," said Aire. "So close to dinner, too."

The building had been in sight for a time, but only as a black beast crouching with closed eyes on the lawn. Now we were some hundred yards or so distant, but had still to go through the gate-house archway if we followed the westward trend of the drive.

I said, "I suppose our friends haven't appeared. I'd make my outing as long as possible, too, having to return at last to this devil's playground."

We passed underneath the arch, crossed the lawn.

"Even the kitchens looked dark from down below. Can't tell about them from this side, though. I certainly expected the motorists to be back by this time; didn't you?"

"Yes, I did."

"It looks like a tomb."

I was aware that Aire had made a swift movement; then I saw him stock still, with his hand part way to his lips in a gesture of surprise.

"No lights, no. But there's someone in the conservatory."

"What!"

"I saw the gleam of a face at the window of the tower. Just a white blotch. See that?"

"Righto."

We made across the lawn at a run, entered the Hall of the Moth by the unfastened french window, and encountered two figures emerging from the conservatory.

"I'm so glad you've come!"

"Miss Lebetwood!"

"Yes, it's Millicent and I. Don't—don't be afraid," she added with a little, unsteady laugh.

"Are you alone? Is there something the matter with the lights?"

"The lights are all right. Yes, we're alone."

Aire demanded, "Aren't the servants here?"

"They're all here, I guess. I meant our people, you know. They brought us to the bridge, so we could come up and have an hour or two of rest before dinner. They didn't want to come in yet; so they drove on again."

"But why didn't you switch on the lights?" Aire queried. "With all deference to your courage, I should think you would have felt easier in your minds—"

"We didn't dare turn on the light," said Miss Lebetwood.

Aire and I barked astonishment.

Miss Mertoun, who had been clinging to the American girl's arm, said, "Do go on, Paula. Tell them what we saw."

"It's very little after all," said Miss Lebetwood. "We had driven down to the Wye Valley, had tea, and come back again by five-thirty, and someone suggested going north to Ludlow before returning to the House. But Millicent and I said we'd rather be excused; so one car waited on the main road while the other brought us up and dropped us at the bridge. We walked very slowly, and it wasn't until about half an hour ago that we reached the House. It was pretty dark, you know, even then, but light from one or two kitchen windows showed in the garden; so we weren't scared at all."

"Ah," remarked Aire. "You didn't come by the drive, then?"

"Oh, no, it was too dull for us. We came round through the grove under Whimble and across the lawn south of the House to the cat-head door. The door wasn't latched, and we simply walked into the vestibule, and we would have gone straight upstairs, but Millicent remembered a book she had left in the Hall of the Moth. So she went in there to get it, and I waited by the steps, but a moment later I heard her give a small scream. I ran in—"

"What had you seen, Miss Mertoun?" asked Aire, turning to the English girl.

"Something looked in the window. Paula saw it, too."

"'Something' is a trifle vague, isn't it?"

"But we don't know what it was."

"Well, what was its shape, and how was it dressed?"

"It was as tall as a man, maybe taller," said Miss Lebetwood, "and it was wrapped in a long black robe from the top of its—head to the ground."

"That's the creature Oxford and I saw on the lawn that first night," I exclaimed.

Aire asked, "What was its face like?"

Miss Lebetwood spoke in a matter-of-fact tone. "It didn't have any face."

Aire actually staggered back a step, and I reached out for something to support me, but encountering nothing, concluded to stand upright.

I found my voice. "You mean you couldn't see any."

"On the contrary, I was quite near the window—that one by the armoury door. Millicent had left her book on the cabinet there, and had reached the place before she saw the shape, and I naturally went to her side. We had all the light there was, and would have seen a face if there had been any there."

Stricken by a memory, I put my hand on Aire's arm. "Remember, Doctor, how Maryvale put no face in his portrait?"

He ignored me, and said, "What then?"

"We were petrified, of course. It seemed to peer in, if you can understand, even without a face. The whole attitude of the thing was inquiring, curious. And then perhaps it saw us, for suddenly it twisted and hurried away."

"Why didn't you get the servants?" I put in.

"Things were bad enough without that."

"What shall we do, Bannerlee?"

"Go after it, don't you think?"

"Right. You have a torch, haven't you?"

"Yes; I'll fetch it. You stay here to guard the womenfolk."

I made dizzy haste up the spiral stairs and down again, and found the three outside the french window where the intruder had stood. Aire was lighting matches in search of footprints, but as had been predicted, vainly. We agreed that it would be best for the two girls to return to the conservatory and keep watch through the windows, having care to remain invisible. If anything untoward happened, they were to signal us by switching on the light, at the same time ringing for the servants if danger was evident.

Aire and I went side by side over the lawn toward the small solitary copse. First one of us flashed the light along the sward while the other tried to penetrate the darkness ahead; then we reversed duties. As for footprints, if there were any they were exceedingly light and vague, and singularly small, but we could not even agree there was a definite trail.

The distance from the House to the cypresses was over two hundred feet, and before we had covered the distance the Vale was filled with a soft illumination, as if twilight had re-begun. On our right, the moon was rising over Whimble, a crescent moon glowing like white-hot metal. Then Aire, who had been looking ahead, drew up.

"Something's among the trees for sure."

While he spoke, I saw movement underneath the horizontal branches, and that black-robed, conic figure—unmistakably the same I had seen on the evening of my arrival—swiftened from the shelter of the cypresses toward the expansive darkness of the park where the summer-house stood. The long loose-flying sleeves flapped curiously as if there were no arms within them. The wide garment spread along the ground, but we had no sight of legs or feet, and I admit I felt uneasy at the thought that if we caught this unknown, it might prove to have no face.

We ran in pursuit, but I was careful not to outstrip Aire, lest the thing should turn and fell us separately. In consequence, we barely maintained our distance, and had the mortification of seeing the black robe merge with the night among the sycamores of the park.

"Hear that?"

"It's jumped into the stream."

"Or fallen in."

A little way within the park we found the steep-sided channel of the brook which flowed across the farm of the sisters Delambre, later on passed beneath the elaborated bridge, and eventually joined Aidenn Water. The bank at this point was five or six feet high.

"What next?"

Aire slid and floundered down to the edge of the rivulet which whispered along the channel.

"Can't tell for certain, but I believe it went toward the bridge."

I got down beside him, and we sped between the banks, which gradually lifted above us. Dry land was scarce, and we did a deal of splashing in the brook, but by the aid of my torch I seemed to see ahead muddy traces of other splashing before ours. A wild rose growing on the edge of the water had been trampled down.

A couple of short turns in the course of the brook brought us to the stone bridge, a structure magnificently heavy in the body, but leaving a semicircular arch only about eighteen inches high for the passage of water.

"It's a blind alley. No man—or woman—could have gone through there. There isn't room for a good-sized dog."

I bent down and shot the light underneath; there was nothing but water there.

"Well—"

"Up the bank, did it go?"

I flashed the torch up and down both sides of us. On the one hand was a miniature precipice more than ten feet high, on the other was a wall of earth nearly vertical, thickly grown with ivy-leaved toad-flax showing no sign that anything larger than a mite had travelled over it.

"I never—" Aire began.

I could not repress a tremor when he suddenly looked skyward, showing that the spell of magic could exist in his bones. I turned my gaze up, too, as if I really expected to see a black-robed figure floating over the ruined summerhouse or receding into the depths of the night sky. But it was eastward that Aire was looking, and while we stared, some solitary winged form flapped across the narrow surface of the moon.

"We're beaten," said Aire.

"Let's get out of here. I need a tonic."

"Shall we go back?"

"No; I'll give you a leg up, and you reach down a hand to me."

In this wise we crawled up the toad-flax, and a minute later our wet feet were taking us back toward the cypress grove again. I kept my light running along the ground, though my hope was feeble of discovering any traces of the unknown. But when we had reached the grove itself, Aire darted forward with a chortling cry.

No need to tell me what the white thing was that he picked up and held in a trembling hand. He tried to decipher it in the moonlight before my torch made the letters clear:

LoOk OUT FoR mE ToNIGhT

There was singularly little reaction on the part of anyone; I think most of the minds in the House are drugged with dangers and alarums.

"But, I say," protested Charlton Oxford. "The beastly placard says to-night, y'know."

"Can you use a pistol?" asked Crofts.

"Yes, but—"

"You can have mine, then. As for me, I'm going to sleep with one ear and one eye open, and shan't be surprised at anything, including being murdered."

Alberta rang for someone to remove the coffee-cups. "And nobody must whisper a word of it to the servants, must they, Crofts?"

"Of course not."

Blenkinson himself entered, slipped about the room with deferential soft-footedness, collected the débris, and carried it out on two trays. I noticed his eyes once or twice sliding into their corners while he stole an inscrutable look at Miss Lebetwood.

"Extraordinary staff of servants you have," remarked Aire, as soon as the butler had departed.

"I'm paying double wages," said Crofts shortly.

"I agree with Stephen," declared Belvoir. "And I don't think wages alone cut much figure."

"Tell them, Crofts," said Alberta.

Her husband looked a bit abashed, but having encountered the steady beam of her eye, growled, "Blenkinson."

"Elucidate," I said.

"Blest if I know," confessed Crofts. "But there's the fact. The fellow's a perfect lord among the community, and somehow he's induced the lot to believe that he's able to protect 'em. I don't know his method. He just assured me I could depend on him."

Silence fell, in which the clock was audible, and I noticed that it was a quarter to ten.

Alberta yawned and made a gesture of weariness. "What do you say to ten o'clock bed, people?"

Assent was unanimous.

* * * *

Those gate-house towers that nod to me across the lawn—may they harbour the Parson? Those locked cellars that no one has seen for years. Who or what may not be down there? There are persons unaccounted for in the Vale. And where now is the drowning-pit? In olden days this castle must have had one. Discovering it, would I know more about the Parson, or about the perfidious tree, or about the cat's claw?

Some of these questions I may be able to answer, if—

Yes, just now, at eleven minutes to twelve, I tossed a sixpence to decide. It fell spinning on the table, wobbled provokingly, and said, "Go forth."

Let the Parson beware! If I catch him—or her—tonight!

Five minutes to twelve.

Great God, through my open window—

Some woman's voice, very faint.... I am not sure whose. It is not Paula Lebetwood's.

It called "Sean, poor Sean!" many times, and died away.

CHAPTER 21

THE MIDNIGHT EXPEDITION

October 8. 11 A.M.

Furtively, yet with a strange half-fearful pleasure, I made my way in safety to the top of the stairs and down. I knew it was useless to inspect the rooms which had been examined many times by day during the past week. So I would have passed the library entrance without a moment's check in my rapid movement, had not a streak of light shot forth from beneath the door just as I reached the bottom stair. Someone had lit the chandelier.

I felt shock. I curdled. To investigate is one thing; to run point-blank on revelations in the wrong place is another. I had a panicky impulse to slip up-stairs again and lock myself in. But instead I loitered where I stood, staring at the yellow drugget spread from the lintel.

The door was slightly ajar, and I saw a portion of the panelling of the library wall; yet no sound came from within. A pale screen of light, of which the edge drew a line on the opposite side of the corridor, indicated that I might peep into the room through the slit of the door. And though my curiosity had somehow turned sick within me, presently I found myself with my eye at the crack.

My legs seemed to wilt. If it had been Cosgrove himself, burly as life, I could not have had a worse turn. A trim young fellow, clad in dinner clothes and wearing a black cap, was inside, and he was a stranger!

He had been standing beyond the table, apparently in thought, his head three-quarters from me, so that I caught only the remote profile of his smooth face, and a narrow slice of his white shirt-front. But now he moved across the room to a bookcase just within my triangle of vision, drew open its glass doors, and commenced looking for some volume. He stood in full view with his back toward me, turning his head from side to side in a survey of the upper shelves. I could see then that though slight of stature, he was, for his height, no mere skeleton, but of fairly solid build, being even a bit broader across the hips than at the shoulders.

A minute later he was beneath the light, his chosen volume lay open before him. I recognized it instantly as the Book of Sylvan Armitage. With his face cast into shadow by the peak of his cap, he leaned across the table with one hand flat on the red velvet, while the other ran through the pages. I could tell that the outspread hand was delicate and tapering, an "artistic" hand; but what I wanted to see plainly was that clean-shaved face.

Of a sudden he picked the book up from the table, pushed himself erect from his leaning position, walked toward the armoury door and beyond my range of vision. There was a click, and the chandelier faded out; a moment later I heard a tiny jingling sound, as of curtain rings disturbed. The young man was restoring the portières to their original places. Then—nothing.

The debonair manner I discerned in this youth even during observation so brief and cramped, the easy, natural way in which his dapper feet carried him across the floor, as if the place belonged to him—all so much at variance with the stealthy habits of a lawless intruder—rather increased the numb, foreboding ill-ease I felt.

At last I ventured into the library, and found it, as I expected, in moon-bathed vacancy. The armoury and the Hall of the Moth were also empty save for their furnishings. I stood in the midst of the Hall, wondering where the young chap had betaken himself, whether out of doors, which seemed un-likely, whether into some crypt or cove in the massive walls, which seemed unlikely, too, or into thin air, which, in spite of the compulsion of ancient sor-ceries, seemed less likely than either. Anyhow, he was gone, and it remained for me to consider what course to take.

No need to retail my devious thoughts. In the end I saw no good in rous-ing the house, particularly since I must reveal my secret projects. I went on as before, with caution redoubled.

The corridor—no one there, apparently. The dinner-room—no one there for certain. The kitchen—now I was in unknown territory. I waited, listened, breathless. Only the whistle of a bat outside, the creak of a timber within. I ran the shifting circle of my torch about the walls, across the floor. A cock-roach, devil's coachman, fled across the flags, and a great moth with eyes glimmering green fluttered toward me from some corner. There on its pillar hung the gate-house key; there, beside the chimney-place where a modern stove presided, was the door I sought.

With prodigious care I passed through this portal, for besides leading ultimately to the bowels of the earth, it ushered me at first into a passage off which opened the precincts of the servants. These half-subterranean cham-bers lay beneath the dinner-room and conservatory. While I stole past the doors, I had audible evidence a-plenty that the dwellers within were sleeping soundly enough.

This passage I was traversing had a distinct downward tendency and stretched underneath the corridor of the ground floor. It terminated in a door which, when I passed my light over it, appeared very black and cumbrous. The key was in the lock.

To my surprise, when by a series of graded pressures I commenced to turn this key, it moved easy and soundless, as if very recently oiled. Beyond was a winding stone stair.

By way of sensible precaution I removed the key and brought it with me, having no wish to be immured in the depths for any cause whatsoever. The stairs, a dozen or so in number, brought me to the entrance of another passage beneath the first, leading me in exactly the opposite direction. While it proceeded it widened into a goodly cellar, and I made out the yawning mouths of bins on either side, a comforting sight. There were dark archways leading to other caverns. And when I stamped, an unmistakable hollow sound came from below, proof that some buried chamber existed there.

The trap-doors by which one gained these sub-cellars, Crofts had said, were long disused, inch-deep in dust. And a few seconds later I came upon one of them, a heavy iron plate in the floor, clamped down with a clumsy padlock—but the dust was cleared away, and the padlock was not fastened at all! I picked the thing up from where it was lying by the flange, and stared at it stupidly. It would never lock anything again; it had been forced.

Now, surely, this was none of Salt's work; he had promised to do no more than inspect the dust-covered entrances. It became increasingly evident that someone had preceded me in this search, someone careful not to be detected while he came, but careless whether it was known that he had been. God forbid that he was still below!

With one fierce tug I lifted the door by a ring in the centre; it fell backward with a heavy clang, and an atmosphere of choking damp came up from the hole it left.

A stair descended therein, very steep and narrow, with a thinnish fuzzy coating which must have been dust, though where it came from would have been difficult to tell. In the dust there were footprints, big footprints.

I didn't like it, but I went on down. The rough stone walls were crumbling with water-rot and the sheer decay of age. While the air grew more smothering, I ran my head into stalactitic cobwebs and rubbed elbows with evil fungi sprouting in every crevice.

It seemed as if there must be a hundred of those steps, though actually they were about the same number as had been in the winding stair. At length I saw that I had come to the last of them, for the big footsteps tramped across a lumpy floor, athwart the glistening path of a snail. The door was earth, soggy and covered with that same thin dust-layer.

Midnight was midnight there indeed. Without my torch, I should never have returned a sane man. Nor did my light, dancing about from wall to wall, make it endurable. Fungi grew riotously everywhere, and the cobwebs, black as a funeral, hung down thick from the vaulted ceiling, like infamous hair. One or two spiders darted out and scurried immediately back into their loathsome jungle. Whenever I shifted my light, I had a feeling that from the place left in darkness the vile growth was reaching out tentacles to grasp and cling to me.

I intended to make my business here as brief as possible, but first I must find what the other visitor had been doing before me. I followed the big footprints across the marshy floor, and noted a thick mark drawn beside them. Something had been dragged.

Then the traces ceased, and I drew back suddenly with a cry at my lips. I had had a narrow escape.

There was little to tell that the floor stopped here, for like it the water was covered with an unclean growth. I stood on the brink of the water-pit, where Aidenn's lord had once drowned thirty wretches in a single day! If ever a place was accurst for the cruelties performed there, this is it.

Over the stagnant pit the ghastly festoons hung so thick that the torchlight could scarcely pierce the darkness to the farther wall. From that wall a strange shape protruded, round like an enormous barrel, but too vague to be identified.

I suddenly caught sight of an object beside me on the verge of the water. A stake had been driven into the earth through the gathered-up mouth of a large cloth bag. The bottom of the bag hung over the edge and down into the water, and the weight of its contents drew the whole bag taut.

I gave a prolonged look through the shaggy gloom, where the black streamers faintly shivered in the air my body had stirred. Was some obscene presence spying on me from the murk?

Banishing fear, I wrenched up the stake, lifted the bag from the pool, and let its burden fall upon the floor. Stark and stiff, with its eyes staring, its tongue thrust out, its fur tousled into knarls and lumps, its claws extended, the enormous cat of the sisters Delambre lay outstretched at my feet. I stooped over the body; my fingers touched a cord drawn tight about the neck.

So Maryvale had made this abysmal journey before me, and there had been substance in his madness when he announced that Parson Lolly is no more. Since bullets would not kill, with cord and water he made assurance double. The long despairing cry will never shudder down the Vale again.

I must have stood there a long while almost oblivious, gazing into the invisible, until the darkness seemed to enter my brain. The most infinitesimal sounds crept into my consciousness: the muffled murmur of water in motion somewhere, the charnel breath of the things that drooped from the vault, the very voice of silence! Then disgust at my surroundings mounted in an instant almost to nausea, and I wheeled about in flight to the cellar above.

I took the stairs in a leap and a scramble, the trap-cover closed with a shout behind me while I darted among the bins and arches to the winding steps. At the top of these I paused to replace the key but not to turn it, then made tiptoes past the doors until I gained the kitchen. With the key of the gate-house in my hand I passed into the dinner-room, thence through the corridor into the conservatory, one of whose smaller windows I proposed to use as a means of egress.

The valley seemed pale and quiet in the moonlight. In a trice I had the casement open and had stepped through to the ground, concealed beneath those outside stairs leading to the door at the end of the first floor corridor. I pushed the window shut, and on the instant the long screech of some predatory night-bird shrilled from the summer-house park. If it was an omen, it was not for good—and my path lay among those shadows!

This was for secrecy. If I passed directly across the lawn, some wakeful eye in one of the long range of windows might find me out; so I had no choice but a long three parts of a circle screened by trees. First I stole behind the birches where I concealed myself at dawn the other day on catching sight of the red-bearded runner, next through the cypresses, then the sycamores of the park, and finally the strawberry trees. These last extended far enough south to enable me to reach the towers from the side opposite the House. The door was on the other side, unconcealed, but I had to risk being seen while I unlocked it.

I stood still beneath the twin, mute towers for a minute or two before gathering determination for my effort. Salt, of course, visited this place the day after his arrival, but has kept his discoveries secret. My hope, of course, was that someone came here *after* Salt, in particular the black-robed object of our pursuit tonight.

I noticed that the moon was near setting, since it had but a short progress to make from eastern to western hill. When it was down, the Vale would be dark indeed. Was it worth waiting until that happened?

Impatience decided not. I sped around the tower that contained the door, turned the monumental key, got safely inside the entrance, and stood with bated breath. Seen or unseen, I was in for it now. Heaven help me if I found a presence inside these walls.

My light showed the beginning of the spiral stair; there was absolutely no sound. I commenced to climb.

It was a long way up. My stockinged feet were all but noiseless on the overlapping stony steps, and more than once I checked myself, thinking that I heard footfalls following mine. The torch, directed downward, revealed the empty stair winding into nether darkness. This delusion persisted; indeed, when I was at the point of entering the little room atop the tower, I thought that I heard even the breath of some stealthy climber. The light showed only the bare winding beneath me, and I spoke a murrain on the narrow tower which had no well to enable me to see clear to the bottom.

My imagination cooled down, and I set about examining the circular chamber. Owing to the thickness of the walls, it was only some five feet in diameter. It was low, and save in the centre, where the pointed roof gave space, I could not stand upright. For windows it had three slots, through one of which the moon cast a slanting beam. The floor was thickly daubed with mud, but this in itself was not surprising when one considered that Salt had sloshed through here on the morning of the downpour.

But that mud would have dried long ago, and this showed signs of damp!

Eagerly, critically, I bent and studied the floor in the full glare of my torch. There were dubious faintly moist impressions, of feet, I believed; but I could make nothing of them. No entire footprint was evident. Over the general surface of the dirt, however, something sopping wet had recently been trailed, but not so heavily as to disturb the topography of the mud. The little ridges and knolls left by Salt's rubber boots remained intact, but portions of that microscopic countryside looked as if they were recovering from an inundation; in one or two hollows there were positive pools, one-sixteenth of an inch deep.

Something exceedingly wet, but not very heavy—what else but the gown of the creature that had fled from Aire and me and plunged into the stream? Only, how in the name of magic did that creature evade us to get here, unless it skipped *up* the stream, which both Aire and I are prepared to attest on oath it did not do?

A flat-headed aperture led the way across the bridge between the towers. In that direction the water-trail appeared to tend, although at the edge of the dirt, where the gown had been drawn along the stones themselves, almost complete evaporation had taken place. Further along there was no sign of damp at all; I suppose the intruder had observed the puddles he was making and had lifted the garment clear from the floor, perhaps doffed it and rolled it under his arm.

I had to crouch nearly double in that low passageway to reach the inner room, which now I believed to be the headquarters of Parson Lolly. My light, cast ahead, showed that it was a chamber of identical mould with the one I had just quitted, and, much to my relief, it was empty. One difference there was, indeed: the corresponding stairway which led down from this tower had for some reason been walled up. I tested the mortared stones; I pounded them with my fist; I butted them with my shoulder. They were sound and secure, leaving no doubt that those stairs condemned to everlasting darkness held no secret connected with the present mysteries.

When I had reached this comfortable certainty, I made a detailed search of the turret. Someone, for sure, had been in the habit of coming there; I found what appeared to me sufficient evidence of occupation, and of hurried, perhaps permanent, departure.

There were pencil-whittlings on the floor, from an indelible pencil; I know the nasty taste of the aniline preparation. Now, when I re-examined the Parson's placard inside the House this evening, I saw, though I did not comment on the fact, that such a pencil had been used in writing it.

There were two or three dark stains, splashes now quite dried, which yet had a dim, offensive odour when my nose was close to them. To my mind, no more proof is needed that a young pig was murdered here.

There were a few short lengths, an inch to four or five inches, of some pliant fibrous wood, perhaps bamboo, which I cannot account for. With these, perhaps, are associated the fragments of black crepe I found cut in wedges, rhombs, and various irregular shapes.

I detected, while bending near one of the slender openings, a sub-acrid, faded scent, which seemed specially localized on the sill, so to speak, of the window, as if some pungent stuff had once been spilt there and removed. In its proper context the source of the odour would, I am sure, have been obvious in an instant; yet here it baffled me.

Last I found a torn end of paper. The side uppermost was blank, but to my joy the other proved to contain printed words. The piece was obviously detached from the title-page of some old book, octavo size, with which I am not acquainted, though "CATTI" looks obscurely familiar. I shall hardly have any trouble in identifying it.[5]

I felt actual elation, for Salt would never have overlooked this, or left it here, supposing he had found it in the course of his inspection.

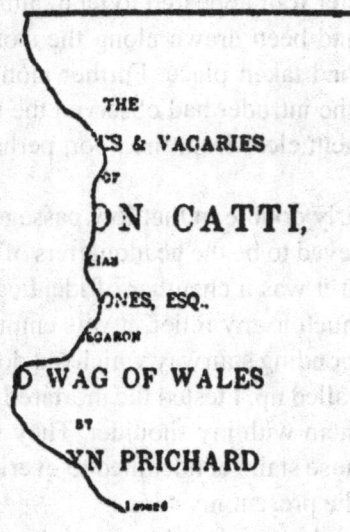

```
        THE
'S & VAGARIES
    OF

N CATTI,
  IAS
NES, ESQ..
GARON

O WAG OF WALES
   BY
N PRICHARD
```

---

5   *Satis*. Reproduced on following page. (V. MARKHAM.)

Five minutes had revealed these things; an hour could not reveal more. I tucked the slip of paper into my breast pocket and departed from the turret. Half-way across the bridge I was again aware of the sound of footsteps climbing to the first chamber, but dismissed the idea as a renewal of the delusion which had troubled me before.

But there was no mistake this time, as I realized very soon. The pad-pad of the unknown feet was growing louder, coming nearer. At once I was terrified, yet possessed of reason. I knew it might be fatal to let this creature see me before I saw him—it—her. Particularly disastrous it would be to be caught in this low passageway where I must go with my head almost touching my knees. I snapped off my light, staggered into the room beyond, and stood at the edge of the stair-head, leaning perforce on account of the funnel-roof. It was a position of vantage. There I was in darkness, whereas whatever was coming must emerge into the moonlight that shot through the opposite slit. I might even escape undetected down the stairs if the creature hurried past me to the bridge and the farther tower.

But this hope was abortive. The creature knew I was there: that belief stuck like a knife in my heart.

The steady steps were only ten feet below, one twist of the stair. They were like the steps of any ordinary man.

The moon must have been nearly swallowed by the hills all this time, for now it went down with appalling suddenness and left the room in thick and absolute night. I could not see my foe in darkness; could it see me?

Every nerve in me was ringing its own alarm. The subtle glue that holds the body-cells in friendly ties dissolved; it was every cell for itself. I was fleeing in all directions.

The creature actually passed me by; I felt the touch of some part of it, cold as an Arctic stone, on my arm.

It was like awakening from an evil dream. My fear welled up in fury. Silently I launched an attack; with the torch I held I let fly in blind and murderous onslaught. I struck something a blow that glanced; the torch slipped from my grasp, but the creature staggered and sank to the floor. I had my hands on its body now, and a crazy exultation took hold of me when I realized that my opponent was merely a man like myself and at my mercy. The stroke I had given blindly seemed to have stunned him, for he made no resistance, but lay crumpled up, as I found by groping. His breath came harsh and irregular.

Who was he? For what seemed immeasurable time I searched, but I could not find my torch.

Obviously I had made an important capture, and the best thing to do, since my light was lost, would be to lock the fellow-prisoner in and go for reinforcements.

I had a handkerchief; so had he. With their assistance I triced him in a position from which he would not easily free himself. I placed him face downward, with his head turned aside for breathing and his legs doubled back, and I clipped each wrist to the opposite ankle.

Then I groped my way down the long turnings, found the darkened world again, locked the tower door, and made for the House.

The rest was like the return of horrid dreams. With the moon gone, still the stars gave a grey cast to the darkness. I saw some fluttering-draped figure descend from the first storey by the outside stairs; I heard distracted sobbing. I saw vague forms that followed one another on the lawn, heard phantom calls and a strange hysteric laughter. The place seemed more alive by night than at any hour of day.

Maryvale, I discovered afterward, had come out again, clambered down all the way by the ivy. Lib, in the room next his, had heard him this time, caught sight of him, fled across the passage to Mrs. Bartholomew, shared that lady's dismay on finding me also flown, summoned Pendleton, who had roused Aire and come helter-skelter in pursuit of the errant man of business. Lib and Mrs. Bartholomew, in different styles of negligée, now stood spectators of the course. Millicent Mertoun, too, had come crying out of doors by those northern stairs, in her sleep, as she had come that first night with the American girl watchfully by her side.

But tonight she roved alone. Where was Paula Lebetwood, whose room is next the stairs, and who, however soundly she may have slept, must have heard her dear friend's weeping?

Lights were awakening in various chambers. Maryvale, much surprised at the solicitude of his captors, was explaining courteously that he had merely descended to "pick herbs." Alberta Pendleton had appeared and was taking Miss Mertoun back to the House.

By the time I had called attention to myself and had caused my story to penetrate Crofts' brain, many minutes had gone by. Four of us, followed by those audacious females, Lib and Mrs. Bartholomew, approached the towers. The door stood open. The intruder, securely trussed and locked in by me, had made off. He had taken my torch, invaluable as both light and weapon.

CHAPTER 22

THE BEGINNING OF THE END: PARABOLA

Same day. 3 P.M.

In spite of early bed last night, no one was downstairs early this bright morning, Sunday. I myself wanted breakfast at nine, but then I am the one person in the House who has anything concrete to do (to wit, this writing)—hence I require the less repose.

I visited the library before I went for food. To my grim pleasure, the Book of Sylvan Armitage was back on its shelf. I am always grimly pleased nowadays when anything baffling turns up. Crofts, by the way, has proved blatantly sceptical about my experience last night; he said that if I must go crawling about the House when decent folk are abed, I mustn't hold him responsible for what I think I see.

The telephone jangled in the corridor while I was at the table. I heard Soames answer and take some message. Presently the servant came to me.

"Superintendent Salt is holding on, sir, if you please."

"Me, he wants?"

"He asked for any of the gentlemen, sir. Would you mind speaking to him?"

"Not at all." A few moments later I was saying, "Hello, Superintendent; this is Bannerlee. Anything I can do for you?"

"Thanks very much, Mr. Bannerlee. Would you mind givin' a message to the doctor—Doctor Aire, I mean?"

"Delighted."

"I've been lookin' up *his* whereabouts the two days before he came down to Radnorshire."

"*His!*"

"Yes. Nothing like thoroughness, is there? He might like to know he's not the Parson. Tell him he's absolved, clean character, goes scot-free."

"He'll be grateful, I'm sure."

"Certain to be. Another thing, too, sir. I took the liberty—unpardonable—of checkin' *you* also."

"*Me!*"

The sound must have deafened Salt, for it was a little while before he resumed, with smothered amusement. "Couldn't help it, sir. All in the way of routine. You're acquitted, too, and can go your ways."

"Thanks awfully."

"Don't mention it. By the way, I just told that man to inform Mr. Pendleton that I'm comin' up there this afternoon early, around dinner-time. I'm bringin' someone with me."

"Oh? Any harm in asking who it is?"

"None at all," chuckled Salt. "Good-bye."

It was about one o'clock when I came downstairs again, after setting down the record of last night's expedition. I think everyone was in the Hall, surrounding Salt and a young fellow in a neat grey suit, who was lank and had freckles and brown hair. His appearance and manner—he was smiling most of the time—were engaging. Salt also wore a respectful grin; in fact, everyone looked brighter for this chap's presence, especially Crofts.

"Come on, Bannerlee," he said; "let me introduce the beginning of the end. You can guess who this is."

I had a flash of genius. "Yes, I can, by George. It's Harry—Mr. Heatheringham."

"Right!" declared the young man. "But after all, Mr. Bannerlee, you've an unfair advantage in this guessing business."

"You mean—?"

He winked, took my torch out of his pocket, and handed it to me with a low bow, such as I had seen somewhere not long before. "Many thanks for this. I had to borrow it when my own failed last night."

"Gods! Was it you I hit? I'm most awfully sorry."

"It didn't hurt, really, but for a little while I didn't know where I stood— er, that is, I wasn't standing at all." He felt a place on the back of his head. "It's hardly the size of a teacup—I mean the bump. And I wasn't dazed for long either."

"I'm glad to hear it," I avowed. "You certainly lost no time waking and legging it."

"Oh, I was awake, wide enough, when you were fastening me up—and a neat job, that."

"You don't mean to say—"

"Yes, but I thought it was better to let you do your worst and untie myself afterward. I wasn't sure that the time for explanations had come, and I wasn't sure—then—just what you yourself were up to."

"But if I'd been someone else, you might have been killed."

His eyes were merry. "I knew it wasn't somebody else. Suppose we call it a draw."

"We're dying to hear how you escaped," said Lib. "Why do you keep it bottled up?"

"It's my living, you see," returned Heatheringham apologetically, but with his customary smile. "I have to be up to a few of the little secrets of my trade, or I don't get any bread and butter. Some do it on the stage for money, but in my business it comes in valuable in good earnest to carry a few skeleton keys and know how to twist a hand out of a knotted handkerchief."

Gradually, while talk went on, we disposed ourselves in chairs, making a group about this young man who showed from the first minute of acquaintance such a winning, and even naïve, nature. He sat in the midst of us now, busy parrying all sorts of questions, and I noticed that while he spoke lightly, he glanced from person to person, making brief, sharp studies of us. Particularly he kept stealing looks at Miss Lebetwood and the two younger Americans.

I had returned the study intensively, striving to capture some elusive recollection. "Pardon me, Mr. Heatheringham, but really I believe I've met you somewhere—another time, I mean. Am I right?"

"Yes, indeed, we have met. We've been having lovers' meetings all over the place. You recollect the umbrella?"

The menagerie-keeper! I uttered a great gasp. "That was never you in the crooked black beard!"

"Wasn't it, though?" he retorted brightly. "I can see your eyes popping now, Mr. Bannerlee, when I said, 'I won't need finger-nails.'"

"Incredible! That man was bulbous." I pointed to the detective's hands, which were brown and lean. "Don't tell me you owned the great red wrists and fingers that fellow had."

"Try a tightly-bound cuff or any other constriction around the wrist and keep your arms down—see what happens. Your hands will look like hams. The rest was just a matter of accessories, an inflated chest-protector, some dowdy clothes, some black hair. A bad disguise, on the whole."

"On the contrary, your twin brother wouldn't have recognized you."

"No, but he would have had me arrested. Disguise should be unobtrusive, but that one shouted all over the place. To tell the truth, I used it more to give my friend Crofts Pendleton something to worry about than for any other reason."

"Oh, you did, did you?" said Crofts.

"Yes, old man. I didn't realize the situation here might actually be serious. I merely supposed some sneak-thief was snooping in the neighbourhood. But it did seem a good chance to have a little sport with you. You will let yourself in for it," he accused our muttering host. "I thought I'd make myself up into a figure of fun and have a reconnaissance of the scene a couple of nights, just to assure myself there was no cause for alarm. Then I'd be seen on purpose by some good honest yokels and perhaps a village idiot or so, and pop in in a day or two to see what the effect had been in the Vale. But matters turned out differently from what I had expected, and by the time I met with you, Mr. Bannerlee, the last thing on earth I wanted was to have it known I was in the neighbourhood. So I improvised some unnatural eccentricities and made up a line of desperate talk that I knew would spoil the last chance of Crofts' guessing it was me, in case you told him of your experience, as I felt certain you would."

"But I didn't."

"No, you didn't. And it made no difference, for what I said about the bothersome watch-dogs wouldn't have made much impression, would it, unless our friend knew where it came from? All those men you sent out," he told Crofts, "kept treading on my toes. I had to leg it twice to slip away from them. And that was after I had made some very material discoveries and would have given a year of my life not to be seen."

"How was I to know that?" said Crofts. "What discoveries do you mean?"

"I ran into a chap who must have been Sir Brooke Mortimer from what I know now. He seemed to have lost his way, quite a distance up the Vale. I set the gentleman going in the right direction and watched him start back downstream. A bit unsteady, I thought he was—oh, nothing wrong with him that way, but I could see his eyes weren't too good. He didn't seem able to pick his footing, and he might have stepped into a hole as big as a house without knowing what had happened to him."

"And do you mean to say that he followed your directions unhesitatingly when according to yourself you looked like something out of Grimm's Fairy Tales?" asked Lord Ludlow, who had been playing finger-exercises on his knees.

"I don't believe he quite took me in, my Lord. I'm telling you his eyesight couldn't have been good. He might have thought I was a gentleman-farmer, for all I know—and he seemed like an unsuspicious, trusting little chap."

I saw that the subject was a painful one to be discussed in full session this way, and I wanted to divert the course of conversation. I nodded to Salt.

"The discovery of Mr. Heatheringham knocks one off the list of your favourite suspects, eh, Superintendent?"

"Can't say it does," he rejoined, with that slow smoulder of humour underneath the surface. "I've known about Mr. Heatheringham since he arrived in our little community over a week ago."

He had! More surprises were let loose. As a measure of sensible precaution the detective had reported his presence to Salt as soon as he arrived in New Aidenn. In the early dawn after meeting me, having learned that there was something worth attention in the way of mystery in the Vale, the young man discarded the crooked black beard of the menagerie-keeper and glorified his chin with a rich red one, finely adapted to his complexion. This emblem he had attached properly, using separate hairs at the edges and trimming the whole to a nicety. He commenced a campaign of deceit.

First Foggins' driver was tempted from the path of duty with a five-pound note, and reported sick. While Foggins the milkman was tearing his hair, in walked the unblushing detective, and Foggins fell victim to his wiles. That very noon the newly-employed had driven the milk cart up the Vale. He had explained at the kitchen door, with a certain amount of wit, though with his ready tongue all the time in his cheek, why the service was so much delayed and how he had fallen heir to the position. The listener to this merry tale was Rosa Clay. It gained the young man a means of contact with affairs inside the House which might have been extremely valuable had the storm not cut off the Vale from Foggins' circuit.

During the week Heatheringham formed with the Post Office attendant a mushroom friendship that passeth all legality. So it came about that Crofts' impassioned letters were handed to their recipient direct, without going to Worcester and back. It was, moreover, the detective himself who had been on the Post Office end of the 'phone when Crofts dictated his telegram Thursday afternoon with many maledictions on the stumbling clerk who took the message.

The dinner-bell had rung and we were on our feet. Salt announced he mustn't stay, but would leave the field clear for the younger man. "Do what he tells you," he said. "He has an idea from time to time."

Heatheringham drew me apart, until the rest were gone, even waving Crofts ahead.

"You can do me a favour, Mr. Bannerlee, if you will," he said with a laugh in his voice, as if he might have something in the way of a surprise to try on me.

"I suppose I owe you a month's hard labour for battering you last night—but, of course, I want to help you if I can. What shall it be?"

"You're keeping a written record of events, aren't you?"

"Crofts told you!" I exclaimed reproachfully—reproachfully in reference to Crofts, that is.

"Not a bit of it—just my prowling. I've noticed your candles burning until all hours, and last night I brought a small telescope with me and had a squint at you from a tree way out by the Water. I could hardly think that you wrote letters all night, could I?"

"Well, your guess is right, as it happens, but my penmanship is rather free and easy, and I don't think you'll find much value—" I was speaking slowly but thinking fast. Had I put down anything positively libellous, anything I'd hesitate to sign my name to?

"Let me try, all the same. You and I are both detached onlookers in this thing, Mr. Bannerlee, and I shouldn't be surprised if we supplement each other pretty fully. I'm quite frankly selfish, you see," he admitted easily. "I want to know all you know without telling you what I know."

"Oh, I'll trust you to repay me, not later than noon tomorrow," I said. "Come along upstairs with me while I get the sheets for you—unless you'll wait until after dinner."

"There's no after dinner for me; I'm not taking dinner," he answered, and we went up the stairs together. "I had a snack in New Aidenn with something like this in prospect. Time's what counts. It will be dark too soon to suit me."

Same day. 7 P.M.

Please God, the experiment is over. It was not long.

About five this afternoon Heatheringham came into the library where I was writing about the events of the day. He had wrestled with my script since I had left him to go down to dinner, and he seemed even better-humoured than before.

"I want some tea," he said. "I want some tea, and yet, while there's light, I want a little assistance from the people here."

"Are you commandeering the servants, too?"

"No, I can do without the servants, except that one who brought the hot water."

"Soames?"

"Right."

"Well, you'll find the rest of us in the conservatory, waiting for both tea and you. Since the tragedy outside the Hall, the venue of tea has been shifted."

"I suppose they could wait fifteen minutes for their feeding, if I suffered with them?"

"We have been in training for martyrdom all week. But what on earth is this rigmarole you're going to put us through?"

"I want you to rehearse a little drama you have already performed without rehearsal."

It was just that.

"I'm sorry if this is painful to some of you," he said later in the conservatory. "But it's vital. I need to check some observations, and there's no way else. I'm awfully sorry to trouble you; really I am, but it's my living, you know." He gave a sly smile. "It's my living, and it will help you to escape from here tomorrow. Is it a bargain?"

From the time Cosgrove left the Hall until Miss Lebetwood found him dying outside may have been an hour. We were asked to re-enact as precisely as possible our movements during the last quarter of this period.

"You would be asleep, sir, over by the gate-house, if I'm not mistaken," said Heatheringham to Oxford. "I'll let you off the sleeping. Just be on hand, if you don't mind. You," addressing Belvoir, "would be coming toward the towers and meeting Miss Mertoun and Lord Herbert. Presently you'd commence monkeying with the winch." He spoke to me. "You were returning from the Delambre cottage, weren't you? Doctor Aire and Mr. Maryvale must see you from the summer-house. I think you'll all work into it."

"But how silly!" said Miss Lebetwood. "All I can do is to wander about the strawberry trees looking for tennis balls I know won't be there."

"It's all make-believe, you know," answered Heatheringham. "And I can't change the parts around, can I?"

"I don't see how my doing that can help."

"Still," insisted the detective deferentially, "it will assist me a lot if you'll just go through the motions. Now, is everybody clear about what he's to do?"

"Shall I fetch hot water for Mr. Bannerlee, sir?" asked Soames, who had been admitted to our company.

"That's hardly essential. But you might carry an empty pannikin to give mental support. Now, shall we commence? Some of the ladies may need coats. It's beginning to blow a bit."

"Not fair unless you tell us what you're going to do yourself," protested Lib.

"I'm going to be here, there, and everywhere," said Heatheringham. "You may even hear me giving a few stage directions. Come on, people, I want my tea. One, two, three, go."

Little gusts of wind were stirring. Evening frost had caused a marvellous change in the foliage, and the air was chromatic with flying leaves. They blew in my face while I breasted my way to the north end of the sycamore park, where I turned to retrace my steps. Through the dim light of the wood, I saw the black forms of Maryvale and Doctor Aire together on the porch of the abandoned summer-house. They nodded when I came nearest them. I reached the bridge, the cypresses, the lawn, the mansion itself. I saw people beyond the gate-house.

Suddenly I remembered that to keep in character I must peer into the Hall, and my flesh began to crawl at the thought of seeing the grim, phantasmal bone. I would not see it, of course, but if I did—

Then I caught a glimpse of Heatheringham over a hundred yards south of the House. He seemed to be waving me on, and I assumed that I must be a little behind my schedule. Without a glance into any of the windows I obediently rounded the library tower, entered the half-opened door, not omitting to ring, since I had done so on the previous occasion. The footman answered the bell with what would have been appalling suddenness had I not known he had been waiting for me. He received my instructions for hot water with the same obeisance and the same perfunctory words in the identical tone as before. I climbed the empty House to my room.

I was in a quandary, for it would do no manner of good to take off my coat and repeat the little battle with myself whose result had been a wounded finger. I certainly wouldn't subject my digit to the safety-razor's mercies a second time. But for the sake of keeping in the rhythm of the other day I might perform some of the milder motions. First I must go out to the balcony, where I had picked up the odd little scrap of rope.

I pressed through the window and, standing on the roof outside, saw the forms of people anticking about the tower and heard the rasp of the winch. Someone was on the lawn a little distance beyond the walk that skirts the House—Heatheringham himself.

"Hello!" I called aloud in the high wind. "Everything working smoothly?"

He must have seen me before, for he answered quickly, cupping his hands. "Yes, I think they're all in their places. You did come out there the other day, didn't you?"

"I did, and should go in again now if I keep in step."

"Did you order that hot water?"

"Yes, indeed."

"How did the servant behave?"

"Admirably; he didn't turn a hair."

"No, I should think not. Well, carry on. I'm bound this way." He shouted the last words in a bristling wind, and set off walking toward the north.

"Good hunting," I called after him.

I had now been on the roof for nearly five minutes and had equalled the span of time I spent there before. I returned to my chamber.

I laid my watch on the table and timed my own part of the programme, to make as near the proper *rapprochement* with Soames as I could. I allowed half a minute for divesting myself of coat and shirt, and as long again for my struggle with the oak chest and my mishap with the stool. (The handle of the chest was gone now; no use repeating that fracas.) Thirty seconds more of searching for a place to attach my strop, perhaps the remainder of the minute spent in that unhappy stropping (for luck and devilment I gave the curlicued bracket a jerk and a smash), fifteen seconds to stare like a fool at the place where I had formerly cut my finger, a few moments for crossing to the door and listening for Soames—

My heart missed a beat or two. Someone *was* climbing the stairs!

It was silly of me, of course, to be taken aback by the very thing I was waiting for, I had heard no one but Soames himself ascending at his proper time.

But the slam of the door down below and the deep brawling laughter which followed— Dear God! They, too, reverberated, and the sound of that inhuman mirth now held a ghastly message which it had not on the first occasion.

And early above the sound of the laughter had I heard a single sharp explosion, like the report of a firearm?

I leaped across to the window. This time there was no fan of light spreading from the Hall, but I saw indecipherable forms criss-crossing on the lawn, and the sound of conflicting cries floated up in the lapse of the wind.

To leave the chamber, to reach the stair-head, took but a second or two. Again I saw Soames green as an old statue, a grotesque caricature of Aquarius, stony-lipped with mortal fear, the little empty water-can dangling from his hand.

I ignored him, but heard his feet pound down the stairs behind me. Down at the front entrance, just outside the door, I caught sight of Lib, still as wax. We looked at each other, mirroring the dread we saw.

"Did you hear it?" I said at last.

Her voice was weak. "The shot, you mean?"

"Was there a shot?"

"There was if my ears are working."

"Where?"

She shook her head miserably. "I—I don't know. I think it was out on the lawn."

"Then why were you coming in?"

She clenched both little fists and shook them tremblingly. "I was only doing what the detective told me to do. Besides, he—he came in first."

"*He came in!*"

"He went in this door while I was quite a way from the House."

"Then what's become of him? He couldn't have fired that shot outside!"

"Don't ask me. Don't ask me. I don't know anything about it. I got to the door in time to hear the tail-end of that laugh—that was enough for me. I don't want to lead the searching-party. This is the last time I officiate for any detective."

"Come along with me, then. He must be here somewhere."

"I think they're trying to find him outside, sir," said Soames, who had stepped warily to the corner of the House.

"That's because they don't know he went in here. Come along, both of you."

We passed into the portrait-corridor, and I shouted Heatheringham's name a couple of times, without effect.

Several of the servants had emerged from their quarters and were clustered about me while I stood at the door beneath the musicians' gallery, scrutinizing the vast gloom of the Hall. Somehow, I was loath to enter or to switch on the light ready to my hand.

"Nobody here," said Lib beside me, in a tone of relief.

I still moved my glance through the spaces of the room. Feet were pouring through the front door. I heard Crofts' voice raised:

"Heatheringham's missing. What in thunder are you up to?"

Then I saw something limned against the dark expanse of the central window of the Hall: the shape of a man who leaned heavily against the window-frame, looking out to the lawn. The moment my eyes had distinguished him, I knew it was Heatheringham. But he was awfully still! Why hadn't he heard my shout?

"Heatheringham!" I called, and was shocked how strained the syllables crept from my lips. "Heather—"

"Where is he? Do you see him?" demanded Crofts, pressing to the door. "Why didn't you light up—good God!"

He had switched on the electricity. From outside, beyond the window, came cry upon excited cry when the form of the detective was revealed by the blazing chandelier. But we who were behind Harry Heatheringham could see why he did not answer us, why he did not move. There was a gaping wound at the base of his brain, and the whole back of his trim grey coat was black with blood.

"Lawks!" cried Soames, and seemed about to faint.

Persons were rushing in from outside now, through the french windows. Doctor Aire took one look at the wound, and his face was filled with the most complete astonishment. His little dark eyes came out of their hiding-places, and even his tobacco-leaf complexion went several shades wan.

"Keep the women away," he snapped at Soames, "and don't let Maryvale come in here."

"This is horrible, horrible," Crofts kept saying.

"Is—is he dead?" asked Bob Cullen timidly, but no one smiled.

"He is," answered the Doctor. "Men with holes in their heads like this are dead as Pharaoh."

I ventured to touch the left hand that hung with such dreadful listlessness. "Why, he's stiff!" I blurted, and a great shudder shook me. "He's stiff! He must have been dead a long time. But, Doctor, I was talking to him less than five minutes ago!"

"You were!" exclaimed Crofts in an incredulous bull-voice.

"Quite so," said Aire. "I noticed it the moment I saw the poor fellow." He, too, touched the left hand. "Stiff, yes, but not cold yet."

"What's it all mean?" asked Belvoir.

"He could never be leaning there in that semi-lifelike manner if it weren't the case," said Aire. "I observed it, as I said, when I had the first glimpse of him. I have heard of it, but I've never seen a case before."

"A case of what?"

"Instant *rigor mortis*. It occurs sometimes, under certain conditions, in sudden death."

Ludlow, who stood near the body on the other side, was regarding it with awe, but his sharp face quickened with discovery. "Have you looked at his other hand? There's a revolver in it."

"Then he did fire the shot," I cried.

"I'll stake my life the shot was from somewhere outside," avouched Crofts.

"I'm sure it was," said Belvoir quietly.

"The point I wish to make," said Ludlow, "is that the revolver is outside. He's put his hand right through."

It was so. Concealed by the fact that the body pressed close to the window, the right arm half-way to the elbow had been thrust through the glass and the wrist was supported by one of the cross-bars between the small panes. The weapon was tightly clutched in the hand, and its nose pointed upward!

"What in the name of reason could he have fired at up there?"

It was when we laid the dead detective, stiff in the original posture, revolver clamped in hand, on the carpet spread over the *Brocade de Lyons* creation that we looked beyond that article of elegance and saw what had been concealed behind it.

Splashes of blood from Heatheringham's wound were on the floor at our feet, between the body and the couch. Now we beheld more blood, a trail of it across the floor in drops that led in a long, irregular, parabolic curve from the couch to the open door by the clock-corner, and so out into the corridor. There the track ceased abruptly.

"Hm," said Aire, standing at the spot. "Here's where the assailant tucked his bludgeon away." He looked up and down the gallery. "Friend Crofts, why not have another search and see if one of these priceless paintings doesn't conceal a door?"

"There has never been, and is not any secret passage in the House," said Crofts decisively. "You can say amen to that."

Aire shrugged his shoulders. Lord Ludlow shook his head several times, though what at no one could tell. Belvoir stared at the last drop of blood where it stained the blue-carpeted floor as if he were fascinated by it. Bob Cullen pursed his lips and whistled a ditty of no tone. Crofts kept putting his hands in his pockets and taking them out again.

Insensibly, instinctively, we drew the tiniest bit closer to one another. Spiritually, we huddled. We were all little men, badly frightened, in the great House where murder stalked invisible.

* * * *

If this is "the beginning of the end," what will the end itself be like?

CHAPTER 23

MISS LEBETWOOD AND A CAMPSTOOL

October 9. Noon.

"No," said Miss Lebetwood, "I certainly didn't do what he wanted me to. What good would that have been?"

Salt's brow was very grave, but his eyes were narrowly upon her. "You watched him, you say?"

"Yes, as long as he was in sight from the edge of the strawberry trees."

"What happened?"

She bit her lip. "Nothing that will really help you."

"Let me be the judge of that," said Salt gently. "What did you see?"

"By the time I reached the strawberry trees and looked back, the lawn was empty. It was still empty when—"

"Excuse me, Miss; what about the gate-house?"

"I couldn't see the towers from that spot; I was on the wrong side of the knoll that overlooks the court."

"Quite. Thank you, Miss."

"So I watched the lawn and the House. I could almost see it growing darker while I waited, the light changes so rapidly in the Vale. And I hate the twilight—all the really terrible things here happen then." She broke off, and we knew that she must be thinking of that one terrible thing in the gloaming of a week ago. Alberta made a movement as if to check her from continuing. "No, it's all right. I was just realizing what a fool I am. The time of day can't possibly make any difference."

"I don't believe it does," acquiesced Salt. "But go on, if you please."

"It was darkening so suddenly that I thought I shouldn't be able to recognize anyone who might appear. But when Mr. Bannerlee came out of the park, I saw him quite plainly. He seemed to hesitate when he came past the Hall, but then he went on faster and disappeared in the direction of the front entrance."

"Heatheringham beckoned me to hurry," I put in.

"There was nobody in sight then, but I believe I heard the winch working under the towers. A minute or two later Mr. Heatheringham appeared from down below, looking this side and that, and occasionally glancing upward."

"Are you sure?" asked Salt.

"Yes, because he caught sight of Mr. Bannerlee, who had come out his window and was standing on the roof. Mr. Bannerlee waved his hand, and I could just hear the sound of his voice when he hailed Mr. Heatheringham, the wind was rushing on so just then. After that I heard nothing of their voices, but soon afterward Mr. Bannerlee went in and Mr. Heatheringham commenced to walk quickly up toward the cypresses. He was looking this side and that again; I thought he was more intent than before. He broke into a run, but while he was running he turned—"

"Turned!"

"Yes, and ran all the way back to the south end of the House. At the library corner he slowed to a walk and went out of sight. Then Lib came along from down the lawn, and she had almost disappeared beyond the library tower—going toward the main entrance, you know—when I heard the crack of the revolver. Lib rather tightened up then, and I saw her look every way at once, but she apparently decided to disbelieve her ears, for she went on out of sight."

"And met Soames and me," I said.

"Well, everybody seemed to have heard the shot, though nobody knew where it had come from. Mr. Pendleton, Lord Ludlow, and the rest began crossing the lawn this way and that, shouting directions at one another that nobody heeded. I came on from the trees, but nobody seemed to see me. After that—well, you know."

Salt nodded. "Mr. Pendleton's told me how they found the body. Just one question more, Miss, and thank you very much. You couldn't have seen anything in the air that Heatheringham might have some reason to take a shot at? No large bird of any description?"

"No, sir."

"You didn't hear something like a bird call—something that might have attracted his attention?"

"I could hear nothing but the wind. Anyhow, Mr. Heatheringham was inside the House."

"Of course he was," said Salt.

But he is no longer. The detective's body was taken to New Aidenn in the dead of night.

Salt's laborious questions to each one of us went on until eleven, but the problem of Harry Heatheringham's taking off remains today more cryptic than Cosgrove's. The Superintendent acknowledged defeat, and had the Chief Constable on the 'phone shortly after eleven. Scotland Yard will be with us presently, although the lack of decent train connections out of Worcester will prevent the Inspector from reaching New Aidenn before late dinner time tonight.

Six burly constables, in pairs, were patrolling the grounds from nine o'clock until morning, but I think most persons within the House kept anxious vigil as well. For my own part, I flung myself on my ancient four-poster and found sleep—sleep, but not rest, for I was visited by tormenting dreams. The world was mist seethed, and through the long black lanes between the billows swept a procession of the souls of murdered ones. Down from the invisible above the swirl sounded a terrible voice: "Let traitors beware," and from time to time a blaze of light burst through, throwing on the curtain of fog the gigantic shadow of an arm.

I awoke, and lay awake in a world of real mist until I could endure inactivity no longer. I dressed and went downstairs, earlier than ever before, save on that morning when I tried to discover "lost content" on the hills. It did not surprise me to find Salt already hard at work; he was examining with almost microscopic care the gouted trail of blood. But a surprise awaited me.

It was much too early for breakfast; yet Miss Lebetwood was standing at the window of the dining-room. Attired in a navy blue sweater and serge skirt and high laced boots, she appeared very alert and full of business.

Seeing that I "took her in," she smiled and said, "I'm going to follow in your steps this morning. As soon as I've had some breakfast, I'm off for the hills."

"On account of—?"

"Yes."

I simulated a groan. "I should never have let you have it if I thought it would make you reckless."

Now, the fact is that she struck me in a heap last evening by coming straight up to me and asking to read this diary. How *she* ever came to hear of it I can't imagine, and she was obdurate to my demands for enlightenment. Only she told me very seriously that since no one else seemed certain to grapple successfully with the many problems in the Vale, she was going a step beyond "thinking" and would take an active course.

"Somehow I'm sure I'll be the best detective of the lot," she said. "I have kept my mind unprejudiced, you see. And really, Mr. Bannerlee, I'm positive you have several facts locked away in your book that I never knew."

The end was that she marched away with the book, I may say entirely against my sense of discretion, while I shuddered at the thought of her perusing some of the personal comments I had included.

And now she was bound for the hills!

I looked through the window, and saw the landscape grey. A bank of fog stood motionless about the base of Whimble.

"This is scarcely the day for it, is it? It's easy to be lost up there in the mist."

She turned from the drear panorama and looked at me kindly. "I can tell from your voice that you're very much concerned about me, but really you shouldn't be. I've had harder climbs than this heaps of times, and you can depend on me to be back early this afternoon. You may begin to worry about two o'clock if I don't appear then"—her chin tilted with determination—"with what I want."

I returned her kind look. "Really, Miss Lebetwood, I hope my, er, jottings haven't set you on some false lead."

"There's a lot more in your journal than jottings," she said, with serious lines of thought about the eyes. She gave me a glancing look. "I see you are sceptical."

"It's hardly fair," I laughed, "that because you've turned detective in earnest, you should try to mystify me like the other sleuths."

"What's this? what's this?" asked Salt, presenting himself.

She beckoned him in. "Mr. Salt, have you finished with that horrible gore for now? Because I want you to 'phone a telegram for me when the Post Office opens. Will you, please?"

"With pleasure, Miss. But why honour me with Mr. Bannerlee so handy?"

"I believe you're fishing! But didn't you appoint yourself censor and want to know all the messages that go out of the Vale?"

"Not any more, Miss," responded Salt, running his eye over a slip of paper she had brought from a skirt pocket. He raised his brows. "To the Welsh National Library, eh? Aberystwyth, of course." Again, more slowly, he perused the message. "H'm, very interestin', Miss. I'll send it without delay, and you'll know by the time you get back if the bookworms have the information."

"Show it to Mr. Bannerlee, please," she said. "I don't want him to think I'm rude."

"No, not for the world," I smiled, with negative hand raised to decline the proffered paper. "Since I'm to be denied the pleasure of accompanying you this morning, I wash my hands of the whole affair. You shall not have my invaluable advice."

"If you went with me this morning," said Miss Lebetwood, making a small grimace, "I could promise you one thing: you'd be unutterly bored. Well, thank goodness, at last here comes my breakfast."

Now, a quarter of an hour later, when my own special breakfast had arrived on a tray, hers had disappeared. We had been talking of tramps and journeys, comparing experiences, but I noticed that for the last few minutes her remarks had been very general and not wholly relevant. It was obvious that she was preoccupied. At last, having built up a little tower of sugar cubes and toppled it with her finger, she said:

"I was the man in the library."

Naturally, this was too much for me to comprehend and adjust myself to in a split-second, and I was still groping like a man stunned when she continued:

"Yes, the cap was my own, and I had borrowed Bob's tuxedo and come down to get that book; it had a fascination for me, and I must say I was surprised"—with a careful inclination of the head toward the corridor—"that *he* hadn't kept it under lock and key."

"Quite so."

"So you see why I didn't come out even when Millicent was wandering again. I had gone back to my room the way I'd come—that was by the outer stairs and through one of the french windows I'd undone the catch of after Blenkinson had gone the rounds—and I was gobbling up the book, still in borrowed plumage, when the commotion began. I couldn't have appeared without starting more fuss than ever; I suppose I shouldn't have much more than a rag of reputation left. They wouldn't be so surprised in America at a girl's dressing like a man—the movies have helped a lot there."

"Well, you needn't take the appalling risk again," I promised her. "If you should wish to gorge yourself clandestinely on the pages of Sylvan Armitage, you may have my copy in perfect secrecy."

"Oh, your copy came? Don't get up, please, and please excuse me if I don't wait. Your breakfast will all get cold if I keep you talking."

"Not at all. Yes, my copy came through."

She had arisen and walked to the door. I had noticed a small campstool folded and leaning against the wall, and now was surprised to see her pick it up and tuck it beneath her arm.

"Are you taking that?"

She held it so that it opened, showing its green canvas seat. "Yes, aren't you in favour of it?"

"It's æsthetic, if that's what you mean. But how odd! If you want something to sit on, why not take a blanket or an old coat?"

"Perhaps this isn't to sit down on."

I gaped. "What—what do you mean?"

She folded the stool and tucked it away again. Her smile was very sweet and provoking, and it held that little token of wistfulness which had never left it since Cosgrove's death.

The skirt swung briskly out, and the sound of the little boots receded and died away. On what wild search was she bound?

Then I stopped eating, while the idea that grew in my mind spread its ugly branches. What might a stranger think? Not I, of course, who would stake my life she is better than gold, but some newcomer from the outside world, such as the Scotland Yard official due here this evening? Might it not seem a pose? This resolve to play the rôle of detective, this secret roaming through the House in man's attire, this interest in my diary, and this secretive hunting on the hills—would they not appear parts of an assumed character? Ridiculous, of course—unthinkable, in actuality—but might it not be thought? And what trouble, even disaster, might not follow such a false impression?

Somehow I was not at all amused toward noon by an argument that sprouted up in the library between Crofts and Aire in connection with some phase of the Parson Lolly legend. Aire was devil's advocate in this discussion, and Crofts persisted in pooh-poohing the tale as all nonsense, tommy-rot, and rubbish.

"I thought you were a scientist," bullied our host, but Aire contented himself with a chuckle, and moved toward the Hall, whence the voice of Lord Ludlow came in a kind of shrill moan:

"...fundamental decencies...civilized life."

And I judged that Belvoir had just uttered some devastating platitude about the geisha girls or the way women choose their husbands in British Guiana. It occurred to me then a bit strongly that Belvoir plays the fool, and that if he really thinks our British morality unsuitable for a civilized temperament (*i. e.* his) he had better emigrate to the bush or to Terra del Fuego, where he may be uncramped among the broader and merrier folkways.

I have mentioned more than once, I believe, the sub-irritant effect Mrs. Belvoir has upon me; her hazy personality, taken with the odd remarks she lets fall, hint at something I can't quite define, but would like to very much.

When Aire went through the armoury door, only four of us were left in the library: Mrs. Belvoir, Alberta, Crofts, and I (in the seclusion of the tower). Mrs. Belvoir watched the Doctor's departure, then turned to Crofts with the promptitude of one who has at last the opportunity she has been waiting for.

"I do hope you won't mind tonight," she said.

It would not have been surprising if Crofts had failed to extract a meaning from this wish, but he seemed to grasp it. His cheek remained at the same full flush it had reached during the Aire controversy, while he turned his eyes slowly toward Mrs. Belvoir, and I thought that the lady had not chosen the likeliest time for wooing his good graces.

"You don't mean to say—" he rumbled.

"But dear Alberta doesn't mind—do you?" she asked in sudden appeal that was answered with ardour rather less than half its own.

"I didn't think it could do any harm," said Alberta, divided between a reassuring smile at her guest and a warning frown at her husband. "Probably the Scotland Yard man—"

"But it's for him I especially want to give a demonstration," declared Mrs. Belvoir with emphatic faintness. "I can help him so much. I think that perhaps the real difficulty we have had all along is that we have not looked beyond the visible. I do so wish Sir Brooke were here; he was so sympathetic. There were always such things of *real value* learned when he was present."

"I have it!" I exclaimed from my obscurity, striking my thigh. "Mrs. Belvoir, you are a spiritualistic medium!"

They all regarded me with amazement bold on their faces, and I turned my blatancy into apologetic curiosity. "Sorry, but I didn't know before, you see. How frightfully interesting. I hope you do give us a séance tonight, Mrs. Belvoir."

"Oh, all right," muttered Crofts. "But it's the police you'll have to convince, really."

"I'll deal with the police," said Mrs. Belvoir.

"As for Sir Brooke's absence," I remarked, "why may he not be present? Perhaps we shall have a message from him, Mrs. Belvoir."

I think she discerned levity in me. "Really, Mr. Bannerlee, you may be surprised by having that very thing happen." She glided from the room.

Crofts looked at me bitterly, as if he held me responsible for the whole business, but instead of pouring out vials of wrath he said, "How about a drink, Bannerlee? I need one."

"Oh, Crofts," reproached Alberta, "you know it's still morning."

"Well, I haven't had one so far, have I?" he retorted, ringing, and stared in oafish surprise when she departed promptly from the room. "What have I done now, I'd like to know?"

"You *are* getting peppered from all directions," I laughed. "But cheer up, old man," I added, hearing a measured tread in the corridor. "This staff of servants of yours certainly outdoes the crew of any sinking ship I've ever heard of in devotion to duty. After last night's catastrophe—well, they deserve medals, platinum ones."

Soames slid in and Crofts said, "Whiskey," cocking an eye at me to see if I approved.

"Yes, and by the way, Soames," I called, while the servant turned on his heel, "just tell us the truth, will you? Why aren't you and Morgan and the rest fifty miles away from here and running for your lives?"

His face was a flat mask, with expression ironed out of every feature. "I—I beg your pardon, sir? I don't understand."

"Oh, yes, you do. Come on, man," I rallied him. "What's this hold Blenkinson's got over you?"

His countenance remained under rigid muscular control, but his legs gave a little shiver. He looked at me, and his face was empty of thought, but then his gaze met his master's. He paled, for Crofts' glare demanded rather than invited confession.

"It's—it's Mr. Blenkinson's, er, theory, sir."

"My God, has Blenkinson a theory too!" Crofts shouted. "A speculative butler! What next? I don't pay him to have theories."

"No, sir," agreed Soames. "We all 'ave the greatest confidence in Mr. Blenkinson."

"No doubt," I said. "And Soames, ah, what is the nature of Mr. Blenkinson's theory?"

The servant had the look of a man ground between millstones. His neck undulated in a series of gulps.

"Out with it," I urged. "Confession is good for the soul."

Soames turned an imploring look at me, his eyes like those of a wretch *in extremis*.

"Oh, Blenkinson's theory be damned," growled Crofts impatiently; "but don't tell him I said so. Fetch the whiskey."

The servant dashed for the door, and it was Toby who brought in the decanter and glasses.

It is now 2.30 P.M.

An hour ago it was clear and mild; then the mist redoubled and a chill came into the air, something we have not experienced before by day.

She has not returned. I shall try to organize a searching party at once, and if no one else regards the situation seriously, I'll go alone to find her.

CHAPTER 24

BANNERLEE'S SECRET

2.45 P.M.

Salt shared my perturbation. Indeed, he adopted the idea of a searching expedition with such alacrity and energy that one might suppose Miss Lebetwood to be fleeing from justice!

There were some bitter things said of her, though, by those, even, who volunteered readiest for the search. Repressed criticisms of her seemingly callous behaviour since Cosgrove's death outcropped now. I stood by, a coward, for hot answers rose to my lips and I suppressed them. I remembered that from these hostile thoughts, thoughts more sinister might spring.

Just as they were going, I observed that Maryvale was not present. (Aire, too, was not among us.) Tenney volunteered the information, gained from Harmony, that Maryvale has again locked himself in his room. Seeking admittance in her morning round of the bedrooms, she found the door fastened and received a gruff intimation that she need not trouble to knock again until further notice.

I am almost as unwilling to leave Maryvale to his own devices as to leave Paula Lebetwood unsought for on the hills. But we *must* find her!

7.45 P.M.

The last stragglers have not even yet returned from the uplands.

Hours of starved hope they were, while I stumbled along the half-blind paths, often bewildered, once quite lost myself. It was dogged work. I never should have struggled through without an inexorable motive and the faintest glimmer of a clue, a clue offered me by Salt many days ago. Had he not told how in his boyhood he had found "something like" the oratory of St. Tarw? I had kept the directions he had given, and now in a forlorn hazard I followed them, since they alone might lead me to some definite place that she, too, might have sought.

In observing Salt's tuition, I was obliged to keep for the most part below the crown of the hills. The flanks were cut by gorges where water had eaten its way. In these places I made but indifferent progress. In a dusky dingle I did no better, and although I gasped in relief at finding what seemed a path, it proved unfriendly, for it led me into a covert of dogwood whose small green berries were turning purple-black, and deserted me there. I got out somehow, although spines clutched me. Before me, stretching into the upper fog, extended a curtain of rock and gravel. I attacked it with feet and hands.

It seemed to go up and up forever. In that frantic climb, out of a bottom soon invisible, up to a summit veiled in fog, I tore a finger-nail and broke into the flesh of my left palm. I paused on a splintery ledge to bind my handkerchief over the wound, and rested there awhile. It was then that I thought of looking, not up or down, but sidewise.

A brief cry escaped me. I could see further on the left, and what I saw quickened my heart.

A few yards away the rock curtain ended somewhat abruptly, and beyond appeared a brief slope full of stunted trees. Even further in the same direction, the trees gave place to shorter, tangled growth intermixed with grassy patches. Here and there a monolith thrust up from the surface, which on the whole was fairly level, though a vague darkness in the background showed that this clearing was not the summit of any hill, but a platform more or less below the highest elevation.

Along the outer edge of the cleared space stood a regiment of trees, whose ranks were quite dense enough to conceal what lay behind from eyes in the hollow of the Vale. Having gained the grassy platform with its curious black stones sprouting and littered about, I found that while I continued in the same direction over the tumbled grass full of small scarlet toadstools, the ground grew higher and the dark mass of the hilltop closer, while the platform narrowed.

My hope caught fire and blazed. I kept peering ahead and slightly upward, for the gentle slope persisted. Suddenly I saw Miss Lebetwood, very dim in the mist.

She was seated close under the shadowy brow of the hill, with her face away from me, and her head thrown back, leaning against something.

A lovely picture she had been that first night by the gate-house tower; now again I paused, rapt by the grace of her languid, lissome body, by the pale abstraction of her face—against the ancient gloom of the oratory of St. Tarw!

There was not the slightest doubt that this had been the devotional cell of the saint. Here stood the rude arch, still discernible though one or two of its stones had been displaced and the rest were mantled in moss and grass grown downward from above. The projection beside the door, where her head leaned, had surely once upon a time been the support of a holy shrine. These scattered rocky benches: on them had sat the small, dark, half-savage hill-folk, the strange congregations of the venerable man.

No, I would not rouse her from that mood of thought or vacancy; I would be still until she turned and looked at me. So minutes passed, while her image impressed itself in my mind, in my very heart of hearts. While I stood there in the grass, awaiting the first movement of her weary head, even breathing softly that she might not be disturbed, for the first time I dared to say to myself, bold and unafraid, "I love her."

She did quicken from her inanimate pose, she did turn her head and see me. She rose swiftly; already I had come very near to her.

When she attempted to speak, her voice faltered. "So—so you found me?"

"Yes, Paula," I said.

"I was waiting. I heard—"

My own voice filled the pause. "You don't mean that—you were waiting—for me?"

"Yes."

"You heard the others calling, and you waited for me?"

"Yes."

Then—I cannot describe what was, only what must have been, for the white-heat of those moments has annihilated the memory of them—she was close within my arms, and my lips reached hers. Yes, for that ineffable once, I must have kissed her, since I remember too well that when I would have drawn her to me again, she put me away with a gentle pressure of her hand against my arm.

She shook her head slowly, her gaze searching mine. "You—misunderstood, I think. I—I let you because of what I saw in your eyes. They were soft and wistful for a moment."

"But—Paula—"

"Now I think that you must never do that again."

My mind went cold and grey as the world about us. "I'm sorry, then. Indeed, I must have misunderstood."

I saw that some change had rushed over her. Her face became dull and sad, as if the clammy gloaming that darkened about us had penetrated to her heart. "Don't misunderstand me all over again; please don't. Your kisses might be very sweet, and their meaning might be dear to dream about. But you know that I have to set all the woman in me aside.... I must forget dreams," she said bitterly, and to my astonishment she put both hands across her eyes and commenced to sob, sinking down on the stone seat again. I stood by and felt the iron grind into my soul.

But half a minute later she looked up with a rueful smile through her tears. "How perfectly ridiculous of me. What must you think! Don't imagine for a minute that I was crying for any such preposterous reason as I said. It's just that I'm awfully, awfully tired, and I *felt* tired that moment. I was up nearly all last night over your diary. Please, have you a handkerchief I can use? I've nothing but one of these silly little women's affairs."

I handed over a fairly clean one. "Up all last night and in the hills all day! You're a Trojan. But at least you found what you were looking for?"

She ceased dabbing for a moment to give me a half-moist look. "Here, do you mean?"

"Why, of course."

"I found what I wanted, but it wasn't here. This was afterward. I somehow had a feeling that you would come here and discover me sooner or later. These *inane* tears."

I brooded on this for a while, while she removed the last traces of them. "I suppose it's no good asking where you found what you really wanted?"

"Why, yes—up there on Mynydd Tarw."

"But at least you aren't bringing it back with you as you declared you would, are you?"

She gave a strange laugh. "It was too big, a million times too big. So I have to be satisfied with carrying it here." She placed a finger against her forehead. "Now I am ready, sir, if you'll take me back down with you. Please let's go now. There is so much to be done tonight."

"You shall rest tonight, nothing else."

"On the contrary—don't think I'm rude—there's everything else. Yes, yes, really. Come, let's go."

She picked up the little campstool, but I took it from her. Slowly we turned and went away from that place, and while we passed through a huddling hazel wood where sheep had made a track before us, the sun at last thridded the mist with hazy golden beams. While we descended the glen, I looked at her face with the light playing upon its firm, rounded surfaces and gleaming in her eyes. She was weary, indeed, with what seemed more than physical exhaustion; I slipped my arm about her when she appeared almost unable to pick her footing on the precarious slope. But, "Oh, no, no," she said, resisting so softly that I pitied her, and took my arm away.

When we had discovered the path that led down to Aidenn Water and were well on our slanting way to the valley bottom, she found more strength in the smoother footing. Suddenly I felt that she was scrutinizing me, and I turned my head to hear her ask:

"What did it remind you of—that place up there?"

"A graveyard," I answered almost without thought.

"Just so. Tell me honestly; have you never been there before?"

"Before?—there?" I repeated, quite truly surprised.

"Don't temporize, please. Confess that you were there before but didn't set it down when you wrote your journal. That was the place where you fell when you escaped from the bull, and it was where you took shelter from the storm the day you saw the rainbow. Wasn't it?" I did not answer but she insisted. "I suppose you had some foolish fear that if you wrote about it and someone—like poor me—read of the discovery before you had published it to the world, you might lose the credit for it. Yes? For it *was* your discovery, and I only followed the hints you gave."

"Yes," I said promptly, since my secret was guessed. "It was my discovery, and I wanted to preserve it for myself. I thought I had written enough, without being explicit to the point of revelation, to sustain any claim I might need to make afterward. I suppose you think I was a very large and egregious idiot?"

For a little while she did not answer. When I turned to look at her, her eyes seemed to dwell not on the present but on the past, and there was the intention of a smile in her face. "No; I think you were an—antiquarian. Ah, you scholars!"

"Well, in archæological circles you know—" I broke off.

"Archæological circles seem about as important as ant-hills to me, just now. One thing, though, I really learned last night and today—a platitude I never quite believed in."

"A platitude—and not yet discredited?"

She gave a little laugh. "I mean the one about boxing up truth. You can hammer down board after board, but the truth is like smoke: it always finds a new chink in the cover to escape from. Don't you see"—she gave a smothered laugh—"the moment you began keeping your archæological cat in the bag, you had to use all kinds of devices of wire and rope to keep it there, and more often than not it was you and not the cat who was tangled!"

I looked at her in comic dismay. "Well! If you've found that out from the diary you must be a perfect demon of ratiocination!"

"Hardly; it was obvious. For instance, when Mr. Salt offered you his suggestions for finding the oratory, you felt obliged to skid all around the truth that you already knew where it was. You even said that finding it seemed 'superfluous.' That was rather neat, I thought."

I grinned. "So do I. As a fact, I followed his route to the oratory today. And now I have a gleam in my prophetic soul that you found discrepancies in the rainbow section of the diary."

She weighed her answer. "Well, I don't know. I saw the discrepancies readily enough. You never were on Whimble all that afternoon, were you, in spite of the suggestions you scattered to that effect? I always thought archæologists were profound people, but I had no idea they were so sly."

I mused. "Hm. You are perfectly right. 'I headed straight for Whimble....'"

"Yes, and afterward, 'It would take me some time to get from where I was to the edge of Mynydd Tarw.' That was so, no doubt, but I'd bet a—a lot that you were on Mynydd Tarw all the while."

"Naturally, but I wasn't going to say so, when the oratory was under the edge of that particular hill. Yes, you're right: my secret entailed quite a number of peccadilloes."

I saw her smiling at me. "They became quite inveterate, didn't they? But the whole thing goes back to the platitude. Squeeze the truth in one place and it sticks out in another. Because you *would* have the secret of the oratory all to yourself, you had to conceal the innocent fact that you accidentally left a book there."

I stared at her as at a miracle, which indeed she was. "Come, come; this is on the thick side. You must have been shadowing me."

"Only in brain-waves. It was your copy of the Book of Sylvan Armitage, wasn't it? How did you happen to leave it there? I can guess you had it out of your knapsack and studied it for comparison with the place you had fallen to. Then, perhaps, you laid it down—"

"I did, and leaned back to rest, just as I found you doing this afternoon. The Book slipped off the stone and fell inside the shelter of the oratory. I didn't notice it when I started up and left the place. But how on earth did you know?"

"You mustn't think it was so wonderful for me to see a plain nose on a plain face. To begin with, I was surprised to death when I learned that you hadn't brought your own copy of the Armitage with you, but had to send for it from Balzing. Was it likely that you would leave behind the one work which referred to the oratory of St. Tarw? Then that evening in the library after the rainbow, some of Lib's remarks—'Having the hump,' and so forth—sounded as if you might be concealing something that you had brought with you under your coat. And finally—well this alone would have been enough to tell me—the day you were supposed to receive it through the mail, you didn't call at the Post Office for it; when you came home from Old Aidenn, you gave New Aidenn a wide berth and crossed the Smatcher."

"Out of my own inkwell I stand condemned," I laughed. "It's uncanny, that's what it is, the way you get inside my cranium and read my secret thoughts. Still, you haven't told me what the fundamental deduction was. It couldn't have been a mere guess. How did you *know* that I wasn't on Whimble when I drew the map?"

"I think you are playing Doctor Watson on purpose. Why, that was the essence of simplicity. Why, a *primitive* mind could have told that. What do you suppose I brought the campstool for? It was as simple as—as rule of three. You'll have to discover that for yourself."

After silence:

"What was that you said—about the rapture you felt the first time you wandered on the uplands? You never could feel the same freedom? You never could be so happy again?"

"I think I never shall."

"Nor I. I hate this place. It has robbed me of something—something more than love or any little thing like that."

"What do you mean?" I asked, appalled—and when she did not answer, I asked again, with my hand clenched about her wrist and my eyes burning into her face, "What do you mean?"

"I'm not sure...but I suppose I mean...innocence. Since I came here, something has happened that I never can forget. I think it will make all my life worse."

We went on. The sunlight was dying. The trees became spectral. In me, who walked beside this wonderful, clear-spirited girl, a monstrous horror welled.

I had a sense of vast, dark, insufferable wings hovering down. Was it fated that I should need to protect her against herself? Long before we reached the House, that I had sworn to do, at all costs, whatever should betide.

CHAPTER 25

THE FLIGHT OF PARSON LOLLY

(There ended my diary. Thenceforth I was to be like a man in a maelstrom. And now that circumstances have stayed my hand from its task for weeks on end, I have no confidence that I can record with due proportion and emphasis events which seem to have been fantastic and instantaneous as dreams. Frantic suspense, frozen horror, and the rest are now a whirling memory. But I hope, above all else, that whoever reads these lines may feel, as those who knew her did, the splendid nervous courage, the shrewd discernment, and the strange compassion and mercy, of Paula Lebetwood!)

Make no mistake. The weary, faltering girl at my side—never, never for an instant did I suspect her.

Yet while we lagged through a ruined fairyland, past the wreck of Sir Pharamond's first hold, beneath branches where the rooks were brawling, and between the ordered files of the summer-house park—all the way my heart grew blacker, and the incubus weighed heavier on my soul. I feared for her, and fear pressed cold fingers against my lips.

Blasphemous thoughts; they were not mine. I had no thoughts of her but reverence.

They might have been the jangling voices of the birds themselves: "Look! Here comes the foreign woman who was pledged to the Kingmaker, but is going to marry his millions instead! Why has she never wept a tear for the man in his shroud?" What if the trees had voices, these grey and sombre sycamores? "We saw what happened in the two twilights. We know where the golden-haired girl was when Cosgrove met his fate. We know when she left the strawberry grove the day that Heatheringham rushed toward death. We saw her slip across the shadowed lawn—"

No, no! If trees could speak, they would declare her innocence.

Not trees but men would be her judges, cunning men, who might weave about her a web of suspicion with strands as fine and strong as silk.

Scotland Yard might be waiting for us when we returned; that is, a brisk, clear-headed, observant, utterly unprejudiced investigator, a person whose mind as nearly as might be resembled an inductive and deductive machine. He would sweep the ground clear of the débris of false starts and idle speculations, and construct anew.

The deaths: what would the lynx of justice discover immediately in respect of them? He would hear of a motive, money. How should he know better than to impute a sordid impulse to this high-minded girl? He would hear of a quarrel on the afternoon of Cosgrove's death. How should he know that there had been more than mere anger in her mood when she parted from us, that there had been dignity, aloofness, a temper far above reprisal?

But there was worse, much worse. She may have been with Cosgrove the moment he was struck down!

Belvoir, coming toward the towers, had seen the Irishman with canvas lifted regarding the puny battle-axe. In the mixed light, Belvoir had not been positive he *had* seen Cosgrove, but the likelihood was that he had attested to less rather than more than the truth. The American girl might have been beyond the Irishman at that moment, concealed partly by his bulk, partly by the darkness of her gown in the twilight. I, of course, had come past the spot afterward and found the lawn empty, but the two might easily have gone through one of the entrances of the House and re-emerged shortly after I had made my reconnaissance from the parapet. What brief, passionate scene could then have taken place, such as would have ended by Cosgrove's turning away and her hammering him with a rough-and-ready chunk of rock snatched up from the rim of the flower-bed, I left to the professional imagination.

In Heatheringham's death, we knew her insistence that she had disobeyed his bidding, and her declaration of what she had seen. But, again, there was not a tittle of proof of her assertion that she had remained on the edge of the strawberry trees. Quite safely she could have slipped back into the House. I wondered, in spite of the arm thrust through the glass, if the detective might not have been outside the House when he pressed the trigger, and that straightway he rushed into the Hall (pursuing something?)—to meet his death. Who waited for him there? No one could have, save Paula Lebetwood.

Black—it was black.

I tried to gain comfort from the obscurities that would confront Scotland Yard if he tried to build up a theory in this wise. I recalled the bone, the laugh, the pig's gore, and other unsolved conundrums. But Scotland Yard, being an experienced hand, would be sure to fit them in somewhere. I was sick at heart.

Yes, I must protect her against the world, and, if need be, against herself. The proof would be in action. I began wondering whom I could trust.

When we came to the fringe of the sycamore park and passed alongside the cypress trees, one first-storey window showed light in the northern wall of the House, and we could see radiance from others down the long façade.

"Miss Mertoun has returned." It was the only speech either of us had offered in two dark and desolate miles.

"Millicent?" The American girl halted in surprise. "Did they make her go out, too?"

"She volunteered like the rest of the ladies for searching in the Vale itself."

"Darling Millicent. I love her better than anything else on earth. She shouldn't have tried to find me, Mr. Bannerlee. She isn't strong, you know, and this has been a terrible, tragic week for her. She should never have come to Aidenn Vale, but I didn't—understand then, as I do now."

Somehow we did not go straight on, but lingered there by the cypresses with their low-hung darkness.

"But her week has not been as tragic as yours."

Her voice was sombre. "More, much more."

"What!" I came closer, peered into her face, where the dusk had erected shadows. "What do you mean?"

"You haven't wondered, I see, about Millicent and Sean."

"Wondered? Wondered what, in God's name?"

She spoke wearily. "You didn't know Sean, of course. Neither did I, I suppose."

"What do you mean?" I cried again, with an intolerable heaviness in me, remembering Lib.

"Religion and sensuality: they go together often, don't they? I thought that if I recognized that—streak in Sean I might disregard it and it would be like a thing that never was. If that had been all...."

I caught up the silence. "You can never make me believe—that Miss Mertoun—"

"Oh, of course not. She wasn't like the others.... She hasn't offended me; I'm the offender...."

"Paula, you mustn't stop. Tell me what you mean."

"It's beastly of me, I suppose...especially when someone else... I wonder why it is we confide in people we half-know instead of our closest friends. But it's horrible to have a thing pent up in your brain...like a deadly growth."

"Tell me, Paula."

"If I hadn't come along, Millicent would be Mrs. Cosgrove now. It sounds—almost grotesque, doesn't it? But there it was, a fact that months and even years couldn't kill. I never had the least inkling of it—oh, Millicent's been a loyal friend to me—until we were all here and it was—too late. Millicent came, you see, since if she didn't—I would never have had a Bidding Feast without Millicent, and she knew it. But I never guessed…until she told me, after midnight, the night you came."

"She—loved him still?"

"No, hated him then. But the old heart-wound would break out during sleep. His music, as she called it, came to her through her dreams. Then she answered what she believed to be—his call."

A little wind came winding down the Vale and wrapped its chilly arm about us. She said, very low: "That was what I meant, partly, when I spoke of lost innocence a little while ago. I have changed toward people since I came here. I think I can never trust a person again." Then quickly, "We must go in. They'll be wanting to know I'm safe."

I followed where she made a road through the darkness.

We reached the House at seven-fifteen. At the bottom of the stairs she turned. "Thank you—thank you more than I can say. May I have the camp-stool? I must go up now, really. I—I—have to—think over tonight."

I handed over the stool. "If ever—" I commenced, feeling my voice shake in my throat.

The boy Toby, his hair all on end as usual, crossed the corridor from the dinner-room to the Hall. She called his name, and the lad reappeared, coming toward us bashfully. His eyes, turned on her, were filled with something like awe, and I remembered how she had made this seemingly lumpish lad her excellent and devoted scholar. He now carried a few yards of insulated wire.

"Has Superintendent Salt returned?"

"Yes, from the hills, Miss. He came back early, but he's gone away again."

"Did he leave any message?"

"He said you wasn't to mind if he didn't bring his friend from—some-where—"

"Scotland Yard?"

"Yes, that's right. He wouldn't bring him tonight. He said you was to go ahead anyhow because the French womenfolks was coming with Constable Pritchard."

"French women!" I exclaimed in surprise and pleasure. "Does he mean that the sisters Delambre have been brought back?"

"Sure to be," said Toby.

"By George, I'll be tickled to see what they look like. But what does it all mean? No one could imagine—"

Miss Lebetwood silenced me with a gesture and an eager question. "He was working here this afternoon, then, wasn't he?"

"Yes, Miss, but it was a secret or somefing. He put the maids out of the house at half-past three."

"Three-thirty!" I exclaimed again, indignantly now. "He didn't waste much of his precious time in the search!" I asked the lad, "Why did he make the women-servants leave the building? He did, didn't he?"

"Yes, sir; he was going to use some gas from a little tank he had with him all over the ground floor of the House. He said it was a deadly poisonous gas, and unless they were looking for their deaths if they got a whiff they had better go down to New Aidenn for the rest of the afternoon. Wheeler was in the search; so I drove 'em all down to the bridge in the big car," Toby recited with pride.

"And did you come back for a whiff?" asked Miss Lebetwood, smiling faintly.

"No, Miss; I went to my workroom in the stables and did some more on my radio. I only remembered about a quarter past six that I had to fix the lights in the Hall, and when I came to the House I met Mr. Salt and the constable's brother that wasn't here before coming out with the gas tank. 'It's all right,' he said. 'Tell 'em they can go anywhere they like now. I've sucked the gas back into the respirator; so there's no danger for that matter of fact.' And then he told me what I told you."

"I suppose most of our people have returned?"

"Yes, Miss. The ladies are all upstairs or somewhere. There's them back from New Aidenn, too, and Mr. Blenkinson and some of the others from the hills. If you wasn't found by nine o'clock, they was going to 'phone up Penybont and Bleddfa and maybe get a bloodhound and have a grand search like they almost had for Sir Brooke Mortimer."

"Thank you, Toby," said the girl, "and thank you again, Mr. Bannerlee. I *shall* have to do a bit of thinking now." She went quickly, almost lightly, up the steps. Somehow, she had drawn comfort from Salt's strange behaviour.

I followed Toby into the Hall. Quite by chance I had found the person I could trust, one whose allegiance to the American girl might be as great as mine.

He was upon a lofty step-ladder planted beneath the chandelier which hung some distance clear of the musicians' gallery. Below him rested a bushel basket partly filled with electric bulbs.

"Will you be there long, Toby?"

"Only to take out the rest of the bulbs, sir, and connect a bit of wire with the wall-fixture in case they needs it. Only a minute or two, sir."

I drew close to the foot of the ladder and spoke very softly. "Toby—can you get an hour off before very late tonight—to do something for Miss Lebetwood?"

"For Miss Paula?" His funny hair seemed to be a forest of notes of exclamation. "Of *course* I can, sir, for Miss Paula."

"Right! I knew you would. Come down here a minute, and I'll give you directions. This is very secret, mind. If you should meet even Miss Paula herself, remember you're not to show a sign you're the wiser."

I laid the trappings of mystery on very thick, enough to make the souls of a dozen lads lick their lips. I explained how a message might be delivered at the House later on tonight that would make it necessary for Miss Lebetwood, and perhaps Miss Mertoun, to leave without word or warning to anyone by the eleven o'clock train. Secrecy and haste were the points I stressed. He fell into the plot with so much spirit that I felt a little ashamed of the deception I was practising. With eagerness that ran before my suggestions, he promised to be at New Aidenn station when it opened for the 9.40 train, and to purchase with money I gave him two tickets for London available by the late express. He would leave the tickets for me *in the mail*. We went into the armoury and agreed on a definite spot. He would also secrete two ladies' bicycles, property of the Clays, beneath the bush opposite the third oak tree on the left-hand side of the drive after passing the gate-house. We went over that complex direction again and again.

Yes, in these days of the many-tentacled police, the telegraph, and the radio, I was planning for Paula Lebetwood an escape by flight. With two hours' clear start, for I would see that the telephone did not function and that the shaky bridge should go down behind the pursued, I could almost guarantee scot-freedom. For of course those tickets would not be used for getting to London, not when the express connected at Leominster with fast trains running both north and south. To what destination I would direct the fugitives, I had better not say, but it was one which would afford a refuge almost before the wires were singing with the alarm for her capture.

At that moment Aire slipped in from the darkness through one of the french windows. His head was bare, his clothing was somewhat dishevelled, and he seemed to lack for breath. His mouth was set, with its thin bluewhitish lips drawn back from the teeth. He stared at us some time before speaking; then his voice, the first time I had known it to be so, was instinct with fear.

"Bannerlee, seen Maryvale?"

"I've just returned with Miss Lebetwood. What makes you ask?"

"He's—gone."

"He'll come back."

"I'm sure he will. Come in here, Bannerlee."

Quite astonished by his tone, I followed him toward the library, turning at the door to give a pithy glance at the boy, whose hair now looked like a forest of query-notes. When I entered the library, Aire had thrown himself down in one of the big leather arm-chairs in a posture of complete relaxation, and was breathing heavily. Again it was some time before he spoke.

"He's gone, God knows where. He left me an hour ago while we were walking among the strawberry trees. Went snap off, like breaking a stick, while I was in the middle of a sentence."

"Why, Doctor," I exclaimed, with a snort of assumed cheerfulness, "surely you're making too much of this."

He sprang up, paced the breadth of the room, ugly wrinkles on his brow. "I hope I am. I hope I am. But I've bitched the thing so. And this afternoon he seemed in perfect possession of himself. I've been so damned optimistic that now the reverse— He seemed perfectly normal late this afternoon, you understand; in fact the two of us were planning—no matter. I must go out again."

"I'll come along with you."

"No, thanks. I'll have to manage him alone. It will be 'Horse and Hattock in the Devil's name,' and I fancy I'm the only one who can play up to him."

"But you'll be in danger."

He gave a short laugh. "I think not. I'm more afraid of the things that can't hurt." He looked out to the lawn. "Thank God for a clear night, and moonlight. You know, the trees seem to have faces in their trunks; they seem to be grinning and mowing in the wind. That's the sort of drivel this thing's brought me to. Well, I'm off."

He made toward the door, but paused with his hand on it. "Don't say a word of this to anyone, Bannerlee. I'll need a free hand if I'm to bring it off. Cheerio."

He plunged into the night. I saw him cross the silver carpet of the lawn and disappear between the gigantic jaws of the gate-house towers.

A moment later in the corridor I met Harmony carrying a tray up to "the young ladies." She told me that cold viands were laid out in the dinner-room for those lagging in from the hills. But in spite of my three hours' struggle, I was in no humour for feeding, especially since I was bound to encounter the others and would have to repeat my adventures again and again.

I asked the girl if there had been any fresh development during my absence.

"Did you hear about what they dug up this afternoon, sir?"

"Great Scott! You don't mean another corpse?"

"Lor', no, sir, not human. In the garden, it was, where the dogs were scratching the place to pieces. Someone said get a spade and dig and see what's there, and they found it."

"What did they find?"

"A little pig, sir. And it was wrapped in some black cloth they said must be Parson Lolly's gown, only it was all tore up and full of holes and had some funny bits of red paper pinned to it. They do say that Parson Lolly is too tall for a gown like that. We met Superintendent Salt when we were coming back from the town, and he was carrying it with him."

"So," I remarked. "It looks to me as if the Superintendent took advantage of Miss Lebetwood's absence to spend a busy afternoon down here."

"Lor', yes, sir. He was using the gas-expirator and fair drove us out of the house."

"I'm glad he made such a thorough job of inspirating the gas again."

"Yes, sir, or it wouldn't be safe. It's that wonderful, sir."

"It is," I agreed heartily, and cursed—to myself.

She with her tray went down the passage while I went up the second flight, feeling not the shadow of a suspicion of my darling, but the certainty that before the night was past, she would be accused. I hurried past Maryvale's portal with an aching heart.

Yet such was the settled habit of the week that when I reached my own door, the turmoil of my mind was stilled. This lonely chamber, which had such baneful associations for me a week ago, had become a harbour of refuge. Whatever strife and doom might wait outside, here the ceiling aslope, the candle-bracket askew, the oaken chest, and the narrow window before my table invited me to my work.

I fell to. I wrote steadily. I forgot to be hungry. Once the sound of a gong quivered through the House, but not until long after it had died away did I consider what it meant. Then I set down my pen. Mrs. Belvoir's séance must be in progress, and Scotland Yard was doubtless there. I must attend.

I secured my invaluable pocket light before setting out. Past Maryvale's door forbid, down the long stairs, through the corridor of faces—until a murmurous voice reached me from the Hall of the Moth, a voice whose tone I recognized though the words were indistinct. Yes, Mrs. Belvoir was probing beyond the visible.

Softly I opened the door behind the musicians' stair, tiptoed over the threshold, and stood concealed within. Great curtains shut out the moonlight from the Hall, which was dark indeed, save for the circle of bulbs on the circumference of the chandelier. These, cased by Toby in paper, gave very little illumination, and that of a mysterious tinge. At the other end of the room wavered a lazy fire, composed for the most part of bluish flame.

The people seated around the table, which had been placed not far from the musicians' stairs, were so vague that I could not tell their attitude toward the proceedings. I observed at once that Mrs. Belvoir was not going to "bring the spirits and all," not yet, at any rate. For on the table was spread some dark cloth above which I caught the faint glimmer of glass: a crystal sphere. The woman seated deep in her chair before the ball must be the pythoness herself.

Her voice had lapsed when I entered, and a long silence ensued. Then she said: "It's no use. I've lost it again," and I saw a white arm reach up. Instantly a dazzling light shone above her head, from a special globe connected with the wall-fixture, and Mrs. Belvoir was gazing intently into the crystal ball. I now saw that the sphere was erected on a small tripod with legs of different-coloured metals, and that this structure stood upon a square yellow velvet cloth laid over a cloth of blue. A mouldy, triangular crust of bread was placed underneath the crystal, and some statement I had once heard or read, that "bread possesses a potent protective magic against evil forces," occurred to me to explain its presence.

Neither Salt nor any stranger was there. Mrs. Belvoir, attired in pale mauve ninon, a heliotrope band above her forehead, and an amethyst pin at her breast, was brooding over the crystal with eyes that widened and narrowed with the phase of her thought. Those pale sapphire eyes were darkened with intensity, and the customary indistinctness of her face—a mermaid-under-water look—was quite gone. Sometimes her hands clasped or slid about the sphere; sometimes her fingers rested on her temples or tapped them gently. Beyond a doubt, she was sincere.

The assisting parties were either slightly embarrassed or strongly impressed, all save Belvoir, who sat opposite her; on his face lived a smile of scepticism. Up went the arm and the Hall was dim once more.

"I have it now," said the seeress: "I am in fog, deep fog."

"Good," came a *sotto voce* from the other end of the table, but the word was drowned in the current of her speech. Leaning back, but apparently still gazing at the sphere, in trance-life passivity, she seemed not so much to utter words as to let the words flow from her mouth.

"I am in fog, thick fog; it clings about me." Her hands made dim outward movements, as if pressing away the mist that enveloped her. "I am lost, and there is a malignant spirit nearby, but I am not sure I know that—yet. I sit down—on a rock. I am not very hungry, but since there is nothing else to do, I eat what I have brought with me. I wait for light to penetrate the fog. I wish to find something; perhaps I fear the malignant spirit that is near. I wish to find the ancient hermit's cell. It is a place hallowed by good works and piety. The malignant spirit will not dare come near me there. I eat and wait. The mist clears partly away at last. I go on. The sun shines on me; I am glorified...."

I suddenly realized it was my story she told. There was nothing wonderful in this, to be sure, for the narrative of my afternoon on the hills had long been common property. I listened with care, to see if she included some detail proving her version to be a brain-picture really evoked by the crystal and having objective authority. But all she added to the fable was the "malignant spirit" hovering near me all the while, a presence which I certainly had no idea was dogging me on the hilltops.

It became apparent that the seeress was not interested in me but in the spirit, and some time before the dénouement I had an inkling of how the story would end.

"I am fleeing from the malignant spirit in its carnal shape. I allow it to overtake me—so far, no farther. We are approaching the brink of the cliff. I leap aside, and the animal plunges into the gulf. I am saved, and I hear the carnal shape of the spirit go thundering down, down, down. I am saved, and the bull is dead."

Silence.... When Mrs. Belvoir spoke again, her voice had lost its dreaminess and become positive. But she spoke with effort; the phrases seemed wrung out of her.

"The bull is dead.... But spiritual force...is never destroyed.... The bull is dead.... The malignant spirit is living still.... It never ceases to operate.... It is localized...."

A small sound shattered the tension of that moment: merely the opening of one of the french windows.

"My God, what's that?" cried Eve Bartholomew, before someone reached above Mrs. Belvoir's head and lit the bright globe once more. Mrs. Belvoir turned, intending angry remonstrance, but her voice was stilled by one look at Doctor Aire.

He was coatless and collarless, and his shirt and trousers were miry. His small yellow head seemed to have turned almost white, save for a ragged cut across his forehead, and while he spoke the man leaned hard on the back of the *Brocade de Lyons* couch as if in the last throes of exhaustion.

Everyone was standing up; my presence excited no surprise.

"Maryvale's—somewhere near."

"Doctor! What's happened to you?" cried Crofts.

"I've had a bout with him on the tennis court. He was a few stone too heavy for me. I saw him heading for the House—probably wants something that's in his room. I'm afraid—he's insane."

"What shall we do, then?" asked Crofts, become very cool in the crisis.

"Keep a watch at every entrance, enough of us at each place to tackle him safely."

"Stephen, you mustn't go out again. You've done too much already," said Alberta.

But Aire, though he swayed, hung on grittily, and shook his head. "No, thanks. A stiff drink will put me right. Just have the men-servants in here, Crofts, and—"

Miss Mertoun gave a shrill scream. A creature was looking at us through the open entrance behind Aire—a strange creature.

The thing that looked at us was using Maryvale's face, but it was not Maryvale any longer. The countenance, blank of any jot of humanity, had become a mere bag with features. It lingered there only for a moment, staring at us with incomprehension so complete that a pang of pity thrilled through me. A woman sobbed. The face was gone.

Pell-mell the men were gone, too, in a wild chase scattering across the lawn, and I among them. Yet sorry as I was for Maryvale, he did not concern me now. I had sterner work even than trammelling a moonlight madman.

I determined to risk the notice of my absence in order to make certain that the bicycles were properly waiting where Toby had promised to conceal them. Keeping under the shadow of trees where I could, I hastened across the southern lawn toward the oaks that guard the drive below the gate-house towers. I was just in time to see someone drag one of the bicycles from its bushy covert into the full moonlight and bend over the front tyre with a gleaming blade ready to slash. I sprang upon this man, mastered him more by the surprise of my leap than by main strength. He fell face upward, groaning. His knife lay on the grass ten feet away.

"Morgan! What crazy work is this?"

He thrashed about in my inexorable grip, and blurted out his words in speech that reverted toward the primitive. "The killers, the killers! They bikes was for them. I saw the lad fetch 'em and hide 'em, aye I did. 'E's sweet on 'er since she took notice of 'im."

"What are you talking about?" I blustered. "What do you know about the murderers?"

He struggled to rise, but I let my weight bear down, and he relapsed with another groan, though certainly not hurt. "I know who did the killin'. I've known all along."

I shook him roughly by the shoulders. "Don't lie to me. Come, out with it, now, or I'll throttle you."

"Mr. Blenkinson told us. It's the sure truth."

"*Blenkinson!*" I bawled. "By God, Blenkinson's got something to answer for to me. What lies has he been spreading?"

"He has the proofs. It's sure as if 'e saw 'em with 'is own eyes."

"Saw *what*? Saw *who*?"

"Saw the killin's. The three Americans did 'em, and they'll make shares of Mr. Cosgrove's money."

My fingers itched for his throat, but black fear blazed in my heart. "Liar!" I screamed. "They'll hang you sooner than *her*! Don't you know she won't touch a penny of it until the killer's found!"

The man on the ground maintained a sullen obstinacy. "Sometimes them hangs as isn't guilty, and them suffers as finds out. The milkman knew it was 'er, and look what 'appened to 'im."

"You poor, blind fool," I exclaimed bitterly. "There's jealousy and hatred in this somewhere. Damn Blenkinson. Why, there isn't a particle of evidence—"

"There is, there is," he gasped. "There's court evidence to 'ang 'er when Mr. Blenkinson comes out with it."

"What evidence? Tell me!"

He writhed in my clutch. "The beetle-stone as she lost from 'er ring that day. She tried to keep it secret, but it got about. Mr. Blenkinson found it right in the same place as the stone she did the killin' with. There wasn't a foot between 'em."

I pressed my fists against his chest, with a downward thrust now and then for emphasis. "Your fine Blenkinson's a liar, do you hear? His evidence, as you call it, isn't worth a pin. And if he whispers a word of his slander, and it comes to my ears, I'll thrash him within an inch of his life, do you hear? And the same applies to you—you contemptible—"

I stood up quickly. Men were crowding out of the plantation near Whimble-foot and clamouring toward the House. Had the quarry turned? I must be present now at any cost.

This man was cowed sufficiently. He still lay supine; I prodded him with my foot. "Remember!" I warned him darkly, and commenced running toward the mansion, stooping to seize the knife where it glittered on the turf.

Once only I paused for a moment and looked back. Was there something—someone—moving stealthily toward the man, who was sitting up now and feeling himself for bruises? A moment later the figure of a woman emerged from the shadows, crossed quickly to Morgan, and seemed to lift him bodily from the ground. I did not immediately grasp that she had lugged him up by the ear. Now they were arguing, gesticulating, and though I had heard it seldom, I knew the prim voice of Miss Ardelia Lacy.

Smiling to myself, I pressed on.

The half-dozen men who reached the corner of the House more or less in a pack were in the nick of time to see the wretched Maryvale, driven from cover to cover like a hunted beast, drag his body, which had never before seemed ponderous, to the base of one of the gate-house towers. He carried what seemed a club with an enormous broadened head.

He turned there at bay while we closed in upon him, and the awful wreck of his face with its glaring eyes and bared teeth in the moonlight will haunt me to my death. He was a beast. While we stood speechless, he began to climb.

One hand gripped the queer-looking club, but grasping the ivy with one hand alone, he raised himself steadily. It was agony to watch this man-turned-ape mounting where none of us dared to follow. In the thick wavering growth that clung to the tower sometimes he swung pendulum-wise, sometimes was almost buried in the foliage, but his ascent was sure as if he climbed the stairs within. We cried out to him appeals and abuse; I do not think he heard us. Someone ran to the stables, shouting for a ladder.

Maryvale reached the angle where the covered bridge meets the wall of the tower. Here the ivy thins, and the man made a wide stop to the roof of the bridge. Then, surely, I felt the supreme horror, when Maryvale, using the base of a window-slit for foot-rest, lifted himself over the edge of the turret-roof and carefully but expeditiously crawled up the slope of stone toward the pointed top.

We held on shouting, some of us, in sheer desperation. Pendleton made a frenzied effort to climb the ivy, failed. Maryvale crept on, his whole body flat against the roof, save for the arm which held the club-like mass. He reached the pinnacle and lifted himself to a precarious standing posture, one foot firm on the very apex, the side of the other foot pressed against the slope.

For a few moments he bent over the object he had carried; then when he straightened his body, his arm above his head brandished a flaming, sizzling torch, and he uttered the only words I had heard him speak that day. He called out to the night at large:

"Lolly, Lolly, Parson Lolly!" His voice gloated above the hiss of the torch. "Who's the Parson? I'M THE PARSON! AND NOW I'M GOING OVER THE HILLS: PARSON LOLLY FLIES!"

The torchlight danced in his face while he laughed shrilly. Then he launched himself into the air in an enormous leap.

He fell almost but not quite clear of the sloping roof. Striking it all awry, he dashed against the roof of the bridge and on down. Mercifully, he was hurled toward the wall of the tower, and his foot caught for a second in some loop of the ivy-twine twenty feet from the ground. His swinging body struck the wall a terrific blow, and he hung head downward for a moment; his torch, which had drawn a flaming mark across the night, now blazed upward enveloping him with its flames. Only for an instant, however. The impact of the collision with the wall had stunned him, and the torch fell from his hand. The ivy gave way, and the madman, part of his clothing afire, fell insensible to the ground at our feet.

CHAPTER 26

BLOOD ON THE PORTRAIT

We had carried Maryvale down to the bridge, and the ambulance from the Cottage Hospital at Kington had been waiting to take the unfortunate man away. We did not know until later, of course, that Maryvale would never walk again, though the delusion which had unhinged his mind no longer held him in thrall.

Now we were returning to the House, I and the remnant of the men of the Bidding Feast. We were a straggling squad. The sense of Fate, of dark wings closing down, of stern gates clashing, swept over me again while I wondered which of us would be the next to suffer. One by one our little group reassembled in the library. There the women were waiting; there, too, stood Maryvale's picture of the headless Parson, more enigmatic than before. Yes, even with the madman's words ringing in our ears, none of us could believe that he had indeed been the arch-lord of disorder who may have destroyed two men.

Mrs. Belvoir, purpureal priestess, was making agitated efforts to reassemble her devotees that she might reveal the further activities of the "malignant spirit"; but the devotees were very slippery. Indeed, it was natural that after the catastrophe of Maryvale, other things should disintegrate, and although the terror spread through the House tightened the little knot of us, soon we might have wandered off to bed, unless a sudden loud knocking had been audible.

"The front door, isn't it?" asked Miss Lebetwood.

Our host said it was, and added he wondered what the devil—

"It is a sign for me, I think." Addressing Mrs. Belvoir: "Marvel, you must let me take charge now."

"Why, what do you mean?" demanded the seeress.

"We shall see in a moment."

Alberta's firm hand had restrained Crofts from jumping into the corridor to answer the knock himself. Presently Soames sidled into the room with a salver which he presented to Miss Lebetwood. Regarding him closely, I thought he gave her a slanting, snake-like look of mingled fear and malevolence—and yet on the surface his countenance remained perfectly respectful.

"A telegram for you, Miss."

"Thank you."

Lib gurgled, "Why, Paula, someone's had the cheek to open it!"

"I know," answered Miss Lebetwood, withdrawing two closely-filled sheets from the envelope already slit. "Those were my instructions."

Crofts asked sharply, "Don't they know those should be 'phoned here?'"

"My directions again," said the American girl evenly, without glancing up from the sheet in her hand. Her brief, self-possessed words made us realize of a sudden that she had assumed leadership quietly and confidently. "There will be no answer, Soames," she remarked, and the man slid out shadow-wise.

A silence supervened, while we stared at her and she read the message to the very end. When she was through, her clear blue eyes were bright with exultation.

"Yes, it's what I expected! I think, people, that we will see the end of our ghastly bewilderment tonight. Won't you be glad? Oh, I will!"

Mrs. Belvoir, aware that she was likely to lose the post of cynosure, countered vaguely. "What do you mean?" she repeated. "I haven't finished—"

"You won't need to, Marvel dear. I have found a better way to deal with the malignant spirit you spoke of. I have Mr. Salt's approval for what I do. In fact"—she smiled slightly—"I am his deputy."

Lord Ludlow's eyebrows gave a jerk. "His deputy?"

"Yes, and I believe I am to have a Police-Constable to enforce my authority. And the—the Frenchwomen from the farm, the Delambres, have kindly consented to be present here tonight as witnesses."

"Well, I'll be damned," said Crofts. "Will people be coming in here all night? Who owns this place, anyhow?"

Alberta struck a counter-blow. "Of course, Paula dearest, we shall do anything you like. Shall we have to wait long for those strange old women?"

"*They* are waiting for *you*," said the American girl, standing by the door which led through the armoury into the Hall. "Will you enter, please, and take your seats as before?"

"I don't like this," objected Crofts, blocking our way. "In my opinion there should be no jiggery-pokery without Salt or this Scotland Yard man he was supposed to bring. Why doesn't he do as he intended?"

"Hush, dear," said Alberta, "or Paula will have her Constable arrest you and lock you up in the gate-house."

"He may appear later on, of course," the American girl suggested, not very hopefully. "You can trust me, though, to—"

"Later? Later?" Crofts grumbled. "Are we going to be kept up all night?"

But now Paula Lebetwood ignored him. "Please follow me," she said, brushing past, and Crofts gave way.

Like creatures under a spell we moved into the Hall, a place still obscured from the moon and illumined now only by the pale ring of lights from the chandelier by the gallery. I offered to switch on the other chandelier, which hung near the chimney-piece, but she said she wished it to remain dark for the present. While she spoke, she lit the one bright globe beneath which Mrs. Belvoir had sat, and took her own place beneath it.

"Please interrupt me as little as possible," she requested, "especially in this early part where I know my way. I'll try not to waste time, though I don't expect this to be a really short meeting. No, don't say anything, yet."

It was hard to repress some exclamation of wonder when I saw the two women who sat in semi-darkness near the great expanse of the chimney-piece. Very quiet they had been, and took no notice of us while we entered. They seemed to be absorbed in the embers of the fire, from which only an occasional blue flame winked like an eye. One of them, the squatter of the two, seemed particularly aloof, and only her flattish nose and broad forehead peeped beyond the old-fashioned hood still drawn over her head. The other, who wore an expansive coverchief, was taller and more stalwart, with a strong face, large chin, and eyes which shone even in the gloom. She appeared from time to time to take some interest in us and our proceedings. But on the whole the presence of these foreign sisters was eerie and evasive.

More stolid than either of these appeared the bovine Constable who sat near them and seemed to have them in charge.

"Geewhilikins!" emitted Bob, and the state of Lib could be imagined from the fact that she brazenly allowed him to clutch her hand and keep it.

Paula Lebetwood indicated the sisters Delambre with a gesture. "These—gentlewomen: you know who they are, of course. Before tonight is over we shall all be grateful to them for coming here. But it's late, I know, and you are all anxious to hear my—revelation; so I'll commence at once."

Her revelation! God grant that no prank of fate should cause *her* to be snared in whatever trap she was setting!

"Don't think, please, that I am certain myself what tonight's result is going to be," she went on while we settled into our seats around the shadowy board. "If I did, I wouldn't waste your time. But I think—yes, I am almost certain—that you will find out before you leave your places. And perhaps I had better put this in evidence first."

She picked up the creased sheets of the telegram which lay on the table before her and handed them to Charlton Oxford. "It's the answer to a wire Mr. Salt sent for me this morning. As you see, it's from the Welsh National Library at Aberystwyth."

"That is surely far afield," remarked Ludlow.

"It may seem so. But I believe that when Mr. Salt hears of it, he'll agree with me that it's an important item in our list. In fact, my Lord, it's the keystone of my arch."

While his eyes travelled along the lines, Oxford's face was blank. Obviously he did not perceive the slightest link between the matter of the telegram and the matter in hand. He was not even puzzled; he was irretrievably befogged.

"Will someone repeat it aloud, please? It will save so much time."

Crofts snatched the sheets from Oxford's fingers and commenced to read. The eagerness in his voice subsided while he went on to an uncomfortable conclusion with an air that he was being made a fool. Our confusion increased with rapt attention, but the sisters Delambre seemed utterly uninterested, and I believe that the Constable had already dropped into a doze. The message ran about as follows[6]:

ADEQUATE DESCRIPTION MANUSCRIPT IN CATALOGUE MOSTYN COLLECTION TO WHICH IT FORMERLY BELONGED STOP ORIGINAL NOW IN CARDIFF UNIVERSITY LIBRARY STOP COPIES MAY EXIST STOP MOSTYN SAYS ELIS GRUFFYDD SELF STYLED SOLDIER OF CALAIS WAS NATIVE GRONNANT UCHAIN PARISH LLANASSA FLINTSHIRE LIVED ABOUT 1490–1560 STOP CUSTODIAN WINGFIELD PALACE SEVEN YEARS BEFORE JOINING RETINUE AT CALAIS STOP BEST KNOWN AS AUTHOR AND SCRIBE OF LARGE POLYCHRONICON IN WELSH IN TWO MANUSCRIPT VOLUMES STOP FIRST BEGINS CREATION ENDING BATTLE OF HASTINGS STOP SECOND CONTINUES TO 1552 STOP FOLIOS 365–657 CONTAIN EYE WITNESS ACCOUNTS MANY TRANSACTIONS INCLUDING TRIALS IN STAR CHAMBER STOP NO MENTION IN MOSTYN OF REFERENCE TO CWM MELIN OR AIDENN VALE STOP CAN ASSURE YOU NO PASSAGE OF THIS MANUSCRIPT HAS BEEN PUBLISHED STOP.

"May I have it back? Thank you. And now straight to the point. People, I suppose you think that if we could only put our fingers down tight on one person, our troubles would be over. I mean Parson Lolly—not the Parson of Mr. Maryvale's sad delusion, but the real one."

"I should say so," remarked Crofts.

---

6   The original has been supplied. (V. MARKHAM.)

"Well," she said very quietly, "if there is one part of these mysteries I know I hold the clue of, it's the Parson. I *know* who the Parson is."

The tableful of us stiffened as if we had been plunged in an electric bath.

"Then who, who, who?" Crofts burst out.

"You mustn't excite yourself. There never was any reason to be excited about Parson Lolly. Parson Lolly is a dud."

"Yes, he is!" hooted Bob incredulously.

"Yes, he is, I tell you. I can't believe for a minute that he has any unusual power. You can hardly say that he has any power at all; at least, it's delusive rather than formidable. Why, he's done nothing but deliver threats and make gestures, and some of us have been imagining we're the victims of supernatural pranks."

"Supernatural or not," growled Crofts, "I'll give him a fine quarter of an hour when I lay hands on him. Who is he?"

The American girl looked him straight in the eye, severely, and he subsided with vague rumblings. "Now, I stipulate that you shall do nothing of the sort. If you intend to make this the excuse for working off your surplus bad temper, I won't go any further."

"I'll go bail for him," promised Alberta.

"Oh, don't pay any attention to me," said Crofts.

The American girl leaned her chin in her hand and studied the table with thoughtful eyes. She spoke slowly, tentatively. "Suppose I set the evidence before you and see if your conclusion isn't the same as mine. Beginning, perhaps, with that night Millicent wandered out on the lawn, and I with her. It was the clock in the corner there that started all the trouble; neither the Parson nor any human being here could have foreseen the effect that melody would have on Millicent when she heard it through her dreams. But somewhere on the lawn we two collided, you might say, with a separate series of events. First of all it was the devilish, goggling face that glared down at us from an instant from the air. And let me remind you that it was not only an enormous face—I was frightened, but I'm not exaggerating—it was also high up in the air. We know the Parson is tall when he stands full length, but even he can't extend indefinitely. Well, we saw this perfectly hellish face, just for an instant, and it hasn't been seen again—that way. Mr. Salt took most of it away with him when he left the Vale this evening."

"What's that?" jogged in Crofts.

"Let me go on, please. The head was one thing. Then there was the placard: 'Parson Lolly sends regards. Look out for Parson Lolly.' That was the first of a number of such messages that have been found all about the place, and why *this* one, at any rate, should have caused us such great alarm, I can only account for by supposing that we'd caught the spirit of panic from the servants. On sober reflection, I should think that that placard demonstrated a sort of ingenuousness in Parson Lolly."

"A damned funny sort of ingenuousness," remarked our host. "What about the axe and the blood we found?"

"I was just going to remind you of them. The blood, as you know, we learned to be that of one of a batch of little pigs, and its carcass was found this afternoon along with the head. As for the axe, you remember that Doctor Aire pointed out how light and impracticable it was, and how it had been removed from low down on the armoury wall. The final thing was that Mr. Bannerlee's hat had been deposited on the lawn. The rest was merely excitement. I am able, though, to add a point or two borrowed from Mr. Bannerlee."

I received a burning glance from Crofts. "From you? Have you been holding something back all this time?"

The American girl swiftly continued. "These are notes from the diary Mr. Bannerlee commenced that night."

They all exclaimed, "Diary!"

"Yes, yes; don't be so surprised at everything, or we shan't get through. Don't let them bother you, Mr. Bannerlee. A little later I'll say something more general about the diary, but now I confine myself to a pair of small points. One is that while he came down the path from the uplands to the Vale, he heard a voice somewhere in the fog below, shouting—an indeterminate sort of voice with a quality he couldn't quite describe. Now, I believe that was Parson Lolly's voice, the same odd voice we heard the night before Mr. Bannerlee came. And the second point is this. Late in the afternoon before Sean met his death, Mr. Bannerlee was standing on the roof outside his window. Crofts had told him how the sun strikes the tumulus in Great Rhos at sunset. Mr. Bannerlee looked down, as it chanced, and saw a tiny piece of rope beneath the parapet that runs along there. It was lying at the edge of one of the merlons, which have been scraped fairly smooth and have their corners sharp. It is my belief that this scrap was part of the clothes-line rope and that it had something to do with Parson Lolly's visit the night the conservatory window was smashed, also on the night previous to Mr. Bannerlee's advent."

"Look here," Crofts broke in. He had gradually been sliding to the edge of his chair again. "Why can't you give up beating about the bush and tell us out and out?"

"I'd have to go over it all anyhow," returned Miss Lebetwood. "I'm wondering if these straws seem to you to point the way I think they do. You must let me tell this in my own way. There isn't much more, and for that I have to thank Mr. Bannerlee also."

"You mean my visit to the tower?" I asked. "The Superintendent could help you there. He must have scoured the place long before me."

"He did, as it happens. But he left matters there as he found them, and it was through reading your diary that I heard of the variegated lot of objects which probably belonged to the Parson. For instance, you found shavings from the pencil which had written the placards. You also saw some splashes, unquestionably the blood of the little pig. Then there were fragments of wood and scraps of crêpe, left over from the construction of the head. Another thing was a pungent smell that you couldn't identify. I think that was all except a torn-off corner of the title-page of a book; something ending in 'CATTI.' I would have telegraphed for information about that, too, this morning, but when I asked the Superintendent, he was able to tell me right away what the book is. It's been quite a common one in Wales for generations: 'The Adventures and Vagaries of Twm Shon Catti,' who is described as a wild wag of Wales. He was a real person two hundred years ago, Mr. Salt told me, and a great many legends have sprung up about him, so that his exploits as a highwayman and a hero and a man of chivalry make up quite a readable book. It was borrowed from your library, Crofts, but I noticed this morning that it was back in its place."

Our host now seemed sunk in meditative gloom. "What of it?"

"Well, suppose I recapitulate. As I see it, the night before Mr. Bannerlee came, the Parson intended to invade the House, but his plans were awry. Although the head was made, he didn't bring it with him; this was to be an experimental sortie. He came by way of the kitchen yard, and took down the clothes-line that was hanging there and brought it with him. He made a loop, a lasso, with one end of the rope and flung it up the side of the House until he succeeded in drawing it tight about one of the merlons of the battlement. Then he began shouting through a megaphone, and even if you had heard his voice previously you wouldn't have recognized it then. And he was still shouting while he commenced to walk up the wall of the House."

I thought Crofts was going to levitate from his chair. "A megaphone!"

"But, my dear young lady," objected Aire, "the man must have had a hand too many. I grant you, he might have hauled himself up the outside of the House, but he'd need both hands for it; where does the megaphone come in?"

"You people will interrupt," said the American girl. "The explanation is simple. The megaphone came from old Watts' storeroom, of course. Don't you remember that there are relics in there of early days of sport—even some oars and a sliding seat from a shell? A rowing coxswain uses a megaphone, doesn't he, and there's an attachment for keeping it tight against his mouth while both hands are occupied with the rudder chains. Parson Lolly, I imagine, can manage as well as most coxswains. Anyhow, he *was* climbing, and he *was* shouting when his foot slipped and there he dangled. Instead of letting go the rope, he held on, and the result was that he began to sway back and forth. Of course he tried to steady himself by reaching one foot out to the wall, but instead of checking his momentum he kicked away from the wall, and his pendulum swing carried him neatly through the window of the conservatory. He wasn't as much as scratched."

"Unbelievable," declared Crofts. "And supposing by a miracle he wasn't cut to pieces, what became of him?"

The American girl went on quietly. "When my brother was a high-school lad, he had a soccer ball at home. One evening in an unlit hall he stepped on it accidentally and it sent him clean through a glass door without his losing a drop of blood. It isn't an unusual thing, after all. As for how the Parson got away, he really didn't—then. You see, the swing of the rope had gradually ground it to bits where it rubbed against the sharpened merlon. When the Parson swung through the window, the rope broke and he came down on his feet inside the conservatory. Lucky for him, perhaps, that he did, if he wanted to evade us, for all he had to do was to draw the rope in after him and wait until we had spent our patience looking for him in the grounds. None of us had a thought of searching inside."

"Well, I'm—" Crofts muttered, breaking off into stupefaction. No one else said a word, only stared at the American girl, and waited.

"That night we may assume Parson Lolly escaped as soon as the coast was clear. But he escaped only to plan new mischief for the next evening. And again his schemes miscarried. I think it is easier to reconstruct what happened this time. For one thing, he brought the head with him." Crofts seemed about to break in, but desisted. "He was carrying the blood as well; he must have slaughtered the piglet a little while before he set out from the tower, for the blood had not begun to clot. Earlier, he had been prowling inside the House and had pilfered the little battle-axe and the cap belonging to Mr. Bannerlee."

"But, dearest, you aren't making it a bit clearer," said Alberta. "What could it have all been for?"

"It was to give us the scare of our lives."

"And didn't it?" muttered Oxford. "Dash him!"

"But not as planned. Sean pointed that out at once, I believe. The Parson's intention that night was to stage a fictitious murder. There were the weapon, the gore, and the hat which was to be discovered reeking with blood. We were to find these things, and in the midst of our excitement we were to be thrown into a panic when the head—went off—probably somewhere on the battlement, or even above."

"The head, the infernal head!"

"Yes, Crofts; it appeared when they dug it up this afternoon—Harmony told me—that it had been constructed somewhat like a kite and could have been flown quite easily. That occurred, in fact. When Millicent and I inadvertently crossed the Parson's path and he dropped everything and legged it, the kite did fly up a little way, and then—went off." She addressed me. "When it crashed to the ground, Mr. Bannerlee, the Parson still held the cord, and you distinguished the head as a black mass sliding across the lawn."

"I grant you the kite and the rest of the fol-de-rol," cut in Lord Ludlow, in a voice like the broken edge of a cake of ice. "I fancy, however, that this 'going off,' as you call it, needs more explanation than you'll readily find."

"The hellish thing couldn't have been lit with a match like a Hallowe'en turnip," added Crofts.

The American girl slowly shook her head and smiled. "On the contrary, for me that was about the easiest guess of all as soon as I read how Mr. Bannerlee smelt powder in the tower. Don't you see, the Parson must have carried a small dry battery connected by a length of wire with the magnesium charge in the head? It was an ordinary flash-light powder such as is used for taking photographs."

There was a long interval of sagging silence. I cannot speak for others, but my own mind struggled with an obstacle it could not grasp. There must be some egregious contradiction involved in this idea. Flashlight! Who had owned a flashlight?

"But, Miss Lebetwood, you yourself—it can't be—you're the photography expert here. You didn't—yourself—"

"Wait a moment! I've got it!" Aire whistled. "Someone told me other other day—you'd been teaching Toby how to take flashlight photographs. Didn't you bring down some old apparatus of yours and give it to him last week?"

"Quite right," said the American girl. "It's been Toby all along, of course."

"Toby!" Crofts was only beginning to see the light.

"Toby, who else?"

"God!" Crofts seemed to choke for breath. "Do you mean to say that lad killed Cosgrove—killed Heatheringham? I can't believe it."

"He never killed anybody. Don't you see, Parson Lolly has no connection with these murders?"

"Eh, what?"

"Well, what do you know about that?"

"I'll be switched!"

"I'll be damned!"

The American girl gave Ludlow a particular look. "It hardly needed the new psychology to give us the right lead. I'm amazed, really I am, that no one has thought of it before. Why, what activities did the Parson engage in? His plots were just the sort of thing that an artless—and artful—child would plan to frighten a grown person."

"Or a grown person to frighten a child," appended Aire.

"Yes, I think so, but there could be no such intention here, of course. As soon as I got my wits about me the night Mr. Bannerlee arrived, I suspected some juvenile escapade. The details unfolded to fit the theory. There was the little battle-axe from low on the wall, whereas the big ones hung out of reach. That later night, who but a small boy could have crawled underneath the arch of the bridge in the park when the Doctor and Mr. Bannerlee were so brisk on his trail? Then there was the book: hardly anyone but a lad nowadays would take much interest in a work as naïve as 'Twm Shon Catti.' A boy, however, might be much struck with it, and it probably fired Toby to emulation of Twm—a bloodyish emulation. There was his cloak, too—that was rather puerile, although it was a neat dodge all the same."

"Where does the neat dodge come in?" I asked.

"Why, to add to his stature. A tiny Parson Lolly would be in danger of being identified with a boy, if there happened to be a boy in the neighbourhood. That was the reason for the exceedingly large and flowing garb. He must have had strapped to his shoulders one of those contrivances that magicians use to 'produce' objects, an apparatus that could be folded or extended by pressure on some spring. No wonder Millicent and I saw no head on him! That sort of stunt is as old as conjuring, I believe, and the appliance probably came from the exhaustless variety of old Watts' attics."

The American girl leaned back in her chair, settling her head against the leather and closing her eyes, as if grateful for a chance to rest. The accumulation of details which she had picked out left no doubt whatever that the houseful of us had been hoaxed and flummoxed by a child, that Aidenn Vale was Cock Lane repeated on a twentieth century scale.

But it could not be!

There were facts, cold, stony facts, that loomed mountain high, cutting off this path. These facts could not be avoided.

"But, Miss Lebetwood!" I cried hoarsely, "it won't do."

"Won't do!" resounded the voice of our host, a man of imponderable mind.

"The placards!" I insisted. "Why, I remember clearly the one in Cosgrove's room had been left after Toby had gone to wherever-it-was to fetch my bag—absolutely no question about that. That afternoon, too, the one Mrs. Bartholomew picked up by the library tower: I'll swear by the beard of the Prophet it wasn't there when I went past a few minutes before the tragedy occurred. And Toby was peeling potatoes then. It's inconceivable—absolutely inconceivable—that he could have had anything to do with them."

Her eyes still shut, Miss Lebetwood said quietly, "I think I can tell who it was. Not Toby, I'll admit, but that doesn't alter the rest of what I've said about him. Toby didn't write those placards, or leave them, and I am sure he knows no more about them than he knows about—that one there!"

The hair at the back of my neck prickled, and my spine seemed to be wriggling in convulsions. A dozen cries, loud or stunned, sounded as if from one multi-vocal throat. For the American girl's eyes were open now, and her arm pointed to the musicians' gallery. Indistinct, hanging outside the bright zone of the globe, but unmistakable, a fifth placard was suspended from the rail of the balustrade.

"My God!"

"I'll take oath that wasn't there when we came in," declared Crofts, and many voices supported him.

It was I who rose like a brisk automaton, kicked my chair back against the wall, and sped up the stairs to the gallery, where I had never set foot before. The placard hung by a black thread attached to a pin. I seized it, carried it down to the light. Now we might have been some multi-headed creature studying the inscription:

TOnigHT my LAst NiGHt BeSt REGards
PARSON LOLLY

Only the American girl remained limp in her chair, not bending forward for a sight of the words. While my gaze, as it must, fell on her and lingered there, ever such a shadowy smile crept from her lips to her eyes.

"Good people, good, good people, please don't misjudge me. That placard has been hanging there since long before you came in. You didn't see it because you weren't on the look-out for it."

"You knew it was there?" Crofts boomed. "And you didn't warn us?"

"Warn you? Against myself?"

"Against yourself, dearest?" cried Millicent Mertoun, her face suddenly worn with anxiety.

Miss Lebetwood said, "I wrote that placard. I wrote it this evening and put it up there after Marvel's crystal-gazing tonight. I did it just to show you that anybody could make a placard like that. This is the fifth, and perhaps the four others were done by four different persons."

Accompanying the last words of her speech, the first strokes of twelve began to sound from the clock in the corner. There was a spell in the sound of its old music. We were hushed.

For the only time I saw Lord Ludlow's face absolutely grey with fear. "There's something moving in the wall!"

"Not in the wall—on the wall!"

Indeed, high up, above our solitary light, something rubbed and scraped near the portrait of Sir Pharamond. From somewhere else in the room came a soft murmur, as of a smooth-running reel. Belvoir caught hold of the bulb by its brass top and raised it overhead. Within the brightness now, the colours of the portrait were sharper and more brilliant than they had appeared in the austere dimness of the Hall.

But Sir Pharamond was not still; he writhed and rocked, and a loud outcry was evidence we saw the blood oozing from the wound upon his cheek.

A moment later down fell Sir Pharamond with a sound of splintering wood and ripping canvas. The wall where the portrait had been was quite smooth and blank.

The quiet chime of the old clock had not ceased to ring.

CHAPTER 27

THE PURR OF THE CAT!

Blood on the pallid cheek of Sir Pharamond, and his downfall, as had been prophesied in the olden time! I saw no one else, heard no one else, only gaped at the ruined portrait and was conscious of the clock's melodious voice. An epoch seemed to pass before my senses ceased to dance, and I found myself one of the faltering semicircle which closed about the shattered portrait.

But beyond the area of brightness I made out indistinctly the most amazing thing of all. The sisters Delambre sat by the fireplace precisely as they had been since we entered the Hall. The short, stodgy one seemed quite absorbed in the flickering embers; the taller of the two had merely turned her head in our direction. Even the Constable seemed bereft of reflexes. This lack of surprise, this apathy, this uncanny silence impressed me just then as a thing more incredible than the disaster close at hand.

I still stared at the strange pair, while conscious that Aire had slipped before us, standing over the wreck of the portrait. He turned and faced us, and the small voice of the man seemed charged with a booming importance.

I heard him vaguely. "I told Salt," came in somewhere, and then, "Crofts put me up to it, really."

"You're crazy, crazy," claimed Crofts.

"I tell you it never would have happened if you hadn't been so fractious this morning. I said this sort of thing might conceivably take place. Well, it has, that's all."

Eve Bartholomew ventured. "You mean that you—you—"

"Very simply indeed." Aire hunched his shoulders appreciatively. "A matter of two spools and a bit of string connected with the mechanism of the chimes. A scurvy conjurer's trick; that's all. I apologize."

"But the blood!" I cried in a sudden access of emotion. "Spools and strings don't produce blood. I saw it oozing from the cheek!"

Aire smiled, shook his head slightly. "No, they don't. But then, you didn't see blood oozing from the cheek."

Half a dozen hot affirmatives contradicted him.

"I tell you no. You're all acquainted with the prophecy of the bloody cheek, and you were all hypnotized."

"Don't try to tell me," bullied Crofts, brushing the little man aside and bending to the wreckage.

Aire smiled dryly. "That's not blood, you see; it's painted blood."

"What!" cried Crofts, holding up a portion of the canvas. "You daubed this stuff on my painting?"

"Not I; Maryvale. And that's not your painting, by the way."

Crofts could only mutter.

"Don't be disturbed, my friend. This portrait is a rush order, as they say in America, a copy done for me this afternoon by Maryvale. You'll find the original under his mattress, poor chap."

"Well, of all—" Crofts relapsed into dumb glowering.

Aire made a slight movement of disdain. "Why be so upset? It was only a trick—a cheap trick, I admit—and I take the full responsibility, ladies and gentlemen. I almost wish it hadn't occurred, but dogmatic people sometimes get on my nerves. And now let's forget about it and get back to the table; we were really learning something there. Paula, I hope this hasn't too awfully disconcerted you? You can go on with it?"

She forced a smile. "Yes, certainly. Do come on, people; it's getting awfully late."

We returned to our places not much more comforted than when we had sprung from them a few minutes before. It was all very well to speak of parlour tricks, but there was no ease in sitting around the table in that darkened room with those images of lethargy dwelling by the fire, and no cheer in waiting through the lonesome night, wondering from what direction some new terror might leap upon us. But there we were.

"...bearings of Sean's death," Paula Lebetwood was saying. She went on in a strange voice: "He was struck and fell dying where I found him by the tower. Then the weapon, as we now know, was hurled down there, too. But we have to admit that as far as we can tell none of us could have been at the tower at that time. Nobody except Wheeler met Sean—or will admit he did—after our quarrel in the Hall. So, stated in those terms, there is an irreconcilable contradiction in Sean's death. Only there is no contradiction save in words; for we know, well enough, that somebody *must* have struck him, and therefore somebody must have been there.

"In Mr. Heatheringham's death there were differences, though in some respects it was much the same. In the first place, he must have seen something hostile or there would have been no revolver shot. The trail of blood across the floor, too, showed what had been the murderer's line of retreat. But the most unusual thing, surely, is one that Doctor Aire can explain better than I. Will you, Doctor?"

Aire looked at her inquiringly. "I suppose you mean the rigidity—cadaveric spasm, as we call it? What do you want me to—?"

"It shows something about the way he was killed, doesn't it?"

"Yes, it does. The topic is of great interest to one of my profession; we come across it so seldom, save on the battlefield. We know something about it, though, enough to be sure that there are certain definite predisposing factors."

She nodded. "Yes, I meant that. Please go on."

"*Sudden* death is one, and death due to violent disturbance of nervous system. Then the last contraction of the muscles during life persists with more rigidity even than in the usual *rigor*."

"I'm sure you people see what I mean by harping on these gruesome things," said the girl. "Thank you, Doctor. This abnormal state of things taken with the shot through the broken window proves that Mr. Heatheringham was killed right where we found him. I mean he couldn't have been bludgeoned outside—say where I found Sean lying—and have crawled back into the Hall and raised himself to the window to fire at whoever might have been there. So far, we have no idea who was with him; yet I think it must have been one of the servants or one of us—more likely one of us."

No one chose to say anything in the brief silence she left. Presently, in a fresher tone, she resumed.

"That's how the problem stood yesterday: just death, simple and inexplicable—violent death without a real motive—violent death without an agent, apparently. Even the discovery of the stone has been no help in finding the agent; anybody could have grabbed a stone from the rockery."

Crofts muttered, "Why go over all that again? We've known it from the start."

"I apologize. I only mentioned those things to go on to say that it's useless to think about them any longer. We could continue for weeks and months mulling over motive and method—mulling over time and place and all the rest of it that makes an endless circle. Last night, though, I thought of a new way."

"New?" the words sprang from Belvoir's lips.

She paused and looked about the table. "I—I'm a little nervous about telling you my idea. The thing was, I suddenly thought of Mr. Bannerlee's diary."

"That's a fine one!" I put in ironically. "You thought of it when nobody but Crofts and Heatheringham had ever heard of it—unless Heatheringham told Salt!"

"As it happens, I've known about it all along. A few minutes before luncheon the day of Sean's death, you and Crofts came upstairs to the first-storey landing together. I had changed after playing tennis and was just going downstairs. Although the two of you suddenly lowered your voices when you saw me, I had already heard you, Mr. Bannerlee, say that you had been up till nearly morning and had done more than five thousand words. Crofts said he hoped you had got it straight, and that left no doubt what you had been writing. But I was much too polite, then, to let you know I guessed what you were doing.... And before I go on, people, let me say that as far as I can tell, no record has ever been written with fewer mistakes."

"Thank you," I acknowledged.

"Humanly and"—here she slipped in a smile—"archæologically speaking, that is. You can't expect one person to write a story that would satisfy every question that flits through another person's mind. I'm not sure that I like his style, either," she remarked, rather abstractedly, "though you couldn't judge it very well in that fragmentary state—except, I think, he fancies his power of description and likes to make a passage effective now and then. But while I read, I began to feel the diary was just suited to the purpose I had in mind."

"Which was—?" said Lord Ludlow, who gave the impression of long-suffering patience.

"I wanted to find the killer without bothering how he killed. I expected the diary would help me to look on all you people divested of my own prejudices. Through the diary I could judge you more fairly, and more strictly than I could in my own mind. Meeting you there would be like meeting new persons, all of you except Crofts and Alberta being new to Mr. Bannerlee. The diary is really full of side-lights on people and little bits of character. Maybe, though, I was expecting too much from Mr. Bannerlee. How could he come to know us in a day, or a week? He couldn't. He saw us only from the outside and the diary reveals only the outside of us. Without being disrespectful either to you or to Mr. Bannerlee, I must say I was reminded of clowns in a circus. Most of us seemed to be doing the same thing over and over again. Ted Belvoir and Lord Ludlow were eternally carrying on a silly debate; Eve was making a fresh prophecy every day, and not one of them came true; Crofts seemed to be growing grouchier every time he was mentioned; Gilbert Maryvale spent most of his afternoons leaving cryptic remarks about, so to speak; Lib's mission in life was talking gibberish to Mr. Bannerlee. Everyone seemed to be posing as an idiot, quite an innocent idiot. Well, it turned out that my most important discovery in the diary wasn't a character after all, but a fact."

"A fact you didn't know before?" asked Belvoir.

The American girl smiled faintly. "First of all, though, if Mr. Bannerlee doesn't mind, I want to tell you the big secret he's been keeping from us. Do you mind, Mr. Bannerlee?"

I bowed the responsibility on to her shoulders with a smile. "I think you should tell us beforehand how you found out—what you did. I'd like to know myself."

"I was going to. People, you remember the other day, Mr. Bannerlee went on the hilltops again, and he was so taken with the view of distant mountains that he drew sighting lines on his map to show which ones were visible. The sighting lines, of course, were drawn from the same spot, and that spot was on Whimble. After orienting his map, he squinted across it, looking toward the Malvern Hills and the Black Mountain and elsewhere to establish lines of vision. He could even see to Plinlimon; that's about thirty miles away. You did see Plinlimon that day, didn't you?"

"Certainly."

"Well, that was how I knew you hadn't been on Whimble, whose highest point has an elevation of about 1950 feet. The highest point on Plinlimon is less than 2500. Thirty miles apart and only five hundred feet difference. Now, if Mr. Bannerlee stood anywhere on Whimble and he looked toward Plinlimon, Great Rhos, just across the Vale, would be between him and the mountain. Great Rhos is a flattish sort of hill, and its elevation is 2166. Think that over."

"How idiotically, infernally stupid of me!" I cried.

"But I don't see—" said Eve Bartholomew blankly.

Others about the table uttered exclamations that showed their understanding or betrayed their confusion.

The American girl turned to Mrs. Bartholomew. "You see, dear, if you were nineteen feet high and wanted to see something ten yards away that was five feet higher than you, you couldn't do it if there was a wall a foot higher than you less than a yard away."

To give her credit, Mrs. Bartholomew grasped the point instantly. But she still was dubious. "Then how did Mr. Bannerlee see the mountain?"

"He must have been somewhere else."

"But you said he *said* he was on Whimble."

I laughed. "No, I didn't say so, Mrs. Bartholomew. I was satisfied to let people think so, though."

"Why was that?" interjected Lord Ludlow sharply.

The American girl turned to him. "He wanted to reserve a little share of glory for himself. Why should he have told us his special secret, or even write it down in the House, before he knew what kind of people we were? I think Mr. Bannerlee was very sensible."

I smiled, recalling a somewhat different reaction to my "antiquarianism" that afternoon.

"But what does it all mean?" Mrs. Bartholomew came in plaintively.

"That's what I wondered this morning," answered the American girl. "Mr. Bannerlee, I suppose by this time you know the reason why I took that campstool; in fact, you had written the reason yourself somewhere. 'What a difference a few feet make in the prospect!' You are a bit taller than I am, and there was just that barest risk that you could see further from Whimble than I could. But when I reached the tippy-top of the hill and set my campstool there and stood on it, I knew I had as good a chance as you of peeping over Great Rhos. But I couldn't. So I knew you must have been somewhere else when you saw Plinlimon, and I could only suppose that the reason you'd hidden your whereabouts was your discovery of the oratory, after three hundred years."

"The oratory!" Doctor Aire reached out a hand to me. "My congratulations, Bannerlee!"

"And mine!" said Belvoir.

"After three hundred years!"

"The oratory!" cried Lib. "Bannerlee, you've been false to me. Couldn't you trust lil' Lib?"

"So that was it," muttered Crofts. "You needn't have been so close about it."

"Really a downy bird," giggled Alberta.

I faced the American girl. "This is almost—gratuitous, you know. These unfortunate people are waiting for you to cast some light upon their darkness, not to herald any trifling discovery of mine."

"Yes, I *had* better be getting on toward solving the mystery, if we're ever to be done tonight. The weird thing is that guessing about Mr. Bannerlee's discovery is what put me on some sort of a track. In fact, if Mr. Bannerlee's matches hadn't given out that afternoon he saw the rainbow, I never, never would have seen the path—that sounds like a figure of speech almost, and a paradox, but I mean just that."

"Matches!"

"Yes, Mr. Bannerlee, by the time you had reached the House you might have been excused for thinking Fate was playing with you. And, by the way, people, a little while ago Mr. Bannerlee explained to me how he had brought his quarto of Sylvan Armitage to Radnorshire with him after all. Naturally, when he left it in the oratory by chance, he did not care to tell us about it, on account of his precious secret. So he had just recovered his copy and was bringing it down the Vale with him that afternoon."

"Aren't you going to get out of the sixteenth century?" inquired Ludlow. "It seems to me that you are leading this discussion along the lines of a wranglers' tea-party."

"Do forgive me for wasting so much time. The Book of Sylvan Armitage interests me so much; indeed, it helped me tremendously. Mr. Bannerlee caught me reading it the other night; did he tell you?"

"Nothing criminal in that," said Belvoir.

"Nno, but it was slightly—unconventional. The passage where Armitage happened upon the oratory was an admirable parallel to Mr. Bannerlee's account in his diary, as I learned later. Yes, I came to be very glad indeed that I had stolen down at midnight to get the Book.... Now, people, I can't go any further without telling you another secret about Mr. Bannerlee. He won't forgive me for this, I'm afraid. But he's not only a gentleman and a scholar"—I suppressed my indignation at this outrageous statement—"not only a discoverer of things so old that they are new—he is also an altruist!"

I bowed my head giddily under this monstrous charge, and heard her go on to say: "He is defending one of us, one, I think, whom he had never seen before!"

If dismay were a sign of guilt, there was not an innocent one among them. Their alarm testified, I think, to the fact that they had hoped, and hope begot belief, that the crime would be traced at last to someone outside the Vale. They had all been innocent to each other before; now to suppose the murderer sat among them was a shock as great as murder itself.

"Someone in this room?" whispered Crofts in a voice far different from his bullying voice.

"Someone at this table?" asked Eve Bartholomew.

"Someone at this table."

Belvoir made a show of pulling himself together. "See here, Bannerlee, is this true?"

"That's not a fair question, is it?" said the American girl. "Mr. Bannerlee cannot know how much I know about—"

I said, "Frankly, Miss Lebetwood, you are not being as direct as you promised to be. I am at a loss as to the 'altruism' you refer to. Tell us plainly what you mean, and perhaps I can be of some assistance. You are mistaken if you believe that I would shield anyone for a moment who had deliberate murder at his door."

"That's fair. Well, my trump-card is that I know who burned the evidence that incriminated one of us; no matter how I know. You burnt it, Mr. Bannerlee, you yourself."

Their haggard white faces were turned on me. I felt my cheeks flush. "I think you are alarming our fellow-guests without good reason. Why, granting, as you believe, I *did* drop the paper in the fire, and supposing there were the least connection between the writer and the crime—which seems improbable—the mere fact that the Book at this moment belongs to Crofts' library doesn't indicate that one of you discovered the parchment during some visit here and filled an idle hour doing its contents into an obsolete style of English. None of you, as far as I know, are Celtic experts."

"Emphatically!" declared Lord Ludlow, fixing a reproachful gaze on the American girl. "Miss, you are confusing a wild shot in the dark with the reasoning process. This piece of translator's work, probably done by someone outside this Valley and quite unknown to us, can have no connection with any atrocity committed here. You are far afield, and I do not think you will help us much unless, as I said, you lift us from the plane of a wranglers' tea-party."

"You may be right," she confessed. "I shan't try to convince you. But it was a tempting lead. And surely it's not true to say there's no connection between the parchment story and events which have occurred this week." Elbows on table, she rested her head on her hands, speaking very thoughtfully. "For instance, in the old story Hughes related after lunch that day he called this place the castle on the mill-site. An old, old map in the library gives Aidenn Vale as 'Cwm Melin,' which means 'Mill Valley,' I've learned, and that is what the Vale was called in the manuscript; do you remember? The parchment explains, too, what was meant by the 'spanning and roofing of the waters,' one of Mr. Maryvale's mystifying utterances. It referred simply to the fact that when Sir Pharamond built his second castle here, he roofed in the Water; I suppose the present stream beyond the towers is a deflected one and the channel where Sir Brooke was found is the original course. That may seem far-fetched, but the proof is that Doctor Aire took from Sir Brooke's forehead a splinter of the petrified wood of the mill-wheel itself. When Sir Brooke was carried down the subterranean stream, his body must have collided with the edge of the mill-wheel, and passed on. Mr. Bannerlee, in his expedition to the cellar, must have actually seen the casing of the wheel, all overgrown with hideous fungi. So there *are* connections, of a sort."

"Quite interesting in the abstract," said Ludlow tartly. "We are looking for something, however, which has a tangible link with a crime of violence. May I suggest that if you have nothing more to offer us, this meeting adjourns?"

She had not lifted her head; her fists ground into her forehead. "I shall try to satisfy you, sir, again with Mr. Bannerlee's assistance. I think you will recall that there was a sentence in the parchment to the effect that Sir Pharamond disposed of his enemies 'with no more trouble than snuffing a night-light.' Now, within five minutes after reaching the House, Mr. Bannerlee discovered a curious thing. Looking through the armoury window, he saw *you*, Ludlow. *And what were you doing there? You were snuffing a candle that stood in the old bracket on the wall!*"

Ludlow's chair was flung back. He was on his feet, putty-faced, staring at her in utter consternation.

"Are you accusing me?"

Before she could answer, our attention swung to the other end of the Hall. From somewhere in that semi-darkness came a muffled rasping sound, as of some huge beast that purred.

Crofts was on his feet now, with eyes that strained to overcome the gloom. He called, "What's that?"

Aire strode half-way to the fireplace, turning his head this way and that. "There *is* something moving in the wall this time. Only where?"

"No!" I shouted, above the increasing hubbub. "IT'S THE PURR OF THE CAT! The purr of the cat means death! Clear the Hall!"

But I was too late. A glaring light leaped from nowhere, light so intense it pierced the brain. The walls and roof blazed with white fire. The persons in the Hall were like figures of clay, presented and fixed for all eternity in one or another cast of horror. Some had cowered back beneath the gallery, some had their hands before their faces, some were forever fleeing, foot lifted, toward the door.

The Constable and one of the sisters had retreated from the chimney-piece, while the other woman stooped low before the fireplace. A thing with the size and form of a man had been lying there at their feet, unseen. In this white instant I saw the woman grasp this figure, raising it above her head.

The collapse of the mantelshelf—a black projectile flying toward me and veering away—a stunning crash—a long greedy laughter rising from below, clutching us, tearing us, subsiding in a sudden burst of silence.

Darkness succeeded light. The strong arm of the Delambre woman still held the man upright: a headless body.

CHAPTER 28

THE CRASH

Again I smelt powder.

In tingling silence some of us crossed the Hall and regarded the headless thing. Belvoir lit the other chandelier, and in its sparkle, to my immeasurable relief, the figure proved to be the scarecrow which had served in the sisters' field. The woman who had stooped in the fireplace and held the effigy in the path of the leaping, swinging bar sat in her chair, again impassive. I noted her admirable hands, strong and hairy like a man's, her face, broad and full of flesh, but firm and capable. The bumpkinish policeman touched me on the sleeve and pointed to the table, a sign we should keep to our own end of the Hall.

I noted a disturbance there. Crofts, towering over the American girl, shook her with rude fingers clamped into her shoulders.

"You—you—"

While I returned to our group, I was struck with the curious feeling that someone was missing there. Someone had slipped out. Vaguely I wondered who it had been, and whether his absence would be revealed when we took our places once more. But we were not to sit down together again that night.

The American girl had drawn away from Crofts and stood looking at him, not angrily, but with a certain speculation in her gaze. My blood rushed up when I saw her white skin bruised by the marks his fingers had made. She said, "You think I—?"

"Murderess!" That was like Crofts.

Several of us protested at his folly; the rest were horrified into dumbness.

Her steady gaze did not fail. "You do suspect me. So did Mr. Heatheringham—and Mr. Blenkinson has done me the honour also. But I didn't do it, people, and—sometimes—I wonder if anybody did...at least in the sense we've been thinking."

"Nobody did! With that damned engine—that thunderbolt! Nobody did!"

"Don't shout so. That engine, as you call it, was Mr. Salt's discovery this afternoon while the House was cleared. I had nothing to do with it just now."

Crofts' jaw fell. "Cleared? The House cleared? There wasn't anything in this 'lost' business?"

"Very little. I did want to find Mr. Bannerlee's oratory, but principally I hoped to draw you kind people out of the Vale. Mr. Salt and I have been associated in a lawful conspiracy. He and the Scotland Yard Inspector—"

"Who?"

"The Scotland Yard man. He was to arrive at New Aidenn by motor early in the afternoon since the trains were slow. While the House was empty, they investigated, and found this machine. Mr. Salt expected something like it. This was the real weapon, of course; that stone half buried in the loam was a blind."

"You've known this—long?"

"How could I? I had a hint of it when I kept finding in so many places how the old castle here was built on a mill-site: Cwm Melin, you know. It even happened that Mr. Bannerlee knew that name and that name only for this place. He had never heard of Aidenn Vale."

"The devil with Bannerlee. What's a mill got to do with it?"

"The mill-wheel, don't you see, winds up the spring of the machine. It must be quite automatic, and I dare say at this moment the cat's claw—I suppose that's what it is—the long heavy arm of iron, is ready to leap out again."

Doctor Aire's face revealed a ferment within. "By jingo—I think I have it. That mocking roar—hideous—was the sound of water tumbling into a cistern, or a heavy cask. Then if the cistern discharged over the wheel, the gear actuating the arm would wind until—yes, by thunder, that's it!"

"What's what?"

"We heard the purr. That was the gear winding against the resistance of the spring—a sword-spring, perhaps. When the tension exceeded the strength of the spring, the accursed thing let fly. There must be a shaft...." The Doctor lapsed into mumbling.

"Beneath the perfidious tree!" screamed Mrs. Bartholomew so suddenly that we all jumped. "What does that mean?"

Miss Lebetwood answered, "There was once a cross—see the traces—carved on the chimney."

Aire had his eye shrewdly on her. "We can credit you with the flashlight, can't we?"

She nodded. "Yes; the camera's in the gallery, and there were powders attached to several places on the wall. Constable Pritchard manipulated the electric button that ignited them. I hope we have obtained a decent picture of the claw in mid-air."

"But who—who's responsible?" asked Mrs. Bartholomew plaintively, with outspread hands.

"Dead too long to make any difference," said Aire.

"Could this, er, machine last for centuries?" Crofts demanded, shouldering his way to the Doctor.

"For millenniums, without oiling," returned Aire. "Why not? The really important thing is—"

"I've got it!" I cried. "About your question, Mrs. Bartholomew. Remember, Miss Lebetwood, what Maryvale told me the day he finished his picture? Someone, he said, of the house of Kay. And, by heaven, he was right!"

"The really necessary thing," persisted Aire, "is to dismantle this machine without getting killed. It will be ticklish work, though, since it's automatically prepared to lunge out with its claw on five seconds' notice. We'll have to make a start with the cistern and the wheel."

"That's not the first thing, Doctor," said the American girl.

Aire turned toward her in surprise. "Nothing can be more urgent. You wouldn't leave this thing for a night or for an hour, would you, like a gun primed and cocked? Why, at any moment, sooner or later, the equilibrium—"

"I think not, and if we hear the purr again we can keep our distance. Something needs to be done, however, before you take the machine apart. We must find the real murderer."

We gave vent to all kinds of sounds, mainly incredulous.

"Listen! We have *not* discovered yet the person here who knows Welsh and whom Mr. Bannerlee is shielding."

I commenced a vain "I haven't admitted—" but my speech was charged down.

"I can prove you are!" she cried. "Yes, sir! I want to know why you are shielding him, or her. All day long I haven't got my mind off those matches you wanted so badly after recovering your own copy of the Book. Do you know, it's my belief you knew you were carrying evidence dangerous to someone, and you wanted to destroy it before you reached the House. I think it was the translation you actually did destroy later on."

"Look here—" put in Crofts, reaching out a hand. His face might have been that of a man sinking under water for the third time. "Look here—"

"Crofts!" cried Alberta, her eyes bright with agony.

"The parchment and translation were in old Watts' copy," Belvoir snapped.

I doubt if she heard them, intent as she was on the molten stream of her thought. "This translation, done off-hand, betrayed someone of us who had a competent knowledge of Welsh and consequently a head-start, at any rate, in knowledge of the cat's claw."

"It was in old Watts' copy," muttered Belvoir.

"When you came into the library, Mr. Bannerlee, you were about satiated with your attempts to burn the paper. But even if you couldn't destroy it, you could get it off your person, and you did that. You told how you 'reached your hand up into a dark corner,' and you might have added 'and changed my quarto with the one on the shelf.' What happened a few minutes later when you and Lib were looking over your copy? A flake of moss fell to the floor; Lib must have noticed it, for you were scrupulous to mention it in the diary, and you passed it off with some remark about careless dusting. But I read in Armitage about moss, and I read about mossy stones in the diary, and I've seen plenty of mossy ones around the oratory, and you can't tell me that the copy with the parchment in it wasn't the one you'd left up there last week. So I imagine you knew well enough what Lib had found when she called out to you while you were leaving the library."

"How absurd!" I cried.

"'Imagine' is a well-chosen word," said Lord Ludlow crisply. "I am not much edified by this botanical excursion. You can't accuse a man of being accessory to murder because of the way he turns a phrase."

"Thanks, Ludlow," I nodded. "There's no need, really—"

"The thing I am driving at," said the American girl in a quiet little voice that drilled its way into our brains, "is that you, Mr. Bannerlee, wrote the translation yourself. There is no other conclusion, is there?"

"Wilder and wilder!" I exclaimed. "This is too bad, Miss Lebetwood, when you've realized all along that I have no knowledge of Welsh."

Our speech had settled into a duel with unmerciful give-and-take. "Are you sure? Consider this: In the diary your early references to the Welsh language were all natural and ambiguous, which puzzled me mightily when I came to other things later on. Then I saw that you must be taking advantage of those early references to conceal the fact that you are really quite adept in Welsh."

"Took advantage? That's rather strong, isn't it?"

"Well, just think. You made a pun on the name of St. Tarw, which means 'bull.' You even went out of your way to use an American expression, that it was a 'bully name.' A little later, when the man you call the gorilla-man shouted at you in Irish, you knew quite definitely that he did *not* shout in Welsh, although Welsh and Irish belong to the same race of languages, and that particular expression must sound about the same in one language as in the other.

"But these were trivial compared with the point they hinted at, and that telegram there clinches the point. You told Lib all about how you read Ellis Griffiths' history, and now we know the manuscript has never been printed, let alone translated."

She came close to me, still speaking, and I yielded a step before the accusations she flung out like weapons. "You destroyed the manuscript you yourself had made. You hurled the stone from the rockery into the earth from the balcony outside your room. And at the same time you dropped the placard the wind carried down to the corner of the House, and it was you who left the earlier placard in Sean's room that morning when everyone else was downstairs."

My voice sounded horribly ineffective in its attempt at surprise. "You accuse *me*! You accuse *me*—of—?"

"I do, I do! Haven't I been putting you on your guard all morning and all afternoon—ever since I showed you the campstool? Haven't I been telling you what I know and hinting what I've guessed? Haven't I done enough—?"

My laugh, to show contempt, was also a failure. "Preposterous. It's a—vertebrate without a skeleton: your theory. I didn't want to kill your lover. What motive could I have had?"

Those blue eyes could be as sharp as steel. She seemed to be the embodiment of intellect become passionate. "Motive? Something overwhelmed you stronger than any motive: impulse. If you had thought two minutes, Sean would be alive today. You had motive, yes, though I'm ashamed to describe it, but the impulse dwarfed the cause behind it, for once. You had been thinking about it, hadn't you, ever since the night before, and all day long, or there would have been no threatening message in Sean's room—but it was that chance, that chance in a thousand that settled it. I understand now what has always seemed to me the greatest mystery of all: the motive you had for the diary and the tremendous trouble you took in writing five thousand words overnight."

"I set down the reason plainly: I wanted to clear up the muddle we all were in."

"That may have been so when you took up your pen, but before you laid it down the diary had become a greater thing than any mere alignment of facts; it had become your defence! You were someone else, Mr. Bannerlee; the bright and cheery, affable, not-too-scholarly, antiquarian and athlete—all that part of you subservient now to something else: Iago!"

"Who was Iago?" asked Mrs. Bartholomew with troubled mouth. "Something in Shakes—"

"The spider spins its web with all its cunning bound up in instinct. While you spun your web, Mr. Bannerlee, all your cunning was bound up in intellect, and you loved each shrewd knot and strand. Yes, that was it; you came to be in love with artifice, you laughed in your sleeve at Salt and Doctor Aire and Heatheringham and me—all people who were trying to break through your web."

I had hold of myself now, in spite of the tumult of my heart, and could return blow for blow. "What nonsense! What a fool I'd be if I killed a man to preen myself for intellectual superiority. I tell you again, I never wanted to kill your lover. What reason had I?"

Her eyes fell for a moment before mine, and a little storm of wrinkles crossed her brow. "Impulse, impulse, I said, didn't I? I think you wrote of it, three times at least. That first night by the tower—when I and the Parson's sign were together inside the circle your torch had cast? Again, after Sean and I had quarrelled, and yet again as you walked up the Vale in the twilight and could not forget the quarrel. Afterward too, when you were so depressed on learning that I was to be immensely rich. You covered it well, oh, yes! But could I fail to know what was tugging at you all the while?" She raised her eyes to mine for a long, grave look. "I suppose you would call it being in love with me, wouldn't you?"

I fought down the thing in my throat. "And suppose I was—suppose I am—what difference does it make? Must I plead guilty to a crime I never dreamed of because I had the bad luck to take a fancy to the face of a woman who's denied to me? I was well enough when I walked on the mountain and felt as if I could move the earth. I wish to God I had stayed up there, and not come down into this place where Fate takes the strings and plays her hellish tricks!"

She gave me the most mournful look I have ever seen on any face. "That's why I can't despise you, you know, though I've tried. I can't look on you as a—a thing of horror. You've played the game right through: you put down every prevarication and evasion you had made, and then you let me read the diary. You just—gave yourself away, and did it without a murmur. When you were up there alone on the Forest and exulted in your loneliness, you were a man any woman would have given a lot to march beside. And then you came down here among us—and how quickly you proved that all our gods have feet of clay."

My indignation howled at highest pitch. "I tell you for the last time that I deny absolutely the trumped-up charge you keep senselessly repeating."

She shook her head. "Denial's no good. Do you think, as everyone seems to believe, that terrible machine worked by chance just now, by some overplus of pressure or loss of equilibrium? No, Mr. Bannerlee; a man set the cat purring and the claw lunging. Do you know where he is?"

Silence....

"A man did it?" I repeated, my voice parched and scraping, my body numb as a block of wood. "A man—did it?" I remembered I had felt that one of us had secretly left the Hall. But no—that had been after the deviltry of the machine.

"A man in this House—in your room, Mr. Bannerlee. Twelve-fifteen was the time set."

I saw faces leaping and jigging around me, one of them with great blue eyes and crown of golden hair swinging enormous toward me and swinging giddily away again. The door into the corridor, which I had not seen opened, was suddenly closed from outside. I heard a sea of voices, and above them shot out the voice of Crofts, booming like a huge wave:

"But my God, how was it done?"

"They found out this afternoon," said the American girl, "and Mr. Salt scratched off a few details for me. The mantelpiece is as old as the castle, and looks and feels sound enough, but it swings down by means of an invisible hinge. The claw operates it. The claw must be articulated in some way with a shaft driven from a water-wheel in the wall below. The purring sound from the clash of the teeth would draw anyone toward the fireplace, just in the path of the flying bar as he stooped to find where the noise came from. The blow was so terrific it drove Sean through the opening of the french windows, to crawl a yard or two—and die. Heatheringham was already dead when he was hurled against the glass, and his arm striking upward and through the pane that way caused the revolver he was carrying cocked to explode. I think— that's all."

She had recited all this with the most studied coolness and precision, this account of the machine—a device surely the creation of a haunted and tortuous brain. The account completed, the driving-force which had sustained her was gone, and she looked weary almost to haggardness. Pity and shame and grief wrenched me for the part I had played in the fatal story. When Mrs. Belvoir ended her close-lipped listening of an hour with a querulous question, I heard someone, Alfred Bannerlee, speaking as if from far away.

"I'll tell you about that. It was the cats' heads stuck everywhere about here that made me wonder if I hadn't dropped into Cwm Melin, as it was called in the parchment account. 'Hear the cat purring under the perfidious tree' was fresh in my mind. There was a cat's head on the firearch, and there had been a cross above. I can't say that, er, gave the show away, but it stirred me up a bit. Upstairs, though, when I saw the bracket on the wall and thought of 'no more trouble than snuffing a night-light,' an idea seemed spread out as plain as an open book. I never thought of the mechanism as a certainty, only as a possibility—barely that. I swear that when I tugged with my razor strop and brought the wretched bracket down, I had no idea what might happen. From what I hear, there must be some sort of weighted valve controlling the flow from the cistern to the water-wheel. A chain from the bracket operates the valve and sets the whole damned business in motion. But I didn't understand that then. It was all like a dream—what happened—"

The faces passed into a blur again, jerking up and down. Voices roared and voices were thin echoes shivering into silence. Everything was moving, even the sisters Delambre. One strode across the room like a tempest, tossing her garments this way and that. The other came waddling after, and was engaged in a mighty struggle with her hood. The hood came away, revealing a goodly beard.

A comic-opera transformation had taken place. Suddenly it was Salt who was standing before me, Salt and a giant of a man with beefy face. Salt's expression was ridiculous, for he was doing his best to make it stern and menacing. The words in the air seemed to come from his lips:

"Quietly, Mr. Bannerlee."

Then I thought that I had fainted. But I had not; instantaneous, utter darkness had swept into the Hall.

CHAPTER 29

RESCUE

Like an imbecile, I waited stock-still in the darkness for the light to return. The sudden eclipse, however, had checked my foes as well. I heard their footsteps cease like those of men who had walked over a cliff.

Not a gleam penetrated the murk. There were cries for light, and someone tried to scratch a match, ineffectually. I began to move.

I partly lost my balance, lurched against a man, and heard his Lordship's bitter plaint from the level of my knees. I blundered into the passage without disabling anyone else. Intuition kept me from blundering toward the front entrance; later I realized that would have been too obvious a way. I groped to the left, feeling along the right-hand wall.

I seemed to wake up in the dinner-room.

Someone else was in there. I heard an anxious whisper: "Bannerlee… Bannerlee…that you?"

I recognized a friend. "Yes."

From the invisible a small, damp, clutching paw clasped my hand. "You gotta get out of this. Out the window. Snap into it."

We were together on the east lawn, running. Thank God the moon had gone down. Thank God the servants were asleep.

"It's a—wise egg that knows—its own rooster. Bannerlee, your off-springs—couldn't spot you—as the bloke that finished Cosgrove. Step on it! I can—keep up."

"What happened to the lights?"

"I happened to 'em—that's all."

We approached a black smudge across the greater dark: a band of trees. We entered into their depths. I stopped, held her back.

She whispered frantically, "Step on it! You can't stay here!"

"No, but I have to decide what comes next. Steady on! Don't worry about me; I'll come clear. What did you do? Are the lights finished for good?"

"Did you notice I'd sneaked out? I was afraid the lid 'ud blow off, soon and I wanted to do my bit. I had the dickens of a time finding the fuse-box in the kitchen. I pulled off the handle of the big switch com*pletely*, and gave the rest of the works a kick so a lot of stuff fell down to the floor. I also cut the telephone connection into bits to round off a good night's effort."

"Wonderful. I'm surprised you weren't killed by the current."

"Never mind wonderful. I know my electricity. All in the good cause. Only step on the gas!"

"By Jove, I will!" I cried, divining the sense of this saying. "I must get a tin of petrol—no, two tins. First, though, listen. Will you do something more for me?"

"Yes, yes—anything. But make it snappy."

"I want my diary. Get hold of it and wait for word from me. Where can I write you safely?"

"You're crazy. They'll trace you sure as—"

"Not if you do this right. The book is in the desk drawer in my room. It's not locked. It's your part to conceal the thing, here, until the wind blows over a bit. The police will believe I have it, and I want it—for a good reason. Eventually you can recover it and mail it to the name and address I write you. Where can a letter reach you safely?"

"I don't know. American Express, London."

"No good. Are you going to be in the Continent this winter?"

"I think so. Mummy's hipped on Nice."

"American Express, Nice, then. You can send for my letter if you don't go there after all. By the way, it will be addressed to Miss, er, Sarah Vale. Can you remember?"

"Yes, yes; I'll write it down when I get in." She hung on my arm imploringly. "Step on it now! You'll get caught if you keep hanging around with these by-the-ways and can-you-remembers. My God, you've only a couple o' minutes' leeway. I don't see how you'll make it."

I laughed and patted her shoulder. "My dear Lib, I have a start of at least two hours, probably more. But I shan't be foolhardy and lessen the time I have. Goodbye, Lib. I can never thank you for what you've done."

"Good-bye forever, Bannerlee." Dim white arms reached around my neck, and her lips touched mine in a brisk little kiss. "I'm awful sorry Paula had to spill the beans. She took the line Cosgrove was her man, and—and all that sort of rot. Say you aren't mad at me, or anything. 'Cause I'm to blame for all this trouble, I guess."

"No! How could you be?"

"I saw you drop the translation in the fire that night, and like an ass I let Paula find it out. But I didn't mean any harm; honest I didn't."

I touched her cheek with my fingers. "You're absolved, little Lib. It could have made no difference, eventually. You're going to be Mrs. Cullen some day, aren't you?"

"Oh, gee, I don't know. I s'pose I'll have to be, to get some peace and quiet."

"I shall send you a beautiful present from Central Africa or Siam or elsewhere. May I kiss the bride again?"

I might. And yet again.

I turned away, but swung back. "Tell her—I'll never forget her. And I'll always be sorry for the pain I've caused her. That's all."

"I will; sure I will. But, Bannerlee, I want to say something. I think it's the limit a real man like you has to light out because something happened to that doggone Irishman. I think it's a goldarn pity Paula couldn't have fallen for you—hard. Then she would have kept quiet if they'd torn out her fingernails, instead of seeing her duty and doing it tonight, like a fool. I'm awful sorry. *Now step on it!*"

She glided and glimmered away. I was a lone outlaw against the world.

Not a moment squandered now. I dashed for the stables, with which I was fairly familiar. Cautiously using my torch, I penetrated the section transformed into the garage. A minute later, with two petrol tins hugged to my breast, I fled down the Vale for life. There had not been a single shout from the environs of the House.

I carried the tins across Aidenn Water and set one down, returning with the other to the temporary log bridge, which I must burn behind me. It must have made a comfortable blaze, soaked as it was with petrol, but I could not stop to witness this holocaust to Mercury.

Salt's car was waiting there. I deposited the emergency tin of petrol in the rear, jumped in, and had no difficulty in starting the engine. The key had been left on the dashboard, as I knew it would be. With the fire rising behind me, merrily I rolled out of the mouth of the Vale to the main road and toward New Aidenn, embarking on a brief career of constructive vandalism.

My object was to cut off for as long as might be the communications of my enemies, the inhabitants of the earth. The torch revealed that along the edge of the road eight or ten telephone wires were strung, but shortly before entering the town I jumped out of the car, clambered up the short pole, and with the aid of gloves and other things in the tool-box snipped both right and left.

There were no street lamps in New Aidenn, I had heard, and I thought it safe to assume that no constable would venture out of doors there as late as one o'clock in the morning to recognize my borrowed motor. Not a soul was stirring; the Police Station was dark. I passed through safely, and halted the car on the other side of the town to give some attention to the wires running that way.

My destination was Hereford, but I had until nearly three o'clock to reach there, and no danger of my losing my road. So I often halted in my journey when I had passed a village which might contain a telephone, in order to secure it from business too early in the morning. Thus I reached Hereford about ten minutes before the north-to-west express was due.

I left the useful car in an alley near the station, hoping it would be recognized about dawn and not until then. When the train was puffing beside the platform, I boldly applied at the window for a first-class ticket to Exeter (I had been about to say "Bristol," when I happened to think "Don't be so childishly obvious, like an ordinary criminal. Let Salt think he's up against a real antagonist.") I explained that I had intended to drop off at Hereford, but would not break my journey until further on because a person I had met on the train told me there wasn't a decent hotel in the place. I needed some excuse, of course, for the fact that I was not wearing hat and coat. The booking-clerk seemed rather sleepy, and I remained a little longer talking to him, to insure that he would remember me.

Then I boarded the train and entered a first-class compartment where a gentleman was sleeping. His hat and coat, however, would not fit me. I merely scraped some of the mud (quite distinctive mud that said "Aidenn Vale" as plainly as words) on the floor there. I thought of leaving more "clues," but decided not to butter the bread too thick. I passed on to another compartment in search of vestments. From a gentleman who was slumbering with his head hanging off the seat I obtained not only hat and coat, but a mackintosh which from a distance would look just as well inside-out.

I then found an empty compartment and sat there, wearing my new-found raiment, until the engine snorted and hunched its shoulders and commenced crawling southward. When the train had left the platform, I glanced from the off window to insure that the station yard was dark, then unlatched the door and dropped safely to the ground.

All immediately required was to keep out of sight until the corresponding express from west to north should come in. It should have arrived a quarter of an hour afterward, but to my disgust it was late, and I had a worried thirty minutes among some coals. I devoted the time to cleaning my boots with my handkerchief, which I stuffed in my pocket, to be burned later. At length the express pulled in, and when all appeared ready for departure, I walked quickly up the track beside it. The south-bound platform was deserted now. This fact enabled me to choose an empty compartment and enter it by the off door.

Suddenly remembering my plans for the morrow, however, I stepped out on the platform and bought some fruit from a yawning lad who conducted a buffet on wheels. I had thought at first of stealing the stuff, but buying it would be less ostentatious. When I had paid for what I had chosen, I took the first opportunity to steal quite a bit more.

I had really been very lucky. During my absence from the compartment, tickets had been inspected and doors locked. Lacking a ticket for this particular train, I might have been embarrassed. Now I walked hurriedly toward the end of the train, past the ticket-inspector, around the rear coach, and along to the off door of my empty compartment again.

I rode north.

At Shrewsbury I alighted for precaution just before the train drew into the platform, and re-entered my compartment when the engine had been changed. Near Crewe I definitely abandoned the train, climbed the bank of a shallow cutting, and got over the hedge. It was still rather dark, but I had no difficulty in finding a satisfactory bit of woodland where I might lie hidden all day.

I was staking everything on one chance, that Paula Lebetwood had remembered the references to the Bonnet yacht and that my ticket-taking and perhaps the mud from my boots would serve to concentrate the attention of the authorities upon Bristol. If Jack and Mary hadn't altered their plans, they would be slipping out of harbour this morning with the tide, probably five hours before the dogs of righteousness would arrive hungry at the docks. It seemed reasonable that the authorities should assume that I was aboard the barque. I knew for certain that she carried no wireless, and that barring an unexpected encounter there was no chance of police disillusionment until she put in in Norway—or Africa.

I intended never to be seen unless for urgent cause, and then, if possible, by the under-intelligent. Empty compartments on fast trains by night were to be had for the taking, and even if the expresses should be crowded, the stopping trains were available, though on them it would be necessary to turn out at every station. In the barely credible contingency of my being nipped and made to pay my fare, I had plenty of money, for I had cashed a fairly large cheque before setting out for Aidenn Forest, and I had not stopped to tip the servants before leaving Highglen House. The train by night and secluded slumber by day; these were indicated for my recovery.

I shall not detail my week-long, decidedly boring expedition to Hull. After a couple of days my personal appearance became run-down, and I dropped into a small market town on market day, asked a constable directing traffic to assist me to a hairdresser's, found the place down a dark dead-end and up a shaky stair, and enjoyed a haircutting, shampoo, and shave. I told the attendant that I looked and felt a new man, bought a packet of safety-razor blades, tipped him enough but not too much, chatted pleasantly about the price of heifers, and departed.

About nine that evening, in a restaurant in a larger town, I expressed a predilection for pickled walnuts.

Not long afterwards I stepped out of a station wash-room, an unobtrusive dark gentleman to the roots of my hair, with eyebrows that gave a special appearance to my face.

I carried a passport, thanks to Jack and Mary. From Hull one Albert Barrerdale sailed eight days after Alfred Bannerlee had stumbled out of the Hall of the Moth. Praises be for the men who are supposed to scrutinize the details on passports, and don't.

* * * *

Now on my Mediterranean island (whose name, pardon me, I do not mean to give) I enjoy perpetual sun and the fruits of never-ceasing summer. I might rest here secure for the term of my natural life, and I might achieve a sort of happiness, for here no sensuous pleasure is withheld from man. Air, sea, and land conspire to lull the soul, and at night from the village creep up strains of music sweet and spicy. I might remain—but I think I shall move on.

The Bonnets saved me; no doubt of that. Overweening sleuth-hounds met a sharp rebuff three months later when the Bonnet barque, not having touched at any port, returned to Bristol dock. The emphatic statement of Jack and Mary that I had not been on board, a statement which they later attested in order to dispel public mutterings against their veracity, stunned the police, who had been sitting back and waiting for me to be delivered up to them from India or Madagascar. The hounds then were willing, but found no scent. Moreover, since I had not been aboard the barque, they *knew* that I could not have escaped from England, knowledge that must have proved rather a hindrance than a help.

The diary reached me in a picturesque village in a small Balkan country. Its disappearance that night, by the way, gave rise to the amazing belief among several of my fellow-guests that I had secreted myself within the House, and the consequence was a general desertion next day. After receiving the pages, I carried them with me for weeks before lighting on my isle and commencing my work anew. Now the manuscript is ready to return, rounded, coherent, and decked with proper ornament.

My purpose? I have done it for *her* sake. I don't care a penny for the gaping world; all I ask is, let this book stand as the monument of an ardour which exceeded the orthodox. Let it be a fantastic tribute to a mistress who never can be mine. Let it take the place of a sigh and a sob for love's labours lost. While I handled and recast this matter, I lived near her again in Highglen House, shared hours that held all life's sweetness, and remembered that she did not despise me!

If I may offer a suggestion to you who are to receive this manuscript, I advise that you present it unaltered to the public as a piece of fiction, with the name of some obscure but ambitious author upon the title-page. And if he will be so generous, I trust that Lord Ludlow will write a foreword to give the thing the stamp of reality.

I trust, finally, that I may be forgiven if I remark that this is the *last* that will ever be heard of me.

Paula!

THE COMMUNICATION
OF APRIL 17, 1926

No matter where I am. It is a different place from where you think, and it will be no good tracing this letter, for you'll find only that you are mistaken. The man who is going to take it to Rangoon and mail it two months hence, is an outcast like myself and will certainly keep faith.

Occasionally a paper gets through to me from England, and I read it with more or less amusement. Bloodthirsty wretches, the English, who would like nothing better than to see me suspended between time and eternity. But it shall not be.

There has been some discussion as to what "really" happened the evening Maryvale attempted to shoot the cat. One copy of a newspaper I came across contained a sort of symposium on the subject. One or two letters came near the simple truth, which was that, being afraid of Maryvale's revolver, I took the chance which was offered to remove the bullets from as many cartridges as I could, managing to insure that his first three shots would be ineffective. Hints that I deliberately intended to craze the poor fellow, for whom I had a sincere liking, are false.

Through Lord Ludlow my diary has reached the authorities upon guarantee that it will not be confiscated, and from official announcements it seems they believe it to be an equal mixture of necessary truth and designing falsehood. To my astonishment, moreover, they have reported that it is a masterpiece of indiscretion—which is nonsense. About myself, to be sure, I have perhaps written a thing or two that most men would not care to have known of them during life. But I am dead. Yes, in all that concerns life as I knew it, my friends, my studies, my pleasures—in all that matters—I am dead. The authorities, however, scoff at the diary, and adduce the "mystic bone."

Fools! The episode of the bone hanging white in the gloom was not invention, or delusion either. It was the white patch on Cosgrove's head while he waited in the darkness and surveyed the Hall, planning Noah's Flood and the crisis which would arise when Sir Brooke met the gorilla-man. The close-cropped nape of his neck between his black hair and the black collar of his sportsman's coat, and the knobs that were his ears—I did not comprehend at first that these were what I saw. When my amazement and alarm had subsided, and I realized that Cosgrove was in there—I think I hated him then.

His odious behaviour toward his intended wife and the sinister hint beneath Bob's bitter outbreak had rankled. My survey from outside my window a minute later happened to prove that no one was in the immediate vicinity of the Hall. Otherwise I should hardly have felt the sense of satisfaction snug at the heart of my shivering soul when—after the bracket had given way—I realized that *something had happened*! But not until I reached the lawn did I know that it had happened to Cosgrove. I shall never be sure in my inmost soul whether or not I was quite aware that this trivial act might loose some destructive force—whether I am a murderer or the toy of Fate.

They say, however, that the placards I left and the stone I cast down from the balcony convince me of malice prepense. They do not, though they seem to do so.

The placard I left in Cosgrove's chamber that morning (the bottom of a cardboard box I found in the store-rooms) meant no more than what it said: mischief. I never had any delusion about the supernatural aspect of Parson Lolly; indeed, the stressing of that element had made me a little suspicious of Cosgrove himself. Celts do odd things. I believed that for some clandestine reason he might be behind the manifestations, and I thought it would be good sport to play his own game against him. I merely proved to be wrong.

The second placard was a flash of inspiration, after the bracket had given way and pandemonium burst out below me. There might be a way of shifting the onus, if anything actually catastrophic had taken place!—if there *had* been a cat's claw, and—! Parson Lolly again! It did not take twenty seconds to dash into the storeroom, find the cover of the same box, scrawl the words, and fling the placard out of the window for the wind to carry. Later I destroyed every scrap of the box.

The stone I pitched down late that night. It was an obvious afterthought, and a good one.

As for Heatheringham's death, it was black misfortune and nothing else. It appears that on account of Cosgrove's Will he looked askance on Paula Lebetwood, but even had he suspected me, I do not think I could have been so callous as to wipe him from the earth in a bloody smear. I was doubtful that minute in my room, which was the more prudent course for me: to dash the bracket down, creating a new disturbance, or to leave it untouched. Prudence certainly decided to let the accursed thing alone, but one moment's recklessness defied prudence. I solemnly assert that I believed the Hall was empty and Heatheringham somewhere in the twilight north of the House.

Salt, it seems, was a shrewder fellow than his appearance betokened. He had suspected me from the first night he came to the House. "The way he looked at Miss Lebetwood, or rather the way he avoided looking at her, set me thinking"; such are the words which commence an interview given to one of the more lurid newspapers. Salt's homely yet somehow handsome face, accompanied by well-combed beard, adorns this report, which concludes with an irony I suppose must be accidental: "I am glad Mr. Bannerlee didn't injure my car."

While irony is fresh in mind, irony was never more dramatic than in that business of the water-wheel, facts they found when the claw was dismantled and the channel investigated. That the Knight's dead body, blundering down the channel, should have dislodged the obstruction which otherwise would have prevented the wheel from turning and the claw from darting out! So Sir Brooke, elderly and infirm, stumbling to his death, fulfilled his mission after all.

I have received a message from Lib, and I may as well close with that. It was transmitted to me through an American newspaper, by means of a simple "dictionary" cipher code I explained to her in a farewell letter from that Mediterranean isle of mine:

"Dear Bannerlee Paula's going to marry a guy named Frank Andrews she knew here in the States before she bumped into Cosgrove Bobby and I too as soon as Bobby is twenty one the first boy will be named after you why not I hope you are not too sad in that place wherever you are and I wish you could come and see us sometime but I guess you'd better not a plain-clothes policeman says good morning to me every day when I go round the corner so it wouldn't be healthy for you here I sure wish Paula had met you before this Andrews or Cosgrove there would have been nothing to it and everything would be rosy Paula is terribly sorry but she doesn't hate you Love Lib."

Well, some day in the forties, when the Radnorshire riddles are buried in oblivion beneath the ashes of a hundred other mysteries—I shall return! I shall visit little Lib, and find it difficult to recognize in her matronly staidness a trace of the dash and frankness of her liking for me. Perhaps, too, I shall pat that "first boy" on the head.

Shall I dare to see *her*? Or, shall I stand outside her lighted window, remembering. That would be better, I believe. I can be nothing to her then, but once—

After all, she did not despise me!

www.ingramcontent.com/pod-product-compliance
Lightning Source LLC
Chambersburg PA
CBHW011351010726
47494CB00008B/2264

* 9 7 8 1 6 6 7 6 4 0 8 3 9 *